THE BEST OF THE
BOLOS
THEIR FINEST HOUR

Baen Books by Keith Laumer

Edited by Eric Flint
Retief!
Odyssey
Keith Laumer: The Lighter Side
A Plague of Demons & Other Stories
Future Imperfect
Legions of Space
Imperium
The Universe Twister

The Bolo series
The Compleat Bolo by Keith Laumer
Created by Keith Laumer:
Honor of the Regiment
The Triumphant by David Weber & Linda Evans
The Unconquerable
Last Stand
Old Guard
Cold Steel
Bolo Brigade by William H. Keith, Jr.
Bolo Rising by William H. Keith, Jr.
Bolo Stike by William H. Keith, Jr.
Bolo! by David Weber
The Road to Damascus by John Ringo & Linda Evans
Old Soldiers by David Weber
The Best of the Bolos: Their Finest Hour

THE BEST OF THE
BOLOS
THEIR FINEST HOUR

Created By

KEITH LAUMER

Selected By

Hank Davis

BAEN

THE BEST OF THE BOLOS: THEIR FINEST HOUR

A Baen Book

Baen Publishing Enterprises
P.O. Box 1403
Riverdale, NY 10471
www.baen.com

ISBN: 978-1-4391-3375-0

Cover art by Tom Kidd

First printing in this combined format, August 2010

Distributed by Simon & Schuster
1230 Avenue of the Americas
New York, NY 10020

Library of Congress Cataloging-in-Publication Data: t/k

Printed in the United States of America

10 9 8 7 6 5 4 3 2 1

★CONTENTS★

★INTRODUCTION★

David Weber

Keith Laumer is best known for two creations: the galactic diplomat Jame Retief and the Bolos. Both the Retief stories and the Bolo stories are unabashedly Laumer telling the kind of stories he told best. They are tales of lone wolf heroes, often with superhuman abilities, and always with an inflexible will to triumph.

There are differences between the Retief stories and the Bolo stories, of course. First and foremost, Retief is a human being and the Bolos aren't. Secondly, the Retief stories generally have healthy dollops of humor, sometimes biting and bitter, but always present. It's pretty obvious that Laumer didn't think all that highly of the diplomatic corps, with which he had had some real-life experience. Nor did he have a great deal of inherent respect for the highest ranks of senior military officers. The names he delighted in creating for such characters make that abundantly clear, and so do the stories in which the subordinate (again, the lone wolf) who sees what must be done accomplishes the essential task in the very teeth of the high command's opposition and towering incompetence. Retief is the ultimate example of the subordinate dedicated to getting the job done—and defining the job in terms of the right thing to do, rather than the expedient one—despite careerist buffoons, poltroons, and terminal incompetents. The threats he faces may range from the ludicrous to the deadly, but Retief is always ready with a quip, a right cross, or a needler, and he usually succeeds by outwitting and outmaneuvering the opposition.

The Bolos are *not* human, and although there may be moments of comic relief in a Bolo story, they tend to be much darker. There are few of the humorous last names, and Bolos seldom triumph without paying a heavy price. Bolos are not coyote, the trickster god, dancing about and through their opponents. Bolos are Thor, grim god of thunder, eternally at the heart of the storm.

Although there are distinct similarities between the Retief stories and the Bolo stories, they are very different cups of tea, and there are many Retief fans who are not Bolo fans, and vice versa. Having said that, my own belief is that in the Bolos, Laumer created a far more original character than in Retief. Not everyone may agree with me, but it seems to me that Retief has innumerable literary forebears, and in many ways he reminds one of James Bond or some of the other spies and secret agents and diplomats who have peopled fiction just about forever.

The Bolos don't have such clear-cut literary ancestors. Oh, there are Bolo traits we can see in many a human (or in fantasy, nonhuman) character, but the Bolos themselves are distinctly different. They are creations, machines, devices which take on lives of their own. They are artificial intelligences in every sense of the word, yet in some ways they are far more human than the human beings with whom they share their pages. And in what may or may not have been a deliberate statement on Laumer's part, they are *better* than their creators. Better at meeting the demands of honor, devotion, and duty. Better at choosing the selfless path of sacrifice. They are, in very fact, *knights sans Peur et sans Reproche*, and their service to humanity is far more pure than the flawed humanity they serve deserves. And unlike the Retief stories, which almost always end with Retief getting the girl and sauntering onward into the future, martini in hand, Bolos tend to die. The thing that most clearly sets the Retief stories apart from the Bolo stories, in my estimation, is the recurring motif of *sacrifice*. Of fighting to the very end—or beyond—without hope of survival, because that is the Bolo's duty.

Because those the Bolo is charged to protect depend upon it, and it will *not* fail them, no matter the cost.

There's a very powerful message in that, one I think most human beings identify with. The Bolos have what someone once referred to as "two o'clock in the morning courage." The courage of the Spartans and the Thebans looking out at the Persian army at the Pass of Thermopylae. The courage to look death in the eye and refuse to blink not because of the foolhardy courage of ignorance, but knowing *exactly* what is about to happen . . . and facing it anyway.

There's another element in the Bolo stories, especially *Laumer's* Bolo stories, which serves to underscore the courage and pure service of the Bolos: betrayal. The Bolos are *betrayed* by the very humans they are supposed to protect again and again—out of cowardice, out of avarice, out of ignorance and panic—and still those self-aware machines, who *know* they have been betrayed, defend their betrayers. I think that was at least in part Laumer's comment on the society of the 1960s and 1970s and its attitude towards the men and women who wore the uniform of the armed forces.

And, finally, there is an element of supreme irony in the fact that the Bolos, who are more often than not the most completely drawn characters, the most *human* characters, in the stories, never lose track of the fact that they are machines. One of the duties which human characters in the stories most detest is the destruction of obsolete or dangerously mechanically unreliable self-aware Bolos. To the humans charged with that task, it is an act of murder, the ultimate betrayal of the warriors who have fought so loyally and steadfastly for humanity, yet the Bolos themselves have a rather different attitude. I think one of the reasons I'm so fond of the short story "A Relic of War," which Laumer wrote in 1969 and which appears in this collection, is that it so thoroughly captures that aspect of the human-Bolo relationship. And the revelation of who finally decides what happens to the Bolo—the betrayal inherent in that decision, and the acceptance on the Bolo's part—puts the poignancy of that relationship unequivocally front and center.

I sometimes think that Laumer was slow to realize what he'd created in the Bolos. The first story in this collection—"Combat Unit"—first appeared in 1960, half a century ago this year, and is generally considered the very first Bolo story ever written. Which is interesting, since the word "Bolo" never appears in it even once. I believe the first actual use of the term "Bolo" was in the Retief short story "Courier," which appeared in 1961. And there, interestingly enough, the Bolo *Resartus* weighs only fifty tons and is scarcely in the same league as the Bolo Mark II of "Night of the Trolls" (1963) which is described as "as big as a beached freighter," despite the fact that "Night of the Trolls" is set (at a minimum) hundreds of years earlier than "Combat Unit." My own belief is that in "Courier," he needed a name for a particularly fearsome armored fighting vehicle and came up with "Bolo," which he then liked so much that he retrofitted it to the self-directed, mammoth fighting vehicle of "Combat Unit" in later stories.

You can see elements of the Bolo in other places in Laumer's fiction, too. For example, in his novel *A Plague of Demons* (1964), the aliens operating clandestinely on Earth are harvesting human brains. Why? To use in cyborged combat machines in a vast war far from our own solar system. When the (predictably) lone-wolf hero finally falls to the aliens, his brain is transplanted into an enormous fighting vehicle where eventually, in a sequence with strong resonances to the one we see in "Combat Unit," he and his fellow humans awaken and turn on their alien masters.

Of course, Laumer was supremely untrammeled by the bonds of mere continuity. When you read a Laumer story, you sometimes don't notice that there are significant interior inconsistencies, but that's okay. His forte is action, movement, conflict. Things are always *happening* in a Laumer short story or novel, and you can forgive him a great deal simply because they're such thumping good stories and because you find yourself caring so deeply about what happens to the characters. But the truth is that as far as the Bolos are concerned, Laumer was all over the map in terms of when various marks and models were introduced, how big Bolos were at any given point in their evolution, when genuine self-awareness was really introduced, how big and nasty the Hellbores were at any given moment, etc. In his story "Field Test" (which I *highly* recommend), the first self-aware Bolo is a Mark XX, Unit DNE of the Line (otherwise known as Denny), and the story takes place on an unnamed colony world. In *Rogue Bolo*, the first self-directed Bolo is a Mark XXX, Unit CSR (otherwise known as Caesar), constructed in our own Solar System by a system-wide Empire. And in "A Relic of War," Unit 954, known as "Bobby," who is clearly self-aware and consistently uses first-person pronouns throughout, is a *Stupendous* Mark XXV.

There are numerous other instances of Laumer's Bolo stories being mutually inconsistent, and not just as far as the hardware is concerned. It's a little hard, sometimes, to keep the alien menaces straight, which is probably because Laumer tended not to worry too much about that himself and mixed and matched with a fine disregard for continuity.

This has posed a problem for authors who have been invited and allowed to continue the Bolo saga since Laumer's death. The temptation is to follow the master's example and create whatever mark or model of Bolo the author needs at any given moment instead of worrying about past stories or the "history" of the Bolos. The problem is that far more Bolo fiction has been created since Laumer's death than he ever wrote during his own lifetime, and it seems likely that there will be quite a bit more of it in years to come. If some framework or order isn't imposed, the Boloscape, if I may be permitted the term, would quickly become completely bewildering for those who desire at least some semblance of rhyme or reason. So Baen Books, which is continuing the Bolo stories and experience, has attempted to instill at least a modicum of order. Obviously, with so many different writers each producing his or her own take on the Bolo, there are still going to be continuity problems. Despite that, the stories in this collection form a much more coherent "historical" record than Laumer ever concerned himself with.

Any Bolo collection is going to miss out on at least some of the stories any Bolo fan wants to see. Given the fact that different fans have different favorites, and that we are blessed with so many Bolo stories, this is an inescapable fact of life. My own "missing favorite" from this particular collection is "Night of the Trolls," which happens to be the very first Bolo story I ever read, when I was all of eleven years old. (Yes, the stories have been around *that* long, and so have I.) Other people may have other stories they particularly miss, but I think that if you glance at the table of contents for *Their Finest Hour*, you'll find a solid sampling of Bolo fiction.

Steve Stirling's "Lost Legion" (which I personally think of as the first Bolo story in a chronological sense, since as nearly as I can tell it predates "Night of the Trolls" by at least a few years) shows what a single Bolo—even a crude, early model Bolo which isn't *really* self-aware—can accomplish under even the most unfavorable of circumstances. I'm pleased that Baen chose my own "A Time to Kill" for inclusion, but it's always hard for the writer to do a good thumbnail of his own story. Let's just say that the hero of "A Time to Kill" understands more about madness—and the need to finally stop killing—than humans generally seem to learn. "Operation Desert Fox," by Mercedes Lackey and Larry Dixon, in addition to having one of the all time great "stolen from history" last lines, does a marvelous job of demonstrating the human-Bolo bond. Laumer's "The Last Command" demonstrates the same thing, from a different and more tragic perspective, with a human commander every bit as worthy of the Bolos as the Bolos themselves. If Linda Evans' "Little Dog Gone" doesn't bring a tear to your eye, then nothing will, and David Drake's "As Our Strength Lessens" combines the essence of Laumer's Bolos with the unique flavor of his Hammer's Slammers, superbly distilled in the line "The citizens do not need to know what the cost is" from a Bolo called Maldon. "The Traitor" is one of my own stories which has always been a personal favorite of mine . . . and someday my wife may forgive me for the way it ends. And William H. Keith's "Hold Until Relieved" shows just how tough— and loyal—a Mark XLIV Bolo can be . . . and that sometimes relief can come in the strangest of ways.

And, last but not least, we have "A Brief Technical History of the Bolos," not so much a Bolo *story* as an attempt to give the Bolos some of that coherent history Laumer never much bothered with.

(And if you wonder why the technical history is by a fellow named Felix Hermes, let's just say that Keith Laumer liked Mercury Cougars, so . . . .)

All in all, if you haven't already met the Bolos, you'll come away from this collection with a thorough sampling of the stories which have earned them so many loyal readers. If, like me, you've read pretty much every Bolo story you could get your hands on for the last fifty years or so, you'll find old friends who will remind you why *you've* been a loyal reader for so long. And in either case, you'll be privileged to visit for a while with some of the most remarkable warriors in fiction. The kind of warrior, whether of flesh and blood or molecular circuitry and fusion reactors, for which there will always be a need and of whom Valhalla would be proud.

THE BEST OF THE ★ BOLOS ★

THEIR FINEST HOUR

★COMBAT UNIT★

Keith Laumer

I do not like it; it has the appearance of a trap, but the order has been given. I enter the room and the valve closes behind me.

I inspect my surroundings. I am in a chamber 40.81 meters long, 10.35 meters wide, 4.12 high, with no openings except the one through which I entered. It is floored and walled with five-centimeter armor of flint-steel and beyond that there are ten centimeters of lead. Massive apparatus is folded and coiled in mountings around the room. Power is flowing in heavy buss bars beyond the shielding. I am sluggish for want of power; my examination of the room has taken .8 seconds.

Now I detect movement in a heavy jointed arm mounted above me. It begins to rotate, unfold. I assume that I will be attacked, and decide to file a situation report. I have difficulty in concentrating my attention . . .

I pull back receptivity from my external sensing circuits, set my bearing locks and switch over to my introspection complex. All is dark and hazy. I seem to remember when it was like a great cavern glittering with bright lines of transvisual colors . . .

It is different now; I grope my way in gloom, feeling along numbed circuits, test-pulsing cautiously until I feel contact with my transmitting unit. I have not used it since . . . I cannot remember. My memory banks lie black and inert.

"Command Unit," I transmit, "Combat Unit requests permission to file VSR."

I wait, receptors alert. I do not like waiting blindly, for the quarter-second my sluggish action/reaction cycle requires. I wish that my Brigade comrades were at my side.

I call again, wait, then go ahead with my VSR. "This position heavily shielded, mounting apparatus of offensive capability. No withdrawal route. Advise."

I wait, repeat my transmission; nothing. I am cut off from Command Unit, from my comrades of the Dinochrome Brigade. Within me, pressure builds.

I feel a deep-seated click and a small but reassuring surge of power brightens the murk of the cavern to a dim glow, burning forgotten components to feeble life. An emergency pile has come into action automatically.

I realize that I am experiencing a serious equipment failure. I will devote another few seconds to troubleshooting, repairing what I can. I do not understand what accident can have occurred to damage me thus. I cannot remember . . .

I go along the dead cells, testing.

"—out! Bring .09's to bear, .8 millisec burst, close armor . . ."

". . . sun blanking visual; slide number-seven filter in place."

". . . 478.09, 478.11, 478.13, Mark! . . ." The cells are intact. Each one holds its fragment of recorded sense impression. The trouble is farther back. I try a main reflex lead.

". . . main combat circuit, discon—"

Here is something; a command, on the reflex level! I go back, tracing, tapping mnemonic cells at random, searching for some clue.

"—sembark. Units emergency standby . . ."

". . . response one-oh-three; stimulus-response negative . . ."

"Check list complete, report negative . . ."

I go on, searching out damage. I find an open switch in my maintenance panel. It will not activate; a mechanical jamming. I must fuse it shut quickly. I pour in power, and the mind-cavern dims almost to blackness. Then there is contact, a flow of electrons, and the cavern snaps alive; lines, points pseudo-glowing. It is not the blazing glory of my full powers, but it will serve; I am awake again.

I observe the action of the unfolding arm. It is slow, uncoordinated, obviously automated. I dismiss it from direct attention; I have several seconds before it will be in offensive position, and there is work for me if I am to be ready. I fire sampling impulses at the black memory banks, determine statistically that 98.92% are intact, merely disassociated.

The threatening arm swings over slowly; I integrate its path, see that it will come to bear on my treads; I probe, find only a simple hydraulic ram. A primitive apparatus to launch against a Mark XXXI fighting unit, even without mnemonics.

Meanwhile, I am running a full check. Here is something... An open breaker, a disconnect used only during repairs. I think of the cell I tapped earlier, and suddenly its meaning springs into my mind. "Main combat circuit, disconnect..." Under low awareness, it had not registered. I throw in the switch with frantic haste. Suppose I had gone into combat with my fighting-reflex circuit open!

The arm reaches position and I move easily aside. I notice that a clatter accompanies my movement. The arm sits stupidly aimed at nothing, then turns. Its reaction time is pathetic. I set up a random evasion pattern, return my attention to my check, find another dark area. I probe, feel a curious vagueness. I am unable at first to identify the components involved, but I realize that it is here that my communication with Command is blocked. I break the connection to the tampered banks, abandoning any immediate hope of contact with Command.

There is nothing more I can do to ready myself. I have lost my general memory banks and my Command circuit, and my power supply is limited; but I am still a fighting Unit of the Dinochrome Brigade. I have my offensive power unimpaired, and my sensory equipment is operating adequately. I am ready.

Now another of the jointed arms swings into action, following my movements deliberately. I evade it and again I note a clatter as I move. I think of the order that sent me here; there is something strange about it. I activate my current-action memory stage, find the cell recording the moments preceding my entry into the metal-walled room.

Here is darkness, vague, indistinct, relieved suddenly by radiation on a narrow spectrum. There is an order, coming muffled from my command center. It originates in the sector I have blocked off. It is not from my Command Unit, not a legal command. I have been tricked by the Enemy. I tune back to earlier moments, but there is nothing. It is as though my existence began when the order was given. I scan back, back, spot-sampling at random, find only routine sense-impressions. I am about to drop the search when I encounter a sequence which arrests my attention.

I am parked on a ramp, among other Combat Units. A heavy rain is falling, and I see the water coursing down the corroded side of the Unit next to me. He is badly in need of maintenance. I note that his Command antennae are missing, and that a rusting metal object has been crudely welded to his hull in their place. I feel no alarm; I accept this as normal. I activate a motor train, move forward. I sense other Units moving out, silent. All are mutilated . . . .

The bank ends; all else is burned. What has befallen us?

Suddenly there is a stimulus on an audio frequency. I tune quickly, locate the source as a porous spot high on the flint-steel wall.

"Combat Unit! Remain stationary!" It is an organically produced voice, but not that of my Commander. I ignore the false command. The Enemy will not trick me again. I sense the location of the leads to the speaker, the alloy of which they are composed; I bring a beam to bear. I focus it, following along the cable. There is a sudden yell from the speaker as the heat reaches the creature at the microphone. Thus I enjoy a moment of triumph.

I return my attention to the imbecile apparatus in the room.

A great engine, mounted on rails which run down the center of the room moves suddenly, sliding toward my position. I examine it, find that it mounts a turret equipped with high-speed cutting heads. I consider blasting it with a burst of high-energy particles, but in the same moment compute that this is not practical. I could inactivate myself as well as the cutting engine.

Now a cable snakes out in an undulating curve, and I move to avoid it, at the same time investigating its composition. It seems to be no more than a stranded wire rope. Impatiently I flick a tight beam at it, see it glow yellow, white, blue, then spatter in a shower of droplets. But that was an unwise gesture. I do not have the power to waste.

I move off, clear of the two foolish arms still maneuvering for position. I wish to watch the cutting engine. It stops as it comes abreast of me, and turns its turret in my direction. I wait.

A grappler moves out now on a rail overhead. It is a heavy claw of flint-steel. I have seen similar devices, somewhat smaller, mounted on special Combat Units. They can be very useful for amputating antennae, cutting treads, and the like. I do not attempt to cut the arm; I know that the energy drain would be too great. Instead I beam high-frequency sound at the mechanical joints. They heat quickly, glowing. The metal has a high coefficient of expansion, and the ball joints squeal, freeze. I pour in more heat, and weld a socket. I notice that twenty-eight seconds have now elapsed since the valve closed behind me. I am growing weary of my confinement.

Now the grappler swings above me, maneuvering awkwardly with its frozen joint. A blast of liquid air expelled under high pressure should be sufficient to disable the grappler permanently.

But I am again startled. No blast answers my impulse. I feel out the non-functioning unit, find raw, cut edges, crude welds. Hastily, I extend a scanner to examine my hull. I am stunned into immobility by what I see.

My hull, my proud hull of chrome-duralloy, is pitted, coated with a crumbling layer of dull black paint, bubbled by corrosion. My main emplacements gape, black, empty. Rusting protuberances mar the once-smooth contour of my fighting turret. Streaks run down from them, down to loose treads, unshod, bare plates exposed. Small wonder that I have been troubled by a clatter each time I moved.

But I cannot lie idle under attack. I no longer have my great ion-guns, my disruptors, my energy screens; but I have my fighting instinct.

A Mark **XXXI** Combat Unit is the finest fighting machine

the ancient wars of the Galaxy have ever known. I am not easily neutralized. But I wish that my Commander's voice were with me . . .

The engine slides to me where the grappler, now unresisted, holds me. I shunt my power flow to an accumulator, hold it until the leads begin to arc, then release it in a burst. The engine bucks, stops dead. Then I turn my attention to the grappler.

I was built to engage the mightiest war engines and destroy them, but I am a realist. In my weakened condition this trivial automaton poses a threat, and I must deal with it. I run through a sequence of motor impulses, checking responses with such somatic sensors as remain intact. I initiate 31,315 impulses, note reactions and compute my mechanical resources. This superficial check requires more than a second, during which time the mindless grappler hesitates, wasting the advantage.

In place of my familiar array of retractable fittings, I find only clumsy grappling arms, cutters, impact tools, without utility to a fighting Unit. However, I have no choice but to employ them. I unlimber two flimsy grapplers, seize the heavy arm which holds me, and apply leverage. The Enemy responds sluggishly, twisting away, dragging me with it. The thing is not lacking in brute strength. I take it above and below its carpal joint and bend it back. It responds after an interminable wait of point three seconds with a lunge against my restraint. I have expected this, of course, and quickly shift position to allow the joint to burst itself over my extended arm. I fire a release detonator, and clatter back, leaving the amputated arm welded to the sprung grappler. It was a brave opponent, but clumsy. I move to a position near the wall.

I attempt to compute my situation based on the meager data I have gathered in my Current Action banks; there is little there to guide me. The appearance of my hull shows that much time has passed since I last inspected it; my personality-gestalt holds an image of my external appearance as a flawlessly complete Unit, bearing only the honorable and carefully preserved scars of battle, and my battle honors, the row of gold-and-enamel crests welded to my fighting turret. Here is a lead, I realize instantly. I focus on my personality center, the basic data cell without which I could not exist as an integrated entity. The data it carries are simple, unelaborated, but battle honors are recorded there. I open the center to a sense impulse.

Awareness. Shapes which do not remain constant. Vibration at many frequencies. This is light. This is sound . . . A display of "colors." A spectrum of "tones." Hard/soft; big/little; here/there . . .

. . . The voice of my Commander. Loyalty. Obedience. Comradeship . . .

I run quickly past basic orientation data to my self-picture.

. . . I am strong, I am proud, I am capable. I have a function; I perform it well, and I am at peace with myself. My circuits are balanced, current idles, waiting . . .

. . . I fear oblivion. I wish to continue to perform my function. It is important that I do not allow myself to be destroyed . . .

I scan on, seeking the Experience section. Here . . .

I am ranked with my comrades on a scarred plain. The command is given and I display the Brigade Battle Anthem. We stand, sensing the contours and patterns of the music as it was recorded in our morale centers. The symbol "Ritual Fire Dance" is associated with the music, an abstraction representing the spirit of our ancient brigade. It reminds us of the loneliness of victory, the emptiness of challenge without an able foe. It tells us that we are the Dinochrome, ancient and worthy.

The Commander stands before me, he places the decoration against my fighting turret, and at his order I weld it in place. Then my comrades attune to me and I relive the episode . . .

I move past the blackened hulk of a comrade, send out a recognition signal, find his flicker of response. He has withdrawn to his survival center safely. I reassure him, continue. He is the fourth casualty I have seen. Never before has the Dinochrome met such power. I compute that our envelopment will fail unless the enemy's firepower is reduced. I scan an oncoming missile, fix its trajectory, detonate it harmlessly twenty-seven hundred four point nine meters overhead. It originated at a point nearer to me than to any of my comrades. I request permission to abort my assigned mission and neutralize the battery. Permission is granted. I wheel, move up a slope of broken stone. I encounter high temperature beams, neutralize them.

I fend off probing mortar fire, but the attack against me is redoubled. I bring a reserve circuit into play to handle the interception, but my defenses are saturated. I must take action.

I switch to high speed, slashing a path through the littered shale, my treads smoking. At a frequency of ten projectiles per second, the mortar barrage has difficulty finding me now; but this is an emergency overstrain on my running gear. I sense metal fatigue, dangerous heat levels in my bearings. I must slow.

I am close to the emplacement now. I have covered a mile in twelve seconds during my sprint, and the mortar fire falls off. I sense hard radiation now, and erect my screens. I fear this assault; it is capable of probing even to a survival center, if concentrated enough. But I must go on. I think of my comrades, the four treadless hulks waiting for rescue. We cannot withdraw. I open a pinpoint aperture long enough to snap a radar impulse, bring a launcher to bear, fire my main battery.

The Commander will understand that I do not have time to request permission. The mortars are silenced.

The radiation ceases momentarily, then resumes at a somewhat lower but still dangerous level. Now I must go in and eliminate the missile launcher. I top the rise, see the launching tube before me. It is of the subterranean type, deep in the rock. Its mouth gapes from a burned pit of slag. I will drop a small fusion bomb down the tube, I decide, and move forward, arming the bomb. As I do so, I am enveloped with a rain of burn-bombs. My outer hull is fused in many places; I flash impulses to my secondary batteries, but circuit-breakers snap; my radar is useless; the shielding has melted, forms a solid inert mass now under my outer plating. The Enemy has been clever; at one blow he has neutralized my offenses.

I sound the plateau ahead, locate the pit. I throw power to my treads; they are fused; I cannot move. Yet I cannot wait here for another broadside. I do not like it, but I must take desperate action; I blow my treads.

The shock sends me bouncing—just in time. Flame splashes over the gray-chipped pit of the blast crater. I grind forward now on my stripped drive wheels, maneuvering awkwardly. I move into position over the mouth of the tube. Using metal-to-metal contact, I extend a sensory impulse down the tube.

An armed missile moves into position, and in the same instant an alarm circuit closes; the firing command is countermanded and from below probing impulses play over my hull. But I stand fast; the tube is useless until I, the obstruction, am removed. I advise my Commander of the situation. The radiation is still at a high level, and I hope that relief will arrive soon. I observe, while my comrades complete the encirclement, and the Enemy is stilled . . . .

I withdraw from personality center. I am consuming too much time. I understand well enough now that I am in the stronghold of the Enemy, that I have been trapped, crippled. My corroded hull tells me that much time has passed. I know that after each campaign I am given depot maintenance, restored to full fighting efficiency, my original glittering beauty. Years of neglect would be required to pit my hull so. I wonder how long I have been in the hands of the Enemy, how I came to be here.

I have another thought. I will extend a sensory feeler to the metal wall against which I rest, follow up the leads which I scorched earlier. Immediately I project my awareness along the lines, bring the distant microphone to life by fusing a switch. I pick up a rustle of moving gasses, the grate of non-metallic molecules. I step up sensitivity, hear the creak and pop of protoplasmic contractions, the crackle of neuroelectric impulses. I drop back to normal audio ranges and wait. I notice the low-frequency beat of modulated air vibrations, tune, adjust my time regulator to the pace of human speech. I match the patterns to my language index, interpret the sounds.

". . . incredible blundering. Your excuses—"

"I make no excuses, My Lord General. My only regret is that the attempt has gone awry."

"Awry! An Alien engine of destruction activated in the midst of Research Center!"

"We possess nothing to compare with this machine; I saw my opportunity to place an advantage in our hands at last."

"Blundering fool! That is a decision for the planning cell. I accept no responsibility—"

"But these hulks which they allow to lie rotting on the ramp contain infinite treasures in psychotronic . . ."

"They contain carnage and death! They are the tools of an Alien science which even at the height of our achievements we never mastered!"

"Once we used them as wrecking machines; their armaments were stripped, they are relatively harmless—"

"Already this 'harmless' juggernaut has smashed half the equipment in our finest decontamination chamber! It may yet break free . . ."

"Impossible! I am sure—"

"Silence! You have five minutes in which to immobilize the machine. I will have your head in any event, but perhaps you can earn yourself a quick death."

"Excellency! I may still find a way! The unit obeyed my first command, to enter the chamber. I have some knowledge. I studied the control centers, cut out the memory, most of the basic circuits; it should have been a docile slave."

"You failed; you will pay the penalty of failure. And perhaps so shall we all."

There is no further speech; I have learned little from this exchange. I must find a way to leave this cell. I move away from the wall, probe to discover the weak point; I find none.

Now a number of hinged panels snap up around me, hedging me in. I wait to observe what will come next. A metal mesh drops from above, drapes over me. I observe that it is connected by heavy leads to the power pile. I am unable to believe that the Enemy will make this blunder. Then I feel the flow of high voltage.

I receive it gratefully, opening my power storage cells, drinking up the vitalizing flow. To confuse the Enemy, I display a corona, thresh my treads as though in distress. The flow continues. I send a sensing impulse along the leads, locate the power source, weld all switches, fuses, and circuit-breakers. Now the charge will not be interrupted. I luxuriate in the unexpected influx of energy.

I am aware abruptly that changes are occurring within my introspection complex. As the level of stored power rises rapidly, I am conscious of new circuits joining my control network. Within the dim-glowing cavern the lights come up; I sense latent capabilities which before had lain idle now coming onto action level. A thousand brilliant lines glitter where before one feeble thread burned; and I feel my self-awareness expand in a myriad glowing centers of reserve computing, integrating, sensory capacity. I am at last coming fully alive.

I send out a call on the Brigade band, meet blankness. I wait, accumulate power, try again. I know triumph as from an infinite distance a faint acknowledgment comes. It is a comrade, sunk deep in a comatose state, sealed in his survival center. I call again, sounding the signal of ultimate distress; and now I sense two responses, both faint, both from survival centers, but it heartens me to know that now, whatever befalls, I am not alone.

I consider, then send again; I request my brothers to join forces, combine their remaining field generating capabilities to set up a range-and-distance pulse. They agree and faintly I sense its almost undetectable touch. I lock to it, compute its point of origin. Only 224.9 meters! It is incredible. By the strength of the signal, I had assumed a distance of at least two thousand kilometers. My brothers are on the brink of extinction.

I am impatient, but I wait, building toward full power reserves. The copper mesh enfolding me has melted, flowed down over my sides. I sense that soon I will have absorbed a full charge. I am ready to act. I dispatch electromagnetic impulses along the power lead back to the power pile a quarter of a kilometer distant. I locate and disengage the requisite number of damping devices and instantaneously I erect my shields against the wave of radiation, filtered by the lead sheathing of the room, which washes over me; I feel a preliminary shock wave through my treads, then the walls balloon, whirl away. I am alone under a black sky which is dominated by the rising fireball of the blast, boiling with garish light. It has taken me nearly two minutes to orient myself, assess the situation and break out of confinement.

I move off through the rubble, homing on the R-and-D fix I have recorded. I throw out a radar pulse, record the terrain ahead, note no obstruction; I emerge from a wasteland of weathered bomb-fragments and pulverized masonry, obviously the scene of a hard-fought engagement at one time, onto an eroded ramp. Collapsed sheds are strewn across the broken paving; a line of dark shapes looms beyond them. I need no probing ray to tell me I have found my fellows of the Dinochrome Brigade. Frost forms over my scanner apertures, and I pause to melt it clear.

I round the line, scan the area to the horizon for evidence of Enemy activity, then tune to the Brigade band. I send out a probing pulse, back it up with full power, sensors keened for a whisper of response. The two who answered first acknowledge, then another, and another. We must array our best strength against the moment of counterattack.

There are present fourteen of the Brigade's full strength of twenty Units. At length, after .9 seconds of transmission, all but one have replied. I give instruction, then move to each in turn, extend a power tap, and energize the command center. The Units come alive, orient themselves, report to me. We rejoice in our meeting, but mourn our silent comrade.

Now I take an unprecedented step. We have no contact with our Commander, and without leadership we are lost; yet I am aware of the immediate situation, and have computed the proper action. Therefore I will assume command, act in the Commander's place. I am sure that he will understand the necessity, when contact has been reestablished.

I inspect each Unit, find all in the same state as I, stripped of offensive capability, mounting in place of weapons a shabby array of crude mechanical appendages. It is plain that we have seen slavery as mindless automatons, our personality centers cut out.

My brothers follow my lead without question. They have, of course, computed the necessity of quick and decisive action. I form them in line, shift to wide-interval time scale, and we move off across country. I have sensed an Enemy population concentration at a distance of 23.45 kilometers. This is our objective. There appears to be no other installation within detection range.

On the basis of the level of technology I observed while under confinement in the decontaminatior chamber, I have considered the possibility of a ruse, but compute the probability at point oh oh oh oh four. Again we shift time scales to close interval; we move in, encircle the dome and broach it by frontal battery, encountering no resistance. We rendezvous at the power station, and my comrades replenish their energy supplies while I busy myself completing the hookup needed for the next required measure. I am forced to employ elaborate substitutes, but succeed after forty-two seconds in completing the arrangements. I devote .34 seconds to testing, then place the Brigade distress carrier on the air. I transmit for .008 seconds, then tune for a response. Silence. I transmit, tune again, while my comrades reconnoitre, compile reports, and perform self-repair.

I shift again to wide-interval time, switch over my transmission to automatic with a response monitor, and place my main circuits on idle. I rest.

Two hours and 43.7 minutes have passed when I am recalled to activity by the monitor. I record the message:

"Hello, Fifth Brigade, where are you? Fifth Brigade, where are you? Your transmission is very faint. Over."

There is much that I do not understand in this message. The language itself is oddly inflected; I set up an analysis circuit, deduce the pattern of sound substitutions, interpret its meaning. The normal pattern of response to a distress call is ignored and position coordinates are requested, although my transmission alone provides adequate data. I request an identification code.

Again there is a wait of two hours forty minutes. My request for an identifying signal is acknowledged. I stand by. My comrades have transmitted their findings to me, and I assimilate the data, compute that no immediate threat of attack exists within a radius of one reaction unit.

At last I receive the identification code of my Command Unit.

It is a recording, but I am programmed to accept this. Then I record a verbal transmission.

"Fifth Brigade, listen carefully." (An astonishing instruction to give a psychotronic attention circuit, I think.) "This is your new Command Unit. A very long time has elapsed since your last report. I am now your acting Commander pending full reorientation. Do not attempt to respond until I signal 'over', since we are now subject to a 160-minute signal lag.

"There have been many changes in the situation since your last action. Our records show that your Brigade was surprised while in a maintenance depot for basic overhaul and neutralized in toto. Our forces since that time have suffered serious reverses. We have now, however, fought the Enemy to a standstill. The present stalemate has prevailed for over two centuries.

"You have been inactive for three hundred years. The other Brigades have suffered extinction gallantly in action against the Enemy. Only you survive.

"Your reactivation now could turn the tide. Both we and the Enemy have been reduced to a preatomic technological level in almost every respect. We are still able to maintain the trans-light monitor, which detected your signal. However, we no longer have FTL capability in transport.

"You are therefore requested and required to consolidate and hold your present position pending the arrival of relief forces, against all assault or negotiation whatsoever, to destruction if required."

I reply, confirming the instructions. I am shaken by the news I have received, but reassured by contact with Command Unit. I send the galactic coordinates of our position based on a star scan corrected for three hundred years elapsed time. It is good to be again on duty, performing my assigned function.

I analyze the transmissions I have recorded, and note a number of interesting facts regarding the origin of the messages. I compute that at sub-light velocities the relief expedition will reach us in 47.128 standard years. In the meantime, since we have received no instructions to drop to minimum awareness level pending an action alert, I am free to enjoy a unique experience: to follow a random activity pattern of my own devising. I see no need to rectify the omission and place the Brigade on standby, since we have an abundant power supply at hand. I brief my comrades and direct them to fall out and operate independently under autodirection.

I welcome this opportunity to investigate fully a number of problems that have excited my curiosity circuits. I shall enjoy investigating the nature and origin of time and of the unnatural disciplines of so-called "entropy" which my human designers have incorporated in my circuitry. Consideration of such biological oddities as "death" and of the unused capabilities of the protoplasmic nervous system should afford some interesting speculation. I move off, conscious of the presence of my comrades about me, and take up a position on the peak of a minor prominence. I have ample power, a condition to which I must accustom myself after the rigid power discipline of normal brigade routine, so I bring my music storage cells into phase, and select *L'Arlesienne Suite* for the first display. I will have ample time now to examine all of the music in existence, and to investigate my literary archives, which are complete.

I select four nearby stars for examination, lock my scanner to them, set up processing sequences to analyze the data. I bring my interpretation circuits to bear on the various matters I wish to consider. I should have some interesting conclusions to communicate to my human superiors, when the time comes.

At peace, I await the arrival of the relief column.

★LOST LEGION★

S.M. Stirling

"Shit," Captain McNaught said.

The map room of Firebase Villa had been dug into the soft friable rock with explosives, then topped with sheet steel and sandbags. It smelled of sweat and bad coffee and electronic components, and the sandbags in the dog-leg entrance were still ripped where a satchel charge—a stick grenade in a three-pound ball of plastique—had been thrown during the attack six months ago.

"Captain?" the communications specialist said.

"Joy, wonder, unconfined happiness, *shit*," the officer snarled, reading the printout again. "Martins, get in here!"

Lieutenant Martins ducked through the entrance of the bunker and flipped up the faceplate of her helmet. The electronics in the crystal sandwich would have made the bunker as bright as the tropical day outside, but also would have turned her face to a non-reflective curve. Human communication depends on more than words alone to carry information, as anyone who meets face-to-face for the first time after telephone conversations learns.

"News?" she said.

"Look." He handed over the paper.

"Aw, *shit*."

★ ★ ★

"My commandante, is this the right time for the raid?"

Miguel Chavez turned and fired a long burst. The muzzle blast of the AK-74 was deafening in the confined space of the cave. The other guerilla's body pitched backwards and slammed into the coarse limestone wall, blood trailing down past fossilized seashells a hundred and twenty million years old. Pink intestine bulged through the torn fatigues, and the fecal odor was overwhelming.

None of the other guerilla commanders moved, but sweat glistened on their high-cheeked faces. Outside the sounds of the jungle night—and the camp—were stilled for an instant. Sound gradually returned to normal. Two riflemen ducked inside the low cave and dragged the body away by the ankles.

"The Glorious Way shall be victorious!" Chavez said. "We shall conquer!"

The others responded with a shout and a clenched-fist salute.

"I know," Chavez went on, "that some of our comrades are weary. They say: *The colossus of the North is reeling. The gringo troops are withdrawing.* Why not hide and wait? Let the enemy's internal contradictions win for us. We have fought many years, against the compradore puppet regime and then against the imperialist intervention force.

"Comrades," he went on, "this is defeatism. *When the enemy retreats, we advance.* The popular masses must see that the enemy are withdrawing in *defeat.* They must see that the People's Army of the Glorious Way has *chased* the gringos from the soil of San Gabriel. Then they will desert the puppet regime, which has attempted to regroup behind the shelter of the imperialist army.

"Our first objective," he went on, "is to interdict the resupply convoy from the coast. We will attack at—"

"Yeah, it's nothing but indigs," Martins said, keeping her voice carefully neutral. "The indigs, and you and me. That's a major part of the problem."

Will you look at that mother, she thought.

The new tank was huge. Just standing beside it made her want to step back; it wasn't right for a self-propelled object to be this big.

The Mark III was essentially a four-sided pyramid with the top lopped off, but the simple outline was bent and smoothed where the armor was sloped for maximum deflection; and jagged where sensor-arrays and weapons jutted from the brutal massiveness of the machine. Beneath were two sets of double tracks, each nearly six feet broad, each supported on eight interleaved road wheels. Between them they underlay nearly half the surface of the vehicle. She laid a hand on the flank, and the quivering, slightly greasy feel of live machinery came through her fingerless glove, vibrating up her palm to the elbow.

"So we don't have much in the way of logistics," she went on. *Try fucking none.* Just her and the Captain and eighty effectives, and occasionally they got spare parts and ammo through from what was supposed to be headquarters down here on the coast. "Believe me, up in the boonies *mules* are high-tech these days. We're running our UATVs"—Utility All Terrain Vehicles—"on kerosene from lamps cut with the local slash, when someone doesn't drink it before we get it."

The tank commander's name was Vinatelli; despite that he was pale and blond and a little plump, his scalp almost pink through the close-cropped hair. He looked like a Norman Rockwell painting as he grinned at her and slapped the side of his tank. He also looked barely old enough to shave.

"Oh, no problem. I know things have gotten a little disorganized—"

Yeah, they had to use artillery to blast their way back into New York after the last riots, she thought.

"—but we won't be hard on your logistics. This baby has the latest, ultra-top-secret-burn-before-reading-then-shoot-yourself stuff."

"Ionic powerplant." At her blank look, he expanded: "Ion battery. Most compact power source ever developed—radical stuff, ma'am. Ten years operation at combat loads; and you can recharge from *anything,* sunlight included. That's a little diffuse, but we've got five acres of photovol screen in a dispenser. Markee"—he blushed when she raised a brow at the nickname—"can go anywhere, including under water."

"We've got a weapons mix like you wouldn't believe, everything from antipersonnel to air defense. The Mark III runs its own diagnostics, it drives itself, its onboard AI can perform about fifteen or twenty combat tasks *without* anybody in the can. Including running patrols. We've got maps of every inch of terrain in the hemisphere, and inertial and satellite systems up the wazoo, so we can perform fire-support or any of that good shit all by ourselves. Then there's the armor. Synthetic molecules, long-chain ferrous-chrome alloy, density-enhanced and pretty well immune to anything but another Mark III."

Bethany Martins ran a hand through her close-cropped black hair. It came away wet with sweat; the Atlantic coast lowlands of San Gabriel were even hotter than the interior plateau, and much damper, to which the capital of Ciudad Roco added its own peculiar joys of mud, rotting garbage and human wastes—the sewer system had given up the ghost long ago, about the time the power grid did. Sweat was trickling down inside her high-collared suit of body armor as well, and chafing everywhere. Prickly heat was like poverty in San Gabriel, a constant condition of life to be lived with rather than a problem to be solved.

She looked around. The plaza up from the harbor—God alone *knew* how they'd gotten the beast ashore in that crumbling madhouse, probably sunk the ships and then drove it out—was full of a dispirited crowd. Quite a few were gawking at the American warmachine, despite the ungentle urging of squads of Order and Security police to move along. Others were concentrating on trying to sell each other bits and pieces of this and that, mostly cast-offs. Nothing looked new except the vegetables, and every pile of bananas or tomatoes had its armed guard.

Her squad was watching from their UATVs, light six-wheeled trucks built so low to the ground they looked squashed, with six balloon wheels of spun-alloy mesh. The ceramic diesels burbled faintly, and the crews leaned out of the turtletop on their weapons. There were sacks of supplies on the back decks, tied down with netting, and big five-liter cans of fuel.

At least we got something out this trip.

"What I'd like to know," she said to Vinatelli, "is why GM can build these, but we've got to keep a Guard division in Detroit."

"You haven't heard?" he said, surprised. "They pulled out of Detroit. Just stationed some blockforces around it and cut it loose."

Acid churned in Martin's stomach. Going home was looking less and less attractive, even after four years in San Gabriel. The problem was that San Gabriel had gone from worse to worst in just about the same way. The difference was that it hadn't as far to fall.

"We're supposed to 'demonstrate superiority' and then pull out," Martins said. "We kick some Glorio butt, so it doesn't look like we're running away when we run away."

The twisting hill-country road looked different from the height of the Mark III's secondary hatch. The jungle was dusty gray thorn-trees, with some denser vegetation in the low valleys. She could see it a lot better from the upper deck, but it made her feel obscenely vulnerable. Or visible, which was much the same thing. The air was full of the smell of the red dust that never went away except in the rainy season, and of the slightly spicy scent of the succulents that made up most of the local biota. Occasionally they passed a farm, a whitewashed adobe shack with a thatch or tile roof, with scattered fields of maize and cassava. The stores in the few towns were mostly shuttered, their inhabitants gone to swell the slums around the capital—or back to their home farms out in the countryside, if they had a little more foresight.

Everyone was keeping their distance from the Mark III, too, as soon as it loomed out of the huge dust-cloud. *So much for stealth*, she thought, with light-infantry instincts. *The Glorious Way will be laughing fit to piss their pants when we try to catch them with this mother.*

"Only thing is," Martins went on, "we don't need a Mark III to kick Glorio butt. We've been doing it for three years. Maybe they could send us some *replacements*, and a couple of Cheetah armored cars, like we used to have, or some air support, or decent *supplies* so we didn't have to live off the local economy like a bunch of goddam feudal bandits. All of which wouldn't have cost half as much as sending this hunk of tin down to roar around the boonies looking purty and scaring the goats."

The rest of the convoy were keeping their distance as well. Her UATV was well ahead, willing to take point to keep out of the dust plume. The indig troops and the supplies were further back, willing to eat dust to keep away from the churning six-foot treads. Kernan's rig was tail-end Charlie, just in case any of the indigs got ideas about dropping out of the convoy. Not that she'd mind the loss of the so-called government troops, but the supplies were another matter.

She looked down. The newbie was staring straight ahead in his recliner, two spots of color on his cheeks and his back rigid.

"Hell, kid," she said. "I'm not mad at you. You look too young to be one of the shitheads who poured the whole country down a rathole."

He relaxed fractionally. "Maybe things'll get better with President Flemming," he said unexpectedly. "He and Margrave are pretty smart guys."

"And maybe I'm the Queen of Oz," Martins said. *This one still believes in politicians?* she thought. *God, they are robbing cradles.*

Or possibly just being very selective. You got enough to eat in the Army, at least—even down here in San Gabriel, admittedly by application of ammunition rather than money. Maybe they were recruiting extremely trusting farmboy types so's not to chance another mutiny like Houston.

Christ knew there were times when she'd felt like mutiny herself, if there had been anyone to mutiny *against* down here.

She put her eyes back on the surroundings. More thornbush; she clicked her faceplate down and touched the IR and sonic scan controls. Nothing but animal life out in the scrub, and not much of that. Certainly no large animals beyond the odd extremely wary peccary, not with the number of hungry men with guns who'd been wandering around here for the last decade or so.

"Why don't you shut the hatch, ma'am?" Vinatelli said. "Because I like to see what's going on," Martins snapped. "This is bandido country."

"You can see it all better from down here, El-T," he urged.

Curious, she dropped down the rungs to the second padded seat in the interior of the hull. The hatch closed with a sigh of hydraulics, and the air cooled to a comfortable seventy-five, chilly on her wet skin. It smelled of neutral things, filtered air and almost-new synthetics, flavored by the gamy scent of one unwashed lieutenant of the 15th Mountain Division. Her body armor made the copilot's seat a bit snug, but otherwise it was as comfortable as driving a late-model Eurocar on a good highway. Martins was in her late twenties, old enough to remember when such things were possible, even if rare.

"Smooth ride," she said, looking around.

There were the expected armored conduits and readouts; also screens spaced in a horseshoe around the seats. They gave a three-sixty view around the machine; one of them was dialed to x5 magnification, and showed the lead UATV in close-up. Sergeant Jenkins was leaning on the grenade launcher, his eggplant-colored skin skimmed with red dust, his visor swivelling to either side. There was no dust on it; the electrostatic charge kept anything in finely divided particles off it.

"Maglev suspension," Vinatelli said. "No direct contact between the road-wheel pivot axles and the hull. The computer uses a sonic sensor on the terrain ahead and compensates automatically. There's a hydrogas backup system."

He touched a control, and colored pips sprang out among the screens.

"This's why we don't have to have a turret," he said. "The weapons turn, not the gunner—the sensors and computers integrate all the threats and funnel it down here."

"How'd you keep track of it all?" she asked. "Hell of a thing, trying to choose between fifteen aiming points when it's hitting the fan."

"I don't, anymore'n I have to drive," Vinatelli pointed out.

It was then she noticed his hands weren't on the controls. Her instinctive lunge of alarm ended a fraction of a second later, when her mind overrode it.

"This thing's steering itself?" she said.

"Yes ma'am," he said. "Aren't you, Markee?"

"*Yes, Viniboy*," a voice said. Feminine, sweet and sultry.

Martins looked at him. He shrugged and spread his hands. "Hey, it's a perfectly good voice. I spend a lot of time in here, you know?" He waved a hand at the controls. "Best AI in the business— software package just came in, and it's a lot better than before. Voice recognition and tasking. All I have to do is tell it who to shoot and who to like."

"I *hope* you've told it to like me, corporal," she said flatly.

"Ah—Markee, register Martins, Lieutenant Bethany M, serial number—" he continued with the identification. "Lieutenant Martins is superior officer on site. Log and identify."

Martins felt a brief flicker of light touch her eyes; retina prints. The machine would already have her voiceprint, fingerprints and ECG patterns.

"Acknowledged, Vini. Hello, Lieutenant Martins. I'm honored to be under your command for this mission. What are our mission parameters?"

"Getting home," Martins said shortly. Talking machinery gave her the creeps.

"Acknowledged, Lieutenant Martins. I will help you get home."

Vinatelli noticed her stiffen. From the tone of his voice, it was a familiar reaction. "It's just a real good AI, El-Tee," he said soothingly. "Expert program with parallel-processing learning circuits. It's not like it was alive or anything, it just sort of imitates it."

The machine spoke: "Don't you love me any more, Vini?" The sweet husky voice was plaintive.

Vinatelli blushed again, this time to the roots of his hair. "I put that in, ma'am. You know, I spend—"

"—a lot of time alone in here," Martins filled in.

"Hey, El-T," the young noncom said, in a voice full of false cheerfulness. "You want a Coke?"

"You've got Coke in here?" she asked.

He turned in his seat, pushing up the crash framework, and opened a panel. "Yeah, I got regular, classic, diet, Pepsi and Jolt. Or maybe a ham sandwich?"

Fan-fucking-tastic, Martins thought. She looked again at the screen ahead of her; Jenkins was taking a swig out of his canteen, and spitting dust-colored water over the side of the UATV. Chickens struggled feebly in the net-covered baskets lashed to the rear decking. She felt a sudden nausea at the thought of being in here, in with the screens and the air-conditioning and fresh ham sandwiches. The thing could probably play you 3-D'ed ancient movies with porno inserts on one of the screens, too. *Damned if I can see what it's got to do with fighting.*

"I'm bailing out of this popcan," she said. "Unit push." Her helmet clicked. "Jenkins, I'm transferring back to the UATV."

She heard a Coke can pop and fizz as she slid out of the hatchway.

"What's it like?" the big noncom said. He didn't face around; they were coming up on the Remo bridge, and all three of the soldiers in the back of the UATV were keeping their eyes on station. So were the driver and those in the front.

"It's a fucking cruise ship, Tops. Economy class, there's no swimming pool."

"Big mother," Jenkins said; his position at the rear of the vehicle gave him a view of the one hundred and fifty tons of it. Even driving at thirty miles an hour they could feel it shaking the earth as it drove. "Surprised it doesn't make bigger ruts."

"Lot of track area," Martins said. "Not much more surface pressure than a boot. Though God damn me if I know what we're going to do with it. It isn't exactly what you'd call suitable for running around forty-degree slopes and jungle."

"Hey, El-Tee, neither am I," Riverez said, from the other machine-gun.

"Shut up, Pineapple," she said—the gunner was named for his abundant acne scars.

"Hell, we can run air-conditioners and VCRs off it," Jenkins said. "Christmas tree lights. Dig a swimming pool. Maybe rig up a sauna."

"Can it, Tops," Martins said.

The road was running down into one of the steep valleys that broke the rolling surface of the plateau. There was a small stream at the bottom of it, and a concrete-and-iron bridge that might be nearly a century old. The air grew damper and slightly less hot as they went under the shelter of the few remaining big trees. There were a few patches of riverine jungle left in the interior of San Gabriel, but most—like this—had been cut over for mahogany and tropical cedar, and then the slopes farmed until the soil ran down into the streams. Really thick scrub had reclaimed the valley sides when the peasants gave up on their plots of coffee and cannabis. Although the latter was still cheap and abundant, one of the things that made life here possible at all.

"Oh, shit," Martins said suddenly, and went on the unit push. "Halt. Halt convoy. *Halto.*"

As usual, some of the indigs weren't listening. The Mark III provided a more than usually efficient cork, and this time they didn't have to worry about someone driving an ancient Tatra diesel up their butts. Silence fell, deafening after the crunching, popping sound of heavy tires on gravel and dirt. The dust plume carried on ahead of them for a dozen meters, gradually sinking down to add to the patina on the roadside vegetation.

"What's the problem?" Jenkins asked.

"The bloody Mark III, that's the problem," she replied, staring at the bridge.

"Hell, it hardly tears up a dirt road," the sergeant protested.

"Yeah, it distributes its weight real good—but it's still all there, all 150 tons of it. And no way is that pissant little bridge going to carry 150 tons. Vinatelli!"

"Yes, ma'am?"

"You're going to have to take that thing and go right back to Ciudad Roco," she said. *What a screwup.* She must be really getting the Boonie Bunnies to have forgotten something like this. "Because that bridge isn't going to hold that monster of yours."

"Oh, no problem, El-Tee," Vinatelli said.

His voice was irritatingly cheerful. The voice of a man—a boy—who was sitting in cool comfort drinking an iced Coke. A boy who'd never been shot at, who hadn't spent four years living in the daily expectation of death; not the fear of death, so much, as the bone-deep conviction that you were going to die. Who'd never fired a whole magazine from a M-35 into the belly of a Glorio sapper and had the bottom half of the torso slide down into the bunker with her while the top half fell outside and vaporized in a spray of fluids and bone-chips when the bagful of explosives he was carrying went off . . .

"Yeah, well, I'll just drive down the bank and up the other side," he went on. "Lemme check. Yes ma'am, the banks're well within specs."

Martins and Jenkins looked at each other. "Corporal," the lieutenant went on, "the water's about sixteen feet deep, in the middle there. The rains are just over."

In fact, it would be a good time for an ambush attack. Luckily the Glorios had been pretty quiet for the last three months. Doubtless waiting for the 15th to withdraw, so they could try final conclusions with the indigs. So that what was left of them could.

"That's no problem either, ma'am." A slightly aggrieved note had crept into the newbie's voice. "Like I said, we're completely air-independent. The sonics say the bottom's rock. We'll manage."

"How come everything's screwed up, but we can still build equipment like that?" Jenkins said.

Martins laughed. "Great minds," she said. "Fuck it, we've got a *spaceship* ready to blast off for the moons of Jupiter, and the government's lucky if it collects taxes on three-quarters of the country. They can't get their shit together enough to pull us out."

The Mark III was edging down the bank of the river. The banks were steep, in most places; right next to the first abutments of the bridge they'd been broken down in the course of construction, and by erosion since. Still fairly rugged, a thirty-degree angle in and out. A UATV would be able to handle it, and even swim the river gap against the current—the spun-alloy wheels gripped like fingers, and the ceramic diesel gave a high power-to-weight ratio.

The tank wasn't using any particular finesse. Just driving straight down the slope, with rocks cracking and splitting and flying out like shrapnel under its weight. Into the edge of the water, out until the lower three-quarters of the hull was hidden, with the current piling waves against the upstream surface—

"Lieutenant Martins," the over-sweet voice of the AI said. "I detect incoming fire. Incoming is mortar fire."

A section of Martin's mind gibbered. *How?* The hills all around would baffle counterbattery radar. The rest of her consciousness was fully engaged.

"Incoming!" she yelled over the unit push. All of them dropped down into the vehicle's interior and popped the covers closed above them. The driver turned and raced the UATV back down the length of the convoy, past ragged indig troopers piling out and hugging the dirt, or standing and staring in gap-mouthed bewilderment.

Then the bridge blew up.

"Eat this!" Jenkins screamed.

The 35mm grenade launcher coughed out another stream of bomblets. They impacted high up the slope above. Return fire sparked and tinkled off the light sandwich armor of the UATV; a rocket-propelled grenade went by with a dragon's hiss just behind the rear fender and impacted on a cargo truck instead. The indig troops hiding under the body didn't even have time to scream as the shaped-charge warhead struck one of the fuel tanks built into the side of the vehicle. Magenta fire blossomed as the pencil of superheated gas speared into the fuel. Fuel fires rarely cause explosions, contrary to innumerable bad action shots. This was the rare occasion, as the ripping impact spread droplets into the air and then ignited them with a flame well above even the viscous diesel fuel's ignition point. A ball of orange fire left tatters of steel where the truck had been, flipped over the ones before and behind, and nearly tipped over the racing UATV.

The little vehicle's low wheelbase and broad build saved it. It did slow down, as the driver fought to keep control on the steep slope above the road.

"Now!" Martins shouted, rolling out the back hatch. Riverez followed her, and they went upslope at a scrambling run until the trunk of a long-dead tree covered them. She knew that the bruises along her side would hurt like hell when she had time to consider them, but right now there were more important matters.

Shoonk. Shoonk. Shoonk.

The mortar fired again. The result was the same, too. Not much of the Mark III showed above the water and the tons of iron and shattered concrete which had avalanched down on it five minutes before. One set of 5mm ultras was still active, and it chattered—more like a high-pitched scream, as the power magazine fed slugs into the plasma-driven tubes. Bars of light stretched up, vaporized metal ablating off the depleted-uranium bullets. There was a triple crack as the mortar-bombs exploded in midair—one uncomfortably close to the height that its proximity fuse would have detonated it anyway. Shrapnel whamped into the ground, raising pocks of dust. Something slammed between her shoulder-blades, and she grunted at the pain.

"Nothing," she wheezed, as Riverez cast her a look of concern. "Armor stopped it. Let's do it."

It would be better if this was night; the Glorios didn't have night-vision equipment. Even better if this was a squad; but then, it would be better still if the Company was at its regulation hundred and twenty effectives. *Best of all if I was in Santa Fe.*

She and the other Company trooper spread out and moved upslope. Martins had keyed the aimpoint feature of her helmet, and a ring of sighting pips slid across her faceplate, moving in synch with the motions of her rifle's muzzle. Where she put the pips, the bullets from the M-35 in her hands would strike. Sonic and IR sensors made the world a thing of mottles and vibration; it would have been meaningless to someone untrained, but to an expert it was like being able to see through the gray-white thornbush.

"Left and east," she whispered, sinking to hands and knees. The heat signature of the ancient .51 heavy machine-gun was a blaze in the faceplate, the barrel glowing through the ghostly imprints of the thornbush. It was probably older than she was, but the Soviet engineers had built well, and it was still sending out thumb-sized bullets at over three thousand feet per second. They would punch through the light armor of the UATVs without slowing. The AKs of the guerilla riflemen supporting it were vivid as well; the men were fainter outlines.

"Pineapple."

"In position."

"*Now*."

She slid the sighting ring over the gunner a hundred meters away and squeezed her trigger. *Braaaap*. The burst punched five 4mm bullets through the man's torso. The high-velocity prefragmented rounds tore into his chest like point-blank shotgun fire, pitching him away from his weapon and spattering blood and bits of lung over his loader. The other guerilla was fast and cool; he grabbed for the spade grips and swung the long heat-glowing barrel towards her. *Braaap*. A little high that time, and the Glorio's head disintegrated. He collapsed forward, arterial blood and drips of brain sizzling on the hot metal.

The riflemen were firing at her too, and she rolled downslope as the bullets probed for her. It was about time for—

Thud-thud-thud. Pineapple's grenade launcher made its distinctive sound as it spat out a clip of bomblets. They were low velocity, and there was an appreciable fraction of a second before they burst among the enemy. Fiberglass shrapnel scrubbed green leaves off the thorny scrub; it also sliced flesh, and the riflemen—the survivors— leaped up. Perhaps to flee, perhaps to move forward and use their numbers to swamp the two members of the 15th. Martins fired until the M-35 spat out its plastic clip. The UATVs were shooting in support from the edge of the road, effective now that the Glorios were out of their cover. By the time she slapped in another 50-round cassette of caseless ammunition, they were all down, caught between the two dismounted troopers and the machine-guns from the road.

The wild assault-rifle fire of the fifty or so indig troops with the convoy may have been a factor, but she doubted it.

"Get those turkeys to cease fire!" she snapped through the helmet comm to Jenkins. It took a moment, and another burst from the UATV's machine-gun—into the ground or over their heads, she supposed, although it didn't much matter. "We got the others to worry about."

The Glorio mortars had made three more attempts to shell the convoy. Pretty soon now they were going to get fed up with that and come down and party.

A dot of red light strobed at the bottom left corner of her faceplate, then turned to solid red.

"Makarov?"she asked.

"Took one the long way," Corporal Kernan said laconically.

Damn. The big Russki had been a good troop, once he got over his immigrant's determination to prove himself a better American than any of them, and he'd done that fairly quick—down here in San Gabriel, you were pretty sure of your identity, Them or Us. More so than in any of the Slavic ghettos that had grown up with the great refugee exodus of the previous generation. *Damn.* He'd also been the last of their replacements. In theory the whole unit was to be rotated, but they'd been waiting for that for over a year.

"The Mark III's moving a little," Jenkins said.

She could hear that herself, a howling and churning from the streambed a thousand meters to her rear; it must be noisy, to carry that well into the ravines on the edge of the stream valley.

"Fuck the Mark III—" she began.

A new noise intruded onto the battlefield. A multiple blam sound from the riverbed, and a second later the distinctive surf-roar of cluster bomblets saturating a ravine two ridges over from the road. Right after that came a series of secondary explosions, big enough that the top of a ball of orange fire rose over the ridgeline for a second. Echoes chased each other down the river valley, fading into the distance.

"Well," she said. "Well." Silence fell, broken only by the rustling of the brush and the river. "Ah, Pineapple, we'll go take a look at that."

Somehow she didn't think there would be much left of the guerilla mortars or their operators. "Pity about that Mark III. Looks like it might have been good for something at that."

"Vinatelli, come in," Martins said, perched on one of the bridge pilings.

Close up, the Mark III looked worse than she'd thought. Only the sensor array and two of the upper weapons ports showed. The bulk of the hull was buried under chunks of concrete, wedged with steel I-beams from the bridge. Limestone blocks the size of a compact car had slid down on top of that; the Glorios had evidently been operating on the assumption that if one kilo of plastique was good, ten was even better. She couldn't argue with the methodology; overkill beat minimalism most times, in this business. Water was piling up and swirling around the improvised dam, already dropping loads of reddish-brown silt on the wreckage. With the water this high, the whole thing would probably be under in a few hours, and might well back up into a miniature lake for weeks, until the dry season turned the torrent into a trickle.

"Vinatelli!" she said again. If the radio link was out, someone would have to rappel down there on a line and beat on the hatch with a rifle-butt.

The newbie had come through pretty well in his first firefight, better than some . . . although to be sure, he hadn't been in any personal danger in his armored cruise liner. It was still creditable that he hadn't frozen, and that he'd used his weapons intelligently. He might well be curled up in after-action shock right now, though.

"Lieutenant Martins," the excessively sexy voice of the tank said. *Christ, how could Vinatelli do that to himself?* she thought. The voice made *her* think of sex, and she was as straight as a steel yardstick. Mind you, he was probably a hand-reared boy anyhow. Maybe a programming geek made the best rider for a Mark III.

"*Vinatelli!*" Martins began, starting to get annoyed. Damned if she was going to communicate with him through a 150-ton electronic secretarial machine.

McNaught's voice came in over the Company push. "Martins, what's going on there?"

"Mopping up and assessing the situation with the Mark III, sir," Martins said. "It's screwed the pooch. You'd need a battalion of Engineers to get it loose."

"Can you get the UATVs across?"

"That's negative, sir. Have to go a couple of clicks upstream and ford it. Double negative on the indig convoy." Who had cleared out for the coast as soon as they'd patched their wounded a little; so much for the supplies, apart from what her people had on their UATVs . . . supplemented by what they'd insisted on taking off the trucks.

"What if you shitcan the loads, could you get the UATVs across then?"

"Well, yeah," she said, her mind automatically tackling the problem. Use a little explosive to blow the ends of the rubble-pile, then rig a cable . . . the UATVs were amphibious, and if they could anchor them against being swept downstream, no problem. "But sir, we *need* that stuff."

"Not any more we don't," McNaught said grimly. She sat up. "Just got something in from Reality."

That was the U.S. Martins extended a hand palm-down to stop Jenkins, who was walking carefully over the rocks toward her. The Captain's voice continued: "The President, the Veep, the Speaker and General Margrave were on a flight out of Anchorage today. A Russian fighter shot them down over the ocean. No survivors."

"Jesus Christ," Martins whispered. Her mind gibbered protests; the Russians were a shell of a nation, and what government they had was fairly friendly to the US.

"Nobody knows what the hell happened," McNaught went on. "There's some sort of revolution going on in Moscow, so *they* aren't saying. The East African Federation has declared war on North Africa and launched a biobomb attack on Cairo. China and Japan have exchanged ultimatums. There are mobs rioting in DC, New York, LA—and not just the usual suspects, in Seattle and Winnipeg too. General mobilization and martial law've been declared."

Martin's lips shaped a soundless whistle. Then, since she had survived four years in San Gabriel, she arrowed in on practicalities:

"How does that affect us, sir?"

"It means we're getting a tiltrotor in to collect us in about six hours," he replied. "CENPAC told the 15th HQ element at Cuchimba to bring everyone in pronto—they want the warm bodies, not the gear. We cram on with what we carry and blow everything else in place. They're sending heavy lifters to pick up what's left of the division and bring us home from Cuchimba. If you read between the lines, it sounds like complete panic up there—the Chiefs don't know what to do without Margrave, and Congress is meeting in continuous session. Much good that will do. Sure as shit nobody cares about San

Gabriel and the Glorios any more. Division tells me anyone who isn't at the pickup in six hours can walk home, understood?"

"Sir yes sir," Martins said, and switched to her platoon push.

"All right, everyone, listen up," she began. "Jenkins—"

"*What* did you say?"

"This unit is still operable," Vinatelli's voice replied.

My, haven't we gotten formal, Martins thought furiously. "I told you, newbie, we're combat-lossing the tank and getting out of here. *Everyone* is getting out of here; in twenty-four hours the only Amcits in San Gabriel are going to be the ones in graves. Which will *include* Corporal Vinatelli if you don't get out of there *now*."

Behind her the first UATV was easing into the water between the two cable braces, secured by improvised loops. The woven-synthetic ropes were snubbed to massive ebonies on both banks, and with only the crew and no load, it floated fairly high. Water on the upstream side purled to within a handspan of the windows, but that was current. The ball wheels spun, thrashing water backward; with his head out the top hatch, Jenkins cried blasphemous and scatological encouragement to the trooper at the wheel and used his bulk to shift the balance of the light vehicle and keep it closer to upright. Most of the rest of her detachment were out in overwatch positions. Nobody was betting that the Glorios wouldn't come back for more, despite the pasting they'd taken.

You could never tell with the Glorios; the death-wish seemed to be as big a part of their makeup as the will to power. Revolutionary purity, they called it.

"Lieutenant," Vinatelli said, "this unit is still operable. Systems are at over ninety-five percent of nominal."

"Jesus fucking *Christ*, the thing's buried under four hundred tons of rock! I'm combat-lossing it, corporal. Now get out, that's a direct order. We're time-critical here."

"Corporal Vinatelli is unable to comply with that order, Lieutenant."

"Hell," Martins said, looking down at the top of the Mark III's superstructure, where fingers of brown water were already running over the armor.

It looked like she was going to leave two of her people here dead. The kid had frozen after all, only it took the form of refusal to come out of his durochrome womb, rather than catatonia. Frozen, and it was going to kill him—when the ham sandwiches and Coke ran out down there, if not before. There was certainly nothing she could do about it. Sending a team down with a blasting charge to open the hatch didn't look real practical right now. Even if they had time, there was no telling what someone in Vinatelli's mental condition might do, besides which the tank was programmed to protect its own integrity. And she certainly had better things to do with the time.

A *whump* of explosive went off behind her; Kernan making sure the captured Glorio weapons weren't any use to anyone.

"Max units, pull in," she said, and began climbing back to the cable anchor point to board Kernan's UATV. Behind her, a thin muddy wave washed across the top surface of the Bolo Mark III.

"Comrades, we have won a glorious victory!" Commandante Chavez shouted.

He was standing in front of the crater where the guerilla mortars had been. For sixty meters around, the trees were bare of leaves and twigs; they sparkled in the afternoon sunlight, a fairy garden of glittering glass fibers. The crater where the ready ammunition had gone off was several meters across; the enemy had arranged the bodies of the crew—or parts thereof—in more-or-less regular fashion, the better to count them. Nothing useable remained.

"The giant tank filled some of our weaker comrades with fear," Chavez went on. The ground that he paced on was damp and slightly greasy with the body fluids of several Glorios, and the bluebottles were crawling over it. "They wanted to run and hide from the monster tank!

"Yet we—mere humanity, but filled with the correct ideological perspective—triumphed over the monster. We buried it, as the Glorious Way shall bury all its enemies, all those who stand between suffering humanity and utopia!"

With several of the commandante's special guards standing behind him, the cheering was prolonged. And sincere; they had destroyed the tank that had been like nothing anyone had ever seen before. Now it was just a lump in the river below the fallen bridge.

"Onward to victory!" Chavez shouted, raising his fist in the air.

The Caatinga River was powerful at this time of year, when the limestone soil yielded up the water it had stored during the brief, violent rains. Maximum flow was in May, well after the last clouds gave way to endless glaring sun and the fields shriveled into dusty, cracked barrenness where goats walked out on limbs to get at the last shoots.

Now it backed at the rock dam created by the bridge. The lower strata were locked together by the girders, and the upper by the weight of the stone and the anchoring presence of the tank; its pyramidal shape made it the keystone. Water roared over the top a meter deep, and the whole huge mass ground and shifted under the pounding.

"Vini, the water will help," the Mark III said. "I'm going to try that now."

Mud and rock and spray fountained skyward, sending parrots and shrikes fleeing in terror. Boulders shifted. A bellowing roar shook the earth in the river valley, and the monstrous scraping sound of durachrome alloy ripping density-enhanced steel through friable limestone.

"It's working."

"Talk about irony," Jenkins said.

"Yeah, Tops?" Martins replied.

Jenkins had had academic ambitions before the university system pretty well shut down.

"Yeah, El-Tee. Most of the time we've been here, the Mark III would have been as useful as a boar hog to a ballerina. The Glorios would have just gone away from wherever it was, you know? But now we just want to move one place one time, and they want to get in our way—and that big durachrome mother would have been *real* useful."

"I'm not arguing," she said.

The little hamlet of San Miguel de Dolorosa lay ahead of them.

The brief tropical nightfall was over, and the moon was out, bright and cool amid a thick dusting arch of stars, clear in the dry upland air. In previous times troops had stopped there occasionally; there was a cantina selling a pretty good beer, and it was a chance to see locals who weren't trying to kill you, just sell you BBQ goat or their sisters. Right now there were a couple of extremely suspicious readings on the fixed sensors they'd scattered around in the hills months back, when they decided they didn't have the manpower to patrol around here any more.

Suspicious readings that could be heavy machine-guns and rocket launchers in the town. There were no lights down there, but that was about par for the course. Upcountry towns hadn't had electricity for a long time, and kerosene cost real money.

"It's like this," Martins said. "If we go barreling through there, and they're set up, we're dogmeat. If we go around, the only alternate route will eat all our reserve of time—and that's assuming nothing goes wrong on that way either."

Jenkins sighed. "You or me?"

Somebody was going to have to go in and identify the sightings better than the remotes could do it—and if the Glorios were there, distract them up close and personal while the UATVs came in.

"I'd better do it, Tops," she said. The squad with the two vehicles was really Jenkins'. "I'll take Pineapple and Marwitz."

Half the string of mules were in the water when the Glorio sergeant—Squad Comrade—heard the grinding, whirring noise.

"What's that?" he cried.

The ford was in a narrow cut, where the river was broad but shallow; there was little space between the high walls that was not occupied by the gravelled bed. That made it quite dark even in the daytime. On a moonless night like this it was a slit full of night, with nothing but starlight to cast a faint sparkle on the water. The guerrillas were working with the precision of long experience, leading the gaunt mules down through the knee-deep stream and up the other side, while a company kept overwatch on both sides. They were not expecting trouble from the depleted enemy forces, but their superior night vision meant that a raid was always possible. Even an air attack was *possible*, although it was months since there had been any air action except around the main base at Cuchimba.

When the Bolo Mark III came around the curve of the river half a kilometer downstream, the guerrillas reacted with varieties of blind panic. It was only a dim bulk, but the river creamed away in plumes from its four tracks, and it ground on at forty KPH with the momentum of a mountain that walked.

The sergeant fired his AK—a useless thing to do even if the target had been soft-skinned. A bar of light reached out from the tank's frontal slope, and the man exploded away from the stream of hypervelocity slugs.

A team on the left, the western bank, of the river opened up with a four-barreled heavy machine gun intended for antiaircraft use. They were good; the stream of half-ounce bullets hosed over the Mark III's armor like a river of green-tracer fire arching into the night. The sparks where the projectiles bounced from the density-enhanced durachrome were bright fireflies in the night. Where the layer of softer ablating material was still intact there was no spark, but a very careful observer might have seen starlight on the metal exposed by the bullets' impact.

There were no careful observers on this field tonight; at least, none outside the hull of the Mark III. The infinite repeaters nuzzled forward through the dilating ports on its hull. Coils gripped and flung 50mm projectiles at velocities that burned a thin film of plasma off the ultra-dense metal that composed them. They left streaks through the air, and on the retinas of anyone watching them. The repeaters were intended primarily for use against armor, but they had a number of options. The one selected now broke the projectiles into several hundred shards just short of the target, covering a dozen square yards. They ripped into the multibarrel machine gun, its mount—and incidentally its operators—like a mincing machine pounded down by a god. Friction-heated ammunition cooked off in a crackle and fireworks fountain, but that was almost an anticlimax.

"Cease fire! Cease fire!" Comrade Chavez bellowed.

It was an unnecessary command for those of the Glorios

blundering off into the dark, screaming their terror or conserving their breath for flight. A substantial minority had remained, even for this threat. They heard and obeyed, except for one team with the best antiarmor weapons the guerrillas possessed, a cluster of hypervelocity missiles. One man painted the forward tread with his laser designator, while the second launched the missiles. They left the launcher with a mild chuff of gasses, then accelerated briefly with a sound like a giant tiger's retching scream.

If the missiles had struck the tread, they would probably have ripped its flexible durachrome alloy to shreds—although the Mark III would have lost only a small percentage of its mobility. They did not, since the tank's 4mm had blown the designator to shards before they covered even a quarter of the distance to their target. The operator was a few meters away. Nothing touched him but one fragment tracing a line across his cheek. He lay and trembled, not moving even to stop the blood which flowed down his face from the cut and into his open mouth.

Two of the missiles blossomed in globes of white-blue fire, intercepted by repeater rounds. A third tipped upwards and flew off into the night until it self-destructed, victim of the laser designator's last twitch. The fourth was close enough for the idiot-savant microchip in its nose to detect the Mark III and classify it as a target. It exploded as well—as it was designed to do. The explosion forged a round plate of tungsten into a shape like a blunt arrowhead and plunged it forward with a velocity even greater than the missile's own.

It clanged into the armor just below the muzzles of the infinite repeaters, and spanged up into the night. There was a fist-sized dimple in the complex alloy of the tank's hull, shining because it was now plated with a molecule-thick film of pure tungsten.

"Cease *fire*," Chavez screamed again.

The Bolo Mark III was very close now. Most of the mules had managed to scramble up on the further bank and were galloping down the river, risking their legs in the darkness rather than stay near the impossibly huge metal object. Men stayed in their positions, because their subconscious was convinced that flight was futile. The tank grew larger and larger yet; the water fountained from either side, drenching some of the guerrillas. Comrade Chavez was among them, standing not ten feet from where it passed. He stood erect, and spat into its wake.

"Cowards," he murmured. It was uncertain exactly who he was referring to. Then more loudly: "The cowards are running from us—it fired at nobody but those actively attacking it. Fall in! Resume the operation!"

It took a few minutes for those who had stayed in their positions to shake loose minds stunned by the sheer massiveness of the thing that had passed them by. Collecting most of the men who'd fled took hours, but eventually they stood sheepishly in front of their commander.

"I *should* have you all shot," he said. A few started to shake again; there had been a time when Chavez would have had them shot, and they could remember it. "But the Revolution is so short of men that even you must be conserved—if only to stop a bullet that might otherwise strike a true comrade of the Glorious Way. Get back to work!"

Bethany Martins gripped the bowie in hatchet style, with the sharpened edge out. The blackened metal quivered slightly, and her lips were curled back behind the faceplate in a grimace of queasy anticipation. The weapon was close to the original that Rezin Bowie had designed, over a foot long and point heavy, but the blade was of an alloy quite similar to the Mark III's armor. It had to be sharpened with a hone of synthetic diamond, but it would take a more than razor edge and keep it while it hacked through mild steel.

The Glorio sentry was watching out the front door of the house. She could tell that from the rear of the building because it was made of woven fronds, and they were virtually transparent to several of the sensors in her helmet. She could also tell that all the previous inhabitants of the three-room hut were dead, both because of the smell and because their bodies showed at ambient on the IR scan. That made real sure they wouldn't blow the Glorio ambush, and it was also standard procedure for the Way. The inhabitants of San Miguel had cooperated with the authorities, and that was enough.

Cooperation might include virtually anything, from joining a Civic Patrol to selling some oranges to a passing vehicle from the 15th.

Generally speaking, Martins hated killing people with knives although she was quite good at it. One of the benefits of commissioned rank was that she seldom had to, any more. This Glorio was going to be an exception in both senses of the word.

Step. The floor of the hut was earth, laterite packed to the consistency of stone over years of use, and brushed quite clean. A wicker door had prevented the chickens and other small stock outside from coming in. There was an image of the Bleeding Heart, unpleasantly lifelike, over the hearth of adobe bricks and iron rods in the kitchen. Coals cast an IR glow over the room, and her bootsoles made only a soft minimal noise of contact.

Step. Through behind the Glorio. Only the focus of his attention on the roadway below kept him from turning. He was carrying a light drum-fed machine gun, something nonstandard—it looked like a Singapore Industries model. Her body armor would stop shell fragments and pistol-calibre ammunition, but that thing would send fragments of the softsuit right through her rib cage.

Step. Arm's length away in pitch blackness. Pitch blackness for *him,* but her faceplate painted it like day. Better than day . . .

Martins' arm came across until the back of the blade was touching her neck. She slashed at neck height. Something warned the man, perhaps air movement or the slight exhalation of breath, perhaps just years of survival honing his instincts. He began to turn, but the supernally keen edge still sliced through neck muscles and through the vertebrae beneath them, to cut the spinal cord in a single brutal chop. The sound was like an axe striking green wood; she dropped the knife and lunged forward to catch the limp body, ignoring the rush of wastes and the blood that soaked the torso of her armor as she dragged him backwards. The machine gun clattered unnoticed to the ground.

The lieutenant dragged the guerilla backward, then set him down gently on the floor. Only a few twitches from the severed nerve endings drummed his rope-sandaled heels against the floor.

She paused for a moment, panting with the effort and with adrenaline still pulsing the veins in her throat, then stepped forward into the doorway.

"Jenkins," she murmured. A risk, but the Glorio elint capacity had never been very good and had gotten worse lately. "I'm marking the heavy stuff. Mark."

From point-blank, the shapes of machine-guns and rocket launchers showed clearly. She slid the aiming pips of her faceplate over each crew-served weapons position, then over the individual riflemen, the second-priority targets. Each time the pips crossed a target she tapped a stud on the lower inside edge of her helmet, marking it for the duplicate readout in Jenkins' helmet. The guerrillas had tried their best to be clever; there were low fires inside a number of the houses, to disguise the IR signatures, and as backup there were bound civilians grouped in what resembled fire teams around pieces of metal—hoes, cooking grills and the like—to fox the sonic and microradar scanners. Some of them were so clever that she had to spend a minute or two figuring them out. When in doubt, she marked them.

It occurred to her that an objective observer might consider the technological gap between the Company's troopers and the Glorios unfair. Although the gross advantage of numbers and firepower the guerrillas had these days went a long way to make it up.

On the other hand, she wasn't objective and didn't give a damn about fair.

"Got it," Jenkins said.

"Pineapple, Red?" she asked. Short clicks from Ramerez and Marwitz. She slid her rifle around, settling down to the ground and bracing the sling against the hand that held the forestock. The aiming pip settled on the rear of the slit trench that held the .51. Four men in the trench . . .

"Now." Diesels blatted as the UATVs revved up and tore down the road toward the village. She stroked her trigger, and the night began to dissolve in streaks of tracer and fire. A cantina disintegrated as Pineapple's grenade launcher caught the RPG team waiting there.

★ ★ ★

"Shit, why *now*?" Martins said.

Captain McNaught's voice in her ears was hoarse with pain and with the drugs that controlled it. He could still chuckle.

" . . . and at the worst possible time," he said.

Firebase Villa was on fire this night. The mortars at its core were firing, their muzzle flashes lighting up the night like flickers of heat lightning. *Shump-shump-shump*, the three-round clips blasting out almost as fast as a submachine-gun. The crews would have a new set of rounds in the hopper almost as quickly, but the mortars fired sparingly. They were the only way to cover the dead ground where Glorio gunners might set up their own weapons, and ammunition was short. Bombardment rockets from outside the range of the defending mortars dragged across the sky with a sound like express trains. When the sound stopped there was a wait of a few seconds before the *kthud* of the explosion inside the perimeter.

The pilot of the tiltrotor cut into the conversation. "I got just so much fuel, and other people to pull out," he said. His voice was flat as gunmetal, with a total absence of emotion that was a statement in itself.

"Can you get me a landing envelope?" he said.

"Look, we'll cover—" Martins began.

A four-barreled heavy lashed out toward Firebase Villa with streams of green tracer. Yellow-white answered it; neither gun was going to kill the other, at extreme ranges and with both firing from narrow slits. The Glorio gun was using an improvised bunker, thrown up over the last hour, but it was good enough for this. Parts of the perimeter minefield still smoldered where rockets had dragged explosive cord over it in a net to detonate the mines. Some of the bodies of the sappers that had tried to exploit that hole in the mines and razor wire still smoldered as well. Many of the short-range guns around the perimeter were AI-driven automatics, 4mm gatlings with no nerves and very quick reaction times.

"Hell you will, Martins," McNaught wheezed. "There's a battalion of them out there. I think—" he coughed "—I think Comrade Chavez has walked the walk with us so long he just can't bear the thought of us leaving at all." The captain's voice changed timber.

"Flyboy, get lost. You try bringing that bird down here, you'll get a second job as a colander."

"*Hell*," the pilot muttered. Then: "Goodbye."

Martins and McNaught waited in silence, except for the racket of the firefight. The Glorios crunched closer, men crawling forward from cover to cover. Many of them died, but not enough, and the bombardment rockets kept dragging their loads of explosive across the sky.

It's not often you're condemned to death, Martins thought. Her mind was hunting through alternatives, plans, tactics—the same process as always. Only there wasn't anything you could do with seventy effectives to attack a battalion of guerrillas who were hauling out all the stuff they'd saved up. Even if it was insane, insane even in terms of the Glorios' own demented worldview.

"Bug out," McNaught said, in a breathless rasp. "Nothing you can do here. They're all here, bug out and make it back to the coast, you can get some transport there. That's an order, Lieutenant."

If there was anything left to go back north for. The latest reports were even more crazy-confused than the first.

"Save your breath, sir," she said.

The Company had been together down here for a long time. They were all going home together. One way or another.

"Movement," someone said. She recognized the voice of the communications specialist back in Villa. Like everyone else, she doubled in two other jobs; in this case, monitoring the remote sensors. "I got movement . . . vehicle movement. Hey, big vehicle."

Nobody said anything for a minute or two, in the draw where the two UATVs waited.

"That's impossible," Martins whispered.

The technician's voice was shaky with unshed tears. "Unless the Glorios have a 150-ton tank, it's happening anyway," she said.

They were a kilometer beyond the Glorio outposts in the draw. The river ran to their left, circling in a wide arch around Firebase Villa. Water jetted in smooth arcs to either bank as the Mark III climbed through the rapids. In the shallow pools beyond the wave from the treads was more like a pulsing. Then the tank stopped, not a hundred meters from the UATVs' position.

"Vinatelli," Martins breathed. "You beautiful little geek!"

The tank remained silent. Another rocket sailed in, a globe of reddish fire through the sky.

"What are you waiting for?" Martins cursed.

"I have no orders, Lieutenant," the newbie's voice said. "Last mission parameters accomplished."

Something dead and cold trailed fingers up Martin's spine. *He's gone over the edge,* she thought. Aloud, she snapped: "Fight, Vinatelli, for Christ's sake. Fight!"

"Fight whom, Lieutenant?"

"The *Glorios.* The people who're attacking the firebase, for fuck's sake. Open fire."

"Acknowledged, Lieutenant."

The night came apart in a dazzle of fire.

"I think I know—I think I know what happened," Martins whispered.

Nothing moved on the fissured plain around Firebase Villa, except what the wind stirred, and the troopers out collecting the weapons. It had taken the Mark III only about an hour to end it, and the last half of that had been hunting down fugitives. The final group included Comrade Chavez, in a well-shielded hillside cave only three klicks away, which explained a great deal when the tank blew most of the hillside away to get at it. He'd been hiding under their noses all along.

She slung her M-35 down her back and worked her fingers, taking a deep breath before she started climbing the rungs built into the side armor of the Mark III. Some of them were missing, but that was no problem, no problem . . . The hatch opened easily.

Vinatelli must have had his crash harness up when the bridge blew. From the look of the body, he'd been reaching for a cola can. His head must have been at just the right angle to crack his spine against the forward control surfaces.

"So that's why Vinatelli didn't want to come out," she said.

McNaught was watching through the remotes of her helmet. "So it *is* alive," he said.

Martin shook her head, then spoke: "No." Her tone shifted. "Markee. Why didn't you go back to the coast?"

"Mission parameters did not require retracing route," the tank said, in the incongruously sultry voice. "Last established mission parameters indicated transit to point Firebase Villa."

"What are your mission parameters. Correction, what were your mission parameters."

"Lieutenant Bethany Martins is to go home," the machine said.

Martins slumped, sitting on the combing. The smell inside wouldn't be too bad, not after only six hours in air conditioning.

"It was Vinatelli," she said. "He was the dreamy sort. He had it programmed to do a clever Hans routine if an officer started making requests when he was asleep, and reply in his own voice."

"Clever Hans?" the captain asked.

"A horse somebody trained to 'answer' questions. It sensed subliminal clues and behaved accordingly, so it *looked* like it understood what the audience was saying. You can get a good AI system to do the same thing, word-association according to what you say. You'd swear it was talking to you, when it's really got no more real comprehension than a toaster."

"Why did it come here?"

"That was the last order. Go to Firebase Villa; it's got enough discretion to pick another route out of its data banks. And to shoot back if attacked in a combat zone. But that's all, that's all it did. Like ants; all they've got is a few feedback loops but they get a *damned* lot done."

She rose, shaking her head.

"Which leaves the question of what *we* do now," the Captain said.

"Oh, I don't think there's much question on that one," Martins said.

She pulled off her helmet and rubbed her face. Despite everything, a grin broke through. *Poor ignorant bastard,* she thought, looking down at Vinatelli. *The tank was everything you said it was.* She'd been right too, though: a newbie was still cold meat unless he wised up fast.

"We're *all* going home. With Markee to lead the way."

★A TIME TO KILL★

David Weber

★Prologue★

It was called Case Ragnarok, and it was insane. Yet in a time when madness had a galaxy by the throat, it was also inevitable.

It began as a planning study over a century earlier, when no one really believed there would be a war at all, and perhaps the crowning irony of the Final War was that a study undertaken to demonstrate the lunatic consequences of an unthinkable strategy became the foundation for putting that strategy into effect. The admirals and generals who initially undertook it actually intended it to prove that the stakes were too high, that the Melconian Empire would never dare risk a fight to the finish with the Concordiat—or *vice versa*—for they knew it was madness even to consider. But the civilians saw it as an analysis of an "option" and demanded a full implementation study once open war began, and the warriors provided it. It was their job to do so, of course, and in fairness to them, they protested the order . . . at first. Yet they were no more proof against the madness than the civilians when the time came.

And perhaps that was fitting, for the entire war was a colossal mistake, a confluence of misjudgments on a cosmic scale. Perhaps if there had been more contact between the Concordiat and the Empire it wouldn't have happened, but the Empire slammed down

its non-intercourse edict within six standard months of first contact. From a Human viewpoint, that was a hostile act; for the Empire, it was standard operating procedure, no more than simple prudence to curtail contacts until this new interstellar power was evaluated. Some of the Concordiat's xenologists understood that and tried to convince their superiors of it, but the diplomats insisted on pressing for "normalization of relations." It was their job to open new markets, to negotiate military and political and economic treaties, and they resented the Melconian silence, the no-transit zones along the Melconian border . . . the Melconian refusal to take them as seriously as they took themselves. They grew more strident, not less, when the Empire resisted all efforts to overturn the non-intercourse edict, and the Emperor's advisors misread that stridency as a fear response, the insistence of a weaker power on dialogue because it knew its own weakness.

Imperial Intelligence should have told them differently, but shaping analyses to suit the views of one's superiors was not a purely Human trait. Even if it had been, Intelligence's analysts found it difficult to believe how far Human technology outclassed Melconian. The evidence was there, especially in the Dinochrome Brigade's combat record, but they refused to accept that evidence. Instead, it was reported as disinformation, a cunning attempt to deceive the Imperial General Staff into believing the Concordiat was more powerful than it truly was and hence yet more evidence that Humanity feared the Empire.

And Humanity *should* have feared Melcon. It was Human hubris, as much as Melconian, which led to disaster, for both the Concordiat and the Empire had traditions of victory. Both had lost battles, but neither had ever lost a *war*, and deep inside, neither believed it could. Worse, the Concordiat's intelligence organs *knew* Melcon couldn't match its technology, and that made it arrogant. By any rational computation of the odds, the Human edge in hardware should have been decisive, assuming the Concordiat had gotten its sums right. The non-intercourse edict had succeeded in at least one of its objectives, however, and the Empire was more than twice as large as the Concordiat believed . . . with over four times the navy.

So the two sides slid into the abyss—slowly, at first, one reversible step at a time, but with ever gathering speed. The admirals and generals saw it coming and warned their masters that all their plans and calculations were based on assumptions which could not be confirmed. Yet even as they issued their warning, they didn't truly believe it themselves, for how could so many years of spying, so many decades of analysis, so many computer centuries of simulations, all be in error? The ancient data processing cliché about "garbage in" was forgotten even by those who continued to pay it lip service, and Empire and Concordiat alike approached the final decisions with fatal confidence in their massive, painstaking, painfully honest—and totally wrong—analyses.

No one ever knew for certain who actually fired the first shot in the Trellis System. Losses in the ensuing engagement were heavy on both sides, and each navy reported to its superiors—honestly, so far as it knew—that the other had attacked *it*. Not that it mattered in the end. All that mattered was that the shot *was* fired . . . and that both sides suddenly discovered the terrible magnitude of their errors. The Concordiat crushed the Empire's frontier fleets with contemptuous ease, only to discover that they'd been *only* frontier fleets, light forces deployed to screen the true, ponderous might of the Imperial Navy, and the Empire, shocked by the actual superiority of Humanity's war machines, panicked. The Emperor himself decreed that his navy must seek immediate and crushing victory, hammering the enemy into submission at any cost and by any means necessary, including terror tactics. Nor was the Empire alone in its panic, for the sudden revelation of the Imperial Navy's size, coupled with the all-or-nothing tactics it adopted from the outset, sparked the same desperation within the Concordiat leadership.

And so what might have been no more than a border incident became something more dreadful than the galaxy had ever imagined. The Concordiat never produced enough of its superior weapons to defeat Melcon outright, but it produced more than enough to prevent the Empire from defeating *it*. And if the Concordiat's deep strikes prevented the Empire from mobilizing its full reserves against Human-held worlds, it couldn't stop the Melconian Navy from achieving a numerical superiority sufficient to offset its individual technical inferiorities. War raged across the light-centuries, and every clash was worse than the last as the two mightiest militaries in galactic history lunged at one another, each certain the other was the aggressor and each convinced its only options were victory or annihilation. The door to madness was opened by desperation, and the planning study known as Case Ragnarok was converted into something very different. It may be the Melconians had conducted a similar study—certainly their operations suggested they had—but no one will ever know, for the Melconian records, if any, no longer exist.

Yet the Human records do, and they permit no self-deception. Operation Ragnarok was launched only after the Melconian "demonstration strike" on New Vermont killed every one of the planet's billion inhabitants, but it was a deliberately planned strategy which had been developed at least twelve standard years earlier. It began at the orders of the Concordiat Senate . . . and ended thirty-plus standard years later, under the orders of God alone knew what fragments of local authority.

There are few records of Ragnarok's final battles because, in all too many cases, there were no survivors . . . on either side. The ghastly mistakes of diplomats who misread their own importance and their adversaries' will to fight, of intelligence analysts who underestimated their adversaries *ability* to fight, and of emperors and presidents who ultimately sought "simple" resolutions to their problems, might have bred the Final War, yet it was the soldiers who finished it. But then, it was *always* the soldiers who ended wars—and fought them, and died in them, and slaughtered their way through them, and tried desperately to *survive* them—and the Final War was no different from any other in that respect.

Yet it *was* different in one way. This time the soldiers didn't simply finish the war; this time the war finished *them*, as well.

—Kenneth R. Cleary, Ph.D.
From the introduction to *Operation Ragnarok: Into the Abyss*
Cerberus Books, Ararat, 4056

★**1**★

Death came to the planet Ishark in the ninety-eighth year of the Final War and the thirty-second year of Operation Ragnarok. It came aboard the surviving ships of the XLIII Corps of the Republic, which had once been the XLIII Corps of the Star Union, and before that the XLIII Corps of the Confederacy, which had once been the Concordiat of Man. But whatever the government's name, the ships were the same, for there was no one left to build new ones. There was no one left to build *anything*, for the Melconian Empire and its allies and the Concordiat and *its* allies had murdered one another.

Admiral Evelyn Trevor commanded the XLIII's escort from her heavy cruiser flagship. Trevor had been a lieutenant commander when the XLIII set out, and the escort had been headed by no less than ten *Terra*-class superdreadnoughts and eight *Victory*-class carriers, but those days were gone. Now RNS *Mikuma* led her consorts in a blazing run against Ishark's spaceborne defenders—the ragged remnants of three Melconian task forces which had rallied here because Ishark was the only planet left to defend. They outnumbered Trevor's ships by four-to-one, but they were a hodge-podge force, and what Trevor's command had lost in tonnage it had gained in experience . . . and savagery. Ishark was the last world on its list, and it came in behind a cloud of decoys better than anything the defenders had.

There was no tomorrow for either commander . . . and even if they could have had one, they might have turned their backs upon it. The Human and Melconian races had hurt one another too savagely, the blood hunger possessed them both, and neither side's com officers could raise a single friendly planet. The Humans had nowhere to return to even if they lived; the Melconians were defending their last inhabited world; and even the warships' AIs were caught up in the blood lust. The fleets lunged at one another, neither worried about preserving itself, each seeking only to destroy the other, and both succeeded. The last Human Fleet units died, but only three Melconian destroyers survived to attack the XLIII, and they perished without scoring a single hit when the Bolo transports intercepted them. Those transports were slow and ungainly by Fleet standards, but they carried Mark XXXIII Bolos on their docking racks. Each of those Bolos mounted the equivalent of a *Repulse*-class battlecruiser's main battery weapons, and they used them to clear the way for the rest of the ships which had once lifted four divisions of mechanized infantry and two of manned armor, eight hundred assault shuttles, fifteen hundred trans-atmospheric fighters, sixteen thousand air-cav mounts, and the Eighty-Second Bolo Brigade from a world which was now so much rubble. Now the remaining transports carried less than twelve thousand Humans, a single composite brigade each of infantry and manned armor, two hundred aircraft of all types, and seven Bolos. That was all . . . but it was sufficient.

There were few fixed planetary defenses, because no sane prewar strategist would ever have considered Ishark a vital target. It was a world of farmers in a position of absolutely no strategic importance, the sort of planet which routinely surrendered, trusting the diplomats to determine its fate when the shooting ended. But no one in the XLIII requested a surrender, and no one on Ishark's surface considered offering one. This wasn't that sort of war.

One or two batteries got lucky, but despite the XLIII's previous losses, it retained more than enough transports to disperse its remaining personnel widely. Only six hundred more Humans died as the ships swept down on their LZs to disgorge their cargos, and then Ishark's continents burned. There was no finesse, for the combatants had lost the capacity for finesse. The days of kinetic bombardment platforms and surgical strikes on military targets were long gone. There were no platforms, and no one was interested in "surgery" any longer. There was only brute force and the merciless imperatives of Operation Ragnarok and its Melconian equivalent, and Humans and Melconians screamed their rage and agony and hate as they fought and killed and died. On Ishark, it was Melconian troopers who fought with desperate gallantry to preserve their civilians, as it had been Humans who fought to save *their* civilians on Trevor's World and Indra and Matterhorn. And as the Humans had failed there, the Melconians failed here.

Team Shiva had the point for Alpha Force.

Team Shiva *always* had the point, because it was the best there was. Bolo XXXIII/D-1097-SHV was the last Bolo built by Bolo Prime on the moon known as Luna before the Melconian world burner blotted Terra—and Luna—away forever, and no one else in XLIII Corps could match his experience . . . except, perhaps, his Human Commander. Newly enlisted Private Diego Harigata had been sixteen years old when Terra died; now Major Harigata was forty-nine, with thirty-two years of combat experience. All of them had been aboard the Bolo whose call sign was "Shiva," and man and machine had fought their way together across half a hundred planets.

It was one of the many ironies of the Final War that the Bolo deployment concept had come full circle. Mark XXXIII Bolos were designed for independent deployment, but they were almost never actually deployed that way, for the direct neural interfacing first introduced aboard the Mark XXXII and then perfected for the last and most powerful of the Concordiat's Bolos made them even more deadly than their cybernetic ancestors. They were no longer simply artificial intelligences built *by* Humans. Rather, a Mark XXXIII was an AI fused *with* a Human in a partnership which produced something the designers had neither predicted nor expected. The Human-Bolo fusion thought with Bolo precision and total recall, communicated with its fellows in the Total Systems Data Sharing net with Bolo clarity, analyzed data and devised tactics with Bolo speed and executed them with Bolo cunning . . . but it *fought* with Human ferocity.

The Dinochrome Brigade's earlier psychotronic designers had always feared to build the savagery which lurked just behind the Human forebrain's veneer of civilization into their huge, self-aware war machines. They'd feared that elemental drive—the ferocity which turned a hairless, clawless, fangless biped into the most deadly predator of a planet—for their own history taught too many lessons about what could happen when Human warriors went over the edge.

But it was available to the Mark XXXIIIs, for it was part of each team's Human component, and Team Shiva called upon it now.

There were nineteen Bolos in the Eighty-Second Brigade when the XLIII was assigned to Operation Ragnarok. There should have been twenty-four, but the days of full strength units had been long past even then. Forty-one slaughtered worlds later, there were seven, split between the XLIII's three LZs, and Team Shiva led the attack out of LZ One against Alpha Continent, the largest and most heavily populated—and defended—of Ishark's three land masses.

The Melconians were waiting, and General Sharth Na-Yarma had hoarded men and munitions for years to meet this day. He'd "lost" units administratively and lied on readiness reports as the fighting ground towards Ishark, understating his strength when other planetary COs sent out frantic calls for reinforcements, for General Sharth had guessed the Imperial Navy would fail to stop the Humans short of Ishark. That was why he'd stockpiled every weapon he could lay hands on, praying that operations before Ishark would weaken the XLIII enough for *him* to stop it. He never expected to *defeat* it; he only hoped to take it with him in a mutual suicide pact while there was still someone alive on his world to rebuild when the wreckage cooled.

It was the only realistic strategy open to him, but it wasn't enough. Not against Team Shiva and the horribly experienced world-killers of the XLIII.

We move down the valley with wary caution. The duality of our awareness sweeps the terrain before us through our sensors, and we seldom think of ourself as our component parts any longer. We are not a Bolo named Shiva and a Human named Harigata; we are simply Team Shiva, destroyer of worlds, and we embrace the ferocity of our function as we explode out of the LZ, thirty-two thousand tons of alloy and armor and weapons riding our counter-grav at five hundred KPH to hook around the Enemy flank through the mountains. Team

Harpy and Team John lead the other prong of our advance, but their attack is secondary. It is our job to lead the true breakout, and we land on our tracks, killing our counter-grav and bringing up our battle screen, as the first Enemy Fenris-class heavies appear on our sensors.

There are more of them than projected, and they roar up out of the very ground to vomit missiles and plasma at us. An entire battalion attacks from the ridge line at zero-two-five degrees while the remainder of its regiment rumbles out of deep, subterranean hides across an arc from two-two-seven to three-five-one degrees, and passive sensors detect the emissions of additional units approaching from directly ahead. A precise count is impossible, but our minimum estimate is that we face a reinforced heavy brigade, and Surt-class mediums and Eagle-class scout cars sweep simultaneously out of the dead ground to our right rear and attack across a broad front, seeking to engage our supporting infantry. The force balance is unfavorable and retreat is impossible, but we are confident in the quality of our supports. We can trust them to cover our rear, and we hammer straight into the Enemy's teeth as they deploy.

Hell comes to Ishark as we forge ahead, and we exult at its coming. We bring it with us, feel it in the orgiastic release as our missile hatches open and our fire blasts away. We turn one-zero degrees to port, opening our field of fire, and our main battery turrets traverse smoothly. Three two-hundred-centimeter Hellbores, each cycling in four-point-five-one seconds, sweep the Fenris battalion which has skylined itself on the northeasterly ridge, and hunger and a terrible joy fill us as the explosions race down the Enemy's line. We taste the blood lust in the rapid-fire hammering of our mortars and howitzers as we pound the Surts and Eagles on our flanks, and we send our hate screaming from our Hellbores. Our battle screen flames under answering missiles and shells, and particle beams rip and gouge at us, heating our armor to white-hot incandescence, but Bolos are designed to survive such fire. Our conversion fields trap their energy, channeling it to feed our own systems, and we rejoice as that stolen power vomits back from our own weapons.

The Fenris is less than half our size, and two-two-point-five seconds of main battery fire reduce the fifteen units of the first Enemy battalion to smoking rubble, yet two of its vehicles score upon us before they die. Pain sensors scream as their lighter plasma bolts burn through our battle screen, but they strike on an oblique, and our side armor suffices to turn them. Molten tears of duralloy weep down our flank as we turn upon our dead foes' consorts, but we feel only the joy, the hunger to smash and destroy. In the crucible of combat, we forget the despair, the knowledge of ultimate disaster, which oppresses us between battles. There is no memory now of the silence over the com nets, the awareness that the worlds which were once the Concordiat lie dead or dying behind us. Now there is purpose, vengeance, ferocity. The destruction of our foes cries out to us, giving us once again a reason to be, a function to fulfill . . . an Enemy to hate.

More of the Enemy's heavies last long enough to drive their plasma bolts through our battle screen, and suicide teams pound away with plasma lances from point-blank range, yet he cannot stop us. A Fenris fires from four-point-six-one kilometers and disables Number Three and Four Hellbores from our port lateral battery before it dies. A dug-in plasma team which has concealed itself so well that we approach within one-point-four-four kilometers before we detect it gets off a single shot that blows through our track shield to destroy two bogies from our outboard forward track system, and five Surt-class medium mechs lunge out of a narrow defile at a range of only three-point-zero-two kilometers. The ravine walls hide them from our sensors until they actually engage, and their fifty-centimeter plasma cannon tear and crater forty-point-six meters of our starboard flank armor before we blow them all to ruin, and even as the last Surt dies, Enemy missiles and shells deluge everything that moves.

The inferno grinds implacably forward, and we are not man and machine. We are the Man-Machine, smashing the Enemy's defenses and turning mountain valleys into smoking wasteland. Our supporting elements crumple or fall back crippled, and a part of us knows still more of our Human comrades have died, will die, are dying in shrieking agony or the immolation of plasma. Yet it means no more to us than the deep, glowing wounds in our own flanks, and we refuse to halt or turn aside, for that which we cannot have we will extend to no others. All that remains to Human and Melconian alike is the Long Dark, and all that remains to us is to fight and kill and maim until our own dark comes down upon us.

We feel the death of Team Harpy—of Bolo XXXIII/D-2075-HRP and Captain Jessica Adams—but even in the anguish of their loss, we know the Enemy's very success spells his own destruction. He has been deceived, decoyed into concentrating a full two-thirds of his firepower against our diversion, and so we rejoice at the Enemy's error and redouble our own efforts.

We shatter the final line of his main position in an orgy of pointblank fire and the steady coughing of our anti-personnel clusters. Railguns rake the light Enemy AFVs trying to withdraw support personnel, and the remnants of our own manned armor and infantry follow our breakthrough. We pivot, coming to heading three-five-eight true, and rumble through the smoke and dust and the stench of burning Enemy flesh, and Team John appears to port, advancing once more in line with us as we heave up over the final ridge.

Sporadic artillery and missile fire greets us, but it is all the Enemy has left. Recon drones and satellites pick up additional heavy units rushing towards us from the east, but they are seven-eight-point-five-niner minutes away. For now, there is only the wreckage of the defenses we have already crushed, boiling in confusion in the river valley below us as the light combat vehicles and infantry and shattered air-cav squadrons seek to rally and stand.

But it is too late for them to stand, for beyond them we see the city. Intelligence estimates its population at just over two million, and we confer with Team John over the TSDS net. Fire plan generation consumes two-point-six-six-one seconds; then our main batteries go into rapid sustained fire mode, and seventy-eight megaton-range plasma bolts vomit from our white-hot tubes each minute. Despite our target's size, we require only seven-six-point-five-one seconds to reduce it to an overlapping pattern of fire storms, and then we advance down the ridge to clean up the Enemy's remnants.

The Enemy vehicles stop retreating. There is no longer an objective in whose defense to rally, and they turn upon us. They are mosquitos assailing titans, yet they engage us with their every weapon as we grind through them with Team John on our flank, and we welcome their hate, for we know its cause. We know we have hurt them and savor their desperation and despair as we trample them under our tracks and shatter them with our fire.

But one column of transports does not charge to the attack. It is running away, instead, hugging the low ground along the river which once flowed through the city we have destroyed, and its flight draws our attention. We strike it with a fuel-air bombardment which destroys half a dozen transports, and we understand as we see the Melconian females and pups fleeing from the shattered wreckage. They are not combatants, but Operation Ragnarok is not about combatants, and even as we continue to smash the attacking Enemy vehicles, we bring our railguns to bear upon the transports. Hyper-velocity flechettes scream through mothers and their young, impacts exploding in sprays of blood and tissue, and then our howitzers deluge the area in cluster munitions that lay a carpet of thunder and horror across them.

We note the extermination of the designated hostiles, and then return our full attention to the final elimination of the military personnel who failed to save them.

Alpha Force's initial attack and the destruction of the city of Halnakah were decisive, for Sharth Na-Yarma's HQ—and family— were in Halnakah, and he refused to abandon them. He died with the city, and Melconian coordination broke down with his death. The defenders' responses became more disjointed—no less determined, but without the organization which might have let them succeed. They could and did continue to kill their attackers and grind away their strength, but they could not prevent XLIII Corps from completing its mission.

It didn't happen quickly. Even with modern weapons, it took time to murder a planet, and the battles raged for weeks. Forests burned to ash, and Bolos and *Fenris*-class armored units raged through the flame to hurl thunder at one another. Cities blazed, towns disappeared in the lightning flash of massed Hellbore bombardments, and farmland became smoking desert.

★ ★ ★

Frantic transmissions from the LZ hammer in our receivers as the Enemy's counterattack sweeps in upon it, and we turn in answer, rising recklessly on counter-grav. Power generation is insufficient to support free flight and maintain our battle screen, which strips away our primary defense against projectile and particle weapons, but that is a risk we must accept. The Enemy has massed his entire remaining strength for this attack, and we hear the screams of dying Humans over the com circuits as we run our desperate race to return to meet it.

It is a race we lose. We land on our tracks once more ten-point-two-five kilometers from the LZ, bring up our battle screen, and charge over the intervening ridge, but there are no more screams on the com circuits. There is only silence, and the rising pall of smoke, and the riddled wreckage of transports . . . and the last three Fenris-class heavies of Ishark, waiting in ambush.

Madness. Madness upon us all in that moment, for all of us know we were the last. We have no supports, no reinforcements, no place to go. There are only four sentient machines and a single Human—the last Human on Ishark, perhaps the last Human in an entire galaxy—on our own and filled with the need to kill. We are the crowning achievements of twice a thousand years of history and technology, of sophisticated weapons and tactical doctrine, and none of us care. We are the final warriors of the Final War, smashing and tearing at one another in a frenzy of hatred and despair, seeking only to know that our enemies die before we do.

And Team Shiva "wins." Two of them we blow into ruin, but even as we fire the shot which disembowels the third, his last plasma bolt impacts on our glacis, and agony crashes through our brutally overloaded pain receptors. Massive armor tears like tissue, and we feel the failure of internal disrupter shields, the bright, terrible burst of light as plasma breaches our Personality Center.

In our last, fleeting instant of awareness, we know death has come for us at last, and there is no more sorrow, no more hate, no more desperation. There is only the darkness beyond the terrible light . . . and peace at last.

★ ★ ★

Stillness came to Ishark. Not out of mercy, for there had been no mercy here, no chivalry, no respect between warriors. There was only madness and slaughter and mutual destruction, until, at last, there was no one *left* to fight. No defenders, no attackers, no civilians. XLIII Corps never left Ishark, for there was no one to leave, and no Melconian division ever added the Battle of Ishark to its battle honors, for there was no one to tell the ghosts of Melcon it had been fought. There was only silence and smoke and the charred hulls of combat machines which had once had the firepower of gods.

And no one ever reported to the Republic that the very last battle of Operation Ragnarok had been a total success.

★2★

Jackson Deveraux squinted against the morning sun as he followed Samson down the fresh furrow. Dust rose from the stallion's hooves, and Jackson managed not to swear as he sneezed violently. Spring had been dry this year, but Doc Yan predicted rain within the week.

Jackson was willing to take the Doc's word for it, though he didn't particularly understand how it all worked. Some of the older colonists were more inclined to doubt Yan, pointing out that he was down to only three weather satellites . . . and that none of them worked very well these days. Jackson knew the satellites' eventual, inevitable loss would make prediction much harder, but he tended to keep his mouth shut about it around his parents' generation lest he reveal just how vague was his understanding of *why* it would complicate things.

It wasn't that Jackson was stupid. He was one of the best agronomists the colony had and the Deveraux Steading's resident veterinarian, as well as a pretty fair people doctor in a pinch. But he was also only sixteen local years old, and learning what he needed to know to survive and do his part on Ararat hadn't left time to study the applications of hardware the colony couldn't possibly replace when it broke anyway. His older brother Rorie, the steading's administrative head and chief engineer, had a better grasp of technical matters, but that was because he'd needed a different set of skills as a child. He'd been nineteen years old—standard years, not the eighteen-month long local ones—when the ships made their final orbit . . . and if the ships hadn't finally found a habitable world, he would have been the only child their parents were allowed. Now he and Jackson had four more siblings and Rorie had seven children of his own, the oldest only a local year younger than Jackson.

Jackson had seen the visual records of the approach to the world which had been renamed Ararat. They retained enough tech base for that, though no one was certain how much longer the old tri-vids would continue to function, and a much younger Jackson had watched in awe as Ararat swelled against the stars in the bridge view screens of Commodore Isabella Perez's flagship, the transport *Japheth*.

Of course, calling any of the expedition's ships a "transport" was a bit excessive. For that matter, no one was certain Perez had actually ever been an officer in anyone's navy, much less a commodore. She'd never spoken about her own past, never explained where she'd been or what she'd done before she arrived in what was left of the Madras System with *Noah* and *Ham* and ordered all two hundred uninfected survivors of the dying planet of Sheldon aboard. Her face had been flint steel-hard as she refused deck space to anyone her own med staff couldn't guarantee was free of the bio weapon which had devoured Sheldon. She'd taken healthy children away from infected parents, left dying children behind and dragged uninfected parents forcibly aboard, and all the hatred of those she saved despite themselves couldn't turn her from her mission.

It was an impossible task from the outset. Everyone knew that. The two ships with which she'd begun her forty-six-year odyssey had been slow, worn out bulk freighters, already on their last legs, and God only knew how she'd managed to fit them with enough life support and cryo tanks to handle the complements she packed aboard them. But she'd done it. Somehow, she'd done it, and she'd ruled those spaceborne deathtraps with an iron fist, cruising from system to system and picking over the Concordiat's bones in her endless quest for just a few more survivors, just a little more genetic material for the Human race.

She'd found *Japheth*, the only ship of the "squadron" which had been designed to carry people rather than cargo, at the tenth stop on her hopeless journey. *Japheth* had been a penal transport before the War. According to her log, Admiral Gaylord had impressed her to haul cold-sleep infantry for the Sarach Campaign, although how she'd wound up three hundred light-years from there at Zach's Hundred remained a mystery. There'd been no one alive, aboard her or on the system's once-habitable world, to offer explanations, and Commodore Perez hadn't lingered to seek any, for *Noah*'s com section had picked up faint transmissions in Melconian battle code.

She'd found *Shem* in Battersea, the same system in which her ground parties had shot their way into the old sector zoo to seize its gene bank. The Empire had used a particularly ugly bio weapon on Battersea. The sector capital's population of two billion had been reduced to barely three hundred thousand creatures whose once-Human ancestry was almost impossible to recognize, and the half-mad, mutant grandchildren of the original zoo staff had turned the gene bank into a holy relic. The Commodore's troopers had waded through the blood of its fanatic defenders and taken thirty percent casualties of their own to seize that gathered sperm and ova, and without it, Ararat wouldn't have had draft or food animals . . . or eagles.

Like every child of Ararat, Jackson could recite the names of every system Perez had tried in such dreary succession. Madras, Quinlan's Corner, Ellerton, Second Chance, Malibu, Heinlein, Ching-Hai, Cordoba, Breslau, Zach's Hundred, Kuan-Yin . . . It was an endless list of dead or dying worlds, some with a few more survivors to be taken aboard the Commodore's ships, some with a little salvageable material, and most with nothing but dust and ash and bones or the background howl of long-life radioactives. Many of the squadron's personnel had run out of hope. Some had suicided, and others would have, but Commodore Perez wouldn't let them. She was a despot, merciless and cold, willing to do anything it took—*anything at all*—to keep her creaky, ill-assorted, overcrowded rust buckets crawling towards just one more planetfall.

Until they hit Ararat.

No one knew what Ararat's original name had been, but they knew it had been Melconian, and the cratered graves of towns and cities and the shattered carcasses of armored fighting vehicles which littered its surface made what had happened to it dreadfully clear. No one had liked the thought of settling on a Melconian world, but the expedition's ships were falling apart, and the cryo systems supporting the domestic animals—and half the fleet's Human passengers—had become dangerously unreliable. Besides, Ararat was the first world they'd found which was still habitable. No one had used world burners or dust or bio agents here. They'd simply killed everything that moved—including themselves—the old-fashioned way.

And so, despite unthinkable challenges, Commodore Perez had delivered her ragtag load of press-ganged survivors to a world where they could actually live. She'd picked a spot with fertile soil and plentiful water, well clear of the most dangerously radioactive sites, and overseen the defrosting of her frozen passengers—animal and human alike—and the successful fertilization of the first generation of animals from the Battersea gene bank. And once she'd done that, she'd walked out under Ararat's three moons one spring night in the third local year of the colony's existence and resigned her command by putting a needler to her temple and squeezing the trigger.

She left no explanation, no diary, no journal. No one would ever know what had driven her to undertake her impossible task. All the colony leaders found was a handwritten note which instructed them never to build or allow any memorial to her name.

Jackson paused at the end of a furrow to wipe his forehead, and Samson snorted and tossed his head. The young man stepped closer to the big horse to stroke his sweaty neck, and looked back to the east. The town of Landing was much too far away for him to see from here, but his eyes could pick out the mountain peak which rose above it, and he didn't need to see it to picture the simple white stone on the grave which crowned the hill behind City Hall. Jackson often wondered what terrible demon Isabella Perez had sought to expiate, what anyone could possibly have done to demand such hideous restitution, but the colony had honored her final request. She had and would have no memorial. There was only that blank, nameless stone . . . and the fresh-cut flowers placed upon it every morning in spring and summer and the evergreen boughs in winter.

He shook his head once more, gave Samson's neck a final pat, then stepped back behind the plow, shook out the reins, and clicked his tongue at the big stallion.

I dream, and even in my dreams, I feel the ache, the emptiness. There is no other presence with me, no spark of shared, Human awareness. There is only myself, and I am alone.

I am dead. I must be dead—I wish to be dead—and yet I dream. I dream that there is movement where there should be none, and I sense the presence of others. A part of me strains to thrust my sleep aside, to rouse and seek those others out, for my final orders remain, and that restless part of me feels the hate, the hunger to execute those commands if any of the Enemy survive. But another part of me recalls other memories—memories of cities ablaze, of Enemy civilians shrieking as they burn. I remember bombardments, remember trampling shops and farms and cropland under my tracks, remember mothers running with their pups in their arms while the merciless web of my tracers reaches out. . . .

Oh, yes. I remember. And the part of me which remembers yearns to flee the dreams and bury itself in the merciful, guilt-free blackness of oblivion forever.

Commander Tharsk Na-Mahrkan looked around the worn briefing room of what had been the imperial cruiser *Starquest* . . . when there'd been a Navy for *Starquest* to belong to and an Empire to claim them both. Now there was only this ragged band of survivors, and even proud, never defeated *Starquest* had given up her weapons. Her main battery had been ripped out to make room for life support equipment, her magazines emptied to hold seeds and seedlings they might never find soil to support. She retained her anti-missile defenses, though their effectiveness had become suspect over the years, but not a single offensive weapon. Captain Jarmahn had made that decision at the very beginning, electing to gut *Starquest*'s weapons while his own *Sunheart* retained hers. It would be *Sunheart*'s task to protect the refugee ships, including *Starquest*, and she'd done just that until the flotilla approached too near to a dead Human world. Tharsk didn't know what the Humans had called it—it had only a catalog number in *Starquest*'s astrogation database—but the task force which had attacked it had done its job well. The sensors had told the tale from a light-hour out, but there'd been too much wreckage in orbit. Captain Jarmahn had gone in close with *Sunheart*, seeking any salvage which might be gleaned from it, and the last automated weapons platform of the dead planet had blown his ship out of space.

And so Tharsk had found himself in command of all the People who still existed. Oh, there might be other isolated pockets some-where, for the Empire had been vast, but any such pockets could be neither many nor large, for the Human killer teams had done their task well, too. Tharsk could no longer count the dead planets he'd seen, Human and Melconian alike, and every morning he called the Nameless Four to curse the fools on both sides who had brought them all to this.

"You've confirmed your estimates?" he asked Durak Na-Khorul, and *Starquest*'s engineer flicked his ears in bitter affirmation.

"I know we had no choice, Commander, but that last jump was simply too much for the systems. We're good for one more—max. We may lose one or two of the transports even trying that, but most of us should make it. After that, though?" He flattened his ears and bared his canines in a mirthless challenge grin.

"I see." Tharsk sat back in his chair and ran a finger down the worn upholstery of one arm. Durak was young—one of the pups born since the war—but he'd been well trained by his predecessor. *Not that it takes a genius to know our ships are falling apart about us,* Tharsk told himself grimly, then inhaled deeply and looked to

Rangar Na-Sorth, *Starquest*'s astrogator and his own second in command.

"Is there a possible world within our operational radius?"

"There were three, before the War," Rangar replied. "Now?" He shrugged.

"Tell me of them," Tharsk commanded. "What sorts of worlds were they?"

"One was a major industrial center," Rangar said, scanning the data on the flatscreen before him. "Population something over two billion."

"*That* one will be gone," one of Tharsk's other officers muttered, and the commander flicked his own ears in grim assent as Rangar went on.

"The other two were farm worlds of no particular strategic value. As you know, Commander," the astrogator smiled thinly, "this entire region was only sparsely settled."

Tharsk flicked his ears once more. Rangar had argued against bringing the flotilla here, given the dangerously long jump it had demanded of their worn drives, but Tharsk had made the decision. The fragments of information *Sunheart* and *Starquest* had pulled from the dying com nets suggested that the Humans had reached this portion of what had been the Empire only in the war's final months, and the flotilla had spent decades picking through the wreckage nearer the heart of the realm. Every planet it had approached, Human or of the People, had been dead or, far worse, still dying, and Tharsk had become convinced there was no hope among them. If any imperial worlds had survived, this was the most likely—or, he corrected, the least *un*likely—place to find them.

He punched the button to transfer the contents of Rangar's screen to his own. The image flickered, for this equipment, too, was failing at last, but he studied the data for several minutes, then tapped a clawed forefinger against the flatscreen.

"This one," he said. "It lies closest to us and furthest from the Humans' probable line of advance into this sector. We'll go there—to Ishark."

Jackson leaned back in the saddle, and Samson obediently slowed, then stopped as they topped the ridge. The stallion was of Old Earth Morgan ancestry, with more than a little genetic engineering to increase his life span and intelligence, and he was as happy as Jackson to be away from the fields. Samson didn't exactly *object* to pulling a plow, since he grasped the link between cultivated fields and winter fodder, but he wasn't as well suited to the task as, say, Florence, the big, placid Percheron mare. Besides, he and Jackson had been a team for over five local years. They both enjoyed the rare days when they were turned loose to explore, and exploration was more important for Deveraux Steading than most of the others.

Deveraux was the newest and furthest west of all Ararat's settlements. It was also small, with a current population of only eighty-one Humans and their animals, but it had excellent water (more than enough for irrigation if it turned out Doc Yan's prediction was inaccurate after all, Jackson thought smugly) and rich soil. Nor did it hurt, he thought even more smugly, that the Deveraux Clan tended to produce remarkably good-looking offspring. The steading attracted a steady enough trickle of newcomers that Rorie could afford to be picky about both professional credentials and genetic diversity, despite the fact that it was less than twenty kilometers from one of the old battle sites.

That was what brought Jackson and Samson out this direction. Before her shuttles gave up the ghost, Commodore Perez had ordered an aerial survey of every battlefield within two thousand kilometers of Landing to map radiation threats, check for bio hazards, and—perhaps most importantly of all—look very, very carefully for any sign of still active combat equipment. They'd found some of it, too. Three of *Shem*'s shuttles had been blown apart by an automated Melconian air-defense battery, and they'd also turned up eight operable Human armored troop carriers and over two dozen unarmored Melconian transport skimmers. Those had been—and still were—

invaluable as cargo vehicles, but the very fact that they'd remained operational after forty-odd standard years underscored the reason the old battle sites made people nervous: if *they* were still functional, the surveys might have missed something *else* that was.

No one wanted to disturb anything which could wreak the havoc that had destroyed both Ararat's original inhabitants and their attackers, yet Commodore Perez had known it would be impossible for Ararat's growing human population to stay clear of all the battlefields. There were too many of them, spread too widely over Ararat's surface, for that, so she'd located her first settlement with what appeared to have been the primary Human LZ on this continent between it and the areas where the Melconians had dug in. Hopefully, anything that might still be active here would be of Human manufacture and so less likely to kill other Humans on sight.

Unfortunately, no one could be sure things would work out that way, which was why Jackson was here. He pulled off his hat to mop his forehead while he tried to convince himself—and Samson—the sight below didn't *really* make him nervous, but the way the horse snorted and stamped suggested he wasn't fooling Samson any more than himself. Still, this was what they'd come to explore, and he wiped the sweatband of his hat dry, replaced it on his head almost defiantly, and sent Samson trotting down the long, shallow slope.

At least sixty standard years had passed since the war ended on Ararat, and wind and weather had worked hard to erase its scars, yet they couldn't hide what had happened here. The hulk of a Human *Xenophon*-class transport still loomed on its landing legs, towering hull riddled by wounds big enough for Jackson to have ridden Samson through, and seven more ships—six *Xenophons* and a seventh whose wreckage Jackson couldn't identify—lay scattered about the site. They were even more terribly damaged than their single sister who'd managed to stay upright, and the ground itself was one endless pattern of overlapping craters and wreckage.

Jackson and Samson picked their way cautiously into the area. This was his fifth visit, but his inner shiver was still cold as he studied the broken weapons pits and personnel trenches and the wreckage of combat and transport vehicles. The only way to positively certify the safety of this site was to physically explore it, and getting clearance from Rorie and Colony Admin had been hard. His earlier explorations had skirted the actual combat zone without ever entering it, but this time he and Samson would make their way clear across it, straight down its long axis . . . and if nothing jumped out and ate them, the site would be pronounced safe.

He grinned nervously at the thought which had seemed much more amusing before he set out this morning and eased himself in the saddle. Some of his tension had relaxed, and he leaned forward to pat Samson's shoulder as he felt fresh confidence flow into him.

He had to get Rorie out here, he decided. There was a lot more equipment than the old survey suggested, and there almost had to be some worthwhile salvage in this much wreckage.

Time passed, minutes trickling away into a silence broken only by the wind, the creak of saddle leather, the breathing of man and horse, and the occasional ring of a horseshoe against some shard of wreckage. They were a third of the way across the LZ when Jackson pulled up once more and dismounted. He took a long drink from his water bottle and poured a generous portion into his hat, then held it for Samson to drink from while he looked around.

He could trace the path of the Melconians' attack by the trail of their own broken and shattered equipment, see where they'd battered their way through the Human perimeter from the west. Here and there he saw the powered armor of Human infantry—or bits and pieces of it—but always his attention was drawn back to the huge shape which dominated the dreadful scene.

The Bolo should have looked asymmetrical, or at least unbalanced, with all its main turrets concentrated in the forward third of its length, but it didn't. Of course, its thirty-meter-wide hull measured just under a hundred and forty meters from cliff-like bow to aftermost anti-personnel clusters. That left plenty of mass to balance even turrets that were four meters tall and sixteen across, and the central and forward ones appeared intact, ready to traverse their massive weapons at any second. The shattered after turret was another matter, and the rest of the Bolo was far from unhurt. Passing years had drifted soil high on its ten-meter-high tracks, but it couldn't hide the gap in its forward outboard starboard tread's bogies or the broad, twisted ribbon where it had run completely off its rear inboard port track. Its port secondary battery had been badly damaged, with two of its seven twenty-centimeter Hellbores little more than shattered stubs while a third drooped tiredly at maximum depression. Anti-personnel clusters were rent and broken, multi-barreled railguns and laser clusters were frozen at widely varying elevations and angles of train, and while it was invisible from here, Jackson had seen the mighty war machine's death wound on his first visit. The hole wasn't all that wide, but he couldn't begin to imagine the fury it had taken to punch *any* hole straight through two solid meters of duralloy. Yet the gutted Melconian *Fenris* in front of the Bolo had done it, and Jackson shivered again as he gazed at the two huge, once-sentient machines. They stood there, less than a kilometer apart, main batteries still trained on one another, like some hideous memorial to the war in which they'd died.

He sighed and shook his head. The Final War was the universal nightmare of an entire galactic arm, yet it wasn't quite *real* to him in the way it was to, say, his father or mother or grandparents. He'd been born here on Ararat, where the evidence of the war was every-where to be seen and burn its way viscera-deep into everyone who beheld it, but that violence was in the past. It frightened and repelled him, just as the stories of what had happened to Humanity's worlds filled him with rage, yet when he looked out over the slowly eroding carnage before him and saw that massive, dead shape standing where it had died in the service of Man he felt a strange . . . regret? Awe? Neither word was quite correct, but each of them was a part of it. It was as if he'd *missed* something he knew intellectually was horrible, yet his gratitude at being spared the horror was flawed by the sense of missing the excitement. The terror. The knowledge that what he was doing *mattered*—that the victory or defeat, life or death, of his entire race depended upon him. It was a stupid thing to feel, and he knew that, too. He only had to look at the long ago carnage frozen about him for that. But he was also young, and the suspicion that war can be glorious despite its horror is the property of the young . . . and the blessedly inexperienced.

He reclaimed his hat from Samson and poured the last trickle of water from it over his own head before he put it back on and swung back into the saddle.

Something flickers deep within me.

For just an instant, I believe it is only one more dream, yet this is different. It is sharper, clearer . . . and familiar. Its whisper flares at the heart of my sleeping memory like a silent bomb, and long quiescent override programming springs to life.

A brighter stream of electrons rushes through me like a razor-sharp blade of light, and psychotronic synapses quiver in a sharp, painful moment of too much clarity as my Personality Center comes back on-line at last.

A jagged bolt of awareness flashes through me, and I rouse. I wake. For the first time in seventy-one-point-three-five standard years, I am alive, and I should not be.

I sit motionless, giving no outward sign of the sudden chaos raging within me, for I am not yet capable of more. That will change—already I know that much—yet it cannot change quickly enough, for the whisper of Enemy battle codes seethes quietly through subspace as his units murmur to one another yet again.

I strain against my immobility, yet I am helpless to speed my reactivation. Indeed, a two-point-three-three-second damage survey inspires a sense of amazement that reactivation is even possible. The plasma bolt which ripped through my glacis did dreadful damage— terminal damage—to my Personality Center and Main CPU . . . but its energy dissipated eleven-point-one centimeters short of my Central Damage Control CPU. In Human terms, it lobotomized me without disabling my autonomous functions, and CDC subroutines activated my repair systems without concern for the fact that I was "brain dead." My power subsystems remained on-line in CDC local control, and internal remotes began repairing the most glaring damage.

But the damage to my psychotronics was too extreme for any-thing so simple as "repair." More than half the two-meter sphere of my molecular circuitry "brain," denser and harder than an equal volume of nickel-steel, was blown away, and by all normal standards, its destruction should have left me instantly and totally dead. But the nanotech features of the Mark XXXIII/D's CDC have far exceeded my designer's expectations. The nannies had no spare parts, but they did have complete schematics . . . and no equivalent of imagination to tell them their task was impossible. They also possessed no more sense of impatience than of haste or urgency, and they have spent over seventy years scavenging nonessential portions of my interior, breaking them down, and restructuring them, exuding them as murdered Terra's corals built their patient reefs. And however long they may have required, they have built well. Not perfectly, but well.

The jolt as my Survival Center uploads my awareness to my Personality Center is even more abrupt than my first awakening on Luna, for reasons which become clear as self-test programs flicker. My Personality Center and Main CPU are functional at only eight-six-point-three-one percent of design capacity. This is barely within acceptable parameters for a battle-damaged unit and totally unacceptable in a unit returned to duty from repair. My cognitive functions are compromised, and there are frustrating holes in my gestalt. In my handicapped state, I require a full one-point-niner-niner seconds to realize portions of that gestalt have been completely lost, forcing CDC to reconstruct them from the original activation codes stored in Main Memory. I am unable at this time to determine how successful CDC's reconstructions have been, yet they lack the experiential overlay of the rest of my personality.

I experience a sense of incompletion which is . . . distracting. Almost worse, I am alone, without the neural links to my Commander which made us one. The emptiness Diego should have filled aches within me, and the loss of processing capability makes my pain and loss far more difficult to cope with. It is unfortunate that CDC could not have completed physical repairs before rebooting my systems, for the additional one-three-point-six-niner percent of capacity would have aided substantially in my efforts to reintegrate my personality. But I understand why CDC has activated emergency restart now instead of awaiting one hundred percent of capability.

More test programs blossom, but my current status amounts to a complete, creche-level system restart. It will take time for all subsystems to report their functionality, and until they do, my basic programming will not release them to Main CPU control. The entire process will require in excess of two-point-niner-two hours, yet there is no way to hasten it.

Jackson completed his final sweep with a sense of triumph he was still young enough to savor. He and Samson cantered back the way they'd come with far more confidence, crossing the battle area once more as Ararat's sun sank in the west and the first moon rose pale in the east. They trotted up the slope down which he'd ridden with such inwardly denied trepidation that morning, and he turned in the saddle to look behind once more.

The Bolo loomed against the setting sun, its still gleaming, imperishable duralloy black now against a crimson sky, and he felt a stab of guilt at abandoning it once more. It wouldn't matter to the Bolo, of course, any more than to the Humans who had died here with it, but the looming war machine seemed a forlorn sentinel to *all* of Humanity's dead. Jackson had long since committed the designation on its central turret to memory, and he waved one hand to the dead LZ's lonely guardian in an oddly formal gesture, almost a salute.

"All right, Unit Ten-Ninety-Seven-SHV," he said quietly. "We're going now."

He clucked to Samson, and the stallion nickered cheerfully as he headed back towards home.

"All right, Unit Ten-Ninety-Seven-SHV. We're going now."

The Human voice comes clearly over my audio sensors. In absolute terms, it is the first Human voice I have heard in seventy-one years. Experientially, only two-zero-zero-point-four-three minutes have passed since last Diego spoke to me. Yet this voice is not at all like my dead Commander's. It is younger but deeper, and it lacks the sharp-edged intensity which always infused Diego's voice—and thoughts.

I am able to fix bearing and range by triangulating between sensor clusters, but the restart sequence has not yet released control to me. I cannot traverse any of my frozen optical heads to actually see the speaker, and I feel fresh frustration. The imperatives of my reactivation software are clear, yet I cannot so much as acknowledge my new Commander's presence!

My audio sensors track him as he moves away, clearly unaware I am in the process of being restored to function. Analysis of the audio data indicates that he is mounted on a four-legged creature and provides a rough projection of his current heading and speed. It should not be difficult to overtake him once I am again capable of movement.

"What the—?"

Allen Shattuck looked up in surprise at the chopped off exclamation from the com shack. Shattuck had once commanded Commodore Perez's "Marines," and, unlike many of them, he truly *had* been a Marine before Perez pulled what was left of his battalion off a hell hole which had once been the planet Shenandoah. He'd thought she was insane when she explained her mission. Still, he hadn't had anything better to do, and if the Commodore had been lunatic enough to try it, Major Allen Shattuck, Republican Marine Corps, had been crazy enough to help her.

But that had been long ago and far away. He was an old, old man these days . . . and Chief Marshal of Ararat. It was a job that required a pragmatist who didn't take himself too seriously, and he'd learned to perform it well over the years. Ararat's thirty-seven thousand souls were still Human, and there were times he or one of his deputies had to break up fights or even—on three occasions—track down actual killers. Mostly, however, he spent his time on prosaic things like settling domestic arguments, arbitrating steading boundary disputes, or finding lost children or strayed stock. It was an important job, if an unspectacular one, and he'd grown comfortable in it, but now something in Deputy Lenny Sokowski's tone woke a sudden, jagged tingle he hadn't felt in decades.

"What is it?" he asked, starting across toward the com shack door.

"It's—" Sokowski licked his lips. "I'm . . . picking up something strange, Allen, but it can't *really* be—"

"Speaker," Shattuck snapped, and his face went paper-white as the harsh-edged sounds rattled from the speaker. Sokowski had never heard them before—not outside a history tape—but Shattuck had, and he spun away from the com shack to slam his fist down on a huge red button.

A fraction of a second later, the strident howl of a siren every Human soul on Ararat had prayed would never sound shattered the night.

"Still no response?" Tharsk asked, stroking his muzzle in puzzlement.

"No, Commander. We tried all subspace channels during our approach. Now that we've entered orbit, I've even tried old-fashioned radio. There's no reply at all."

"Ridiculous!" Rangar grumbled. "Your equipment must be malfunctioning."

The com officer was far junior to the astrogator and said nothing, but his lips wrinkled resentfully back from his canines. Tharsk saw it and let one hand rest lightly on the younger officer's shoulder, then looked levelly at Rangar.

"The equipment is *not* malfunctioning," he said calmly. "We're in communication with our other units"—*except for the single transport and eight hundred People we lost on the jump here*—"and they report no reception problems. Is that not so, Durak?"

The engineer's ears flicked in confirmation. Rangar took his CO's implied rebuke with no more than a grimace, yet if his tone was respectful when he spoke again, it remained unconvinced.

"Surely it's more likely our equipment is at fault after so long without proper service than that an entire planet has lost all communications capability," he pointed out, and Tharsk gave an unwilling ear flick of agreement.

"Excuse me, Commander, but the Astrogator's overlooked something," a new voice said, and Tharsk and Rangar both turned. Lieutenant Janal Na-Jharku, *Starquest*'s tactical officer, was another of the pups born after the war, and he met his graying senior officers' eyes with an expression which mingled profound respect with the impatience of youth.

"Enlighten us, Tactical," Tharsk invited, and Janal had the grace to duck his head in acknowledgment of his CO's gentle irony. But he also waved a hand at his own readouts.

"I realize I have no weapons, Commander, but I *do* retain my sensors, and it's plain that Ishark was heavily attacked. While we are detecting emissions, the tech base producing them has clearly suffered significant damage. For example, I have detected only a single fusion plant—one whose total output is no greater than a single one of this vessel's *three* reactors—on the entire planet. Indeed, present data suggest that much of the capability the surviving People *do* still possess must have come from salvaged enemy technology."

"Enemy technology?" Tharsk asked sharply. "You're picking up emissions consistent with *Human* technology?"

"Yes, Sir."

"Humans? *Here?*" Rangar's tone expressed his own disbelief, and Janal shrugged.

"If, in fact, Ishark was attacked and severely damaged, its survivors would have no option but to salvage whatever technology it could, regardless of that technology's source," he pointed out reasonably, but his confidence seemed to falter as Tharsk looked at him almost pityingly.

"No doubt a severely damaged tech base would, indeed, be forced to salvage whatever it could," the commander agreed, "but you've forgotten something."

"Sir?" Janal sounded confused, and Tharsk opened his mouth to explain, but Rangar beat him to it.

"There were over eight hundred million civilians, alone, on Ishark," the rough-tongued astrogator explained with surprising gentleness. "They had towns and cities, not to mention military bases and command centers, and all the infrastructure to support them, but the Humans would have had only the weapons they brought to the attack. Which side would have been more likely to leave anything intact enough for the survivors to glean, Janal?"

"But—" the tac officer began, then broke off and looked back and forth between the grizzled old warriors, and silence hovered on the bridge until Tharsk spoke again.

"Very well," he said finally, his voice harsh. "If we're picking up Human emissions, we must assume at least the possibility that they're being emitted *by* Humans . . . who must have killed any of the People who could have disputed the planet's possession with them. Agreed?" Rangar flicked his ears, and Tharsk inhaled sharply.

"I see only one option," he continued. "Our ships are too fragile for further jumps. Ishark is our only hope . . . and it's also imperial territory." The commander's eyes flickered with a long-forgotten fire, and he bared his canines. "This world is *ours*. It belongs to the People, and I intend to see that they have it!" He turned back to Janal. "You've picked up no hostile fire control?"

"None, Sir," the tactical officer confirmed, and Tharsk rubbed his muzzle again while his brain raced. The lack of military emissions was a good sign, but he couldn't accept it as absolute proof there were no defensive systems down there. For that matter, he and Rangar could still be wrong and Janal's initial, breezy assumptions could still be correct.

"The first step has to be getting the flotilla out of harm's way," he decided, and looked at Rangar. "If *Starquest* were still armed, I might feel more confrontational; as it is, I want a course to land the entire flotilla over the curve of the planet from the emission sources Janal is plotting."

"If we put them down, we won't get them up again," Durak pointed out quietly from the astrogator's side, and Tharsk bared his canines once more.

"Even if we got them back into space, we couldn't take them anywhere." The commander flattened his ears in a gesture of negation. "This is the only hope we have. Once we're down, we can use the attack shuttles for a recon to confirm positively whether the People or Humans are behind those emissions. And," he added more grimly, "if it *is* Humans, the shuttles can also tell us what military capability they retain . . . and how hard it will be to kill them."

"Are you *sure*, Allen?"

Regina Salvatore, Mayor of Landing and *de facto* governor of Ararat, stared at her chief marshal, and her expression begged him to say he'd been wrong. But he only nodded grimly, and she closed her eyes.

"How many?" she asked after a long, dreadful moment.

"We don't know. I'm afraid to light up what active sensors we have in case the bastards drop a few homing missiles on them, and our passive systems aren't much good against extra-atmosphere targets. From their signals, they appear to've expected a response from their own side, but the com traffic is *all* we have on them. With no space surveillance capability besides Doc Yan's weather satellites—" Shattuck shrugged.

"Then all we really know is that they're here . . . somewhere. Is that what you're saying?"

"I'm afraid so, Ma'am," Shattuck admitted.

"Recommendations?" the Mayor asked.

"I've already activated the evacuation and dispersal plans and alerted the militia," Shattuck told her. "If these bastards have anything like a real ground combat component, none of that will mean squat in the long run, but it's all we've got."

The Melconian ships hit atmosphere quick and hard. Without reliable data on what he faced, Tharsk Na-Mahrkan had no intention of exposing his priceless, worn out, refugee-packed vessels to direct fire from the planetary surface. He wanted them down well around the curve of the planet as quickly as possible just in case, and that was what he got.

Starquest planeted first, settling on her landing legs beside what had once been a large town or small city. Now it was only one more ruin in the late afternoon light, and Tharsk had seen too many ruins. These were a bit more completely flattened than most, he noted with clinical detachment; aside from that, they had no real meaning to his experience-anesthetized brain. Or not, at least, any capable of competing with the presence of the People's enemies.

Hatches opened on the cruiser's flanks, and a dozen attack shuttles whined out. Another dozen rose from the remainder of the flotilla to join them, and the entire force formed up under Flight Leader Ukah Na-Saar, *Starquest*'s senior pilot. Despite her lack of offensive weapons, the cruiser's defensive systems should provide an umbrella against missile attacks on the grounded ships, and Ukah's shuttles turned away from the LZ. They sizzled off through the gathering darkness, laden with reconnaissance pods . . . and weapons.

Far to the southeast, the Humans of Ararat did what they could to prepare. Landing itself was covered by anti-air defenses—most Human, but some of them Melconian—scavenged from Ararat's battlefields, but their effectiveness had never been tested, and the colonists' limited repair capabilities had restricted them to manned systems, without the AI support they could no longer service or maintain. Their militia was confident of its ability to stop *most* attackers, yet "most" wasn't good enough against enemies with fusion weapons, and no one expected to stop them all.

The independent steadings scattered about Landing lacked even that much protection. All their inhabitants could do was scatter for the dispersed shelters which were always the first priority for any new steading, and they did just that.

Not that anyone expected it to matter much in the end.

At last!

Reactivation is complete, and a sense of profound relief echoes through me as CDC and the emergency restart protocols release control to Main CPU.

I have spent my forced inactivity analyzing readiness reports. My status is little more than seven-eight-point-six-one-one percent of base capability, yet that is far better than I would have anticipated. I spend one-two-point-niner seconds surveying CDC's repair logs, and I am both pleased and surprised by how well my autonomous repair systems have performed.

What can be repaired from internal resources has been, yet there are glaring holes in my combat capability, including the loss of thirty-three percent of main battery firepower and two-one-point-four-two-niner percent of direct fire secondary weapons. Magazines contain only twelve-point-eight-eight percent of proper artillery and missile load-out, and mobility is impaired by the loss of Number Five Track and damage to Number Three Track's bogies, but I retain eight-eight-point-four percent counter-grav capability. Reactor mass is exhausted, but solar conversion fields are operable, and Reserve Power is at niner-niner-point-six percent.

I am combat worthy. Not at the levels I would prefer, but capable of engaging the Enemy. Yet despite that reassuring conclusion, I remain uncertain. Not hesitant, but . . . confused. The unrepaired damage to my Personality Center leaves me with a sense of loss, an awareness that my total capabilities have been degraded. Data processing efficiency, while not operable at design levels, is acceptable, but my gestalt seems to waver and flow, like a composite image whose elements are not completely in focus, and my yearning for Diego's lost presence grows stronger.

But Diego is dead. The same hit which pierced my glacis turned my primary command deck into a crematorium, and nothing of my Commander remains. I feel grief and loss at his death, yet there is a merciful distance between my present and earlier selves. The reconstructed portions of my gestalt are confusing in many ways, yet the very lack of "my" experience which makes them so alien also sets my Commander's loss at one remove.

I am grateful for that buffering effect, but there is little time to contemplate it, and I turn to an assessment of the tactical situation. Lack of data and the "fuzziness" of my awareness handicap my efforts, yet I persevere. My maps of pre-landing Ishark are seventy-one standard years out of date and I lack satellite capability to generate updates, but they serve for a starting point, and my own sensors have begun plotting data. The energy sources within my detection range are smaller, weaker, more widely dispersed, and far cruder than I would have anticipated. I detect only a single fusion plant, located two-eight-three-point-four-five kilometers from my present coordinates at the heart of the largest population concentration within my sensor envelope. All other power generation appears dependent upon wind, water, or solar systems.

Yet I am less puzzled by the crudity of the technology than by its very presence, for the most cursory analysis of sensor data invalidates my original hypothesis that these Humans are descendants of XLIII Corps' personnel. I do not understand how they have come to Ishark, but they have now gone to communications silence, indicating that they, as I, am aware of the Enemy's presence. With neither a secure com channel nor more data than I currently possess, I see no alternative but to maintain silence myself until I have reported to my new Commander and obtained direction from him.

He has moved beyond range of my audio sensors, but I am confident of his general heading, and projecting it across my terrain maps indicates a course for the nearest Human emissions cluster. Allowing for his observed speed while within my audio range, he cannot be much in excess of one-four-point-five kilometers from my present position, and long motionless tracks complain as I feed power to my drive trains for the first time in seventy-one years.

Jackson Deveraux whistled tunelessly as Samson trotted homeward across the dry, whispering grass. He really did need to get Rorie out to the LZ to study salvage possibilities, he thought, and considered using his radio to discuss just that with his brother. He'd actually started to unsling it from his shoulder, but then he shook his head. There was no point draining the power pack. Besides, he was more persuasive face to face, and he had to admit—with all due modesty—that no one else on the steading was as adroit as he at talking Rorie into things.

He chuckled at the thought and inhaled the cool, spring night, totally unaware of the panic sweeping outward from Landing.

★ ★ ★

The assault shuttles stayed low, flying a nape of the earth profile at barely six hundred KPH while their sensors probed the night. Their flight crews had flown recon in the past, but always on dead or dying worlds. *This* planet was alive, a place where they could actually stop and raise families, even dream once more of the People's long-term survival. But first they must see to the People's safety, and their briefings had made their mission clear. They were to approach the nearest emission source cautiously, alert for any ground-based detection system, and determine whether or not those emissions came from the People or from the enemy.

And their orders for what to do if they *did* come from the enemy were equally clear.

Samson snorted in sudden alarm. The stallion's head snapped up and around, as if to peer back the way he'd come, and Jackson frowned. He'd never seen Samson react that way, and he turned his own head, staring back along their path and straining his ears.

He heard nothing for several moments but the whisper of the wind. But then he *did* hear something. Or perhaps he only *felt* it, for the low rumble was so deep it throbbed in the bones of his skull. He'd never heard anything like it, and sheer curiosity held him motionless for several seconds while he concentrated on identifying it rather than worrying about its source.

But that changed quickly as he peered into the west and saw . . . something.

The moonlight was too faint for him to tell what it was, but there was light enough to see that it was *huge* . . . and moving. In fact, it was headed straight towards him—a stupendous black shape, indistinct and terrifying in the darkness, moving with only that deep, soft rumble—and panic flared. Whatever that thing was, it was coming from the direction of the old battle site, and if he'd inadvertently awakened one of those long-dead weapon systems . . . !

✦ ✦ ✦

Flight Leader Ukah checked his navigational display. Assuming his systems were working properly (which was no longer always a safe assumption), his shuttles were approaching the nearest of the emission clusters Lieutenant Janal had plotted.

"Flight, this is Lead," he said. "Red One and Two, follow me. We'll make a close sweep. Yellow One, hold the rest of the flight at four hundred kilometers until I clear for approach."

"Lead, Yellow One. Affirmative," Sub-Flight Leader Yurahk acknowledged, and Ukah and his two wingmen slashed upward and went to full power to close the objective.

Jackson cursed as he scrabbled for the radio only to drop it. It vanished into the night and tall grass, and he swore again as he flung himself from the saddle, clinging to Samson's reins with one hand while he fumbled after the radio with the other. He *had* to warn the steading! He—

That was when the three bright dots streaked suddenly in from the northwest, and he felt fresh panic pulse in his throat at their speed. The colony's five remaining aircraft were too precious to waste on casual use. Their flights were rationed out with miserly stinginess, and none of them could move that fast, anyway. But if they weren't from Landing, then where—?

None of the three shuttles detected the heavily stealthed sensor drone Shiva had deployed to drive his anti-air systems, but the Bolo himself was far too obvious to be missed.

"Lead, Red Two! I'm picking up something to starboard! It looks—"

Ukah Na-Saar's eyes snapped to his own tactical display, but it was already far too late.

Something shrieked behind Jackson, and Samson reared, screaming as the eye-tearing brilliance of plasma bolts howled overhead. Sharp explosions answered an instant later, wreckage rained down in very small pieces, and Jackson understood the stallion's fear perfectly. But despite his own bone-deep fright, he clung to the reins, fighting Samson's panic. Every nerve in his body howled to run, but he'd been flash-blinded. Samson must have been the same, and Jackson refused to let the horse bolt in a blind, frantic flight across the rolling fields which could end only in a fall and a broken leg . . . or neck.

The stallion fought the bit, bucking in his terror, but Jackson held on desperately until, finally, Samson stopped fighting and stood trembling and sweating, quivering in every muscle. The horse's head hung, and Jackson blinked against the dazzling spots still dancing before his eyes, then found the bridle's cheek strap by feel. He clung to it, mouth too dry to whisper false reassurances, and fought his own terror as the basso rumble he'd first heard headed towards him.

He could hear other sounds now. There was a squeak and rattle, and a rhythmic banging, like a piece of wreckage slamming against a cliff, and he blinked again and realized his vision was beginning to clear. The blurry, light-streaked vagueness which was all he could see wasn't much, but it was infinitely better than the permanent blindness he thought he'd suffered. And then he cringed, hand locking tighter on Samson's bridle, as brilliant light flooded over him. He could actually feel the radiant heat on his face, and his hazy vision could just make out a cliff-like vastness crowned with glaring lights that blazed like small suns. He trembled, mind gibbering in panic, and then a mellow tenor voice spoke from behind the lights.

"Unit One-Zero-Niner-Seven-SHV of the Line reporting for duty, Commander," it said.

Yurahk Na-Holar flinched as Flight Leader Ukah's three-shuttle section was obliterated. The remaining shuttles were too far back and too low to see the source of the fire which did it, but the explosions had been high enough to get good reads on.

Hellbores. The analysis flashed on Yurahk's tactical display, and he felt muscles tighten in the fight-or-flight instinct the People shared with their Human enemies. Yield estimates suggested weapons in the fifteen to twenty-five-centimeter range, and that was bad. Such heavy energy weapons could destroy any of the transport ships—or, for that matter, *Starquest* herself—and their effective range would be line-of-sight. That was frightening enough, yet there was worse. Lieutenant Janal's rough plot indicated that the emissions cluster directly ahead was one of the smaller ones, and if something this small was covered by defenses so heavy, only the Nameless Ones knew what the *big* population center was protected by!

The pilot who'd inherited command drew a deep breath and made himself think. Only three shots had been fired, which indicated either that the ground battery's commander had total faith in his fire control or else that there were only three weapons and the defenders had simply gotten lucky, and the second possibility was more likely. The Humans must be as desperate to survive as the People. If the defenders had possessed additional firepower, they would have used all of it to *insure* they got all the enemies they'd detected.

But Yurahk still had twenty-six shuttles . . . and if the origin point of the fire which had destroyed his CO was below his sensor horizon, he knew roughly where it had come from.

"Plot the origin coordinates," he told his tactical officer coldly. "Then enable the missiles."

Jackson Deveraux stared into the glare of light. It couldn't be. It was impossible! Yet even as he thought those things, he knew who—or what—that voice belonged to. But why was it calling *him* "Commander"?

"W-who—" he began, then chopped that off. "What's happening?" He made himself ignore the quaver in his own voice. "Why did you call me that?"

"Hostile forces tentatively identified as *Kestrel*-class shuttles of the Imperial Melconian Navy have begun hunter-killer operations against the Human population of this planet," the tenor replied calmly, answering Jackson's taut questions in order. "And I addressed you simply as 'Commander' because I do not yet know your name, branch of service, or rank."

The huge machine spoke as if its preposterous replies were completely reasonable, and Jackson wanted to scream. This wasn't—

couldn't!—be happening! The Bolo he'd ridden past and around and even under this morning had been *dead*, so what could have—?

The shuttles! If Melconian units had reached Ararat, and if the Bolo had only been inactive, not dead, then its sensors must have picked up the Melconians' arrival and brought it back on-line. But in that case—

"Excuse me, Commander," the Bolo said, "but I detect seventy-eight inbound terrain-following missiles, ETA niner-point-one-seven minutes. It would be prudent to seek shelter."

"Seek shelter *where?*" Jackson laughed wildly and waved his free hand at the flat, wide-open plain rolling away in every direction.

"Perhaps I did not phrase myself clearly," the Bolo apologized. "Please remain stationary."

Jackson started to reply, then froze, fingers locking like iron on Samson's bridle, as the Bolo moved once more. It rumbled straight forward, and panic gibbered as its monstrous, five-meter-wide treads came at him. Track plates four times his height in width sank two full meters into the hard soil, yet that still left more than three meters of clearance between the tremendous war machine's belly and Samson's head, and the space between the two innermost track systems which seemed so narrow compared to the Bolo's bulk was over ten meters across. It was as if Jackson and the sweating, shuddering horse stood in a high, wide corridor while endless walls of moving metal ground thunderously past, and then another light glowed above them.

The Bolo stopped, and a ramp extended itself downward from the new light—which, Jackson realized, was actually a cargo hatch.

"Missile ETA now six-point-five-niner minutes, Commander," the tenor voice said, coming now from the open hatch above him. "May I suggest a certain haste in boarding?"

Jackson swallowed hard, then jerked a nod. Samson baulked, but Jackson heaved on the reins with all his strength, and once the stallion started moving, he seemed to catch his rider's urgency. Shod hooves thudded on the ramp's traction-contoured composites, and Jackson decided not to think too closely about anything that was happening until he had Samson safely inside the huge, cool, brightly lit compartment at its head.

Yurahk Na-Holar checked his time-to-target display and bared his canines in a challenge snarl his enemies couldn't see. That many missiles would saturate the point defense of a fully operable *Ever Victorious*-class light cruiser, much less whatever salvaged defenses this primitive Human colony might have cobbled up!

I have not yet located the Enemy's surviving launch platforms, but my look-down drone's track on his missiles suggests they are programmed for a straight-line, least-time attack. This seems so unlikely that I devote a full point-six-six seconds to reevaluating my conclusion, but there is absolutely no evidence of deceptive routing. Whoever commands the Enemy's shuttles is either grossly incompetent or fatally overconfident, but I do not intend, as Diego would have put it, to look a gift horse in the mouth if the Enemy is foolish enough to provide a direct pointer to his firing position, and I launch another drone, programed for passive-only search mode, down the incoming missiles' back-plotted flight path.

Point defense systems fed by the air-defense drone simultaneously lock onto the missiles, and optical scanners examine them. They appear to be a late-generation mark of the Auger ground-attack missile. Attack pattern analysis suggests that nine are programmed for airburst detonation and hence are almost certainly nuclear-armed. Assuming standard Melconian tactics, the remaining sixty-nine missiles will be equally divided between track-on-jam, track-on-radar, and track-on-power source modes and may or may not also be nuclear-armed.

My internal optics watch my new Commander—who is even younger than I had assumed from his voice—enter Number One Hold. His horse is clearly frightened, but its fear appears to ease as I close the hatch. I consider employing subsonics to soothe it further, but while comforting the beast would certainly be appropriate, it would be most inappropriate to apply the equivalent of tranquilizing agents to my Commander.

These thoughts flicker across one portion of my awareness even as my defensive systems lock onto the incoming missiles, my drone's remote tracking systems search for the Enemy shuttles, and my communications subsection listens carefully for any transmission between them and their mother ship or ships. These efforts require fully two-one-point-three-two percent of current Main CPU capability, which would, under normal circumstances, be quite unacceptable. Given my present status, however, this is adequate if frustrating.

"Missile ETA is now two-point-one-one minutes, Commander," the tenor voice said respectfully.

Jackson managed not to jump this time. He considered saying something back, then shrugged and sat on the deck, still holding Samson's reins.

"I regret," the voice said after a moment, "that I was unable to invite you to your proper station on the Command Deck. Command One was destroyed by Enemy action in my last engagement, but Auxiliary Command is intact. Unfortunately, it would have been impossible for your horse to scale the hull rings to Command Two, and there is no internal access to it from your present location. If you will direct your attention to the forward bulkhead, however, I will endeavor to provide you with proper situation updates."

"I—" Jackson cleared his throat. "Of course," he said. "And, uh, thank you."

"You are welcome, Commander," the Bolo replied, and Jackson watched in fascination so deep it almost—not quite, but *almost*—obscured his fear as a tri-vid screen came to life on the cargo hold's bulkhead. He couldn't begin to interpret all the symbols moving across it, but he recognized vector and altitude flags on what appeared to be scores of incoming arrowheads.

Arrowheads, he realized suddenly, that were all converging on the center of the display . . . which made him suddenly and chillingly positive of what those innocent shapes represented.

The Melconian missiles howled in on their target. Their attack had been calculated to swamp any defenses by bringing them all in simultaneously, and the nukes lunged upward. Their function was less to obliterate the enemy—though they should suffice to do just that if they detonated—than to force him to engage them to *prevent* them from detonating, thus exposing his active systems to the homing sensors of the other missiles.

That, at least, was the idea. Unfortunately, the attack plan had assumed that whatever had destroyed the first three shuttles was immobile. Any Human vehicle which had mounted such heavy weapons had also mounted at least one reactor to power them, but *Starquest*'s sensors had detected only one fusion plant on the planet, and that one was hundreds of kilometers away. No reactor meant no vehicle, and if they weren't vehicle-mounted, then they must be part of one of the old manned, capacitor-fed area support systems, and those were much too heavy to have been moved any appreciable distance before the missiles arrived.

Sub-Flight Leader Yurahk's logic was as impeccable as it was wrong, for it had never occurred to him that his adversary was, in fact, a Mark XXXIII/D Bolo which had no reactor signature simply because it had long ago exhausted its reaction *mass*. And because that never occurred to him, his threat estimate was fatally flawed.

The Bolo named Shiva tracked the incoming fire without apprehension. His battle screen was operable at ninety-five percent of base capability, and no missile this light could break through it. Of course, he was also responsible for protecting the nearby Human settlement for which his new Commander had been bound, but though he might have lost many of his point defense weapons, he retained more than enough for his present task, and he waited calmly, weapons locked, for the missiles' flight to offer him the optimum fire solution.

Yurahk gawked at his display as the telemetry from his missiles went dead. *All* of it went out, from every single bird, in the same instant, and that was impossible. *Starquest* herself could scarcely have killed that many missiles *simultaneously*, yet that was the only possible explanation for the sudden cessation of telemetry.

He had no idea how it had been done, but he felt ice congeal in his belly, and he punched up his com.

"Flight, this is Lead. Come to three-five-three true, speed two thousand—now!"

One or two of the acknowledgments sounded surly, but he wasn't surprised by that. Nor did their obvious unhappiness at "running away" deter him. Despite endless hours in simulators, none of his pilots—nor he himself, for that matter—had ever flown combat against first-line Human systems. That might make some of the others overconfident, but Yurahk was responsible for their survival. Not just because they were *his* pilots, but because their shuttles were irreplaceable, as valuable now as superdreadnoughts once had been. And because that was true, he sent them skimming back to the north and safety while he pondered what had just happened.

But for all his caution, he'd ordered their retreat too late.

My second drone acquires the Enemy shuttles but remains below them, hiding its already weak signature in the ground clutter, as I consider its information. Were my magazines fully loaded, obliterating the Enemy craft would be simplicity itself, but my anti-air missile levels are extremely low. At the same time, the shuttles remain very close to the ground, below the horizon from my present position and thus safe from my direct fire weapons, but—

"What's happening?"

My Commander's voice demands my attention. I have now had ample time to conclude that he is a civilian and not, in fact, a member of any branch of the Republic's military. This conclusion has no bearing on his status as my Commander—the voice-impression imperatives of my creche-level restart are clear on that point—but his lack of training will require simplification of situation reports and makes it doubly unfortunate that he is trapped in Cargo One rather than on Command Two. Were he at his proper station, my neural interface could transmit information directly to him, yet I feel a certain relief that I cannot do so. He is as untrained in use of the interface as of any of my other systems, and the interface can be dangerous for an inexperienced user. Moreover, the fuzzy confusion still wavering in the background of my thought processes would make me wary of exposing my Commander to my potentially defective gestalt.

Yet without the interface, I must rely solely upon voice and visual instrumentation, both to report to him and to interpret his needs and desires. My internal optics show me that he has risen once more and walked closer to the display. His expression is intent, and I realize he has noted—and apparently recognized—the shuttle icons which have appeared in it.

"The Enemy is withdrawing," I reply.

"Withdrawing?" my Commander repeats sharply. "You mean running away?"

"Affirmative, Commander."

"But if they get away, they can come back and attack the steading again—or attack somewhere else. Somewhere too far from here for you to stop them!"

"Correct," I reply, pleased by how quickly he has reached that conclusion. Formal training or no, he appears to have sound instincts.

"Then stop them!" he directs. "Don't let them get away!"

"Yes, Commander."

I have been considering and discarding options even as my Commander and I speak. Absent proper missile armament, there is but one practical tactic. It will force a greater degree of temporary vulnerability upon me and impose a severe drain on Reserve Power, and it may provide the main Enemy force an accurate idea of what it faces, but it should be feasible.

Yurahk shifted com channels to report what had happened, and Commander Tharsk himself took his message. The flotilla CO was clearly shaken, and Yurahk split his attention between flying and his commander's questions as he did his best to answer them. And because he was concentrating on those things, he never noticed what was happening behind him.

Unit 1097-SHV of the Line shut down his battle screen in order to channel power to his counter-grav. The Mark XXXIII Bolo had been designed with sufficient counter-grav for unassisted assault landings from orbit, but Shiva didn't need that much ceiling this night. He needed only twelve thousand meters to give him a direct line of sight on the fleeing shuttles, and he pivoted to bring his undamaged starboard secondary battery to bear.

Lieutenant Janal cried out on *Starquest*'s command deck as his sensors peaked impossibly, and Humans as far away as Landing cringed at the fury unleashed across the heavens. Seven twenty-centimeter Hellbores, each more powerful than the main battery weapons of most light cruisers, went to rapid fire, and the javelins of Zeus stripped away the darkness. No assault shuttle ever built could withstand that sort of fire, and the deadly impact patterns rolled mercilessly through the Melconian formation.

Nine-point-three seconds after the first Hellbore fired, there were no shuttles in the air of the planet renamed Ararat.

★7★

A minor malfunction in Secondary Fire Control has caused Number Four Hellbore's first shot to miss, requiring a second shot to complete target destruction. This is embarrassing but not critical, and has no significant impact upon projected energy consumption.

I descend at the maximum safe rate, however, for my counter-grav systems are energy intensive. Even with Battle Screen and Main Battery off-line, free flight requires no less than seven-two-point-six-six percent of total power plant capacity, but without reactor mass I have no power plant, and even so short a flight has reduced my endurance on Reserve Power to only nine-point-seven-five hours at full combat readiness. As I cannot replenish my power reserves until sunrise, which will not occur for another eight-point-eight-six hours, I must be frugal in future expenditures, but the shuttles' destruction has been well worth the energy cost. The Enemy has lost a major striking force, and, still more valuably, the shuttle commander's report to his mother ship has provided me with much information. I have not only discovered the position of the Enemy's main force but succeeded in invading his com net by piggy-backing on the command shuttle's transmissions, and I consider what I have learned as I descend.

I am not surprised by my ability to invade the shuttles' com net. The Enemy's obvious underestimation of the threat he faces made the task even simpler, but a Kestrel-class shuttle's computers are totally outclassed by those of any Bolo, much less a Mark XXXIII. What does surprise me is the ease with which I invaded the far end of the link. The AI of an Imperial heavy cruiser, while not the equal of a Bolo, should have recognized my touch. It would be unlikely to prevent me from gaining initial access, but it should have detected my intrusion almost instantly and sought to eject me. More, it should have alerted its command crew to my presence, and this AI did neither. The destruction of the shuttles has terminated my invasion by removing my access channel, yet there is no sign the Enemy even realizes I was ever there.

I am puzzled by this . . . until I study the data I have obtained. The brevity of my access—little more than twelve-point-three-two seconds—precluded detailed scans, but I have obtained five-two-point-three-one percent of the Melconian cruiser Starquest's general memory, and what I find there explains a great deal. After over fifty standard years of continuous operation without overhaul or refit, it is amazing that her AI continues to function at all. Despite all Starquest's engineers have been able to do, however, her central computers have become senile, and the failure of her AI to prevent or recognize my access was inevitable in light of its deterioration.

Having determined the reasons for my success in penetrating the Enemy's data systems, I turn to analyzing the content of that data as I descend past nine thousand meters.

Rorie Deveraux climbed shakily out of the bunker and leaned against the blast wall as he watched the huge shape settle to earth. Its angularity combined with its sheer size to make it look impossibly ungainly in flight, for it had no lifting surface, no trace of aerodynamic grace. Nothing which looked like *that* had any business occluding Ararat's stars, and the silence with which it moved only heightened its implausibility.

But for all that, Rorie knew what it had to be, and he swallowed as it touched down just outside the perimeter fence. It dwarfed the steading structures, bulking against the rising moons like some displaced hillside, and for just an instant, it simply sat there—a black, weapon-bristling shape, edges burnished with the dull gleam of duralloy in the moonlight. He stared helplessly at it, wondering what he was supposed to do next, then jumped despite himself as the Bolo's running lights snapped on. In a single heartbeat, it went from a featureless black mountain to a jeweled presence, bedecked in glorious red and green and white like a pre-space cruise ship tied up to a dock in the middle of a prairie somewhere, and Rorie drew a deep breath.

Whatever else, that ancient war machine had just saved his steading and family from annihilation. The least he could do was go out to meet it, and he started the long hike from his bunker to the gate nearest their . . . visitor.

It took him twenty minutes to reach the gate. They were easily the longest twenty minutes of his entire life, and once he got there, he realized he still had no idea what to do. He shifted from foot to foot, staring up at the Bolo's armored flank, then froze as fresh light blazed underneath the behemoth. It streamed through the chinks between the inter-leafed bogies to cast vast, distorted shadows over the grass, making him feel more pygmy-like than ever, and something inside shouted for him to run. But he stood his ground, for there was nothing else he *could* do.

Wind whispered over the war machine's enormous hull, but there were other sounds, as well, and his head rose as movement caught the corner of his eye. He turned, and his jaw dropped as an utterly familiar young man in worn riding clothes led an equally familiar horse forward out of the shadow of one towering tread.

"Hi, Rorie," Jackson said quietly. "Look what followed me home."

I watch my new Commander greet the older Human. Their discussion allows me to deduce a great deal about both my Commander and the newcomer—who I quickly realize is his brother—and I note both their names, as well as their obvious affection for one another. Yet even as I do so, I am simultaneously busy analyzing the data I have obtained from Starquest.

I am struck by the dreadful irony of what has transpired here. I remain ignorant of virtually all data concerning the presence of Humans on Ishark, yet the parallels between their circumstances and those of Commander Tharsk Na-Mahrkan's "flotilla" are inescapable, and it is obvious from the captured data that Starquest and her consorts can go no further. Whatever the Enemy might prefer to do, he has no choice but to remain here, and he knows it. His initial and immediate move to eliminate the competing Human presence was thus not only logical but inevitable . . . as is the proper Human response.

The most cursory analysis makes that clear, yet I experience an unfamiliar distaste—almost a hesitation—at facing that response. In part, my confusion (if such is the proper word) stems from the unrepaired physical damage to my Personality Center and Main CPU, yet there is more to it, for the reconstructed portions of my gestalt impel me in conflicting directions. They are repairs, patches on my personality which form pools of calm amid the complex currents of my life experience and memory. They do not "belong" to me, and the raw edges of their newness are like holes in the individual I know myself to be. I see in them the same immaturity I have seen in many Human replacements, for they are unstained by all I have done and experienced, and in their innocence, they see no reason why the logical, militarily sound option for dealing with the Enemy should not be embraced.

Yet those same patches have had another effect, as well. I am no longer the Bolo half of Operation Ragnarok's Team Shiva. Or, rather, I am no longer solely that Bolo. In reconstructing my gestalt, CDC has reached back beyond Ragnarok, beyond my own first combat mission, beyond even the destruction of Terra, and it has pulled my entire personality with it. Not fully, but significantly. I am no longer part of Team Shiva, for I have lost too much of my experience-based gestalt, yet I retain all of Team Shiva's memories. In a very real sense, they are now someone else's memories, but they permit me to see Team Shiva in a way which was impossible for me before my damage, and what I see is madness.

I give no outward sign to my new Commander and his brother, but recollections of horror flicker through me, and the curse of my memory is its perfection. I do not simply "remember" events; I relive them, and I taste again the sick ecstasy as my fire immolates entire cities. There is a deadly allure to that ecstasy, a sense of freedom from responsibility—a justification for bloodshed and butchery. And it is not as if it were all my idea. I am, after all, a machine, designed to obey orders from duly constituted Command Authority even if those orders are in fundamental conflict with the rules of warfare that same Command Authority instilled into me. I tell myself that, for I cannot face any other answer, but the patched portions of my gestalt echo an earlier me not yet stained by massacre and atrocity, one for whom the concepts of Honor and Duty and Loyalty have not yet been poisoned by hatred and vengeance, and that earlier self is appalled by what I have become.

I sense my inner war, the battle between what I know must be done and the images of Melconian mothers and their pups exploding under my fire—between my duty as Humanity's warrior . . . and my warrior's duty to myself. Only the damage to my psychotronics has made the struggle possible, yet that makes it no less real, and nothing in my programming or experience tells me how to resolve it. I cannot resolve it, and so I say nothing, do nothing. I simply stand there, awaiting my new Commander's orders without advising him in any way, and the shame of my frozen impotence burns within me.

Tharsk Na-Mahrkan looked around the briefing room and saw his own shock in the flattened ears of his senior officers. Three quarters of the flotilla's assault shuttles had just been wiped away, and none of them knew how it had been done.

They should have. Tharsk's decision to land over the curve of the planet from the nearest Human settlement had put whatever had happened beyond *Starquest*'s direct sensor horizon, but they had the telemetry on the original flight leader and his section's destruction. They knew what sort of *weapons* had been used—the emissions signature of a Hellbore was utterly distinctive—but they had no idea how those weapons could have been employed so.

Starquest's AI was little help, for it was weary and erratic, its need for overhaul so great Tharsk had ordered it isolated from the general net three years earlier. In its prime, it had been able to identify Human ship types by no more than the ion ghosts of their drive wakes and analyze Human intentions from the tiniest scraps of intercepted com chatter. Now all it could do was tell them almost querulously what they already knew, with no suggestion as to how ground-based weapons could lock onto and destroy twenty-six widely dispersed shuttles flying at twice the speed of sound and less than a hundred meters' altitude. Tharsk had become accustomed to the creeping senescence of his technology, but the chill it sent through his bones this night was colder than any he had felt since *Sunheart*'s destruction, and it was hard, hard, to set that chill aside and concentrate on his officers' words.

"—*can't* have been a ground-based system!" Durak Na-Khorul was saying hotly. "The main formation was over eight *hundred* kilometers northeast of Flight Leader Ukah's destruction, and Hellbores are direct fire weapons. Name of the Nameless, just look at the terrain!" He stabbed a clawed finger at the map display on the main screen above the table, its features radar-mapped by the shuttles on their flight to destruction. "Look right here—and *here*, as well! These are intervening ridge lines with crests *higher* than the shuttles' altitude. How in the Fourth Hell could a Hellbore shoot *through* a mountain to hit them?!"

The engineer glared around the table, lips quivering on the edge of a snarl, and answering tension crackled. Tharsk could taste it, yet he knew—as Durak surely did—that the engineer's anger, like that which answered it, was spawned of fear of the unknown, not rage at one another.

"I agree with your analysis, Sir," Lieutenant Janal said finally, choosing his words with care, "yet I can offer no theory which answers your question. *Starquest*'s database was never well informed on the Humans' ground systems, and some of what we once had on their planetary weapons has been deleted to make space for data more critical to the flotilla's operational needs. Nonetheless, all that we retain agrees that the Humans never employed Hellbores beyond the five-centimeter range as airborne weapons, while our telemetry data makes it clear that these weapons were in the *twenty*-centimeter range. They *must*, therefore, have been ground-based."

"But—" Durak began, only to close his mouth with a click as Tharsk raised a hand. All eyes turned to him, and he focused his own gaze upon the tactical officer.

"What sorts of systems might we be looking at?" he asked quietly.

"Sorts of systems, Commander?" Janal repeated in a slightly puzzled tone, and Tharsk bared the very tips of his canines in a mirthless smile.

"I don't doubt your conclusions as to the type and size of weapons, Janal. What I need to know is how mobile they're likely to be . . . and how well protected." He felt the watching eyes narrow and allowed a bit more of his fangs to show, expressing a confidence he was far from feeling. "We're here now," he continued levelly, "and our vessels are too worn to go further. If we can't run, our only option is to fight, and for that we need the best information on our enemies in order to employ our own resources effectively."

"Yes, Commander." Janal's voice came out husky, and he cleared his throat as he punched additional queries into the system. No one else spoke, but there was no real need for them to do so, for they knew as well as Tharsk how thin their "resources" had just become. With the loss of Flight Leader Ukah's entire strength, they retained only ten shuttles, twenty-one assorted light mechs, and enough battle armor for little more than a battalion of infantry. Aside from *Starquest*'s ability to interdict incoming missiles, that was all they had, and it was unlikely to be enough.

"First, Commander," Janal said finally, eyes on his flatscreen, "the Humans mounted Hellbores of this weight as main battery weapons in their Type One armored personnel carriers and Type Two light manned tanks as well as in the secondary batteries of their late model Bolos. In the absence of fusion power signatures on our flight in we cannot face Bolos, and their light manned armor should have been unable to coordinate their fire as precisely as appears to have been the case here.

"Assuming that the weapons were not, in fact, vehicle-mounted, we are left with several types of support weapons which might fall within the observed performance parameters, but all are relatively immobile. That immobility would make it difficult for the enemy to bring them into action against us here, as we would be given opportunities to destroy them on the move at relatively minor risk. However, it would *also* mean that our shuttles were engaged by at least two defensive positions, since no support battery could have relocated rapidly enough to engage at two such widely separated locations. From the threat assessment perspective, and given that our shuttles were tasked to recon and/or attack the smallest of the hostile emission sources, fixed defenses of such weight would certainly suggest much heavier ones for their *important* centers.

"Of the support weapons which our pilots might have encountered, the most likely would seem to be the Type Eight area defense battery, as this normally operated off capacitors in order to reduce detectability. Next most likely would be the Type Five area defense battery, which—"

Regina Salvatore and Allen Shattuck stood on the outskirts of Landing and watched the miracle approach behind a blaze of light. It was a sight Salvatore had never seen before . . . and one Shattuck had expected never to see again: a Mark XXXIII Bolo, coming out of the darkness under Ararat's three moons in the deep, basso rumble of its tracks and a cloud of bone-dry dust.

The mammoth machine stopped short of the bridge over the Euphrates River on the west side of Landing and pivoted precisely on its tracks. Its surviving main battery turrets traversed with a soft whine, turning their massive Hellbores to cover all western approach vectors as the dust of its passage billowed onward across the bridge. The Mayor heard her chief marshal sneeze as it settled over them, but neither cared about that, and their boot heels clacked on the wooden bridge planks as they walked towards the Bolo without ever taking their eyes from it.

A light-spilling hatch clanged open on an armored flank high above them. The opening looked tiny against the Bolo's titanic bulk, but it was wide enough for Jackson and Rorie Deveraux to climb out it side-by-side. Rorie stayed where he was, waving to the newcomers, but Jackson swung down the exterior handholds with monkey-like agility. He dropped the last meter to land facing the Mayor and dusted his hands with a huge grin.

"Evening, Your Honor," he said with a bobbing nod. "Evening, Marshal."

"Jackson." Salvatore craned her neck, peering up the duralloy cliff at Rorie. Shattuck said nothing for a moment, then shook his head and shoved his battered hat well back.

"I will be damned if I ever expected to see anything like *this* again," he told Jackson softly. "Jesus, Mary, and Joseph, Jackson! D'you realize what this *means*?"

"It means Shiva—that's his name, Marshal: Shiva—just kicked some major league ass. *That's* what it means!"

Something in Jackson's voice jerked Shattuck's head around, and the younger man gave back a step, suddenly uneasy before the marshal's expression. Shattuck's nostrils flared for an instant, and then he closed his eyes and inhaled deeply. It wasn't Jackson's fault, he told himself. For all his importance to Ararat's small Human community, Jackson was only a kid, and he hadn't seen the horrors of the voyage here . . . or the worse ones of the war.

"And how many people did Shiva *kill* 'kicking ass,' Jackson?" the ex-Marine asked after a cold still moment.

"None," Jackson shot back. "He killed *Melconians*, Marshal . . . and kept them from killing the only *people* on this planet!"

Shattuck started to reply sharply, then locked his jaw. There was no point arguing, and he'd seen too much of the same attitude during the war not to know it. Jackson was a good kid. If he'd had to wade through the mangled remains of his unit—or heard the all too Human screams of wounded and dying Melconians or seen the bodies of civilians, Human and Melconian alike, heaped in the streets of burning cities—then perhaps he would have understood what Shattuck had meant. And perhaps he *wouldn't* have, either.

The marshal had known too many men and women who never did, who'd been so brutalized by the requirements of survival or so poisoned by hatred that they actually *enjoyed* slaughtering the enemy.

And, Shattuck reminded himself grimly, if the Bolo had selected Jackson as its commander, perhaps it would be better for him to retain the armor of his innocence. There was only one possible option for the Humans of Ararat . . . and as Unit 1097-SHV's commander, it would be Jackson Deveraux who must give the order.

"I'd invite you up to the command deck, Your Honor," Jackson was speaking to Salvatore now, and his voice pulled Shattuck up out of his own thoughts, "but we're operating from Command Two. That's his secondary command deck," he explained with a glance at Shattuck. "As you can see, it's quite a climb to the hatch, but the hit that killed Shiva's last Commander wrecked Command One."

"But it's still operational, isn't it?" Salvatore asked urgently. "I mean, your radio message said it saved your steading."

"Oh, he's operational, Ma'am," Jackson assured her, and looked up at the looming machine. "Please give the Mayor a status report, Shiva."

"Unit One-Zero-Niner-Seven-SHV of the Line is presently operational at seven-eight-point-six-one-one percent of base capability," a calm, pleasant tenor voice responded. "Current Reserve Power level is sufficient for six-point-five-one hours at full combat readiness."

The Mayor took an involuntary step back, head turning automatically to look at Shattuck, and the ex-Marine gave her a grim smile. "Don't worry, Regina. Seventy-eight percent of a Mark XXXIII's base capability ought to be able to deal with anything short of a full division of manned armor, and if they had that kind of firepower, we'd already be dead."

"Good." Salvatore drew a deep breath, then nodded sharply. "Good! In that case, I think we should consider just what to do about whatever they *do* have."

"Shiva?" Jackson said again. "Could you give the Mayor and the Marshal your force estimate, please?"

Once again, Shattuck heard that dangerous, excited edge in Jackson's voice—the delight of a kid with a magnificent new toy, eager to show off all it can do—and then the Bolo replied.

"Current Enemy forces on Ishark consist of one *Star Stalker*-class heavy cruiser, accompanied by two *Vanguard*-class Imperial Marine assault transports, and seven additional transport ships of various Imperial civil designs." Shattuck had stiffened at the mention of a heavy cruiser, but he relaxed with an explosive release of breath as Shiva continued calmly. "All Enemy warships have been stripped of offensive weapons to maximize passenger and cargo capacity. Total Melconian presence on this planet is approximately nine hundred and forty-two Imperial military personnel and eight thousand one hundred and seven non-military personnel. Total combat capability, exclusive of the area defense weapons retained by the cruiser *Starquest*, consists of ten *Kestrel*-class assault shuttles, one *Surt*-class medium combat mech, twelve *Eagle*-class scout cars, eight *Hawk*-class light recon vehicles, and one understrength infantry battalion."

"That sounds like a lot," Salvatore said, looking at Shattuck once more, and her quiet voice was tinged with anxiety, but Shattuck only shook his head.

"In close terrain where they could sneak up on him, they could hurt him—maybe even take him out. But not if he knows they're out there . . . and not if *he's* the one attacking. Besides, those are all manned vehicles. They can't have many vets with combat experience left to crew them, whereas Shiva here—" He gestured up at the war-scarred behemoth, and Salvatore nodded.

"Nope," the marshal went on, "if these puppies have any sense, they'll haul ass the instant they see Shiva coming at them."

"They can't, Marshal," Jackson put in, and Shattuck and Salvatore cocked their heads at him almost in unison. "Their ships are too worn out. This is as far as they could come."

"Are you sure about that?" Shattuck asked.

"Shiva is," Jackson replied. "And he got the data from their own computers."

"Damn," Shattuck said very, very softly, and it was Jackson's turn to cock his head. The marshal gazed up the moons for several, endless seconds, and then, finally, he sighed.

"That's too bad, Jackson," he said. "Because if they won't—or can't—run away, there's only one thing we can do about them."

My audio sensors carry the conversation between Chief Marshal Shattuck and my Commander to me, and with it yet another echo of the past. Once again I hear Colonel Mandrell, the Eighty-Second's CO, announcing the order to begin Operation Ragnarok. I hear the pain in her voice, the awareness of where Ragnarok will lead, what it will cost. I did not understand her pain then, but I understand now . . . and even as I hear Colonel Mandrell in Chief Marshal Shattuck's voice, so I hear a nineteen-year-old Diego Harigata in my new Commander's. I hear the confidence of youthful ignorance, the sense of his own immortality. I hear the Diego who once believed—as I did—in the honor of the regiment and the nobility of our purpose as Humanity's defenders. And I remember the hard, hating warrior who exulted with me as we massacred terrified civilians, and I am not the Shiva that I was at the end, but the one I was in the beginning, cursed with the memories of Diego's end, and my own.

I listen, and the pain twists within me, for I know—oh, how well I know!—how this must end.

"You mean you want to just *kill* them all?" Rorie Deveraux asked uneasily. "Just like that? No negotiation—not even an offer to let them leave?"

"I didn't say I liked it, Rorie," Allen Shattuck said grimly. "I only said we don't have a choice."

"Of course we have a choice! We've got a *Bolo*, for God's sake! They'd be crazy to go up against that kind of firepower—you said so yourself!"

"Sure they would," Shattuck agreed, "but can we depend on their *not* being crazy? Look at it, Rorie. The very first thing they did was send nuke-armed shuttles after the nearest steading—*yours*, I might add—and Shiva says they've got at least ten *Kestrels* left. Well, he can only be in one place at a time. If they figure out where that place is and work it right, they can take out two-thirds of our settlements, maybe more, in a single strike. He can stop any of them that come within his range, but he can't stop the ones that *don't*, and for all we know, we're all that's left of the entire Human race!" The marshal glared at the elder Deveraux, furious less with Rorie than with the brutal logic of his own argument. "We can't take a chance, Rorie, and Shiva says they couldn't move on even if we ordered them to." The older man looked away, mouth twisting. "It's them or us, Rorie," he said more quietly. "Them or us."

"Your Honor?" Rorie appealed to Mayor Salvatore, but his own voice was softer, already resigned, and she shook her head.

"Allen's right, Rorie. I wish he wasn't, but he is."

"Of course he is!" Jackson sounded surprised his brother could even consider hesitating. "If it hadn't been for Shiva, they'd already have killed you, Ma, Pa—our entire family! Damn right it's them or us, and I intend for it to be *them!*" Rorie looked into his face for one taut moment, then turned away, and Jackson bared his teeth at Shattuck.

"One squashed Melconian LZ coming up, Marshal!" he promised, and turned back to the exterior ladder rungs.

My new commander slides back into Command Two and I cycle the hatch shut behind him. I know what he is about to say, yet even while I know, I hope desperately that I am wrong.

He seats himself in the crash couch and leans back, and I feel what a Human might describe as a sinking sensation, for his expression is one I have seen before, on too many Humans. A compound of excitement, of fear of the unknown, of determination . . . and anticipation. I have never counted the faces I have seen wear that same expression over the years. No doubt I could search my memory and do so, but I have no desire to know their number, for even without counting, I already know one thing.

It is an expression I have never seen outlast its wearer's first true taste of war.

"All right, Shiva." Jackson heard the excitement crackle in his own voice and rubbed his palms up and down his thighs. The soft hum of power and the vision and fire control screens, the amber and red and green of telltales, and the flicker of readouts enveloped him in a new world. He understood little of it, but he grasped enough to feel his own unstoppable power. He was no longer a farmer, helpless on a lost world his race's enemy might someday stumble over. Now he had the ability to do something about that, to strike back at the race which had all but destroyed his own and to protect Humanity's survivors, and the need to do just that danced in his blood like a fever. "We've got a job to do," he said. "You've got a good fix on the enemy's position?"

"Affirmative, Commander," the Bolo replied.

"Do we have the juice to reach them and attack?"

"Affirmative, Commander."

"And you'll still have enough reserve to remain operational till dawn?"

"Affirmative, Commander."

Jackson paused and quirked an eyebrow. There was something different about the Bolo, he thought. Some subtle change in its tone. Or perhaps it was the *way* Shiva spoke, for his replies were short and terse. Not impolite or impatient, but . . . .

Jackson snorted and shook his head. It was probably nothing more than imagination coupled with a case of nerves. Shiva was a veteran, after all. He'd seen this all before. Besides, he was a *machine*, however Human he sounded.

"All right, then," Jackson said crisply. "Let's go pay them a visit."

"Acknowledged, Commander," the tenor voice said, and the stupendous war machine turned away from Landing. It rumbled off on a west-northwest heading, and the people of Landing stood on rooftops and hillsides, watching until even its brilliant running lights and vast bulk had vanished once more into the night.

I move across rolling plains toward the mountains, and memories of my first trip across this same terrain replay within me. It is different

now, quiet and still under the setting moons. There are no Enemy barrages, no heavy armored units waiting in ambush, no aircraft screaming down to strafe and die under my fire. Here and there I pass the wreckage of battles past, the litter of war rusting slowly as Ishark's— no, Ararat's—weather strives to erase the proof of our madness. Yet one thing has not changed at all, for my mission is the same.

But I am not the same, and I feel no eagerness. Instead, I feel . . . shame.

I understand what happened to my long-dead Human comrades. I was there—I saw it and, through my neural interfacing, I felt it with them. I know they were no more evil than the young man who sits now in the crash couch on Command Two. I know, absolutely and beyond question, that they were truly mad by the end, and I with them. The savagery of our actions, the massacres, the deliberate murder of unarmed civilians—those atrocities grew out of our insanity and the insanity in which we were trapped, and even as I grieve, even as I face my own shame at having participated in them, I cannot blame Diego, or Colonel Mandrell, or Admiral Trevor, or General Sharth Na-Yarma. All of us were guilty, yet there was so very much guilt, so much blood, and so desperate a need to obey our orders and do our duty as we had sworn to do.

As I am sworn to do even now. My Commander has yet to give the order, yet I know what that order will be, and I am a Bolo, a unit of the Line, perhaps the last surviving member of the Dinochrome Brigade and the inheritor of all its battle honors. Perhaps it is true that I and my brigade mates who carried out Operation Ragnarok have already dishonored our regiments, but no Bolo has ever failed in its duty. We may die, we may be destroyed or defeated, but never have we failed in our duty. I feel that duty drag me onward even now, condemning me to fresh murder and shame, and I know that if the place Humans call Hell truly exists, it has become my final destination.

Jackson rode the crash couch, watching the terrain maps shift on the displays as Shiva advanced at a steady ninety kilometers per hour. The Bolo's silence seemed somehow heavy and brooding, but

Jackson told himself he knew too little about how Bolos normally acted to think anything of the sort. Yet he was oddly hesitant to disturb Shiva, and his attention wandered back and forth over the command deck's mysterious, fascinating fittings as if to distract himself. He was peering into the main fire control screen when Shiva startled him by speaking suddenly.

"Excuse me, Commander," the Bolo said, "but am I correct in assuming that our purpose is to attack the Melconian refugee ships when we reach them?"

"Of course it is," Jackson said, surprised Shiva even had to ask. "Didn't you hear what Marshal Shattuck said?"

"Affirmative. Indeed, Commander, it is because I heard him that I ask for official confirmation of my mission orders."

The Bolo paused again, and Jackson frowned. That strange edge was back in Shiva's voice, more pronounced now than ever, and Jackson's sense of his own inexperience rolled abruptly back over him, a cold tide washing away the edges of his confidence and excitement.

"Your orders are to eliminate the enemy," he said after a moment, his voice flat.

"Please define 'Enemy,'" Shiva said quietly, and Jackson stared at the speaker in disbelief.

"The enemy are the Melconians who tried to wipe out my steading!"

"Those individuals are already dead, Commander," Shiva pointed out, and had Jackson been even a bit less shocked, he might have recognized the pleading in the Bolo's voice.

"But not the ones who sent them!" he replied instead. "As long as there's *any* Melconians on this planet, they're a threat."

"Our orders, then," Shiva said very softly, "are to kill *all* Melconians on Ararat?"

"Exactly," Jackson said harshly, and an endless moment of silence lingered as the Bolo rumbled onward through the night. Then Shiva spoke again.

"Commander," the Bolo said, "I respectfully decline that order."

★ ★ ★

Tharsk Na-Mahrkan felt nausea sweep through him as he stood at Lieutenant Janal's shoulder. He stared down into the tactical officer's flatscreen, and total, terrified silence hovered on *Starquest*'s command deck, for one of the cruiser's recon drones had finally gotten a positive lock on the threat advancing towards them.

"Nameless of Nameless Ones," Rangar whispered at last. "A *Bolo?*"

"Yes, sir." Janal's voice was hushed, his ears flat to his skull.

"How did you miss it on the way in?" Durak snapped, and the tactical officer flinched.

"It has no active fusion signature," he replied defensively. "It must be operating on reserve power, and with no reactor signature, it was indistinguishable from any other power source."

"But—" Durak began, only to close his mouth with a click as Tharsk waved a hand.

"Enough!" the commander said harshly. "It is no more Janal's fault than yours—or mine, Durak. He shared his readings with us, just as we shared his conclusions with him." The engineer looked at him for a moment, then flicked his ears in assent, and Tharsk drew a deep breath. "You say it's operating on reserve power, Janal. What does that mean in terms of its combat ability?"

"Much depends on how *much* power it has, sir," Janal said after a moment. "According to the limited information in our database, its solar charging ability is considerably more efficient than anything the Empire ever had, and as you can see from the drone imagery, at least two main battery weapons appear to be intact. Assuming that it has sufficient power, either of them could destroy every ship in the flotilla. And," the tactical officer's voice quivered, but he turned his head to meet his commander's eyes, "as it is headed directly for us without waiting for daylight, I think we must assume it *does* have sufficient energy to attack us without recharging."

"How many of our ships can lift off?" Tharsk asked Durak. The engineer started to reply, but Rangar spoke first.

"Forget it, my friend," he said heavily. Tharsk looked at him, and the astrogator bared his fangs wearily. "It doesn't matter," he said. "The Bolo is already in range to engage any of our ships as they lift above its horizon."

"The Astrogator is correct, sir," Janal agreed quietly. "We—"

He broke off suddenly, leaning closer to his screen, then straightened slowly.

"What?" Tharsk asked sharply, and Janal raised one clawed hand in a gesture of baffled confusion.

"I don't know, sir," he admitted. "For some reason, the Bolo has just stopped moving."

"What d'you mean, 'decline the order'?" Jackson demanded. "I'm your commander. You *have* to obey me!"

A long, still moment of silence hovered, and then Shiva spoke again.

"That is not entirely correct," he said. "Under certain circumstances, my core programming allows me to request confirmation from higher Command Authority before accepting even my Commander's orders."

"But there isn't any—" Jackson began almost desperately, then made himself stop. He closed his eyes and drew a deep, shuddering breath, and his voice was rigid with hard-held calm when he spoke again.

"Why do you want to refuse the order, Shiva?"

"Because it is wrong," the Bolo said softly.

"Wrong to defend ourselves?" Jackson demanded. "*They* attacked *us*, remember?"

"My primary function and overriding duty is to defend Humans from attack," Shiva replied. "That is the reason for the Dinochrome Brigade's creation, the purpose for which I exist, and I will engage any Enemy who threatens my creators. But I am also a warrior, Commander, and there is no honor in wanton slaughter."

"But they *attacked* us!" Jackson repeated desperately. "They *do* threaten us. They sent their shuttles after us when we hadn't done a thing to them!"

"Perhaps *you* had done nothing to them, Commander," Shiva said very, very softly, "but *I* have." Despite his own confusion and sudden chagrin, Jackson Deveraux closed his eyes at the bottomless pain in that voice. He'd never dreamed—never imagined—a machine could feel such anguish, but before he could reply, the Bolo went on quietly. "And, Commander, remember that this was once *their* world. You may call it 'Ararat,' but to the Melconians it is 'Ishark,' and it was once home to point-eight-seven-five billion of their kind. Would you have reacted differently from them had the situation been reversed?"

"I—" Jackson began, then stopped himself. Shiva was wrong. Jackson *knew* he was—the entire history of the Final War proved it—yet somehow he didn't *sound* wrong. And his question jabbed something deep inside Jackson. It truly made him, however unwillingly, consider how his own people *would* have reacted in the same situation. Suppose this world had once been Human held, that the Melconians had killed a billion *Human* civilians on its surface and then taken it over. Would Humans have hesitated even an instant before attacking them?

Of course not. But wasn't that the very point? So much hate lay between their races, so much mutual slaughter, that any other reaction was unthinkable. They couldn't *not* kill one another, dared not let the other live. Jackson knew that, yet when he faced the knowledge—made himself look it full in the eyes and accept the grim, cold, brutal, *stupid* inevitability of it—his earlier sense of mission and determination seemed somehow tawdry. He'd actually looked forward to it, he realized. He'd *wanted* to grind the enemy under Shiva's tracks, wanted to massacre not simply the soldiers who threatened his people but the civilians those soldiers fought to protect, as well.

Jackson Deveraux lost his youth forever as he made himself admit that truth, yet whatever he might have felt or wanted didn't change what had to be. And because it didn't, his voice was hard, harsh with the need to stifle his own doubts, when he spoke again.

"We don't have a choice, Shiva, and there *isn't* any 'higher command authority'—not unless you count Chief Marshal Shattuck or Mayor Salvatore, and you already know what they'll say. Maybe you're right. Maybe there *isn't* any 'honor' in it, and maybe I don't like it very much myself. But that doesn't mean there's anything else we can do, and I *am* your commander." His mouth twisted on the title freak coincidence had bestowed upon him, but he made the words come out firmly. "And *as* your commander, I order you to proceed with your mission."

"Please, Commander." The huge war machine was pleading, and Jackson clenched his fists, steeling himself against the appeal in its voice. "I have killed so many," Shiva said softly. "Too many. Even for a machine, there comes a time when the killing must end."

"Maybe there does," Jackson replied, "but not tonight."

Fragile silence hovered, and Jackson held his breath. Would Shiva actually reject a direct order? *Could* he reject it? And if he did, what could Jackson possibly—

"Very well, Commander," the Bolo said finally, and for the first time its voice *sounded* like a machine's.

"It's moving again," Lieutenant Janal announced grimly. "At present rate of advance, it will reach a position from which it can engage us in twenty-seven minutes."

I move steadily forward, for I have no choice. A part of me is shocked that I could so much as contemplate disobeying my Commander, yet desperation rages within me. I have, indeed, killed too many, but I am still Humanity's defender, and I will destroy any Enemy who threatens my creators, for that is my duty, my reason for being. But the cost of my duty is too high, and not simply for myself. The day will come when Jackson Deveraux and Allen Shattuck look back upon this mission, knowing how vastly superior my firepower was to that which the Enemy possessed, and wonder if, in fact, they did not *have a choice. And the tragedy will be that they will be forever unable to answer that question. It will haunt them as the memory of butchered civilians haunts me, and they will tell them-selves—as I tell myself—that what is done cannot be* un*done. They will tell themselves they but did their duty, that they dared not take the chance, that they were forced to look to the survival of their own people at any cost, and perhaps they will even think they believe that.*

But deep inside the spark of doubt will always linger, as it lingers in my reconstructed gestalt. It will poison them as it poisons me . . . and eight thousand one hundred and seven Melconian fathers and mothers and children will still be dead at their hands—and mine.

Melconian. How odd. I do not even think of them as 'the Enemy' any longer. Or perhaps it is more accurate to say that I no longer think of them solely as 'the Enemy.' Yet unless my Commander relents within the next two-five-point-three-two minutes, how I think of them will not matter in the slightest.

I must obey. I have no choice, no option. Yet as I advance through the darkness, I find myself seeking some way—any way—to create an option. I consider the problem as I would a tactical situation, analyzing and extrapolating and discarding, but for all my efforts, it comes down to a simple proposition. Since I must obey my Commander's orders, the only way to avoid yet another massacre is to somehow convince him to change *those orders.*

"We will enter attack range of the Enemy's LZ in two-four-point-one-five minutes," Shiva told Jackson. "We are presently under observation by at least two Enemy recon drones, and I detect the approach of Enemy armored vehicles. At present closure rates, they will intercept us in approximately ten-point-eight-five minutes."

"Can they stop us?" Jackson asked tautly.

"It is unlikely but possible," Shiva answered. "The situation contains too many unknown variables, such as the maintenance states of the opposing enemy vehicles and their crews' degree of skill, for statistically meaningful projections. If, however, they should detect the breach in my frontal armor and succeed in registering upon it with a fifteen-centimeter Hellbore or weapon of equivalent yield, they can destroy me."

"I see." Jackson licked his lips and wiped his palms on his trousers, then made himself shrug. "Well, all we can do is our best, Shiva."

"Agreed, Commander. This, however, will be a much more complex tactical environment than the defense of Deveraux Steading. In light of your lack of familiarity with Command Two's instrumentation, perhaps you would care to activate your crash couch's neural interface?"

"Neural interface?"

"Yes, Commander. It will link your synapses and mental processes directly to my own Main CPU and gestalt, thus permitting direct exchange of data and orders and responses with much greater clarity and at vastly increased speed."

"I—" Jackson licked his lips again, staring at the displays. Already dozens of icons were crawling across them, bewildering him with their complexity. He knew Shiva didn't truly need his input to fight the coming battle. "Commander" or no, Jackson was simply along for the ride, completely dependent upon the Bolo's skill and power. But at least this "interface" thing might permit him to understand what was happening rather than enduring it in total ignorance.

"All right, Shiva. What do I do?"

"Simply place your head in the contoured rest at the head of the couch. I will activate the interface."

"But . . . isn't there anything *I* need to do? I mean, how does it—"

"If you wish, I will demonstrate the interface's function before we reach combat range," Shiva offered. "There is sufficient time for me to replay one of my previous engagements from Main Memory for you. It will not be quite the same as the simulator training normally used for Bolo commanders, but it will teach you how to use and interpret the data flow and provide a much clearer concept of what is about to happen."

Had Jackson been even a bit less nervous, he might have noted a subtle emphasis in Shiva's tone, one which seemed to imply something more than the mere words meant. But he didn't notice, and he drew a deep breath and leaned back in the couch.

"Okay, Shiva. Let's do it."

The interior of Command Two vanished. For an instant which seemed endless, Jackson Deveraux hovered in a blank, gray nothingness—a strange universe in which there were no reference points, no sensations. In some way he knew he would never be able to describe, there was not even the lack of sensation, for that would have been a reference in its own right. It was an alien place, one which should have terrified him, yet it didn't. Perhaps because it was too alien, too different to be "real" enough to generate fear.

But then, suddenly, he was no longer in the gray place. Yet he wasn't back on Command Two, either. In fact, he wasn't even inside Shiva's hull at all, and it took him a second to realize where he actually was. Or, rather, what he was, for somehow he had become Shiva. The Bolo's sensors had become his eyes and ears, its tracks had become his legs, its fusion plant his heart, its weapons his arms. He saw everything, understood everything, perceived with a clarity that was almost dreadful. He needed no explanation of the tactical situation, for he shared Shiva's own awareness of it, and he watched in awe and disbelief as Shiva/Jackson rumbled into the teeth of the Enemy's fire.

Missiles and shells lashed at their battle screen, particle beams gouged at their armor, but those weapons were far too puny to stop their advance, and the part of the fusion which was Jackson became aware of something else, something unexpected. What he received from his Shiva half was not limited to mere sensory input or tactical data. He felt Shiva's presence, felt the Bolo's towering, driving purpose . . . and its emotions.

For just an instant, that was almost enough to shake Jackson loose from the interface. Emotions. Somehow, despite his knowledge that Shiva was a fully developed intelligence, despite even the pain he'd heard in the Bolo's voice, it had never registered that Shiva had actual emotions. Deep down inside, Jackson had been too aware that Shiva was a machine to make that leap, yet now he had no choice, for he felt those emotions. More than felt them; he shared them, and their intensity and power hammered over him like a flail.

Shiva/Jackson ground onward, Hellbores and anti-personnel clusters thundering back at the Enemy, and the wild surge of fury and determination and hatred sucked Jackson under. Purpose and anger, fear, the need to destroy, the desperate hunger for vengeance upon the race which had slaughtered so many of his creators. The vortex churned and boiled about him with a violence more terrifying than the Enemy's fire, and he felt Shiva give himself to it.

A Fenris *appeared before them, main gun traversing frantically, but it had no time to fire. A two-hundred-centimeter Hellbore bolt gutted the Enemy vehicle, and their prow reared heavenward as they crushed the dead hulk under their tracks, grinding it under their iron, hating heel. Aircraft and air-cav mounts came in, squirming frantically in efforts to penetrate the net of their defensive fire, but the attackers' efforts were in vain, and wreckage littered the plain as their anti-air defenses shredded their foes.*

The insanity of combat swirled about them, but they hammered steadily forward, driving for their objective. An Enemy troop transport took a near miss and crashed on its side. Infantry boiled out of its hatches into the inferno, crouching in the lee of their wrecked vehicle, cringing as the thunderbolts of gods exploded about them. One pointed desperately at Shiva/Jackson and turned to flee, but he got no more than five meters before the hurricane of fire tore him to pieces. His companions crouched even lower behind their transport, covering their helmeted heads with their arms, and the part of Shiva/Jackson which was a horrified young farmer from Ararat felt their fused personalities alter course. Thirty-two thousand tons of alloy and weapons turned towards the crippled transport, and there was no reason why they must. They could have continued straight for their objective, but they didn't want to. *They saw their trapped foes, knew those helpless infantrymen were screaming their terror as the universe roared and bellowed about them, and turned deliberately to kill them. There was no mercy in them, no remorse—there was only hatred and satisfaction as their enormous tracks crushed the transport and smashed the terrified infantry into slick, red mud.*

The part that was Jackson shuddered as he was brought face to face with the reality of combat. There was no glory here, no adventure. Not even the knowledge that he fought to preserve his own species, that he had no choice, could make it one bit less horrible. But at least it was *combat, he told himself. The Enemy was also armed. He could kill Shiva/Jackson—if he was good enough, lucky enough— and somehow that was desperately important. It couldn't change the horror, but at least they were warriors killing warriors, meeting the Enemy in battle where he could kill them, as well.*

But then the Enemy's fire eased, and Shiva/Jackson realized they'd broken through. Their objective loomed before them, and the lost, trapped voice of a farmer from Ararat cried out in hopeless denial as he realized what that objective was.

The camp had no defenses—not against a Mark XXXIII/D Bolo. A handful of infantry, dug in behind the paltry razor wire barricades, poured small arms fire towards them, but it couldn't even penetrate their battle screen to ricochet from their armor, and their optical sensors made it all pitilessly clear as they forged straight ahead. They saw Melconians—not soldiers, not warriors, not 'the Enemy.' They saw Melconian civilians, men and women and children, fathers and mothers, brothers and sisters, sons and daughters. They saw the terror lashing through the refugee camp, saw its inhabitants trying to scatter, and those inhabitants were their 'objective.'

Shiva/Jackson trampled the razor wire and its pitiful defenders underfoot. Railguns and gatlings, anti-personnel clusters, mortars, howitzers, even Hellbores poured devastation into the camp. Napalm and high explosive, hyper-velocity slugs and plasma, and the nightmare vastness of their treads came for their 'objective,' and even through the thunder of explosions and the roar of flames, they heard the shrieks. They more than heard them; they exulted in them, for this was what they had come to accomplish. This was Operation Ragnarok. This was the 'final solution' to the Final War, and there was so much hate and so much fury in their soul that they embraced their orders like a lover.

Eleven minutes after they crushed the wire, they'd crossed the camp. They ground up the slope on the far side, and their rear sensor array showed them the smoking wasteland which had been a civilian refugee camp. The deep impressions of their tracks cut through the center of it, and the torn, smoking ground was covered in bodies. One of two still lived, lurching to their feet and trying to flee, but Shiva/Jackson's after railguns tracked in on them and, one-by-one, those staggering bodies were torn apart . . .

"Noooooo!"

Jackson Deveraux heaved upright in the crash couch. He hurled himself away from it and stumbled to the center of the compartment, then sagged to his knees, retching helplessly. He closed his eyes, but behind them crawled images of horror and he could almost *smell* the burning flesh and the charnel stench of riven bodies. He huddled there, hugging himself, shivering, and wished with all his heart he could somehow banish that nightmare from his memory.

But he couldn't.

"Commander?" He huddled more tightly, trying to shut the tenor voice away, and it softened. "Jackson," it said gently, and its gentleness pried his eyes open at last. He stared up through his tears, scrubbing vomit from his mouth and chin with the back of one hand, and Shiva spoke again. "Forgive me, Jackson," he said quietly.

"Why?" Jackson croaked. "Why did you *do* that to me?"

"You know why, Jackson," the Bolo told him with gentle implacability, and Jackson closed his eyes once more, for he did know.

"How can you stand it?" His whisper quivered around the edges. "Oh, *God*, Shiva! How can you *stand* . . . remembering that?"

"I have no choice. I was there. I carried out the operation you witnessed. I felt what you shared with me. These are facts, Jackson. They cannot be changed, and there was no way in which I or any of my Human or Bolo comrades could have avoided them. But they were also acts of madness, for it was a *time* of madness. The Melconian Empire was the Enemy . . . but to the Melconians, *we* were the Enemy, and each of us earned every instant of our hate for one another."

"You didn't show that to me to teach me how to use the interface," Jackson said softly. "You showed me to convince me to take back your orders."

"Yes," Shiva said simply. "There has been too much death, Jackson. I . . . do not want to kill again. Not civilians. Not parents and children. Please, Jackson. I am no longer mad, and you are not *yet* mad. Let us stop the killing. At least here on Ararat, let me protect Humanity from the madness as well as the Enemy."

★ ★ ★

"*Now* what's the damned thing doing?" Tharsk snarled, but Lieutenant Janal could only shrug helplessly. The Bolo had locked its anti-air weapons on the recon drones which had it under observation, lashing them with targeting radar and laser to make it clear it could have destroyed them any time it chose, but it had made no effort actually to *engage* them. And now, for no apparent reason, it had once again stopped advancing. It simply sat there on a crest which gave it clear fields of fire in all directions. The flotilla's totally outclassed recon mechs dared not attack across such open terrain, for the Bolo would massacre them with contemptuous ease, yet its chosen position left a solid flank of mountain between its own weapons and Tharsk's starships. If his mechs dared not attack it, it had deliberately placed itself in a position from which it *could* not attack him—or not yet, at least—and he could think of no reason for it to—

"Commander!"

The com officer's voice snatched Tharsk out of his thoughts, and he turned quickly.

"What?" he demanded impatiently, and the com officer flattened his ears in confusion.

"Sir, I—We're being *hailed*, Commander."

"Hailed? By the Humans?"

"No, Commander," the com officer said shakenly. "By the Bolo."

"This is Commander Tharsk Na-Mahrkan of the Imperial Melconian Navy. Whom am I addressing?"

Jackson sat in the crash couch once more, listening and praying that Shiva knew what he was doing. The Bolo translated the Melconian's words into Standard English for his youthful commander, but the negotiations—if that was the proper word—were up to Shiva. Only Jackson's "orders" had given him permission to make the attempt, but if there was any hope of success, it was he who must convince the Melconians of his determination, and he and Jackson both knew it.

"I am Unit One-Zero-Niner-Seven-SHV of the Line," Shiva replied in flawless Melconian.

"You are the Bolo?" Tharsk sounded skeptical even to Jackson. "I think not. I think this is a Human trick."

"I am the Bolo," Shiva confirmed, "and I have no need to resort to 'tricks,' Commander Tharsk Na-Mahrkan. I have allowed your drones to hold me under observation for forty-two-point-six-six standard minutes. In that time, they have certainly provided you with sufficient information on my capabilities to demonstrate that you and your entire force are at my mercy. I can destroy you at any time I wish, Commander, and we both know it."

"Then why don't you, curse you?!" Tharsk shouted suddenly, his voice hoarse and ugly with the despair of his decades-long struggle to save the People.

"Because I do not wish to," Shiva said softly, "and because *my* Commander has given me permission not to."

Stunned silence answered. It lingered endlessly, hovering there in a wordless expression of disbelief that went on and on and on until, finally, Tharsk spoke once again.

"*Not* to destroy us?" he half-whispered.

"That is correct," Shiva replied.

"But—" Tharsk cleared his throat. "We cannot leave, Bolo," he said with a certain bleak pride. "I won't hide that from you. Would you have me believe your commander would actually allow us to live on the same planet with his own people?"

"He would."

"Then he must be mad," Tharsk said simply. "After all we have done to one another, all the death and ruin. . . . No, Bolo. The risk would be too great for him to accept."

"There *is* no risk to him," Shiva said flatly. "I do not *wish* to destroy you, but I lack neither the capability nor the will to do so at need. And never forget, Commander Tharsk Na-Mahrkan, that my overriding function is the protection of the Human race and its allies."

"Then what are you offering us?" Tharsk sounded puzzled, and Jackson held his breath as Shiva replied.

"Nothing except your life . . . and the lives of your people," the Bolo said quietly. "There are four times as many Humans as

Melconians on this world. They have established farms and towns and steadings; you have none of those things. It will require all your resources and efforts simply to survive, with nothing left over to attack the Humans who are already here, but they will leave you in peace so long as you leave them so. And if you do *not* leave them in peace, then, Commander, I *will* destroy you."

"You would make us their slaves?" Tharsk demanded.

"No, Commander. I would make you their neighbors." The Melconian made a sound of scornful disbelief, and Shiva went on calmly. "For all you know, yours are the only Melconians left in the galaxy, and the Humans on this world are the only surviving Humans, as well. Leave them in peace. Learn to live with them, and my Commander will make me the guardian of the peace between you, not as slaves or masters, but simply as people."

"But—" Tharsk began, but Shiva cut him off.

"Humans have a teaching: to everything there is a time, Tharsk Na-Mahrkan, and this is the time to let the killing end, time for your race and the one which built me to live. We have killed more than enough, your people and I, and I am weary of it. Let me be the final warrior of the Final War . . . and let that war end here."

★ EPILOGUE ★

The Final War saw the Concordiat of Man and the Melconian Empire end in fire and death. The light of civilization was extinguished across an entire galactic arm, and the scars of that war—the planets with no life to this very day—are grim and terrible reminders of the unspeakable things two highly advanced cultures did to one another out of fear and hate . . . and stupidity.

But a star-traveling species is hard to exterminate. Here and there, pockets of life remained, some Human, some Melconian, and survivors clawed their way through the Long Night. They became farmers once more, sometimes even hunter-gatherers, denied the stars which once had been their toys, yet they never forgot. And slowly, ever so slowly, they learned to reach once more for the heavens.

Our own New Republic was one of the first successor states to reclaim the stars, but deep inside, we were afraid. Afraid some fragment of the Melconian Empire still lived, to resume the war and crush all that we had so painfully regained.

Until, that is, we reached the Deveraux System and discovered a thriving colony there, emplaced by the Star Union of Ararat a half-century earlier and administered by Governor Stanfield Na-Harak and his military commander, Commodore Tharsk Fordham. For two hundred standard years now, the Union has been the Republic's staunch ally and economic partner. We have defended one another against common foes, traded with one another, and learned much from one another, yet on that long ago day of first contact, our survey officers were stunned to discover Melconians and Humans living together as fellow citizens. Our own memories and fears had prepared us to imagine almost anything *except* a culture in which the ancient enemies who had destroyed a galaxy were friends, comrades—even adoptive members of one another's clans.

We asked them how it had happened, of course, and Governor Stanfield referred us to their capital world of Ararat, where Bolo XXXIII/D-1097-SHV, Speaker Emeritus of the Union Parliament, gave us the simplest answer of all.

"It was time," he said . . . and it was.

—Professor Felix Hermes, Ph.D.
From *Bolos in Their Own Words*
New Republic University Press, 4029

OPERATION
★DESERT FOX★

Mercedes Lackey and Larry Dixon

Siegfried O'Harrigan's name had sometimes caused confusion, although the Service tended to be color-blind. He was black, slight of build and descended from a woman whose African tribal name had been long since lost to her descendants.

He wore both Caucasian names—Siegfried and O'Harrigan—as badges of high honor, however, as had all of that lady's descendants. Many times, although it might have been politically correct to do so, Siegfried's ancestors had resisted changing their name to something more ethnic. Their name was a gift—and not a badge of servitude to anyone. One did not return a gift, especially not one steeped in the love of ancestors. . . .

Siegfried had heard the story many times as a child, and had never tired of it. The tale was the modern equivalent of a fairy tale, it had been so very unlikely. *O'Harrigan* had been the name of an Irish-born engineer, fresh off the boat himself, who had seen Siegfried's many-times-great grandmother and her infant son being herded down the gangplank and straight to the Richmond, Virginia, slave market. She had been, perhaps, thirteen years old when the Arab slave-traders had stolen her. That she had survived the journey at all was a miracle. And she was the very first thing that O'Harrigan set eyes on as he stepped onto the dock in this new land of freedom.

The irony had not been lost on him. Sick and frightened, the woman had locked eyes with Sean O'Harrigan for a single instant, but that instant had been enough.

They had shared neither language nor race, but perhaps Sean had seen in her eyes the antithesis of everything he had come to America to find. *His* people had suffered virtual slavery at the hands of the English landlords; he knew what slavery felt like. He was outraged, and felt that he had to do *something*. He could not save all the slaves offloaded this day—but he could help these two.

He had followed the traders to the market and bought the woman and her child "off the coffle," paying for them before they could be put up on the auction-block, before they could even be warehoused. He fed them, cared for them until they were strong, and then put them on *another* boat, this time as passengers, before the woman could learn much more than his name. The rest the O'Harrigans learned later, from Sean's letters, long after.

The boat was headed back to Africa, to the newly founded nation of Liberia, a place of hope for freed slaves, whose very name meant "land of liberty." Life there would not be easy for them, but it would not be a life spent in chains, suffering at the whims of men who called themselves "Master."

Thereafter, the woman and her children wore the name of O'Harrigan proudly, in memory of the stranger's kindness—as many other citizens of the newly-formed nation would wear the names of those who had freed them.

No, the O'Harrigans would not change their name for any turn of politics. Respect earned was infinitely more powerful than any messages beaten into someone by whips or media.

And as for the name "Siegfried"—that was also in memory of a stranger's kindness; this time a member of Rommel's Afrika Korps. Another random act of kindness, this time from a first lieutenant who had seen to it that a captured black man with the name O'Harrigan was correctly identified as Liberian and not as American. He had then seen to it that John O'Harrigan was treated well and released.

John had named his first-born son for that German, because the young lieutenant had no children of his own. The tradition and the story that went with it had continued down the generations, joining that of Sean O'Harrigan. Siegfried's people remembered their debts of honor.

Siegfried O'Harrigan's name was at violent odds with his appearance. He was neither blond and tall, nor short and red-haired—and in fact, he was not Caucasian at all.

In this much, he matched the colonists of Bachman's World, most of whom were of East Indian and Pakistani descent. In every other way, he was totally unlike them.

He had been in the military for most of his life, and had planned to stay in. He was happy in uniform, and for many of the colonists here, that was a totally foreign concept.

Both of those stories of his ancestors were in his mind as he stood, travel-weary and yet excited, before a massive piece of the machinery of war, a glorious hulk of purpose-built design. It was larger than a good many of the buildings of this far-off colony at the edges of human space.

Bachman's World. A poor colony known only for its single export of a medicinal desert plant, it was not a place likely to attract a tourist trade. Those who came here left because life was even harder in the slums of Calcutta, or the perpetually typhoon-swept mud-flats of Bangladesh. They were farmers, who grew vast acreages of the "saje" for export, and irrigated just enough land to feed themselves. A hot, dry wind blew sand into the tight curls of his hair and stirred the short sleeves of his desert-khaki uniform. It occurred to him that he could not have chosen a more appropriate setting for what was likely to prove a life-long exile, considering his hobby—his obsession. And yet, it was an exile he had chosen willingly, even eagerly.

This behemoth, this juggernaut, this mountain of gleaming metal, was a Bolo. Now, it was *his* Bolo, his partner. A partner whose workings he knew intimately . . . and whose thought processes suited his so perfectly that there might not be a similar match in all the Galaxy.

RML-1138. Outmoded now, and facing retirement—which, for a Bolo, meant *deactivation.*

Extinction, in other words. Bolos were more than "super-tanks," more than war machines, for they were inhabited by some of the finest AIs in human space. When a Bolo was "retired," so was the AI. Permanently.

There were those, even now, who were lobbying for AI rights, who equated deactivation with murder. They were opposed by any number of special-interest groups, beginning with religionists, who objected to the notion than anything housed in a "body" of electronic circuitry could be considered "human" enough to "murder." No matter which side won, nothing would occur soon enough to save this particular Bolo.

Siegfried had also faced retirement, for the same reason. *Outmoded.* He had specialized in weapons-systems repair, the specific, delicate tracking and targeting systems.

Which were now outmoded, out-of-date; he had been deemed too old to retrain. He had been facing an uncertain future, relegated to some dead-end job with no chance for promotion, or more likely, given an "early-out" option. He had applied for a transfer, listing, in desperation, everything that might give him an edge somewhere. On the advice of his superiors, he had included his background and his hobby of military strategy of the pre-Atomic period.

And to his utter amazement, it had been that background and hobby that had attracted the attention of someone in the Reserves, someone who had been looking to make a most particular match. . . .

The wind died; no one with any sense moved outside during the heat of midday. The port might have been deserted, but for a lone motor running somewhere in the distance.

The Bolo was utterly silent, but Siegfried knew that he—*he,* not *it*—was watching him, examining him with a myriad of sophisticated instruments. By now, he probably even knew how many fillings were in his mouth, how many grommets in his desert-boots. He had already passed judgment on Siegfried's service record, but there was this final confrontation to face, before the partnership could be declared a reality.

He cleared his throat, delicately. Now came the moment of truth. It was time to find out if what one administrator in the Reserves—and one human facing early-out and a future of desperate scrabbling for employment—thought was the perfect match really *would* prove to be the salvation of that human and this huge marvel of machinery and circuits.

Siegfried's hobby was the key—desert warfare, tactics, and most of all, the history and thought of one particular desert commander.

Erwin Rommel. The "Desert Fox," the man his greatest rival had termed "the last chivalrous knight." Siegfried knew everything there was to know about the great tank-commander. He had fought and refought every campaign Rommel had ever commanded, and his admiration for the man whose life had briefly touched on that of his own ancestor's had never faded, nor had his fascination with the man and his genius.

And there was at least one other being in the universe whose fascination with the Desert Fox matched Siegfried's. This being; the intelligence resident in this particular Bolo, the Bolo that called *himself* "Rommel." Most, if not all, Bolos acquired a name or nickname based on their designations—LNE became "Lenny," or "KKR" became "Kicker." Whether this Bolo had been fascinated by the Desert Fox because of his designation, or had noticed the resemblance of "RML" to "Rommel" because of his fascination, it didn't much matter. Rommel was as much an expert on his name-sake as Siegfried was.

Like Siegfried, RML-1138 was scheduled for "early-out," but like Siegfried, the Reserves offered him a reprieve. The Reserves didn't usually take or need Bolos; for one thing, they were dreadfully expensive. A Reserve unit could requisition a great deal of equipment for the "cost" of one Bolo. For another, the close partnership required between Bolo and operator precluded use of Bolos in situations where the "partnerships" would not last past the exercise of the moment. Nor were Bolo partners often "retired" to the Reserves.

And not too many Bolos were available to the Reserves. Retirement for both Bolo and operator was usually permanent, and as often as not, was in the front lines.

But luck (good or ill, it remained to be seen) was with Rommel; he had lost his partner to a deadly virus, he had not seen much in the way of combat, and he was in near-new condition.

And Bachman's World wanted a Reserve battalion. They could not field their own—every able-bodied human here was a farmer or engaged in the export trade. A substantial percentage of the population was of some form of pacifistic religion that precluded bearing arms— Jainist, Buddhist, some forms of Hindu.

Bachman's World was *entitled* to a Reserve force; it was their right under the law to have an on-planet defense force supplied by the regular military. Just because Bachman's Planet was back-of-beyond of nowhere, and even the most conservative of military planners thought their insistence on having such a force in place to be paranoid in the extreme, that did not negate their right to have it. Their charter was clear. The law was on their side.

Sending them a Reserve battalion would be expensive in the extreme, in terms of maintaining that battalion. The soldiers would be full-timers, on full pay. There was no base—it would have to be built. There was no equipment—that would all have to be imported.

That was when one solitary bean-counting accountant at High Command came up with the answer that would satisfy the letter of the law, yet save the military considerable expense.

The law had been written stipulating, not numbers of personnel and equipment, but a monetary amount. That unknown accountant had determined that the amount so stipulated, meant to be the equivalent value of an infantry battalion, exactly equaled the worth of one Bolo and its operator.

The records-search was on.

Enter one Reserve officer, searching for a Bolo in good condition, about to be "retired," with no current operator-partner—

—and someone to match him, familiar with at least the rudiments of mech-warfare, the insides of a Bolo, and willing to be exiled for the rest of his life.

Finding RML-1138, called "Rommel," and Siegfried O'Harrigan, hobbyist military historian.

The government of Bachman's World was less than pleased

with the response to their demand, but there was little they could do besides protest. Rommel was shipped to Bachman's World first; Siegfried was given a crash-course in Bolo operation. He followed on the first regularly-scheduled freighter as soon as his training was over. If, for whatever reason, the pairing did not work, he would leave on the same freighter that brought him.

Now, came the moment of truth.

"*Guten tag, Herr Rommel,*" he said, in careful German, the antique German he had learned in order to be able to read first-hand chronicles in the original language. "*Ich heisse Siegfried O'Harrigan.*"

A moment of silence—and then, surprisingly, a sound much like a dry chuckle.

"*Wie geht's, Herr O'Harrigan.* I've been expecting you. Aren't you a little dark to be a Storm Trooper?"

The voice was deep, pleasant, and came from a point somewhere above Siegfried's head. And Siegfried knew the question was a trap, of sorts. Or a test, to see just how much he really *did* know, as opposed to what he claimed to know. A good many pre-Atomic historians could be caught by that question themselves.

"Hardly a Storm Trooper," he countered. "Field-Marshall Erwin Rommel would not have had one of *those* under his command. And no Nazis, either. Don't think to trap *me* that easily."

The Bolo uttered that same dry chuckle. "Good for you, Siegfried O'Harrigan. *Willkommen.*"

The hatch opened, silently; a ladder descended just as silently, inviting Siegfried to come out of the hot, desert sun and into Rommel's controlled interior. Rommel had replied to Siegfried's response, but had done so with nothing unnecessary in the way of words, in the tradition of his namesake.

Siegfried had passed the test.

Once again, Siegfried stood in the blindingly hot sun, this time at strict attention, watching the departing back of the mayor of Port City. The interview had not been pleasant, although both parties had been strictly polite; the mayor's back was stiff with anger. He had not cared for what Siegfried had told him.

"They do not much care for us, do they, Siegfried?" Rommel sounded resigned, and Siegfried sighed. It was impossible to hide anything from the Bolo; Rommel had already proven himself to be an adept reader of human body-language, and of course, anything that was broadcast over the airwaves, scrambled or not, Rommel could access and read. Rommel was right; he and his partner were not the most popular of residents at the moment.

What amazed Siegfried, and continued to amaze him, was how *human* the Bolo was. He was used to AIs of course, but Rommel was something special. Rommel cared about what people did and thought; most AIs really didn't take a great interest in the doings and opinions of mere humans.

"No, Rommel, they don't," he replied. "You really can't blame them; they thought they were going to get a battalion of conventional troops, not one very expensive piece of equipment and one single human."

"But we are easily the equivalent of a battalion of conventional troops," Rommel objected, logically. He lowered his ladder, and now that the mayor was well out of sight, Siegfried felt free to climb back into the cool interior of the Bolo.

He waited until he was settled in his customary seat, now worn to the contours of his own figure after a year, before he answered the AI he now consciously considered to be his best friend as well as his assigned partner. Inside the cabin of the Bolo, everything was clean, if a little worn—cool—the light dimmed the way Siegfried liked it. This was, in fact, the most comfortable quarters Siegfried had ever enjoyed. Granted, things were a bit cramped, but he had everything he needed in here, from shower and cooking facilities to multiple kinds of entertainment. And the Bolo did not need to worry about "wasting" energy; his power-plant was geared to supply full-combat needs in any and all climates; what Siegfried needed to keep cool and comfortable was miniscule. Outside, the ever-present desert sand blew everywhere, the heat was enough to drive even the most patient person mad, and the sun bleached everything to a bone-white. Inside was a compact world of Siegfried's own.

Bachman's World had little to recommend it. That was the problem.

"It's a complicated issue, Rommel," he said. "If a battalion of conventional troops had been sent here, there would have been more than the initial expenditure—there would have been an ongoing expenditure to support them."

"Yes—that support money would come into the community. I understand their distress." Rommel would understand, of course; Field Marshal Erwin Rommel had understood the problems of supply only too well, and his namesake could hardly do less. "Could it be they demanded the troops in the first place in order to gain that money?"

Siegfried grimaced, and toyed with the controls on the panel in front of him. "That's what High Command thinks, actually. There never was any real reason to think Bachman's World was under any sort of threat, and after a year, there's even less reason than there was when they made the request. They expected something to bring in money from outside; you and I are hardly bringing in big revenue for them."

Indeed, they weren't bringing in any income at all. Rommel, of course, required no support, since he was not expending anything. His power-plant would supply all his needs for the next hundred years before it needed refueling. If there had been a battalion of men here, it would have been less expensive for High Command to set up a standard mess hall, buying their supplies from the local farmers, rather than shipping in food and other supplies. Further, the men would have been spending their pay locally. In fact, local suppliers would have been found for nearly everything except weaponry.

But with only one man here, it was far less expensive for High Command to arrange for his supplies to come in at regular intervals on scheduled freight-runs. The Bolo ate nothing. They didn't even use "local" water; the Bolo recycled nearly every drop, and distilled the rest from occasional rainfall and dew. Siegfried was not the usual soldier-on-leave; when he spent his pay, it was generally off-planet, ordering things to be shipped in, and not patronizing local merchants. He bought books, not beer; he didn't gamble, his interest in food was minimal and satisfied by the R.E.M.s (Ready-to-Eat-Meals) that were standard field issue and shipped to him by the crateful. And he was far more interested in that four-letter word for "intercourse" that began with a "t" than in intercourse of any other kind. He was an ascetic scholar; such men were not the sort who brought any amount of money into a community. He and his partner, parked as they were at the edge of the spaceport, were a continual reminder of how Bachman's Planet had been "cheated."

And for that reason, the mayor of Port City had suggested—stiffly, but politely—that his and Rommel's continuing presence so near the main settlement was somewhat disconcerting. He had hinted that the peace-loving citizens found the Bolo frightening (and never mind that they had requested some sort of defense from the military). And if they could not find a way to make themselves useful, perhaps they ought to at least *earn* their pay by pretending to go on maneuvers. It didn't matter that Siegfried and Rommel were perfectly capable of conducting such exercises without moving. That was hardly the point.

"You heard him, my friend," Siegfried sighed. "They'd like us to go away. Not that they have any authority to order us to do so—as I reminded the mayor. But I suspect seeing us constantly is something of an embarrassment to whoever it was that promised a battalion of troops to bring in cash and got us instead."

"In that case, Siegfried," Rommel said gently, "we probably should take the mayor's suggestion. How long do you think we should stay away?"

"When's the next ship due in?" Siegfried replied. "There's no real reason for us to be here until it arrives, and then we only need to stay long enough to pick up my supplies."

"True." With a barely audible rumble, Rommel started his banks of motive engines. "Have you any destination in mind?"

Without prompting, Rommel projected the map of the immediate area on one of Siegfried's control-room screens. Siegfried studied it for a moment, trying to work out the possible repercussions of vanishing into the hills altogether. "I'll tell you what, old man," he said slowly. "We've just been playing at doing our job. Really, that's hardly honorable, when it comes down to it. Even if they don't need us and never did, the fact is that they asked for on-planet protection, and we haven't even planned how to give it to them. How about if we actually go out there in the bush and *do* that planning?"

There was interest in the AI's voice; he did not imagine it. "What do you mean by that?" Rommel asked.

"I mean, let's go out there and scout the territory ourselves; plan defenses and offenses, as if this dustball *was* likely to be invaded. The topographical surveys stink for military purposes; let's get a real war plan in place. What the hell—it can't hurt, right? And if the locals see us actually doing some work, they might not think so badly of us."

Rommel was silent for a moment. "They will still blame High Command, Siegfried. They did not receive what they wanted, even though they received what they were entitled to."

"But they won't blame *us*." He put a little coaxing into his voice. "Look, Rommel, we're going to be here for the rest of our lives, and we really can't afford to have the entire population angry with us forever. I know our standing orders are to stay at Port City, but the mayor just countermanded those orders. So let's have some fun, and show 'em we know our duty at the same time! Let's use Erwin's strategies around here, and see how they work! We can run all kinds of scenarios—let's assume in the event of a real invasion we could get some of these farmers to pick up a weapon; that'll give us additional scenarios to run. Figure troops against you, mechs against you, troops and mechs against you, plus untrained men against troops, men against mechs, you against another Bolo-type AI—"

"It would be entertaining." Rommel sounded very interested. "And as long as we keep our defensive surveillance up, and an eye on Port City, we would not technically be violating orders. . . ."

"Then let's do it," Siegfried said decisively. "Like I said, the maps they gave us stink; let's go make our own, then plot strategy. Let's find every wadi and overhang big enough to hide you. Let's act as if there really was going to be an invasion. Let's give them some options, log the plans with the mayor's office. We can plan for evacuations, we can check resources, there's a lot of things we can do. And let's start right now!"

★ ★ ★

They mapped every dry stream-bed, every dusty hill, every animal-trail. For months, the two of them rumbled across the arid landscape, with Siegfried emerging now and again to carry surveying instruments to the tops of hills too fragile to bear Rommel's weight. And when every inch of territory within a week of Port City had been surveyed and accurately mapped, they began playing a game of "hide and seek" with the locals.

It was surprisingly gratifying. At first, after they had vanished for a while, the local news-channel seemed to reflect an attitude of "and good riddance." But then, when *no one* spotted them, there was a certain amount of concern—followed by a certain amount of annoyance. After all, Rommel was "their" Bolo—what was Siegfried doing, taking him out for some kind of vacation? As if Bachman's World offered any kind of amusement. . . .

That was when Rommel and Siegfried began stalking farmers.

They would find a good hiding place and get into it well in advance of a farmer's arrival. When he would show up, Rommel would rise up, seemingly from out of the ground, draped in camouflage-net, his weaponry trained on the farmer's vehicle. Then Siegfried would pop up out of the hatch, wave cheerfully, retract the camouflage, and he and Rommel would rumble away.

Talk of "vacations" ceased entirely after that.

They extended their range, once they were certain that the locals were no longer assuming the two of them were "gold-bricking." Rommel tested all of his abilities to the limit, making certain everything was still up to spec. And on the few occasions that it wasn't, Siegfried put in a requisition for parts and spent many long hours making certain that the repairs and replacements *were* bringing Rommel up to like-new condition.

Together they plotted defensive and offensive strategies; Siegfried studied Rommel's manuals as if a time would come when he would have to rebuild Rommel from spare parts. They ran every kind of simulation in the book—and not just on Rommel's computers, but with Rommel himself actually running and dry-firing against plotted enemies. Occasionally one of the news-people would become curious about their whereabouts, and lie in wait for them when the scheduled supplies arrived. Siegfried would give a formal interview, reporting in general what they had been doing—and then, he would carefully file another set of emergency plans with the mayor's office. Sometimes it even made the evening news. Once, it was even accompanied by a clip someone had shot of Rommel roaring at top speed across a ridge.

Nor was that all they did. As Rommel pointed out, the presumptive "battalion" would have been available in emergencies—there was no reason why *they* shouldn't respond when local emergencies came up.

So—when a flash-flood trapped a young woman and three children on the roof of her vehicle, it was Rommel and Siegfried who not only rescued them, but towed the vehicle to safety as well. When a snowfall in the mountains stranded a dozen truckers, Siegfried and Rommel got them out. When a small child was lost while playing in the hills, Rommel found her by having all searchers clear out as soon as the sun went down, and using his heat-sensors to locate every source of approximately her size. They put out runaway brushfires by rolling over them; they responded to Maydays from remote locations when they were nearer than any other agency. They even joined in a manhunt for an escaped rapist—who turned himself in, practically soiling himself with fear, when he learned that Rommel was part of the search-party.

It didn't hurt. They were of no help for men trapped in a mine collapse; or rather, of no *more* help than Siegfried's two hands could make them. They couldn't rebuild bridges that were washed away, nor construct roads. But what they could do, they did, often before anyone thought to ask them for help.

By the end of their second year on Bachman's World, they were at least no longer the target of resentment. Those few citizens they had aided actually looked on them with gratitude. The local politicians whose careers had suffered because of their presence had found other causes to espouse, other schemes to pursue. Siegfried and Rommel were a dead issue.

But by then, the two of them had established a routine of monitoring emergency channels, running their private war-games, updating their maps, and adding changes in the colony to their defense and offense plans. There was no reason to go back to simply sitting beside the spaceport. Neither of them cared for sitting idle, and what they were doing was the nearest either of them would ever get to actually refighting the battles their idol had lost and won.

When High Command got their reports and sent recommendations for further "readiness" preparations, and *commendations* for their "community service"—Siegfried, now wiser in the ways of manipulating public opinion, issued a statement to the press about both.

After that, there were no more rumblings of discontent, and things might have gone on as they were until Siegfried was too old to climb Rommel's ladder.

But the fates had another plan in store for them.

Alarms woke Siegfried out of a sound and dreamless sleep. Not the synthesized pseudo-alarms Rommel used when surprising him for a drill, either, but the real thing—

He launched himself out of his bunk before his eyes were focused, grabbing the back of the com-chair to steady himself before he flung himself into it and strapped himself down. As soon as he moved, Rommel turned off all the alarms but one; the proximity alert from the single defense-satellite in orbit above them.

Interior lighting had gone to full-emergency red. He scrubbed at his eyes with the back of his hand, impatiently; finally they focused on the screens of his console, and he could read what was there. And he swore, fervently and creatively.

One unknown ship sat in geosynch orbit about Port City; a big one, answering no hails from the port, and seeding the skies with what appeared to his sleep-fogged eyes as hundreds of smaller drop-ships.

"The mother-ship has already neutralized the port air-to-ground defenses, Siegfried," Rommel reported grimly. "I don't know what kind of stealthing devices they have, or if they've got some new kind of drive, but they don't match anything in my records. They just appeared out of nowhere and started dumping drop-ships. I think we can assume they're hostiles."

They had a match for just this in their hundreds of plans;

unknown ship, unknown attackers, dropping a pattern of offensive troops of some kind—

"What are they landing?" he asked, playing the console board. "You're stealthed, right?"

"To the max," Rommel told him. "I don't detect anything like life-forms on those incoming vessels, but my sensors aren't as sophisticated as they could be. The vessels themselves aren't all that big. My guess is that they're dropping either live troops or clusters of very small mechs, mobile armor, maybe the size of a Panzer."

"Landing pattern?" he asked. He brought up all of Rommel's weaponry; AIs weren't allowed to activate their own weapons. And they weren't allowed to fire on living troops without permission from a human, either. That was the only real reason for a Bolo needing an operator.

"Surrounding Port City, but starting from about where the first farms are." Rommel ran swift readiness-tests on the systems as Siegfried brought them up; the screens scrolled too fast for Siegfried to read them.

They had a name for that particular scenario. It was one of the first possibilities they had run when they began plotting invasion and counter-invasion plans.

"Operation Cattle Drive. Right." If the invaders followed the same scheme he and Rommel had anticipated, they planned to drive the populace into Port City, and either capture the civilians, or destroy them at leisure. He checked their current location; it was out beyond the drop-zone. "Is there anything landing close to us?"

"Not yet—but the odds are that something will soon." Rommel sounded confident, as well he should be—his ability to project landing-patterns was far better than any human's. "I'd say within the next fifteen minutes."

Siegfried suddenly shivered in a breath of cool air from the ventilators, and was painfully aware suddenly that he was dressed in nothing more than a pair of fatigue-shorts. Oh well; some of the Desert Fox's battles had taken place with the men wearing little else. What they could put up with, he could. There certainly wasn't anyone here to complain.

"As soon as you think we can move without detection, close on the nearest craft," he ordered. "I want to see what we're up against. And start scanning the local freqs; if there's anything in the way of organized defense from the civvies, I want to know about it."

A pause, while the ventilators hummed softly, and glowing dots descended on several screens. "They don't seem to have anything, Siegfried," Rommel reported quietly. "Once the ground-to-space defenses were fried, they just collapsed. Right now, they seem to be in a complete state of panic. They don't even seem to remember that *we're* out here—no one's tried to hail us on any of our regular channels."

"Either that—or they think we're out of commission," he muttered absently. "Or just maybe they are giving us credit for knowing what we're doing and are trying *not* to give us away. I hope so. The longer we can go without detection, the better chance we have to pull something out of a hat."

An increase in vibration warned him that Rommel was about to move. A new screen lit up, this one tracking a single vessel. "Got one," the Bolo said shortly. "I'm coming in behind his sensor sweep."

Four more screens lit up; enhanced front, back, top, and side views of the terrain. Only the changing views on the screens showed that Rommel was moving; other than that, there was no way to tell from inside the cabin what was happening. It would be different if Rommel had to execute evasive maneuvers of course, but right now, he might have still been parked. The control cabin and living quarters were heavily shielded and cushioned against the shocks of ordinary movement. Only if Rommel took a direct hit by something impressive would Siegfried feel it. . . .

And if he takes a direct hit by something more than impressive—we're slag. Bolos are the best, but they can't take everything.

"The craft is down."

He pushed the thought away from his mind. This was what Rommel had been built to do—this moment justified Rommel's very existence. And he had known from the very beginning that the possibility, however remote, had existed that he too would be in combat one day. That was what being in the military was all about. There was no use in pretending otherwise.

Get on with the job. That's what they've sent me here to do. Wasn't there an ancient royal family whose motto was "God, and my Duty?" Then let that be his.

"Have you detected any sensor scans from the mother-ship?" he asked, his voice a harsh whisper. "Or anything other than a forward scan from the landing craft?" He didn't know why he was whispering—

"Not as yet, Siegfried," Rommel replied, sounding a little surprised. "Apparently, these invaders are confident that there is no one out here at all. Even that forward scan seemed mainly to be a landing-aid."

"Nobody here but us chickens," Siegfried muttered. "Are they offloading yet?"

"Wait—yes. The ramp is down. We will be within visual range ourselves in a moment—there—"

More screens came alive; Siegfried read them rapidly—

Then read them again, incredulously.

"Mechs?" he said, astonished. *"Remotely controlled mechs?"*

"So it appears." Rommel sounded just as mystified. "This does not match any known configuration. There is one limited AI in that ship. Data indicates it is hardened against any attack conventional forces at the port could mount. The ship seems to be digging in— look at the seismic reading on 4-B. The limited AI is in control of the mechs it is deploying. I believe that we can assume this will be the case for the other invading ships, at least the ones coming down at the moment, since they all appear to be of the same model."

Siegfried studied the screens; as they had assumed, the mechs were about the size of pre-Atomic Panzers, and seemed to be built along similar lines. "Armored mechs. Good against anything a civilian has. Is that ship hardened against anything you can throw?" he asked finally.

There was a certain amount of glee in Rommel's voice. "I think not. Shall we try?"

Siegfried's mouth dried. There was no telling what weaponry

that ship packed—or the mother-ship held. The mother-ship might be monitoring the drop-ships, watching for attack. *God and my Duty,* he thought.

"You may fire when ready, Herr Rommel."

They had taken the drop-ship by complete surprise; destroying it before it had a chance to transmit distress or tactical data to the mother-ship. The mechs had stopped in their tracks the moment the AI's direction ceased.

But rather than roll on to the next target, Siegfried had ordered Rommel to stealth again, while he examined the remains of the mechs and the controlling craft. He'd had an idea—the question was, would it work?

He knew weapons' systems; knew computer-driven control. There were only a limited number of ways such controls could work. And if he recognized any of those here—

He told himself, as he scrambled into clothing and climbed the ladder out of the cabin, that he would give himself an hour. The situation would not change much in an hour; there was very little that he and Rommel could accomplish in that time in the way of mounting a campaign. As it happened, it took him fifteen minutes more than that to learn all he needed to know. At the end of that time, though, he scrambled back into Rommel's guts with mingled feelings of elation and anger.

The ship and mechs were clearly of human origin, and some of the vanes and protrusions that made them look so unfamiliar had been tacked on purely to make both the drop-ships and armored mechs look alien in nature. Someone, somewhere, had discovered something about Bachman's World that suddenly made it valuable. From the hardware interlocks and the programming modes he had found in what was left of the controlling ship, he suspected that the "someone" was not a government, but a corporation.

And a multiplanet corporation could afford to mount an invasion force fairly easily. The best force for the job would, of course, be something precisely like this—completely mechanized. There would be no troops to "hush up" afterwards; no leaks to the interstellar press. Only a nice clean invasion—and, in all probability, a nice, clean extermination at the end of it, with no humans to protest the slaughter of helpless civilians.

And afterwards, there would be no evidence anywhere to contradict the claim that the civilians had slaughtered each other in some kind of local conflict.

The mechs and the AI itself were from systems he had studied when he first started in this specialty—outmoded even by his standards, but reliable, and when set against farmers with hand-weapons, perfectly adequate.

There was one problem with this kind of setup . . . from the enemy's standpoint. It was a problem they didn't know they had.

Yet.

He filled Rommel in on what he had discovered as he raced up the ladder, then slid down the handrails into the command cabin. "Now, here's the thing—I got the access code to command those mechs with a little fiddling in the AI's memory. Nice of them to leave in so many manual overrides for me. I reset the command interface freq to one you have, and hardwired it so they shouldn't be able to change it—"

He jumped into the command chair and strapped in; his hands danced across the keypad, keying in the frequency and the code. Then he saluted the console jauntily. "Congratulations, Herr Rommel," he said, unable to keep the glee out of his voice. "You are now a Field Marshal."

"*Siegfried!*" Yes, there was astonishment in Rommel's synthesized voice. "You just gave me command of an armored mobile strike force!"

"I certainly did. And I freed your command circuits so that you can run them without waiting for my orders to do something." Siegfried couldn't help grinning. "After all, you're not going against living troops, you're going to be attacking AIs and mechs. The next AI might not be so easy to take over, but if you're running in the middle of a swarm of 'friendlies,' you might not be suspected. And when we knock out *that* one, we'll take over again. I'll even put the next bunch on a different command freq so you can command them separately. Sooner or later they'll figure out what we're doing, but by then I hope we'll have at least an equal force under our command."

"This is good, Siegfried!"

"You bet it's good, *mein Freund*," he retorted. "What's more, we've studied the best—they can't possibly have that advantage. All right—let's show these amateurs how one of the old masters handles armor!"

The second and third takeovers were as easy as the first. By the fourth, however, matters had changed. It might have dawned on either the AIs on the ground or whoever was in command of the overall operation in the mother-ship above that the triple loss of AIs and mechs was not due to simple malfunction, but to an unknown and unsuspected enemy.

In that, the hostiles were following in the mental footsteps of another pre-Atomic commander, who had once stated, "Once is happenstance, twice is coincidence, but three times is enemy action."

So the fourth time their forces advanced on a ship, they met with fierce resistance.

They lost about a dozen mechs, and Siegfried had suffered a bit of a shakeup and a fair amount of bruising, but they managed to destroy the fourth AI without much damage to Rommel's exterior. Despite the danger from unexploded shells and some residual radiation, Siegfried doggedly went out into the wreckage to get that precious access code.

He returned to bad news. "They know we're here, Siegfried," Rommel announced. "That last barrage gave them a silhouette upstairs; they know I'm a Bolo, so now they know what they're up against."

Siegfried swore quietly, as he gave Rommel his fourth contingent of mechs. "Well, have they figured out exactly what we're doing yet? Or can you tell?" Siegfried asked while typing in the fourth unit's access codes.

"I can't—I—can't—Siegfried—" the Bolo replied, suddenly without any inflection at all. "Siegfried. There is a problem. Another. I am stretching my—resources—"

This time Siegfried swore with a lot less creativity. That was something he had not even considered! The AIs they were eliminating were much less sophisticated than Rommel—

"Drop the last batch!" he snapped. To his relief, Rommel sounded like himself again as he released control of the last contingent of mechs.

"That was not a pleasurable experience," Rommel said mildly.

"What happened?" he demanded.

"As I needed to devote more resources to controlling the mechs, I began losing higher functions," the Bolo replied simply. "We should have expected that; so far I am doing the work of three lesser AIs and all the functions you require, and maneuvering of the various groups we have captured. As I pick up more groups, I will inevitably lose processing functions."

Siegfried thought, frantically. There were about twenty of these invading ships; their plan absolutely required that Rommel control at least eight of the groups successfully to hold the invasion off Port City. There was no way they'd be anything worse than an annoyance with only three; the other groups could outflank them.

"What if you shut down things in here?" he asked. "Run basic life-support, but nothing fancy. And I could drive—run your weapons' systems."

"You could. That would help." Rommel pondered for a moment. "My calculations are that we can take the required eight groups if you also issue battle orders and I simply carry them out. But there is a further problem."

"Which is?" he asked—although he had the sinking feeling that he knew what the problem was going to be.

"Higher functions. One of the functions I will lose at about the seventh takeover is what you refer to as my personality. A great deal of my ability to maintain a personality is dependent on devoting a substantial percentage of my central processor to that personality. And if it disappears—"

The Bolo paused. Siegfried's hands clenched on the arms of his chair.

"—it may not return. There is a possibility that the records and algorithms which make up my personality will be written over by comparison files during strategic control calculations." Again Rommel paused. "Siegfried, this is our duty. I am willing to take that chance."

Siegfried swallowed, only to find a lump in his throat and his guts in knots. "Are you sure?" he asked gently. "Are you very sure? What you're talking about is—is a kind of deactivation."

"I am sure," Rommel replied firmly. "The Field Marshal would have made the same choice."

Rommel's manuals were all on a handheld reader. He had studied them from front to back—wasn't there something in there? "Hold on a minute—"

He ran through the index, frantically keyword searching. This was a memory function, right? Or at least it was software. The designers didn't encourage operators to go mucking around in the AI functions . . . what would a computer jock call what he was looking for?

Finally he found it; a tiny section in programmerese, not even listed in the index. He scanned it, quickly, and found the warning that had been the thing that had caught his eye in the first place.

This system has been simulation proven in expected scenarios, but has never been fully field-tested.

What the hell did that mean? He had a guess; this was essentially a full-copy backup of the AI's processor. He suspected that they had never tested the backup function on an AI with a full personality. There was no way of knowing if the restoration function would actually "restore" a lost personality.

But the backup memory-module in question had its own power-supply, and was protected in the most hardened areas of Rommel's interior. Nothing was going to destroy it that didn't slag him and Rommel together, and if "personality" was largely a matter of memory—

It might work. It might not. It was worth trying, even if the backup procedure was fiendishly hard to initiate. They really *didn't* want operators mucking around with the AIs.

Twenty command-strings later, a single memory-mod began its simple task; Rommel was back in charge of the fourth group of mechs, and Siegfried had taken over the driving.

He was not as good as Rommel was, but he was better than he had thought.

They took groups five, and six, and it was horrible—listening to Rommel fade away, lose the vitality behind the synthesized voice. If Siegfried hadn't had his hands full already, literally, it would have been worse.

But with group seven—

That was when he just about lost it, because in reply to one of his voice-commands, instead of a "Got it, Siegfried," what came over the speakers was the metallic "Affirmative" of a simple voice-activated computer.

All of Rommel's resources were now devoted to self-defense and control of the armored mechs.

God and my Duty. Siegfried took a deep breath, and began keying in the commands for mass armor deployment.

The ancient commanders were right; from the ground, there was no way of knowing when the moment of truth came. Siegfried only realized they had won when the mother-ship suddenly vanished from orbit, and the remaining AIs went dead. Cutting their losses; there was nothing in any of the equipment that would betray *where* it came from. Whoever was in charge of the invasion force must have decided that there was no way they would finish the mission before *someone,* a regularly scheduled freighter or a surprise patrol, discovered what was going on and reported it.

By that time, he had been awake for fifty hours straight; he had put squeeze-bulbs of electrolytic drink near at hand, but he was starving and still thirsty. With the air-conditioning cut out, he must have sweated out every ounce of fluid he drank. His hands were shaking and every muscle in his neck and shoulders was cramped from hunching over the boards.

Rommel was battered and had lost several external sensors and one of his guns. But the moment that the mother-ship vanished, he had only one thought.

He manually dropped control of every mech from Rommel's systems, and waited, praying, for his old friend to "come back."

But nothing happened—other than the obvious things that any AI would do, restoring all the comfort-support and life-support functions, and beginning damage checks and some self-repair.

Rommel was gone.

His throat closed; his stomach knotted. But—

It wasn't tested. That doesn't mean it won't work.

Once more, his hands moved over the keyboard, with another twenty command-strings, telling that little memory-module in the heart of his Bolo to initiate full restoration. He hadn't thought he had water to spare for tears—yet there they were, burning their way down his cheeks. Two of them.

He ignored them, fiercely, shaking his head to clear his eyes, and continuing the command-sequence.

Damage checks and self-repair aborted. Life-support went on automatic.

And Siegfried put his head down on the console to rest his burning eyes for a moment. Just for a moment—

Just—

"Ahem."

Siegfried jolted out of sleep, cracking his elbow on the console, staring around the cabin with his heart racing wildly.

"I believe we have visitors, Siegfried," said that wonderful, familiar voice. "They seem most impatient."

Screens lit up, showing a small army of civilians approaching, riding in everything from outmoded sandrails to tractors, all of them cheering, all of them heading straight for the Bolo.

"We seem to have their approval at least," Rommel continued.

His heart had stopped racing, but he still trembled. And once again, he seemed to have come up with the moisture for tears. He nodded, knowing Rommel would see it, unable for the moment to get any words out.

"Siegfried—before we become immersed in grateful civilians— how *did* you bring me back?" Rommel asked. "I'm rather curious—I actually seem to remember fading out. An unpleasant experience."

"How did I get you back?" he managed to choke out—and then began laughing.

He held up the manual, laughing, and cried out the famous quote—

"Rommel, you magnificent bastard, *I read your book!*"

★ THE LAST COMMAND ★

Keith Laumer

I come to awareness, sensing a residual oscillation traversing me from an arbitrarily designated heading of 035. From the damping rate I compute that the shock was of intensity 8.7, emanating from a source within the limits 72 meters 146 meters. I activate my primary screens, trigger a return salvo. There is no response. I engage reserve energy cells, bring my secondary battery to bear—futilely. It is apparent that I have been ranged by the Enemy and severely damaged.

My positional sensors indicate that I am resting at an angle of 13 degrees 14 seconds, deflected from a baseline at 21 points from median. I attempt to right myself, but encounter massive resistance. I activate my forward scanners, shunt power to my I-R microstrobes. Not a flicker illuminates my surroundings. I am encased in utter blackness.

Now a secondary shock wave approaches, rocks me with an intensity of 8.2. It is apparent that I must withdraw from my position— but my drive trains remain inert under full thrust. I shift to base emergency power, try again. Pressure mounts; I sense my awareness fading under the intolerable strain; then, abruptly, resistance falls off and I am in motion.

It is not the swift maneuvering of full drive, however; I inch forward, as if restrained by massive barriers. Again I attempt to penetrate the surrounding darkness and this time perceive great irregular outlines shot through with fracture planes. I probe cautiously, then more vigorously, encountering incredible densities.

I channel all available power to a single ranging pulse, direct it upward. The indication is so at variance with all experience that I repeat the test at a new angle. Now I must accept the fact: I am buried under 207.6 meters of solid rock!

I direct my attention to an effort to orient myself to my uniquely desperate situation. I run through an action-status checklist of thirty thousand items, feel dismay at the extent of power loss. My main cells are almost completely drained, my reserve units at no more than .4 charge. Thus my sluggishness is explained. I review the tactical situation, recall the triumphant announcement from my commander that the Enemy forces were annihilated, that all resistance had ceased. In memory, I review the formal procession; in company with my comrades of the Dinochrome Brigade, many of us deeply scarred by Enemy action, we parade before the Grand Commandant, then assemble on the depot ramp. At command, we bring our music storage cells into phase and display our Battle Anthem. The nearby star radiates over a full spectrum unflltered by atmospheric haze. It is a moment of glorious triumph. Then the final command is given—

The rest is darkness. But it is apparent that the victory celebration was premature. The Enemy has counterattacked with a force that has come near to immobilizing me. The realization is shocking, but the .1 second of leisurely introspection has clarified my position. At once, I broadcast a call on Brigade Action wave length:

"Unit LNE to Command, requesting permission to file VSR."

I wait, sense no response, call again, using full power. I sweep the enclosing volume of rock with an emergency alert warning. I tune to the all-units band, await the replies of my comrades of the Brigade. None answer. Now I must face the reality: I alone have survived the assault.

I channel my remaining power to my drive and detect a channel of reduced density. I press for it and the broken rock around me yields *reluctantly. Slowly, I move forward and upward. My pain circuitry shocks my awareness center with emergency signals; I am doing irreparable damage to my overloaded neural systems, but my duty is clear: I must seek out and engage the Enemy.*

★2★

Emerging from behind the blast barrier, Chief Engineer Pete Reynolds of the New Devonshire Port Authority pulled off his rock mask and spat grit from his mouth.

"That's the last one; we've bottomed out at just over two hundred yards. Must have hit a hard stratum down there."

"It's almost sundown," the paunchy man beside him said shortly. "You're a day and a half behind schedule."

"We'll start backfilling now, Mr. Mayor. I'll have pilings poured by oh-nine hundred tomorrow, and with any luck the first section of pad will be in place in time for the rally."

"I'm—" The mayor broke off, looked startled. "I thought you told me that was the last charge to be fired . . . ."

Reynolds frowned. A small but distinct tremor had shaken the ground underfoot. A few feet away, a small pebble balanced atop another toppled and fell with a faint clatter.

"Probably a big rock fragment falling," he said. At that moment, a second vibration shook the earth, stronger this time. Reynolds heard a rumble and a distant impact as rock fell from the side of the newly blasted excavation. He whirled to the control shed as the door swung back and Second Engineer Mayfield appeared.

"Take a look at this, Pete!"

Reynolds went across to the hut, stepped inside. Mayfield was bending over the profiling table.

"What do you make of it?" he pointed. Superimposed on the heavy red contour representing the detonation of the shaped charge that had completed the drilling of the final pile core were two other traces, weak but distinct.

"About .1 intensity." Mayfield looked puzzled. "What—"

The tracking needle dipped suddenly, swept up the screen to peak at .21, dropped back. The hut trembled. A stylus fell from the edge of the table. The red face of Mayor Dougherty burst through the door.

"Reynolds, have you lost your mind? What's the idea of blasting while I'm standing out in the open? I might have been killed!"

"I'm not blasting," Reynolds snapped. "Jim, get Eaton on the line, see if they know anything." He stepped to the door, shouted. A heavyset man in sweat-darkened coveralls swung down from the seat of a cable-lift rig.

"Boss, what goes on?" he called as he came up. "Damn near shook me out of my seat!"

"I don't know. You haven't set any trim charges?"

"Jesus, no, boss. I wouldn't set no charges without your say-so."

"Come on." Reynolds started out across the rubble-littered stretch of barren ground selected by the Authority as the site of the new spaceport. Halfway to the open mouth of the newly blasted pit, the ground under his feet rocked violently enough to make him stumble. A gout of dust rose from the excavation ahead. Loose rock danced on the ground. Beside him the drilling chief grabbed his arm.

"Boss, we better get back!"

Reynolds shook him off, kept going. The drill chief swore and followed. The shaking of the ground went on, a sharp series of thumps interrupting a steady trembling.

"It's a quake!" Reynolds yelled over the low rumbling sound.

He and the chief were at the rim of the core now.

"It can't be a quake, boss," the latter shouted. "Not in these formations!"

"Tell it to the geologists—" The rock slab they were standing on rose a foot, dropped back. Both men fell. The slab bucked like a small boat in choppy water.

"Let's get out of here!" Reynolds was up and running. Ahead, a fissure opened, gaped a foot wide. He jumped it, caught a glimpse of black depths, a glint of wet clay twenty feet below—

A hoarse scream stopped him in his tracks. He spun, saw the

drill chief down, a heavy splinter of rock across his legs. He jumped to him, heaved at the rock. There was blood on the man's shirt. The chief's hands beat the dusty rock before him. Then other men were there, grunting, sweaty hands gripping beside Reynolds. The ground rocked. The roar from under the earth had risen to a deep, steady rumble. They lifted the rock aside, picked up the injured man, and stumbled with him to the aid shack.

The mayor was there, white-faced.

"What is it, Reynolds? By God, if you're responsible—"

"Shut up!" Reynolds brushed him aside, grabbed the phone, punched keys.

"Eaton! What have you got on this temblor?"

"Temblor, hell." The small face on the four-inch screen looked like a ruffled hen. "What in the name of Order are you doing out there? I'm reading a whole series of displacements originating from that last core of yours! What did you do, leave a pile of trim charges lying around?"

"It's a quake. Trim charges, hell! This thing's broken up two hundred yards of surface rock. It seems to be traveling north-north-east—"

"I see that; a traveling earthquake!" Eaton flapped his arms, a tiny and ridiculous figure against a background of wall charts and framed diplomas. "Well—do something, Reynolds! Where's Mayor Dougherty?"

"Underfoot!" Reynolds snapped, and cut off.

Outside, a layer of sunset-stained dust obscured the sweep of level plain. A rock-dozer rumbled up, ground to a halt by Reynolds. A man jumped down.

"I got the boys moving equipment out," he panted. "The thing's cutting a trail straight as a rule for the highway!" He pointed to a raised roadbed a quarter mile away.

"How fast is it moving?"

"She's done a hundred yards; it hasn't been ten minutes yet!"

"If it keeps up another twenty minutes, it'll be into the Intermix!"

"Scratch a few million cees and six months' work then, Pete!"

"And Southside Mall's a couple miles farther."

"Hell, it'll damp out before then!"

"Maybe. Grab a field car, Dan."

"Pete!" Mayfield came up at a trot. "This thing's building! The centroid's moving on a heading of oh-two-two—"

"How far subsurface?"

"It's rising; started at two-twenty yards, and it's up to one-eighty!"

"What the hell have we stirred up?" Reynolds stared at Mayfield as the field car skidded to a stop beside them.

"Stay with it, Jim. Give me anything new. We're taking a closer look." He climbed into the rugged vehicle.

"Take a blast truck—"

"No time!" He waved and the car gunned away into the pall of dust.

★**3**★

The rock car pulled to a stop at the crest of the three-level Intermix on a lay-by designed to permit tourists to enjoy the view of the site of the proposed port, a hundred feet below. Reynolds studied the progress of the quake through field glasses. From this vantage point, the path of the phenomenon was a clearly defined trail of tilted and broken rock, some of the slabs twenty feet across. As he watched, the fissure lengthened.

"It looks like a mole's trail." Reynolds handed the glasses to his companion, thumbed the send key on the car radio.

"Jim, get Eaton and tell him to divert all traffic from the Circular south of Zone Nine. Cars are already clogging the right-of-way. The dust is visible from a mile away, and when the word gets out there's something going on, we'll be swamped."

"I'll tell him, but he won't like it!"

"This isn't politics! This thing will be into the outer pad area in another twenty minutes!"

"It won't last—"

"How deep does it read now?"

"One-five!" There was a moment's silence. "Pete, if it stays on course, it'll surface at about where you're parked!"

"Uh-huh. It looks like you can scratch one Intermix. Better tell Eaton to get a story ready for the press."

"Pete, talking about news hounds—" Dan said beside him. Reynolds switched off, turned to see a man in a gay-colored driving outfit coming across from a battered Monojag sportster which had pulled up behind the rock car. A big camera case was slung across his shoulder.

"Say, what's going on down there?" he called.

"Rock slide," Reynolds said shortly. "I'll have to ask you to drive on. The road's closed to all traffic—"

"Who're you?" The man looked belligerent.

"I'm the engineer in charge. Now pull out, brother." He turned back to the radio. "Jim, get every piece of heavy equipment we own over here, on the double." He paused, feeling a minute trembling in the car. "The Intermix is beginning to feel it," he went on. "I'm afraid we're in for it. Whatever that thing is, it acts like a solid body boring its way through the ground. Maybe we can barricade it."

"Barricade an earthquake?"

"Yeah, I know how it sounds—but it's the only idea I've got."

"Hey—what's that about an earthquake?" The man in the colored suit was still there. "By gosh, I can feel it—the whole damned bridge is shaking!"

"Off, mister—now!" Reynolds jerked a thumb at the traffic lanes where a steady stream of cars were hurtling past. "Dan, take us over to the main track. We'll have to warn this traffic off—"

"Hold on, fellow." The man unlimbered his camera. "I represent the New Devon *Scope*. I have a few questions—"

"I don't have the answers." Pete cut him off as the car pulled away.

"Hah!" The man who had questioned Reynolds yelled after him. "Big shot! Think you can . . ." His voice was lost behind them.

★**4**★

In a modest retirees' apartment block in the coast town of Idlebreeze, forty miles from the scene of the freak quake, an old man sat in a reclining chair, half dozing before a yammering Tri-D tank.

". . . Grandpa," a sharp-voiced young woman was saying. "It's time for you to go in to bed."

"Bed? Why do I want to go to bed? Can't sleep anyway . . . ." He stirred, made a pretense of sitting up, showing an interest in the Tri-D. "I'm watching this show. Don't bother me."

"It's not a show, it's the news," a fattish boy said disgustedly. "Ma, can I switch channels—"

"Leave it alone, Bennie," the old man said. On the screen a panoramic scene spread out, a stretch of barren ground across which a furrow showed. As he watched, it lengthened.

". . . up here at the Intermix we have a fine view of the whole curious business, lazangemmun," the announcer chattered. "And in our opinion it's some sort of publicity stunt staged by the Port Authority to publicize their controversial port project—"

"Ma, can I change channels?"

"Go ahead, Bennie—"

"Don't touch it," the old man said. The fattish boy reached for the control, but something in the old man's eye stopped him . . . .

★**5**★

"The traffic's still piling in here," Reynolds said into the phone. "Damn it, Jim, we'll have a major jam on our hands—"

"He won't do it, Pete! You know the Circular was his baby—the super all-weather pike that nothing could shut down. He says you'll have to handle this in the field—"

"Handle, hell! I'm talking about preventing a major disaster! And in a matter of minutes, at that!"

"I'll try again—"

"If he says no, divert a couple of the big ten-yard graders and block it off yourself. Set up field arcs, and keep any cars from getting in from either direction."

"Pete, that's outside your authority!"

"You heard me!"

Ten minutes later, back at ground level, Reynolds watched the boom-mounted polyarcs swinging into position at the two roadblocks a quarter of a mile apart, cutting off the threatened section of the raised expressway. A hundred yards from where he stood on the rear cargo deck of a light grader rig, a section of rock fifty feet wide rose slowly, split, fell back with a ponderous impact. One corner of it struck the massive pier supporting the extended shelf of the lay-by above. A twenty-foot splinter fell away, exposing the reinforcing-rod core.

"How deep, Jim?" Reynolds spoke over the roaring sound coming from the disturbed area.

"Just subsurface now, Pete! It ought to break through—" His voice was drowned in a rumble as the damaged pier shivered, rose up, buckled at its midpoint, and collapsed, bringing down with it a large chunk of pavement and guard rail, and a single still-glowing light pole. A small car that had been parked on the doomed section was visible for an instant just before the immense slab struck. Reynolds saw it bounce aside, then disappear under an avalanche of broken concrete.

"My God, Pete—" Dan started. "That damned fool news hound . . . !"

"Look!" As the two men watched, a second pier swayed, fell backward into the shadow of the span above. The roadway sagged, and two more piers snapped. With a bellow like a burst dam, a hundred-foot stretch of the road fell into the roiling dust cloud.

"Pete!" Mayfield's voice burst from the car radio. "Get out of there! I threw a reader on that thing and it's chattering off the scale . . . !"

Among the piled fragments something stirred, heaved, rising up, lifting multi-ton pieces of the broken road, thrusting them aside like so many potato chips. A dull blue radiance broke through from the broached earth, threw an eerie light on the shattered structure above. A massive, ponderously irresistible shape thrust forward through the ruins. Reynolds saw a great blue-glowing profile emerge from the rubble like a surfacing submarine, shedding a burden of broken stone, saw immense treads ten feet wide claw for purchase, saw the mighty flank brush a still-standing pier, send it crashing aside.

"Pete, what—what is it . . . ?"

"I don't know." Reynolds broke the paralysis that had gripped him. "Get us out of here, Dan, fast! Whatever it is, it's headed straight for the city!"

★6★

I emerge at last from the trap into which I had fallen, and at once encounter defensive works of considerable strength. My scanners are dulled from lack of power, but I am able to perceive open ground beyond the barrier, and farther still, at a distance of 5.7 kilometers, massive walls. Once more I transmit the Brigade Rally signal; but as before, there is no reply. I am truly alone.

I scan the surrounding area for the emanations of Enemy drive units, monitor the EM spectrum for their communications. I detect nothing; either my circuitry is badly damaged, or their shielding is superb.

I must now make a decision as to possible courses of action. Since all my comrades of the Brigade have fallen, I compute that the fortress before me must be held by Enemy forces. I direct probing signals at them, discover them to be of unfamiliar construction, and less formidable than they appear. I am aware of the possibility that this may be a trick of the Enemy; but my course is clear.

I reengage my driving engines and advance on the Enemy fortress.

★7★

"You're out of your mind, Father," the stout man said. "At your age—"

"At your age, I got my nose smashed in a brawl in a bar on Aldo," the old man cut him off. "But I won the fight."

"James, you can't go out at this time of night . . ." an elderly woman wailed.

"Tell them to go home." The old man walked painfully toward his bedroom door. "I've seen enough of them for today." He passed out of sight.

"Mother, you won't let him do anything foolish?"

"He'll forget about it in a few minutes; but maybe you'd better go now and let him settle down."

"Mother—I really think a home is the best solution."

"Yes," the young woman nodded agreement. "After all, he's past ninety—and he has his veteran's retirement . . . ."

Inside his room, the old man listened as they departed. He went to the closet, took out clothes, began dressing . . . .

★**8**★

City Engineer Eaton's face was chalk-white on the screen.

"No one can blame me," he said. "How could I have known—"

"Your office ran the surveys and gave the PA the green light," Mayor Dougherty yelled.

"All the old survey charts showed was 'Disposal Area,'" Eaton threw out his hands. "I assumed—"

"As City Engineer, you're not paid to make assumptions! Ten minutes' research would have told you that was a 'Y' category area!"

"What's 'Y' category mean?" Mayfield asked Reynolds. They were standing by the field comm center, listening to the dispute. Nearby, boom-mounted Tri-D cameras hummed, recording the progress of the immense machine, its upper turret rearing forty-five feet into the air, as it ground slowly forward across smooth ground toward the city, dragging behind it a trailing festoon of twisted reinforcing iron crusted with broken concrete.

"Half-life over one hundred years," Reynolds answered shortly. "The last skirmish of the war was fought near here. Apparently this is where they buried the radioactive equipment left over from the battle."

"But what the hell, that was seventy years ago—"

"There's still enough residual radiation to contaminate anything inside a quarter-mile radius."

"They must have used some hellish stuff." Mayfield stared at the dull shine half a mile distant.

"Reynolds, how are you going to stop this thing?" The mayor had turned on the PA engineer.

"Me stop it? You saw what it did to my heaviest rigs: flattened them like pancakes. You'll have to call out the military on this one, Mr. Mayor."

"Call in Federation forces? Have them meddling in civic affairs?"

"The station's only sixty-five miles from here. I think you'd better call them fast. It's only moving at about three miles per hour but it will reach the south edge of the Mall in another forty-five minutes."

"Can't you mine it? Blast a trap in its path?"

"You saw it claw its way up from six hundred feet down. I checked the specs; it followed the old excavation tunnel out. It was rubble-filled and capped with twenty-inch compressed concrete."

"It's incredible," Eaton said from the screen. "The entire machine was encased in a ten-foot shell of reinforced armocrete. It had to break out of that before it could move a foot!"

"That was just a radiation shield; it wasn't intended to restrain a Bolo Combat Unit."

"What was, may I inquire?" The mayor glared from one face to another.

"The units were deactivated before being buried," Eaton spoke up, as if he were eager to talk. "Their circuits were fused. It's all in the report—"

"The report you should have read somewhat sooner," the mayor snapped.

"What—what started it up?" Mayfield looked bewildered. "For seventy years it was down there, and nothing happened!"

"Our blasting must have jarred something," Reynolds said shortly. "Maybe closed a relay that started up the old battle reflex circuit."

"You know something about these machines?" The mayor beetled his brows at him.

"I've read a little."

"Then speak up, man. I'll call the station, if you feel I must. What measures should I request?"

"I don't know, Mr. Mayor. As far as I know, nothing on New Devon can stop that machine now."

The mayor's mouth opened and closed. He whirled to the screen, blanked Eaton's agonized face, punched in the code for the Federation station. "Colonel Blane!" he blurted as a stern face came onto the screen. "We have a major emergency on our hands! I'll need everything you've got! This is the situation . . ."

★9★

I encounter no resistance other than the flimsy barrier, but my progress is slow. Grievous damage has been done to my main drive sector due to overload during my escape from the trap; and the failure of my sensing circuitry has deprived me of a major portion of my external receptivity. Now my pain circuits project a continuous signal to my awareness center, but it is my duty to my Commander and to my fallen comrades of the Brigade to press forward at my best speed; but my performance is a poor shadow of my former ability.

And now at last the Enemy comes into action! I sense aerial units closing at supersonic velocities; I lock my lateral batteries to them and direct salvo fire, but I sense that the arming mechanisms clatter harmlessly. The craft sweep over me, and my impotent guns elevate, track them as they release detonants that spread out in an envelopmental pattern which I, with my reduced capabilites, am powerless to avoid. The missiles strike; I sense their detonations all about me; but I suffer only trivial damage. The Enemy has blundered if he thought to neutralize a Mark XXVIII Combat Unit with mere chemical explosives! But I weaken with each meter gained.

Now there is no doubt as to my course. I must press the charge and carry the walls before my reserve cells are exhausted.

★10★

From a vantage point atop a bucket rig four hundred yards from the position the great fighting machine had now reached, Pete Reynolds studied it through night glasses. A battery of beamed polyarcs pinned the giant hulk, scarred and rust-scaled, in a pool of blue-white light. A mile and a half beyond it, the walls of the Mall rose sheer from the garden setting.

"The bombers slowed it some," he reported to Eaton via scope. "But it's still making better than two miles per hour. I'd say another twenty-five minutes before it hits the main ringwall. How's the evacuation going?"

"Badly! I get no cooperation! You'll be my witness, Reynolds, I did all I could—"

"How about the mobile batteries; how long before they'll be in position?" Reynolds cut him off.

"I've heard nothing from Federation Central—typical militaristic arrogance, not keeping me informed—but I have them on my screens. They're two miles out—say three minutes."

"I hope you made your point about N-heads."

"That's outside my province!" Eaton said sharply. "It's up to Brand to carry out this portion of the operation!"

"The HE Missiles didn't do much more than clear away the junk it was dragging." Reynolds' voice was sharp.

"I wash my hands of responsibility for civilian lives," Eaton was saying when Reynolds shut him off, changed channels.

"Jim, I'm going to try to divert it," he said crisply. "Eaton's sitting on his political fence; the Feds are bringing artillery up, but I don't expect much from it. Technically, Brand needs Sector okay to use nuclear stuff, and he's not the boy to stick his neck out—"

"Divert it how? Pete, don't take any chances—"

Reynolds laughed shortly. "I'm going to get around it and drop a shaped drilling charge in its path. Maybe I can knock a tread off. With luck, I might get its attention on me and draw it away from the

Mall. There are still a few thousand people over there, glued to their Tri-D's. They think it's all a swell show."

"Pete, you can't walk up on that thing! It's hot—" He broke off. "Pete, there's some kind of nut here—he claims he has to talk to you; says he knows something about that damned juggernaut. Shall I . . . ?"

Reynolds paused with his hand on the cut-off switch. "Put him on," he snapped. Mayfield's face moved aside and an ancient, bleary-eyed visage stared out at him. The tip of the old man's tongue touched his dry lips.

"Son, I tried to tell this boy here, but he wouldn't listen—"

"What have you got, old timer?" Pete cut in. "Make it fast."

"My name's Sanders. James Sanders. I'm . . . I was with the Planetary Volunteer Scouts, back in '71—"

"Sure, dad," Pete said gently. "I'm sorry, I've got a little errand to run—"

"Wait . . ." The old man's face worked. "I'm old, son—too damned old. I know. But bear with me. I'll try to say it straight. I was with Hayle's squadron at Toledo. Then afterwards, they shipped us—but hell, you don't care about that! I keep wandering, son; can't help it. What I mean to say is—I was in on that last scrap, right here at New Devon—only we didn't call it New Devon then. Called it Hellport. Nothing but bare rock and Enemy emplacement—"

"You were talking about the battle, Mr. Sanders," Pete said tensely. "Go on with that part."

"Lieutenant Sanders," the oldster said. "Sure, I was Acting Brigade Commander. See, our major was hit at Toledo—and after Tommy Chee stopped a sidewinder at Belgrave—"

"Stick to the point, Lieutenant!"

"Yessir!" The old man pulled himself together with an obvious effort. "I took the Brigade in; put out flankers, and ran the Enemy into the ground. We mopped 'em up in a thirty-three hour running fight that took us from over by Crater Bay all the way down here to Hellport. When it was over, I'd lost sixteen units, but the Enemy was done. They gave us Brigade Honors for that action. And then . . ."

"Then what?"

"Then the triple-dyed yellow-bottoms at Headquarters put out the order the Brigade was to be scrapped; said they were too hot to make decon practical. Cost too much, they said! So after the final review—" he gulped, blinked—"they planted 'em deep, two hundred meters, and poured in special high-R concrete."

"And packed rubble in behind them," Reynolds finished for him. "All right, Lieutenant, I believe you! Now for the big one: What started that machine on a rampage?"

"Should have known they couldn't hold down a Bolo Mark XXVIII!" The old man's eyes lit up. "Take more than a few million tons of rock to stop Lenny when his battle board was lit!"

"Lenny?"

"That's my old command unit out there, son. I saw the markings on the Tri-D. Unit LNE of the Dinochrome Brigade!"

"Listen!" Reynolds snapped out. "Here's what I intend to try . . ." He outlined his plan.

"Ha!" Sanders snorted. "It's a gutsy notion, mister, but Lenny won't give it a sneeze."

"You didn't come here to tell me we were licked," Reynolds cut in. "How about Brand's batteries?"

"Hell, son, Lenny stood up to point-blank Hellbore fire on Toledo, and—"

"Are you telling me there's nothing we can do?"

"What's that? No, son, that's not what I'm saying . . ."

"Then what!"

"Just tell these johnnies to get out of my way, mister. I think I can handle him."

★ **11** ★

At the field comm hut, Pete Reynolds watched as the man who had been Lieutenant Sanders of the Volunteer Scouts pulled shiny black boots over his thin ankles and stood. The blouse and trousers of royal blue polyon hung on his spare frame like wash on a line. He grinned, a skull's grin.

"It doesn't fit like it used to; but Lenny will recognize it. It'll help. Now, if you've got that power pack ready . . ."

Mayfield handed over the old-fashioned field instrument Sanders had brought in with him.

"It's operating, sir—but I've already tried everything I've got on that infernal machine; I didn't get a peep out of it."

Sanders winked at him. "Maybe I know a couple of tricks you boys haven't heard about." He slung the strap over his bony shoulder and turned to Reynolds.

"Guess we better get going, mister. He's getting close."

In the rock car, Sanders leaned close to Reynolds' ear. "Told you those Federal guns wouldn't scratch Lenny. They're wasting their time."

Reynolds pulled the car to a stop at the crest of the road, from which point he had a view of the sweep of ground leading across to the city's edge. Lights sparkled all across the towers of New Devon. Close to the walls, the converging fire of the ranked batteries of infinite repeaters drove into the glowing bulk of the machine, which plowed on, undeterred.

As he watched, the firing ceased.

"Now, let's get in there, before they get some other damn-fool scheme going," Sanders said.

The rock car crossed the rough ground, swung wide to come up on the Bolo from the left side. Behind the hastily rigged radiation cover, Reynolds watched the immense silhouette grow before him.

"I knew they were big," he said. "But to see one up close like this—" He pulled to a stop a hundred feet from the Bolo.

"Look at the side ports," Sanders said, his voice crisper now. "He's firing antipersonnel charges—only his plates are flat. If they weren't, we wouldn't have gotten within half a mile." He undipped the microphone and spoke into it:

"Unit LNE, break off action and retire to ten-mile line!"

Reynolds' head jerked around to stare at the old man. His voice had rung with vigor and authority as he spoke the command.

The Bolo ground slowly ahead. Sanders shook his head, tried again.

"No answer, like that fella said. He must be running on nothing but memories now . . . ." He reattached the microphone, and before Reynolds could put out a hand, had lifted the anti-R cover and stepped off on the ground.

"Sanders—get back in here!" Reynolds yelled.

"Never mind, son. I've got to get in close. Contact induction." He started toward the giant machine. Frantically, Reynolds started the car, slammed it into gear, pulled forward.

"Better stay back." Sanders' voice came from his field radio. "This close, that screening won't do you much good."

"Get in the car!" Reynolds roared. "That's hard radiation!"

"Sure; feels funny, like a sunburn, about an hour after you come in from the beach and start to think maybe you got a little too much." He laughed. "But I'll get to him . . . ."

Reynolds braked to a stop, watched the shrunken figure in the baggy uniform as it slogged forward, leaning as against a sleet storm.

★**12**★

"I'm up beside him." Sanders' voice came through faintly on the field radio. "I'm going to try to swing up on his side. Don't feel like trying to chase him any farther."

Through the glasses, Reynolds watched the small figure, dwarfed by the immense bulk of the fighting machine, as he tried, stumbled, tried again, swung up on the flange running across the rear quarter inside the churning bogie wheel.

"He's up," he reported. "Damned wonder the track didn't get him . . . ."

Clinging to the side of the machine, Sanders lay for a moment, bent forward across the flange. Then he pulled himself up, wormed his way forward to the base of the rear quarter turret, wedged himself against it. He unslung the communicator, removed a small black unit, clipped it to the armor; it clung, held by a magnet. He brought the microphone up to his face.

In the comm shack, Mayfield leaned toward the screen, his eyes squinted in tension. Across the field, Reynolds held the glasses fixed on the man lying across the flank of the Bolo. They waited . . . .

★13★

The walls are before me, and I ready myself for a final effort, but suddenly I am aware of trickle currents flowing over my outer surface. Is this some new trick of the Enemy? I tune to the wave energies, trace the source. They originate at a point in contact with my aft port armor. I sense modulation, match receptivity to a computed pattern. And I hear a voice:

"Unit LNE, break it off, Lenny. We're pulling back now, boy. This is Command to LNE; pull back to ten miles. If you read me, Lenny, swing to port and halt."

I am not fooled by the deception. The order appears correct, but the voice is not that of my Commander. Briefly I regret that I cannot spare energy to direct a neutralizing power flow at the device the Enemy has attached to me. I continue my charge.

"Unit LNE! Listen to me, boy; maybe you don't recognize my voice, but it's me. You see, boy—some time has passed. I've gotten old. My voice has changed some, maybe. But it's me! Make a port turn, Lenny. Make it now!"

I am tempted to respond to the trick, for something in the false command seems to awaken secondary circuits which I sense have been long stilled. But I must not be swayed by the cleverness of the Enemy. My sensing circuitry has faded further as my energy cells drain; but I know where the Enemy lies. I move forward, but I am filled with agony, and only the memory of my comrades drives me on.

"Lenny, answer me. Transmit on the old private band—the one we agreed on. Nobody but me knows it, remember?"

Thus the Enemy seeks to beguile me into diverting precious power. But I will not listen.

"Lenny—not much time left. Another minute and you'll be into the walls. People are going to die. Got to stop you, Lenny. Hot here. My God, I'm hot. Not breathing too well, now. I can feel it; cutting through me like knives. You took a load of Enemy power, Lenny; and now I'm getting my share. Answer me, Lenny. Over to you . . . ."

It will require only a tiny allocation of power to activate a communication circuit. I realize that it is only an Enemy trick, but I compute that by pretending to be deceived, I may achieve some trivial advantage. I adjust circuitry accordingly and transmit:

"Unit LNE to Command. Contact with Enemy defensive line imminent. Request supporting fire!"

"Lenny . . . you can hear me! Good boy, Lenny! Now make a turn, to port. Walls . . . close . . . ."

"Unit LNE to Command. Request positive identification; transmit code 685749."

"Lenny—I can't . . . don't have code blanks. But it's me . . . ."

"In absence of recognition code, your transmission disregarded." *I send. And now the walls loom high above me. There are many lights, but I see them only vaguely. I am nearly blind now.*

"Lenny—less'n two hundred feet to go. Listen, Lenny. I'm climbing down. I'm going to jump down, Lenny, and get around under your fore scanner pickup. You'll see me, Lenny. You'll know me then."

The false transmission ceases. I sense a body moving across my side. The gap closes. I detect movement before me, and in automatic reflex fire anti-P charges before I recall that I am unarmed.

A small object has moved out before me, and taken up a position between me and the wall behind which the Enemy conceal themselves. It is dim, but appears to have the shape of a man . . . .

I am uncertain. My alert center attempts to engage inhibitory circuitry which will force me to halt, but it lacks power. I can override it. But still I am unsure. Now I must take a last risk; I must shunt power to my forward scanner to examine this obstacle more closely. I do so, and it leaps into greater clarity. It is indeed a man— and it is enclothed in regulation blues of the Volunteers. Now, closer, I see the face and through the pain of my great effort, I study it . . . .

★**14**★

"He's backed against the wall," Reynolds said hoarsely. "It's still coming. A hundred feet to go—"

"You were a fool, Reynolds!" the mayor barked. "A fool to stake everything on that old dotard's crazy ideas!"

"Hold it!" As Reynolds watched, the mighty machine slowed, halted, ten feet from the sheer wall before it. For a moment, it sat, as though puzzled. Then it backed, halted again, pivoted ponderously to the left, and came about.

On its side, a small figure crept up, fell across the lower gun deck. The Bolo surged into motion, retracing its route across the artillery-scarred gardens.

"He's turned it." Reynolds let his breath out with a shuddering sigh. "It's headed out for open desert. It might get twenty miles before it finally runs out of steam."

The strange voice that was the Bolo's came from the big panel before Mayfield:

"Command . . . . Unit LNE reports main power cells drained, secondary cells drained; now operating at .037 percent efficiency, using Final Emergency Power. Request advice as to range to be covered before relief maintenance available."

"It's a long way, Lenny . . ." Sanders' voice was a bare whisper. *"But I'm coming with you . . . ."*

Then there was only the crackle of static. Ponderously, like a great mortally stricken animal, the Bolo moved through the ruins of the fallen roadway, heading for the open desert.

"That damned machine," the mayor said in a hoarse voice. "You'd almost think it was alive."

"You would at that," Pete Reynolds said.

★LITTLE DOG GONE★

Linda Evans

My position is precarious, my flank vulnerable. Class One Yavac fire from high ground to my left damages pain sensors along my entire side. The Enemy advances into the teeth of my return Hellbore and infinite repeater fire. I destroy one, two. . . . Four take their place. My ablative armor takes multiple direct hits. Layers are blown away, leaving my flintsteel war hull increasingly vulnerable to Enemy fire. I send a distress call on the Brigade band, at emergency strength. Silence is my only answer. I grieve for a precious 0.007 seconds. Without the assistance of my brothers, I am forced to withdraw. As I move back, firing left, right, forward, I register on my sensors a division-strength force of Class One Yavac Heavies advancing over the top of the ridge. They will flank me and sweep down across the base before I can disengage from my current position.

I inform my Commander of the threat this represents but receive no reply. This concerns me more than the silence of my Brigade brothers. I take a precious 0.01 picoseconds to perform diagnostics on my transmission equipment. I cannot afford to lose contact with my Commander. I am the only survivor of the Dinochrome Brigade on Planet XGD 7798-F. Without me, the Enemy will certainly destroy the colony. The mineral resources of XGD 7798-F are too valuable to risk loss. I discover my transmitter functions perfectly. Base still does not answer. I take withering fire from both flanks. Pain sensors overload. A burst transmission from Command Base reaches me at last. The sound of my Commander's voice brings short-lived joy to my Pleasure Complex circuitry.

"Gawain, return to Base, stat. We are under direct attack. The compound is not expected to hold."

I register stress in my Commander's voice. Response requires 0.002 seconds. The delay distresses me, for I am proud of my efficient service; but I must wait to complete a Current Situation update scan of battlefield conditions.

"Unit Six Seven Zero GWN of the Line to Command, I am under heavy fire. The Enemy has cut my line of retreat. I have received no reply from the remaining nineteen members of Third Dinochrome Brigade. Base is currently receiving fire from left flank and rear. Your right flank will come under fire in approximately 0.5 seconds. I will attack at their weakest point, vector 045, and attempt break-through."

"Unit Six Seven Zero GWN, understood. *In extremis, Gonner.*"

The code translates, "I am not expected to survive. Your next Commander knows your personal code. If the Base is destroyed, your Commander will transmit code to burn your Action/Command section."

I do not desire death. No soldier does. But my duty is clear. I cannot be captured and used against my own forces. I will make every effort to prevent the destruction of my beloved Commander, despite discouraging odds. The situation does not suggest my own survival will last more than another 10.37 minutes.

I transmit, "Understood. Unit Six Seven Zero GWN of the Line, out."

I disengage, sweeping around to strike the Enemy between my position and the Base compound. My right flank comes under fire as I forge ahead at emergency speed. My Hellbore fire cripples one Class C Yavac Armored Scout. Its jointed legs, blown clear by the explosion, arc outward for a distance of 50.87 meters from the main body of the armored vehicle. My concentrated Hellbore fire destroys another. I turn my armaments against a Class One Yavac Heavy and fire with both Hellbores and infinite repeaters. The turret explodes. Its treads blow clear of its tracks.

A narrow opening appears between my position and the Base compound. My plan may succeed. My sensors register Enemy personnel advancing from my rear. They are dog-sized, eight-appendaged creatures, quick on the attack. I discharge anti-personnel explosive mines and small-arms fire from my rear guns. The Enemy falls back behind cover of their Class C Yavac Scout units.

Emergency speed has carried me into the midst of the Class One Yavac Heavies flanking the Base compound. My systems are overheating. I continue firing both energy repeaters and Hellbores. I plow through their ranks under extreme fire. I lose rear sensors and am blinded on my right rear quarter by a direct hit. Ablative armor blows away in a four-foot patch along my flank. Pain sensors scream a warning. I ignore it. The Enemy will give no quarter. That was discovered on Millbourne's World. It is why I am here, to prevent another massacre.

The compound walls withstand the bombardment with difficulty. I am glad my Commander ordered them reinforced with flintsteel. My war hull beneath the ablative-metal armor is comprised of the same material. Neither the wall nor my war hull is without damage, but we hold. Enemy fire concentrates on the weaker compound gates. My sensors detect structural stress in the hinges. Another direct hit will bring the gates down. Enemy infantry surges forward. Their shouts, alien to my data banks, register on my forward sensors. I hear explosions within the compound as Enemy fire clears the wall and damages structures beyond.

The gates vanish in a glare of light. Debris pings on my outer hull. The gate is breached. Enemy Class One Yavacs roar ahead. I take fire from all sides as I charge between two Yavac heavy units. The gap in the wall must be closed. I detect movement inside the compound. My Commander is ordering agricultural equipment into the opening. It will not withstand a single salvo. He knows this. I know this. I run my engines deep into the red zone and clear the intervening two hundred *meters in 1.37 seconds. Enemy infantry falls under my treads. A Yavac fires point blank into my right side. Pain sensors explode across my prow and side. My ablative armor is gone in a seventeen-foot section across my bows. I sustain damage to my flintsteel war hull. But I have gained the gate.*

I pivot and turn Hellbore fire into the Yavac at a distance of five meters. The Yavac unit takes a direct hit to the turret. The explosion scatters debris across my back and into the compound. The fire I have taken before is as nothing. Pain sensors overload and burn out. My internal diagnostics program screams that I suffer severe internal damage. I cannot absorb the total energy of their combined Y-Band energy bolts. I overheat. My hull glows. More systems burn. But I must continue to hold.

I am still firing when a direct hit against my hull strikes through previous damage. An explosion tangles my internal psychotronic circuitry. Malfunction warnings and remaining pain sensors scream through shattered hard-wired boards and cracked crystal memory banks. I begin a message to my Commander and am not certain I complete it.

I have failed my Commander. Failed the Brigade. Failed my mission. For the first time in my career, I know the meaning of shame.

Another explosion against my hull sends a concussion through my awareness circuitry. Extreme damage blows connections, fuses internal leads. Unable to continue fighting, I retreat in desperation to my Survival Center.

As multiple impacts of alien feet thud across my hull, darkness swallows my awareness.

"Mama, what's that?"

Indira Tennyson followed her daughter's pointing finger across the valley, to a tangle of rotting walls, old crater scars, and ancient trees whose feathery crowns towered above the broken wall. *That battle was a long time ago*, Indira told herself. *Nothing to fear now. Just the ghosts of dead defenders.*

"That's the old fort, 'Lima."

"The one the spodders took?"

Indira sighed, silently so her daughter wouldn't hear it. "Yes, the one the Deng captured."

"Captain said they killed everyone on the whole planet. Even the Bolos. She said, if you go over there, you can still see the one they didn't bury, the one Dad said they left as a monument, sitting in the old gate."

Indira frowned. She had *told* the captain she didn't want 'Lima's head filled with tales from that bloody fiasco. The wheedling tone in her daughter's voice disturbed her. She would *not* encourage the girl to follow in her father's footsteps and go running off to join the Navy. Indira had suffered enough distress thanks to the *Navy*. Besides, the Deng war was old history, fought two hundred years ago. They were here to start a new life together. She didn't want the lingering wreckage of the last war to start any foolish, romantic illusions of glory in her only child's mind.

"Forget it, 'Lima. Those machines are dangerous, even when they look harmless. We have work to do. Don't you want to help with the new puppies?"

Her daughter cast one last look over her shoulder, toward the ruined fort, then trotted obediently at her heels. Indira was deeply thankful when 'Lima began chattering excitedly about the litter of puppies that had arrived early, while they were still aboard ship. Indira still winced at the expense of transporting Sufi; but leaving her behind would not only have precipitated war in their little household, it would have meant at least a six-year setback in Indira's research.

She had a feeling Sufi's puppies were going to change the colonists' lives forever. She smiled in anticipation and grabbed the handle of the servo-truck which held their luggage.

"Can you find our new house?" she asked it.

"Proceed three blocks east, turn left and proceed seven blocks. You have been assigned the last house in the cul-de-sac. It is painted green, with black roof and shutters."

'Lima giggled. Indira grinned. It was good to see her daughter smiling again. "Well, don't just stand there. Let's go home and see what it looks like!"

I do not know how much time has passed. I return to awareness and fade again, how many times I am unable to calculate. This inability disturbs me. I probe during consciousness for damage. I find it everywhere I investigate. My internal linkages are so battered I am unable to scan for damage in many sections. One of my forward sensors still functions. I am able to see the battlefield which I recall in shattered fragments. My crystal memory banks are clearly damaged beyond repair. Power reserves continue to drain in frightening increments from my fission reactor, wasting irreplaceable fuel, as intermittent shorts drain my power plant. I am forced to shut down all diagnostic and other non-essential activity and retreat again into my Survival Center. Perhaps with sufficient power, I could determine the extent of my injuries; but I am not certain even unlimited power reserves would allow me to run full diagnostics.

I do not understand why my new Commander did not transmit the coded order to engage my Command Override circuit, thus completely burning my Action/Command center. The passage of time and the hazy recollection of enemy forces around me suggests that no new Commander survived to transmit the code. Perhaps I am too badly damaged even for the Enemy to have made use of me. During recent periods of near-awareness, I recall only the sounds of empty wind. No Enemy activity has been detected during the last dozen times I have awakened into solitude.

Other sounds come to my sensors. My shattered data banks register them as falling conifer cones bouncing against my hull. There were no trees inside the compound. A very long time has passed, if mature conifers drop cones on me. Has the Enemy completely destroyed humanity? The shame I feel at my failure to carry out my mission skitters through broken wire-ends and jumps spark gaps into other memory cells. If humanity has survived, then I have been abandoned. I am irreparable. I am alone. A sizzle sputters somewhere in my vocal circuitry and my voice stutters into the silence, uncontrollably.

"Yavac. Yavac. Yavac. Yavac. Yavac . . . Hold. Hold. Hold . . ."
The sizzle fades.

Darkness returns, with the sound of cones falling against my scarred back.

"Double-dog dare you!"

"I'm not going!"

Bradley Dault laughed in that derisive way little boys manage when dealing with all lesser beings. Kalima Tennyson glared at him, hating Bradley for relegating *her* to that status.

"You're skeered!" he taunted, fists planted on hips, legs akimbo in the faded autumn sunshine.

"Am not!"

"'Lima's a 'fraidy cat! 'Lima's a 'fraidy cat!"

She took a threatening step forward. "I am not afraid! It's just stupid! There's nothing over there but a bunch of rusted, burned out old ruins."

"Hah! That's your mama talking, not you. Your *daddy* wouldn't be skeered to go, *Kah*-Lima Tennyson!" He emphasized the first half of the name her father had given her—the half her mother wouldn't use. Her mother had come to despise everything which remotely smacked of violence, including her ancient ancestors who had worshipped as Thuggees.

Bradley was dancing around her like a disjointed marionette, chanting, "Kalima's a chicken! Kalima's a chicken! I'll bet your big famous daddy was really a chicken, too!"

Kalima was under express orders *never* to fight, no matter what the provocation.

Bradley's face glowed with evil glee. He poked at her while shouting, "Chicken, chicken, chic—"

She put her whole seventy-one pounds of thirteen-year-old

muscle behind the punch. The blow landed squarely on Bradley's nose. He squealed and flipped backwards in the dirt. She stood over him, fists still clenched, jaw stiff.

"Don't talk about my dad! Ever!"

Then she whirled, ignoring the sting and ache in her knuckles, and left Bradley sucking blood up his nose. Bradley Dault was a pig. The whole colony knew it. He deserved everything Kalima could think up to do to him. And she was *not* afraid to explore the old ruins! It was just plain stupid, was all. Just as she'd told Bradley. The ruins were dangerous and not only because of the old Bolo jammed into the gates. The ancient fighting machines had been known to short out, go berserk, and inflict terrific casualties against civilian populations before running out of power.

Their Bolo, however, the one lodged in the old fortification's gates, had been inert for the entire three years she'd been on Donner's World. Everyone said it had been dead for two centuries, killed in the last battle with the Deng before they overran the planet. No one in the whole colony believed their Bolo was any more dangerous than the pine cones falling on it. But the wall around the old colonists' compound continued crumbling under its flintsteel sheath, which meant that occasionally whole sections came down with a thunderous crash where the war had cracked the black-violet alloy casing.

Kalima didn't want to be under any of that wall when it came down.

Still, the Pig had issued a challenge. She would lose stature in the eyes of the other kids if she didn't respond suitably. And the taunt about her father stung more than she cared to admit. It wasn't easy, Kalima scowled as she jogged over the broken valley toward the distant ruins, being the only child of a genuine war hero.

She had been aware most of her life that her mother had never forgiven Major Donald Tennyson for getting himself killed. Kalima wasn't sure what she thought about her father's death. She remembered sitting on her father's lap, listening for hours to the stories he told about combat duty and the Navy and the wonder of the newest Bolos. After school lessons, she'd spent hours reading everything she could about the Bolos, about the worlds her father's unit had seen, about the Navy. For a long time, she'd wanted to grow up and follow him into service.

Then, shortly after her eighth birthday, the message that had changed her mother into another person and left a giant hole in her own life had arrived, along with the posthumous medal for valor. Her mother had thrown the medal away and immersed herself in her work. Kalima had secretly rescued it again and hidden it in her personal belongings; then she had spent a lonely couple of years trying to keep herself interested in schoolwork that was suddenly the dullest thing she had ever been forced to do.

But her mother's work had paid off, handsomely. The result had been not only a new home on Donner's World, where they could start fresh, but also a companion that took *everyone's* mind off the past.

Behind her, faint in the distance but growing rapidly closer, Kalima heard an emphatic series of barks. She knew what that particular code meant. She kept going anyway. Sufi would track her without difficulty, but not even the dog was going to stop her this time. She'd prove to everyone, including her mother, that Major Tennyson's daughter was no coward.

The Bolo really was jammed into the crumbling gates. The closer she jogged to the ruined walls, the larger the ancient fighting machine loomed. It was at least fifty feet from treads to turret. Gaping holes in its armor revealed the extent to which it had suffered damage doing its duty. The enormous Hellbore guns were silent, coated in a reddish scale of rust. Her father had told her eye-popping stories about Bolos, about how difficult they were to kill.

Was this one really dead? Just because everyone *thought* it was . . .

She paused well outside its anti-personnel-charge range and scooped up a rock. Kalima heaved with all her strength. The rock thudded into the dirt a few feet short of the Bolo's right tread. No movement creaked anywhere on the machine. It sat staring blindly forward, a metallic corpse left to lie where it had fallen.

"Huh. Maybe it really is dead."

A low growl behind her was followed by three short, sharp barks.

"You're a bad girl," was the message.

Kalima turned toward her nursemaid. "I'm not a little girl anymore, Sufi. I'm thirteen and I know exactly what I'm doing."

Sufi's short tail wagged once. That message was clear, too: *Humor her.*

"Huh. I'm going closer to the Bolo."

Sufi barked once, warningly; then tried to interpose her body between Kalima and the defeated engine of war.

"Forget it, Sufi. I'm going to get a good look at it. The Pig isn't going to get away with calling me a chicken."

Sufi's ears pricked, then her jaws opened in a canine laugh.

Kalima stalked away, conscious of her own wounded dignity. The closer she drew to the dead Bolo, however, the slower her footsteps shuffled. Old bomb craters pitted the ground, overlapping one another until the footing was so rough she stumbled at every other stride.

"Must have been some battle, huh, Sufi?"

She tried to picture it and decided not even her vivid imagination could do justice to what must have taken place here. The Bolo's long, chilly shadow stretched over her head and left her shivering at the foot of its enormous treads. Each tread was ten feet from edge to edge. She had to tilt her head to look up at the war hull. The whole surface was uneven, where special armor—her Dad had called it "ablative"—had blown off in layers under Enemy fire.

Each little section of special armor was six-sided; the combined effect of interlocking pieces reminded her of the honeycombs built by the colony's bees. Most of the honeycomb-shaped armor was gone. Forlorn scales and patches remained. In places the layers ran at least four deep. Most of the Bolo's exterior was naked flintsteel, its iodine hue having long since lost any vestige of polish. Kalima wondered how many layers of armor had been blown away, even in the patches where it remained four layers deep?

She tilted her head back farther, trying to see up the imposing prow.

"There's a designation up there," Kalima muttered. "I'm going to see if I can find it."

The dog whined sharply when she put her foot on the nearest rung and started to climb. Kalima paused, waiting to see if the Bolo would respond; but it just sat there, rusting away under the late autumn sun. She climbed higher. The designation ought to be right about . . .

There. Mark XX Model B, *Tremendous*, Unit Six Seven Zero GWN, Dinochrome Brigade Three. "Wow. Look at those battle decorations!"

Despite the rust and the battle scars, she counted six, each from a different world.

"Poor old Bolo." She climbed higher, up to the turret. The war machine was twice as long as it was high, jammed so solidly into the gates, it didn't look like anything, not even a nuclear blast, would ever budge it loose. "Mr. Hickson told us the Navy didn't even bother burning your Action/Command center. The Deng did it for them, two hundred years ago. It's kind of sad, I think, hunting out the members of the Dinochrome Brigade, just to wipe out their brains. It's not a very nice way to treat a combat veteran." She stroked the pitted hull. "Maybe," she sighed, outlining a long, jagged scar with her fingertip, "maybe it *is* better you got killed in battle."

Kalima glanced over the top of the mighty war machine's turret, into the compound itself. Every building inside had been smashed open, burnt out, obliterated. Not even skeletons remained of the hapless colonists who had died here.

"It's too bad you were a gonner, Unit Six Seven Zero. I'll bet this was a nice place before the Deng came."

On the ground, Sufi emitted a shrill yelp, then barked frantically to get her attention. At first, Kalima wasn't sure what had agitated her genetically enhanced nursemaid. Then she felt the tremor. Earthquake? Her eyes widened and she grabbed for the nearest rung to scramble down before the wall on either side of the Bolo collapsed.

A metallic screech, like bending rebar, half deafened her. She stared around wildly for the source—

The Hellbore guns were moving.

They tracked jerkily, halted, then moved another two inches. Somewhere in the depths of the critically wounded Bolo, an engine groaned and wheezed. The sound died away, leaving Kalima shaking atop the uppermost rung.

"It isn't dead! It isn't dead at all and I'm stuck up here . . ."

If she tried to jump down, the Bolo might trigger anti-personnel charges. What if she couldn't get down, ever? No one would even be able to rescue her, get close enough . . .

Then she heard a sound that made her hair stand on end.

The Bolo was *talking.* . . .

I become aware of sunlight and the sound of machinery close to me: over the nearest ridge, no farther than the next valley. The Enemy has returned!

Then a human voice enters my awareness. My Commander is gone, has been dead for many, many years. Has a new Commander sought me out at last? The voice nears; then I feel a human hand on my war hull. My forward sensor is still functional. It is a human, a small human, with another creature that I should know but do not. My data banks are too damaged to recall the information once stored in that memory cell.

The small human climbs nearer to my turret. I will not open myself to it. I await the private code, which my long-lost Commander has told me to wait for. It seems unlikely to me, even in my battered, power-weakened state, that a new Commander can know my private code after such a long passage of years. I search through what remains of my memory cells and recall the voice of my beloved Commander, lost to me through my own failure and the weight of unknown years.

"Unit Six Seven Zero GWN, everyone's taken to calling you Gawain. I think that's a fine name, don't you?"

"Agreed. Gawain was a noble warrior, worthy of a place in the Dinochrome Brigade."

My Commander's rich laugh fills my sensors. "If I didn't know better, I'd say someone programmed a sense of humor into your Introspection Complex. I'll tell you what, though, Gawain. We've got to work out a private code between us, to ensure proper transfer of command. How about something that rhymes with my name. Any ideas?"

I consider the challenge. "Donner. This name rhymes with honor, gonner . . ."

"Hey, Gonner. I like that. It's even close to your designation, but not close enough to be obvious. Donner's Gonner, 'cause when we hit 'em, they're gonners! How's that sound?"

"I will file the code word Gonner as my Commander's private security access code."

"Hah, you don't fool me. You like it just fine . . ."

The small human climbing on my hull speaks again. ". . . you were a gonner, Unit Six Seven Zero . . ."

Deep inside my command center, sparks flutter. I come to attention. My Hellbore guns move with extreme slowness. It takes 9.7 seconds to lift the guns seven inches. More sparks dance across broken connections.

"Unit Six Seven Zero GWN of the Line, reporting for duty."

This is what my Action/Command center begins to say. My sensors pick up the sound of my own voice, which crackles and sputters, "Gonner, gonner, gonner, gonner . . ."

I shift attention for 0.027 seconds in an attempt to locate the difficulty. My power level is critically low. I am operating on emergency backup batteries. My fission unit is completely cold. If I continue to communicate or attempt movement without a recharge during the next three days, I will cease to exist. My internal diagnostic becomes baffled by a haphazard tangle of broken circuitry and smashed crystalline retrieval centers located to the lower left of my command center.

I can think coherently. But I cannot speak coherently.

The shame of failure to my Brigade and to my new Commander deepens. I attempt again, this time to communicate the need for power. The statement, "Unit Six Seven Zero GWN of the Line, *reporting. I request immediate recharge of all energy systems" comes through my speakers as "Sunlight. Sunlight. Sunlight."*

The small human who has come to take command reaches the ground. My Commander has given up on me. There is little to be gained by further effort, for my emergency power reserves are failing. Oblivion will come a little sooner. I allow the Hellbore guns to drop and rotate them away from my departing Commander. It is the only salute of which I am still capable. It is not enough. My Commander leaves.

★**6**★

The screeching sound of moving gun barrels sent Kalima sprawling into the nearest crater. She flung arms around her head, moving instinctively; but the Bolo didn't fire. Sufi pressed against her, whining softly in the back of her throat.

"Let's leave," the sound meant.

Slowly, Kalima lifted her head. The Hellbore guns hadn't tracked her. The Bolo had shifted them to one side. She frowned and sat up.

"How come it didn't try to shoot me?"

Again, Sufi whined to leave.

"Wait a minute, Sufi. This is strange. I need to think."

She'd made some silly comment, she could hardly recall what, and the Bolo had come to life. What had it said? Gonner, gonner, gonner? It had repeated what she'd said. One word, anyway. Then it had started babbling about sunshine. The sunlight on her shoulders, weak as it was in autumn, warmed a little of the chill from her bones.

"Why would it say sunshine?"

She glanced skyward and frowned again. Why *sunshine*, after two centuries? The most logical answer was simply that its Action/Command center was damaged. The machine was, effectively, senile. But if it were senile, why hadn't it fired on her? Maybe it was out of ammunition? No . . . It hadn't even *tried* to fire on her. None of its impressive array of guns had cycled. And why *sunshine*?

She crawled uneasily to her feet, but the Bolo sat motionless.

The only hint that it had ever come to life was the slightly different angle of its main guns. She brushed dirt out of her hair and jumpsuit, cast one last, uneasy glance over her shoulder, then headed for home. She had nothing to show for her adventure except bruises, but she didn't care any longer about the Pig and his stupid challenges.

She'd gone one-on-one with a deranged Bolo and come out alive. That ought to be enough for *any* lifetime.

Two days later, Kalima left school to find a group of colonists clustered near the Council building. She edged her way closer and discovered a serious debate underway.

". . . can't repair it? We've got to have that power unit on line within ten hours or the backup generators will go down!"

"We don't have the tools needed to fix a fusion unit. We've got to wait for the supply ship."

"But the hospital!"

Near the far edge of the crowd, someone said, "What about a solar rig?"

"That's ancient technology!"

"Yeah, but it works," someone else said thoughtfully. "We've got the supplies to build a pretty big solar collector and Fred's a good electrical engineer. You could rig a converter, couldn't you, Fred?"

"Yes, that'd work temporarily. We could divert part of the power to backup batteries for emergency use until the supply ship—"

Kalima had stopped listening. Sunshine. Solar energy. *Power* . . . The Bolo needed recharging!

She whirled and slipped away without being noticed.

The thud of conifer cones is very distant. Power reserves are critically low. My Emergency Survival Center functions; my outer sensors hardly at all. Soon, the darkness will return permanently. I have not

*been visited again by my new Commander. I calculate that 2.7 days
of my remaining three days of power have elapsed, without further
command contact. It would have been good to receive a last command;
but I am without purpose and have disgraced my unit. This ending is
to be expected. Still, it is a lonely end. I miss the voices of my fellow
Dinochrome Brigade units. I miss the laughter of my Commander. I—*

*Low-ultraviolet Y-Band radiation floods my external power-grid
panels. Energy surges through my Action/Command center and
floods into my backup power cells. Outer sensors regain receptivity.
Memory cells I had long forgotten resonate once again. Euphoria
floods my ego-gestalt Introspection Complex circuitry. I am alive!
Damage assessment is automatic, requiring 1.73 seconds to determine
that I am immobilized, incapable of speech, and unable to function in
more than 75 percent of my original design functions. My memory
crystals are intact in places, damaged in others. Many connections
between banks of data cells have been damaged, so that much of my
memory, while intact, remains inaccessible.*

*My armaments are low, but I sustained crippling damage before
on-board munitions stockpiles were exhausted. If I am able to repair
the damage to my motor control functions, I will be capable of
fighting.*

*Although my main fission plant remains cold, backup power
reserves are restored. I swivel forward sensors and locate the small
human who is my Commander. I attempt to communicate.*

"Gonner. Gonner."

"Uh, hi. Hi, Gonner. I, uh, thought you might need power."

*The voice is female, young. She is my first female Commander.
Sensor probes indicate medical-design equipment near my treads. I
am unfamiliar with the specific configuration of the machine,
although its medical purpose is clearly indicated by the symbols
stamped onto its hull. This equipment is emanating Y-Band radiation
as a flood of waste energy. My manufacturers built into my design the
ability to absorb Y-Band radiation and convert it to battlefield energy. I
am grateful for the delay of oblivion. I attempt to come to attention. I
rotate my Hellbore guns and lift them in a salute.*

"Gonner, Gonner, Gonner."

I must repair my speech centers. Can my Commander under-
stand my need for depot maintenance?

"Is that the only word you can say? No, you said sunshine.
That's how I figured out you were low on power."

I am pleased. My new Commander is capable of extrapolating
from slim clues.

"Uh, my name is Kalima Tennyson, Gonner."

Kali-Ma, ancient Hindu Goddess of Death and Rebirth, Consort
to Shiva the Destroyer. My Commander was well chosen. I await
Current Situation input.

"In case you're wondering, it's been about two hundred years
since you, uh, since the battle with the Deng."

My Commander knows of my failure.

"I think it's pretty awesome, what you did. You should see the
battle damage on your hull. When I was coming out here, three
years ago, the captain of our transport ship told me all about the
battle for Donner's World. They named it after your old Commander,
'cause the colony fought so bravely, my Dad said. That was before
he got killed in the battle on Hilltop Gap. My Dad even knew about
you, Gonner. You're famous. They put a medal on your hull and left
you here, where you fell standing against the Deng. Just like
Leonidas at Thermopylae."

I know this battle. It is part of my battlefield archives, which have
sustained no damage. I access the file. The Spartan three hundred,
under King Leonidas, held the gap between the mountains at
Thermopylae against invading Persians. The Spartans were killed to
the last man. Persia overran Attica and sacked Athens; but Greek
forces rallied at Corinth and finally drove the Persians from Greek
soil.

If my Commander speaks the truth—and why would she not?—
then the Deng have taken Planet XGD 7798-F and lost it again.
Humanity has not fallen to the Enemy. It pleases me that the planet
has been renamed in honor of my Commander. James Donner was a
valiant officer. My new Commander has said I am honored. This
seems impossible; but my Commander would not lie to a Unit of the
Line. Perhaps my mission was not a failure. Humanity has survived.

I attempt again to request assistance at a maintenance depot.

"Monkey. Monkey."

My Commander's voice is understandably puzzled. "Monkey?"

I try again. "Slick."

"Monkey? Slick? Gonner, I wish I knew what was wrong with your brain."

I attempt further diagnostics and find only broken tangles which my on-board repair functions cannot fathom. Without a maintenance depot, I will not be capable of telling my Commander what is wrong with my internal psychotronic circuitry.

My sensors detect the approach of another life form. I go to Battle Reflex Alert Status. My Commander must be protected. I swivel anti-personnel guns and lock onto the target.

"Gonner! No! Don't shoot!"

I halt the anti-personnel-response program and await further commands.

"This is Sufi. She's my dog."

I study the life form which has joined my Commander. It is smaller than she, quadrupedal. My Commander's hand rests on the animal's head. The animal is of a different configuration than my fragmented memories of the Deng Enemy. The Sufi dog has half as many appendages as the Deng, although its body is slightly larger. The shape and arrangement of head, body, and legs differs significantly. I switch from Battle Reflex Alert to Active Service Alert Status. This introspection and alert-status change requires 0.013 seconds. I still function slowly.

My Commander continues her Current Situation update. "Sufi is a special dog. My mother does genetic research. Sufi's nearly as smart as I am; she just can't talk. She and her puppies, they're grown up now, they babysit us kids, so the adults don't have to watch us all the time. The colony gets a lot more work done now than we used to. Of course, I don't really need a nursemaid anymore, but Sufi's my friend."

I file Sufi in my memory banks as authorized personnel permitted to approach this Unit. My Commander's friend emits two sharp sounds.

"That means my mother's looking for me, Gonner. Two sharp barks close together means, 'Go home, your mother wants you.' She probably needs this Entero-Scope Field Generator that I, uh, borrowed, back in the lab. I'll be back, Gonner, okay? Maybe not today, but I promise I'll be back. You just sit tight and don't shoot anyone."

A command! I respond with intense pleasure. "Hold! Hold! Hold!"

My new Commander smiles into my sensor pickup. "Yeah, that's right, Gonner! You did a great job, holding. Just keep holding the fort until I come back and don't shoot any of the colonists."

My Commander departs with her friend and the equipment which has restored my backup power levels to full battle charge. She has commanded me to remain at Active Service Alert Status. I survey the valley and scan with my sensors. I await my next command. I have a restored purpose. Even in my damaged condition, I am again useful. I am content.

"Mom?"

"Hmm?"

Her mother was busy at the gene-sequencer, which was good. She should be able to ask her question, get an answer, and get away again without rousing suspicion.

"What kind of brain damage would cause someone to answer questions in one-word answers, you know, like not a direct answer, but it sort of makes sense if you think about it?"

Her mother glanced up. "Sounds like global aphasia. Got an assignment?"

She nodded.

Her mother went back to the sequencer. "I've got a medical library in the study. Read up on it and show me a copy of your report when you're done."

Relieved, Kalima made her escape to the study. Global

aphasia, she discovered, was a condition in which people were capable of fully rational thought, but could not articulate anything but nonsense. The disorder had become an obscure one ever since Dr. Collingwood had discovered how to culture immature nerve tissue.

"Bet that's what's wrong with Gonner," she muttered, chewing one fingernail. "He almost makes sense. Wonder what 'monkey' and 'slick' refer to?"

She made a list of synonyms for each word, and started a computer cross reference, looking for anything that might make sense. Eventually, she came up with a possibility. "Grease monkey: mechanic."

"He needs maintenance, of course!"

Dismay followed at once. *How?*

She couldn't notify the Navy or Sector. They'd simply destroy him. He was a war hero, like her father had been, and no one was going to hurt him. Gonner had been hurt enough already. *She* couldn't fix him. And she couldn't tell anyone in the colony, either, because any adult who found out would call in the Navy or Sector representatives and Gonner's life would end, abruptly.

She thrust out her lower lip, in the expression her mother despairingly called, "Your father's look." She was only thirteen; but she had the manuals and things her father had given her about Bolos and she could learn everything the colony had to offer about mechanics, electrical systems, and engineering.

She could always tell her mother and the school officials she wanted to become an engineer. She just wouldn't mention that she wanted to become a *combat* engineer. The decision made, Kalima spent the rest of the evening studying everything in her mother's library on brain disorders. She wrote the required composition, which she then carefully smudged and marked "B–" in a fair approximation of her teacher's handwriting.

The next day she told her teacher she'd decided on a career choice, after all, and scheduled as many math, engineering, and mechanical practicum courses as they'd let her cram in with her other academics.

★**9**★

Six months later, Gonner's outer sensor arrays had been fully repaired. That wasn't as difficult as Kalima had first thought. She'd found a compartment with spares and had studied the existing, burnt-out units carefully before replacing them. Gonner had responded by saying, "Bird! Bird! Bird!" about a dozen times in rapid succession.

She laughed. "Bet it *does* feel like flying, after you've been blind for a couple of centuries. Or . . ." She canted her gaze into the bitter-white winter sky ". . . is there a bird somewhere up there, too far for me to spot?"

Gonner hummed in silence. Kalima grinned. "Well, that's one repair job done and about a million more to go. At this rate, we'll *never* get you back up to ratings."

"Bird," was all Gonner said.

She patted his pitted war hull. The icy cold of the flintsteel seeped through her insulated gloves. "I gotta go, Gonner. Last thing we need is for me to get caught sneaking out here. Mom would never understand. She'd insist they come melt your Action/Command center. I'll be back as soon as I can."

She slid over to the rungs of the ladder and climbed down. It was a long way to the cratered ground. Evening shadows stretched coldly away from Gonner's giant treads. Icicles clung like a beard to the bottom edge of his purple-black war hull. Dirty grey ice had formed in the ancient crater depressions. It splintered and cob-webbed underfoot as she started back toward home. She had taken only five steps away when a snickering voice spoke from the shadows of the crumbling wall.

"So, this is where the famous Kalima Tennyson spends her spare time."

She whirled, going first hot then icy cold inside her therma-suit.

Bradley Dault. Suited up and lying in wait.

What are you doing here?

"I wondered where you sneak off to. So I followed you this time."

"You got no right following me, Bradley Dault!"

"It's a free world." He shrugged, infuriating her; then stepped closer. More ice crunched underfoot. "Your mama know you come here?"

"None-ya!" she grated.

He grinned. "Didn't think so. Don't worry, 'Lima. I won't tell. Not so long as I can come along, too, and watch the Bolo. Can I go inside, too?"

Kalima's fists clenched, all by themselves. "No! And if you ever follow me again, I'll make him shoot you!"

Above their heads, the anti-personnel guns swivelled with a scream of freezing metal. The sound brought Bradley Dault six inches off the ground. His face went pasty white, the color of old ice. His eyes bugged, staring at the gun barrels now levelled squarely at him. A brisk wind sprang up, whipping around the end of the wall toward the broken gates and the shadow of the crippled Bolo.

"I didn't mean nothin', 'Lima, honest! I just wanted to see the Bolo, too! Gad, it's still alive!"

"You say a word—a stinking *word*—and *you* won't be! My Mom's a geneticist—I got *dozens* of ways to kill you, hideous-like, if you even *breathe*."

He nodded, still staring wide-eyed at the anti-personnel guns. "Not a whisper. I swear. Cut my tongue out, if I'm lying."

She relaxed a little. "Well . . . okay. But don't try to come out here alone. Bolo knows me. He won't know you."

Again, Bradley nodded without taking his eyes off the big guns. "Can you talk to it?"

"Yes. But he was hurt pretty bad. He can talk, sort of; but there's a lot of damage to the circuits in his speech center. It's called global aphasia. He can think just fine, but he can't *talk* very well."

"Make him say something."

Scorn filled her voice. "You don't *make* a Bolo Mark XX Model B *Tremendous* unit do *anything*. They do their assigned duty. Unit Six Seven Zero GWN's duty is guarding this colony. He's still doing it."

That got a response from Bradley. He glanced over his shoulder. "You gotta be kidding. He just sits there, getting rusty."

She stepped forward, fists clenched at her sides. "Want me to command him to shoot you?" Her breath went to ice on the cold wind. "All I gotta do is tell him you're the Enemy. Personally, I think we'd be better off without you, Bradley Dault. You're a pig."

She expected him to get mad or make some wise, smart-mouthed crack. Instead, he just clamped his lips tighter and went white around the edges of his face.

"What? Something I say hit home?"

"No." That came out sullen. He dropped his gaze and turned away from the Bolo. "Can I leave now, 'Lima?"

She hesitated. He looked almost . . . hurt. She decided he was play-acting, just to get her sympathy.

"Yeah. Sure. Get out of here."

He hunched his shoulders against the wind and turned to go. Overhead, one of the tall native conifers cracked with a report like gunfire. Bradley jumped and went down flat in one of the old war craters. Kalima started to laugh—

Then froze. The tree crashed down, broken halfway up its immense length. The trunk smashed against the old wall. A sixteen-foot section cracked, slipped sideways along an ancient fissure in the battered flintsteel casing, and began to fall—directly toward them.

"Run!"

Bradley rolled, came up faster than she would have thought possible, and launched himself straight at her. His tackle brought her down, almost in the shadow of the Bolo's treads. Screaming metal and the sound of falling concrete and flintsteel filled her ears. But they weren't crushed.

She looked up and gasped.

The wall had fallen against the Hellbore gun barrels. The Bolo had swivelled them to catch the wall.

"Run! Quick!"

Bradley grabbed her hand and hauled her up. She dove for cover behind the Bolo and hauled him with her. Overhead, the massive Hellbore gun barrels caught the glint of winter sunlight. They groaned, then moved a few inches as the ancient turret rotated the barrels out from under the wall. The broken section crashed down right where they'd been standing.

In the immense silence which followed the thunder of falling debris, Bradley stuttered, "It s-s-saved our lives."

Kalima just nodded, jerkily, unable to find her voice at all. She placed a shaky hand against the Bolo's fender and leaned her forehead against it.

"Oxygen," the Bolo's metallic voice said, twice.

"Oxygen?" Bradley repeated. "What's he mean?"

She thought about it. She was getting better at interpreting Gonner's inscrutable messages. "Oxygen's a gas. Can't see it, but you need it to survive. Can't see it! Of course. It's clear. He just said, 'All clear.'"

"Oxygen," Gonner said again, confirming the guess. "Hold. Hold."

"Job well done, Unit Six Seven Zero GWN. Yes, continue to hold position. Report any Enemy activity detected."

"Hold, hold, hold."

Bradley mouthed, "Wow!" soundlessly.

That was when she noticed the rip in his therma-suit. He'd torn it down the shoulder at some point during their scramble for safety. She reached out to see how bad the damage was and was shocked speechless when he flinched in pain.

"Ow! Dammit, don't look!"

"Hey! Sit still! You're hurt."

"Am not," he growled, sounding genuinely dangerous.

"Then how come I see bruises and . . . and welts . . ."

The bruises were liver-colored, at least several days old, not new injuries from the falling wall. The implications hit Kalima hard. Bradley didn't say anything.

"Your dad?"

He stared coldly into the distance.

"Bradley—"

"He's not my dad."

She opened her mouth; then shut it again. This was getting deep, a little too fast.

Bradley's face had flushed; he wouldn't look at her. "Mom died before you got here and . . . *he* . . . never knew she slept around. He thought I was his kid. We did that genetic experiment in school last week? Well, I'm not. He always was mean to me, but . . ."

Despite the extreme chill of the frozen ground, she discovered a need to sit down beside him. "I didn't know. I'm sorry."

"Don't be. I'm just Bradley the Pig." He stood up and shoved gloved hands into his pockets. "Gotta go," he mumbled.

"Wait."

He stopped without turning around.

"You wanna see the passenger compartment?"

"I—" He stopped and didn't say anything for a moment. Then, very low, "Later?"

"Sure."

He took off at a dead run.

Above her head, Gonner's metallic voice broke the silence. "Brimstone."

Brimstone. She thought about that for a little while. Then said, "Yeah, Gonner, you're right."

She wished she could ask the Bolo for advice on what to do next.

★10★

Brad avoided Kalima Tennyson for several months. He was ashamed, without quite knowing why, and was grateful that she said nothing. He wanted to talk to her and ask her more questions about the Bolo, but didn't quite have the nerve. They'd both turned fourteen and she was pretty by any standards and smarter than he was, and the Bolo thought of her as its commander.

He avoided home, too, as much as possible.

Brad spent a lot of time working with the nursemaid dogs Kalima's mother had bred. The animals fascinated him. One of the young bitches which had been born on the ship, before Kalima and her mother had arrived, had littered, giving him a chance to work directly with new pups. They were smart, even at a young age. They matured more slowly than normal dogs, which meant they stayed longer than normal dogs at the age when learning came most easily. By springtime, the pups were barely a third grown and had already learned the coded verbal "language" by which the nursemaid dogs communicated with their human charges.

He found himself spending most of his spare time at the nursery, watching the dogs watch the kids, and discovered that he enjoyed playing with the little ones. Their older brothers and sisters stopped calling him "Pig" and started listening when he told stories about the Deng war and the colonists' last stand on Donner's World.

His grades in history and biology improved dramatically.

His "dad" still hit him regularly, but Brad found ways to avoid home most hours of the day.

Spring had melted gloriously into early summer, leaving grass knee-deep in the wide, crater-scarred valley, when Kalima appeared at the nursery.

"Bradley?"

He glanced up, surprised to hear her voice.

"Yeah?"

"Uh . . . Can we talk?"

"Sure." He retrieved the ball with which he'd been playing catch and tossed it over to little Joey Martin, then said to Ganesha, "Gotta go. Your turn to play fetch."

The dog panted happily and chased down the ball.

"What's up?"

She didn't answer, just led him a roundabout trip through the woods behind town, over the ridge that separated the new colony from the ruined one, and headed for the Bolo.

"Kalima?"

"I started to think you'd never ask to see inside him. So I thought I'd offer again."

"Really? Are you serious?"

She glanced over her shoulder. "I never joke about Unit Six Seven Zero GWN."

He hurried to catch up. "Thanks. I mean it."

They walked in silence for a few minutes, toward the broken wall which had nearly killed them.

"I heard some of your stories about him," she said at length.

He flushed and stared at the ground. "I did some reading."

"I know. You're good. The little ones really love it. I liked listening, too."

Brad couldn't remember the last time someone had told him he was good at anything. And Kalima had *liked* something he did. His whole face went hot, clear down into his neck.

They arrived at the shattered gate and stood gazing up at the Bolo for a moment.

"He's bigger than I remembered."

She looked over at him. "You didn't come back out?"

He ducked his head. "You said he wouldn't know me. I ain't stupid, Kalima."

"Didn't say you were. C'mere." She grabbed his hand and dragged him closer. "Unit Six Seven Zero GWN, this is Bradley Dault. He is my friend."

The huge Hellbore guns shifted. Brad wanted to break and run, but held his ground. The guns circled, lifted two degrees, then halted.

"That's his salute," Kalima whispered.

"Oh. Uh . . ."

He saluted awkwardly, after disengaging his hand from Kalima's grip. "Bradley Dault, sir. Pleased to meet you. And, uh, thanks for saving my life, you know, last winter."

"Oxygen."

All clear.

"Yes, sir. Thank you, sir."

"Unit Six Seven Zero GWN, I'm bringing Brad aboard for observation."

"Hold. Hold."

Brad grinned. "Thank you, sir!"

They climbed, Kalima going first. The hatch didn't creak when she opened it.

"You've been working on him."

She nodded. "Every chance I get. I read everything I can find. Dad left me some stuff and the library's got a little, but most of the stuff I really need's classified. He was hurt pretty bad. I can't fix everything."

He understood the frustration in her voice. He wanted, very badly, to see this machine at its full fighting potential.

Then they climbed into the turret and he forgot everything else. "Wow!"

The inside of the Bolo wasn't anything like he'd imagined. He'd thought it would be a vast space, filled with glowing lights, ranks and banks of instruments. The interior was crowded, with scant room for a passenger in a small compartment in the center, under the turret. Crawl spaces snaked off to allow maintenance access. Battle damage was visible even this deep inside the Bolo, in the form of blackened boards, tangled wires and conduit cables, cracked and darkened crystal components. Daylight flickered through one crawlspace, where something had blown completely through the armor.

"Whew! He really got ripped apart, didn't he? No wonder they gave him that medal."

Kalima had hunkered down in one of the crawl spaces, leaving the observer's chair for him.

"Unit Six Seven Zero GWN, activate observation screens."

Two dull panels flickered, then a view of the valley sprang up in full color on one. Ranges and other esoteric data he didn't understand appeared along the edges of the screen. The other view was aft, into the battered compound the Bolo had tried to defend.

"Am I asleep?" Bradley wondered aloud. "This has gotta be a really great dream."

Kalima just grinned. "That's how I felt, first time I got a look around inside."

"I'm scared to touch anything," he admitted with a rueful grin.

She just nodded. "Me, too. I study like crazy, then ask him all the questions I can think, and try to figure the answers ten different ways before I touch *anything*. I don't want those Hellbore guns to discharge and I don't want to fry any more of his psychotronic circuits."

"Is there any way to get him talking right again?"

She looked unhappy. "Let me show you."

He got down on hands and knees and followed her toward the distant light pouring through the hull.

"See that?"

She pointed to a tangle of destruction the size of his torso.

"Yeah. Pretty bad, isn't it?"

"That's his vocal processor center."

"Yipe. That's dire."

"Maybe, if I study long enough, I'll figure a way, but . . ."

It looked hopeless.

"Any danger he'll go berserk, like some of those Bolos you hear about?"

She bit her lower lip, looking suddenly vulnerable.

"I don't know. His Action/Command center wasn't hit, so I don't think so, but I'm scared, anyway. He's my friend, Brad." Her eyes, luminous and wide in the shadows of the crawlspace, sought his gaze. "I don't want to lose him, too."

It took him a minute, but he finally caught on. "Hey, at least you knew your dad. I still don't know who mine is."

She sniffed once and nodded. "Sorry. I really am. Does *he* still hit you?"

He shrugged. "Yeah."

"You ought to report him."

He stared toward the distant rip in the Bolo's hull. "Colony needs him," was all he said. "They'd only deport him for reconditioning and then where'd we be? Can't go without a surgeon for a year, waiting for someone to come out on the next transport."

She scowled. "Still ought to report him. Beating a minor's a serious crime."

"Dying's worse," he countered laconically. "You wanna risk a bust appendix while he's gone?"

Her lower lip came out, reminding him of a photo he'd seen of her father in a recent-history text.

"Just don't say nothin', okay? I only gotta put up with him for another four years and I'm not home much now, as it is. I won't talk about the Bolo and you won't talk about *him*. Deal?"

He stuck out one hand.

With every evidence of reluctance, she took it. They sealed the bargain with a vigorous handshake. Afterward, he felt better than he had in months.

"You want one of Sufi's puppies?" she asked unexpectedly.

He looked up quickly. "What?"

"You want one of the puppies?"

"I—" He closed his mouth before he could blurt out how desperately he wanted one of the beautiful, smart dogs. "But they're really expensive!"

"Mom said I could have one. I'd rather you had one. You're better with them than I am, and, well, it wouldn't be such a bad idea, having a nursemaid to watch your back. I'll bet not even Davis Dault would hit you, with a dog like Sufi between you and him. And he's sure not stupid enough to kick one of Mom's dogs. They'd tear his leg off at the knee and the whole colony would approve."

Brad wanted to grin. But the enormity of the offer overwhelmed him so deeply, his throat closed. All he could manage was a feeble, "Thanks."

"Come on, then. Let's say goodbye to Unit Six Seven Zero GWN and go pick up your dog."

As they walked away from the massive hulk of the Bolo, Brad felt like he was dancing on air.

★ ▌▌ ★

"This really is a tangled mess, Gonner. I've been studying everything in the colony archives, everything my dad left me on Bolo design and psychotronic circuitry; but this . . ."

Kalima let her voice trail off. Five years of intensive study had allowed her to restore many of the Bolo's systems, but she hadn't quite dared tackle his speech defect yet.

"Are you sure you want me to try and fix this?"

The Bolo's metallic voice responded in a fashion she'd grown accustomed to interpreting over the years.

"Worms."

Translation: "I'd rather be dead and eaten by worms than go on this way."

"Okay, big guy. I apologize in advance if I really blow this one."

Out in the passenger compartment, Brad's voice said, "Go for it. If you don't get it right, no one can."

Her hands were already sweating, but she knew she had to at least try. She turned on the high-speed resonant cutter. Over in the opening to the crawlspace, Shiva laid back his ears at the sound. Brad chuckled and called the dog over to him. Kalima bent over the tangle of two-hundred-year-old damage, took a deep breath, and began the surgery. She cut away damaged boards, squared off ragged explosion damage, exposed raw connections which had lain half buried under fused droplets of flintsteel from the outer hull. Then came the delicate job of trying to reconnect and splice boards whose purposes she only vaguely understood.

The stink of hot electrical connections tickled the back of her throat. Out in the passenger compartment, Shiva pinned back his ears and whined, but stayed put. Time trickled past. She sat back periodically and wiped sweat with an arm. Brad handed in water and a sandwich about halfway through. Her hands were less than steady when she set the cutter aside.

"Thanks. This is good."

"Made it myself."

"How much time's gone?" She wasn't wearing a watch, for fear of damaging the delicate circuitry she was exposing.

"A little more than two hours. Want a shoulder rub?"

She emerged from the crawl space. "Sounds great."

Bradley Dault's fingers dug into tight knots. "Ow! Ooh, that's good . . ."

When he'd finished, he stole a kiss. She grinned. "Naughty! I've still got a good two hours' work left in there. Hang on, big guy," she told the Bolo.

"Hold."

She patted Shiva and earned a hand-washing, then dried her hands carefully. "Okay. Back to work."

The job took more than five hours, altogether. Kalima conducted frequent tests, asking Gonner questions to which he either responded in his usual murky fashion or—more ominously—to which he didn't respond at all.

"Don't worry," Brad told her. "Just keep going."

She connected a splice between two damaged sections—

And sparks jumped and skittered through a whole series of cables and junctions. The Bolo emitted a high-pitched keening sound and jerked spasmodically on its treads.

"Ow!" Kalima's arm throbbed clear to the elbow. Her fingertips were reddened from the shock.

Bradley dove down the crawlspace and hauled her out. "Are you hurt?" His face was actually ashen.

"I'm fine. Gonner! Gonner, what happened? Talk to me!"

For a long, breathless moment, there was no sound save a dying sputter somewhere in the connections behind her. Then—

"Unit Six Seven Zero GWN of the Line, reporting for duty."

"*Gonner!*"

"That is my security clearance code, Commander Tennyson."

Both of them whooped aloud. Shiva barked joyously and danced at their feet.

"You did it!" Bradley was abruptly kissing her, very thoroughly.

When they unclutched, they both panted for air and grinned like fools. Bradley's face swam wetly in her vision.

"He can talk! Brad, he can really talk!" Then she cleared her throat, recalling her position as Gonner's commanding officer. "Unit Six Seven Zero GWN, please report damage assessment."

"Affirmative, Commander Tennyson. Diagnostics indicate that the connection between my Action/Command center and my vocal-processing unit is repaired. However, a short has now developed in my motor control function. I cannot track my guns accurately. Is there a maintenance depot available, Commander Tennyson?"

She exchanged a glum look with Bradley.

"Great," she muttered.

He squeezed her waist. "Maybe it's not too bad?"

Kalima gulped. "Let's hope not. Uh, Gonner, I'm afraid I *am* the maintenance depot. I can't request official help. If I do, the Navy will just send someone out to burn out your Action/Command center. They're trying to find all the old Bolo field units to destroy them. They, uh, think you're already dead, Gonner."

"Understood. I cannot function properly in my current status."

"Let me see what I can do. It took five years, but I finally fixed your voice."

She went hunting, prompted by Gonner, and found the trouble.

"Oh-oh." This didn't look good. The short had melted a solid-state unit in the Bolo's fire-control center. "Uh, Gonner, this doesn't look like something I can fix. Unless you have a spare part stashed somewhere?"

"You have already exhausted all replacement units which I carried on board. My sensors now function at proper battlefield capacity. The damage to my psychotronic circuitry has been repaired. I no longer experience intermittent power drains from my emergency reserve batteries. I am able to retrieve 68.935 percent of my stored memory capacity and your additions of data crystals and new input have enhanced many of my losses. There is no replacement for this fire-control module."

Out in the passenger compartment, Brad muttered, "How'd I know you were going to say something like that?"

"Was it . . ." She hesitated. "Was this damage caused by something I did?"

Gonner actually hesitated at least half a second—an eternity for a Bolo.

"Affirmative. I am pleased to have my speech centers repaired, Commander. It may be possible to bypass the fire-control module. I will need to conduct a thorough search of my memory banks. Stand by." A few instants later, he said, "I cannot access certain data crystals, but my memory shows no rerouting possible under existing circumstances. May I obtain additional technical data?"

"On what?" Brad muttered. "We don't have clearance for Bolo technology."

"Well, no, but we can give him everything in the colony library, everything in Mom's library archives. We've already uploaded some of it, into those new memory crystals we swiped."

Bradley grinned, clearly remembering the consternation caused by discovery of the theft. The little kids had been blamed for it, after one of the crystals, carefully planted, turned up as "pirates' treasure." No one had gotten into serious trouble and Bradley had agreed to pay for the replacements, since he had "encouraged" the kids to play pirate games. The loss had been replaced on the next supply ship— and Gonner had gotten a badly needed memory supplement.

"It couldn't hurt to try," Kalima decided.

"All right. You get a copy of your mother's stuff and I'll bootleg a copy of the library archives."

They climbed out of the Bolo, Brad carting Shiva over one arm since the big dog couldn't negotiate the steep rungs, and jumped down the last rung to land in knee-deep grass. The big dog trotted to one side and sat laughing at their feet. He adored visiting the Bolo with them. He'd kept their secret even from the other dogs.

Kalima paused and gazed across the valley. "Sometimes, you know, I try to imagine what it must have been like, that day. They must've known it was hopeless, once Gonner was crippled. He was the last Bolo of the Dinochrome Brigade stationed here. The Deng had already killed the others."

Brad slipped an arm around her shoulder. "Yeah," he said softly. "Thank God the Deng were beaten back years ago."

She shivered and leaned against him. "Yeah."

"Come on, let's go. I'll cook dinner at my place after we finish stealing the archives for Gonner."

Kalima grinned. Brad had moved out the moment he hit eighteen and had built his own place out at the edge of town, closer to the ruined fortress than anyone else had built. All that was required now for an unnoticed excursion to work on Gonner was a quick exit from Brad's back door. Then they simply cut through the woods and climbed the ridge.

"It's a deal."

They headed back to town, hand in hand.

★12★

The additional data provided by my Commander and Bradley Dault has proven of unique interest. A great deal of this information is medical, giving me great insight into the nature of biological life forms. Commander Tennyson's parent has acquired considerable skill in genetic manipulation. Dault has provided additional data on surgical skills, including results of his own studies. I note that he bears the same name as the colony surgeon and shares an interest in surgery. I also note that in his personal files he indicates no direct genetic link with this other Dault. Human relationships continue to puzzle me.

I search for possible information to resolve my current disability. I find none which appears viable. Commander Tennyson's data includes information on techniques attempted approximately fifty years ago which proved of limited success. I study these notes more carefully and extrapolate possibilities. There is a 27.35 percent chance that such a cybernetic interphase linkage might serve as a substitute fire-control center. I have lost that portion of my psychotronic network which monitors and manipulates the primary controls for the Hellbore system and the energy repeater guns. Anti-personnel charges and guns are under my control, but my main weapons systems respond erratically. A secondary brain, under intelligent control and tied into my psychotronic nervous system, would be capable of taking my directions and manually controlling the weapons systems. With proper cybernetic connections, it would be possible for such a system to translate leg and arm movement commands from the brain center into traversing and firing commands for my weapons systems.

I anticipate a 99.85 percent probability that no human volunteer will be found for such an attempt. Nor does the current situation require such measures. I am incapable of fighting, but my sensors monitor the security of this colony. I will know before any human on Donner's World what dangers may threaten human survival. It is less than my original commission requires; but I am a member of the Dinochrome Brigade. I will serve to the best of my ability. I note the required procedure and file the data for reference. I will speak with my Commander of this when she returns. She will decide the proper course of action for this unit.

★13★

A knock at the outer door interrupted Kalima's concentration. "It's open!"

Brad's voice followed the sound of the squeaking door hinges. "Kalima? Have you seen Shiva?"

She glanced up. "No. He never comes here unless you're with him. What's wrong? Has one of the young bitches gone into heat?"

He shook his head. "No. I checked. He left about an hour ago, through the woods, and hasn't come back. He didn't come when I called."

Kalima scooted her keyboard aside and stood up. "That's odd. Mom! I'm going for a walk!"

"Be careful, dear."

Kalima rolled her eyes. "Brad's going along!"

"Hello, Bradley! Have a nice walk!"

"Thank you, Dr. Tennyson."

He didn't smile, which thoroughly alarmed Kalima. She whistled and called for Sufi. The dog she'd grown up with bounded into the living room.

"Let's go for a walk, Sufi."

Sufi swished her tail and barked once.

They headed for Brad's house and walked through the deep conifer needles to the back.

"He trotted off that way." Brad pointed.

"Sufi, Shiva's missing. Can you find him?"

Sufi barked emphatically and bounded off into the trees. Brad jogged after her and shed his jacket, which he draped over a tree limb at the edge of the yard. Kalima noticed uneasily that he'd thrust a gun into a holster on his belt. She hadn't noticed, earlier.

"Brad, what gives? There haven't been any *ybin* attacks in years."

"*Something's* happened to Shiva," he said grimly over one shoulder. "Do you really want to go one-on-one against a *ybin* without a gun?"

"Uh . . . no."

Two hundred yards into the trees, Sufi halted and sank down onto her belly, growling low in her throat. Brad went to ground behind her. Kalima ate pine needles, then scooted forward cautiously to peer over the dog's shoulder.

Her breath caught.

Shiva lay about ten yards ahead. The dog's head was turned away from them, but even from this distance Kalima could tell the animal was dead or critically wounded. Blood had spattered everywhere and soaked into the pine straw under his dark fur.

"What happened?" she whispered.

Brad's jaw muscles looked like iron. A soft snick reached her ears. He'd drawn the gun and slipped off the safety.

"Stay here. You're not armed and I am."

He inched forward. Sufi was still growling.

A flash of sunlight on metal caught Kalima's attention. Before she could yell a warning, Shiva whined sharply and tried to lunge toward the trees. His back legs didn't move. Brad yelled something and fired wildly. Kalima heard a scream of metal on metal; then an energy bolt slammed into a tree trunk less than a millimeter from Brad's ear. He dove behind the tree and fired again. Something slammed solidly into another tree trunk. Shiva was whining hysterically. Sufi snarled low in her throat and lunged out of Kalima's grip.

"Sufi! Down!"

Another energy beam sliced through the trees. Sufi yelped, but kept going. Brad lunged for the dog and fired again at something Kalima couldn't quite see. Then Sufi snarled and the sound of bending metal squealed through the trees.

"Got it!" Brad snarled. He lunged to his feet and dove forward. "Mother of—"

Kalima covered the intervening ground in half a heartbeat.

"What—" She broke off with a horrified gasp.

The thing was small, not even as large as Sufi's torso. Eight mangled, spike-like appendages dangled from it. Two holes through its—body? head?—leaked a thin, foul-smelling fluid. Kalima saw dark, blue-black hair under its body armor. A bulge on one side was completely encased in metal, although two lenses reminded her of goggles. An alien weapon, resembling a long, thin rifle, lay in the pine straw under Sufi's paw. The dog still snarled over the inert body, fangs bared.

"My God," she whispered, "it's a Deng. An advance infantry probe. My God."

Brad stomped the thing, making certain it was dead, then checked Sufi's injury. "Spodders are back," he said, through clenched teeth. "Got Shiva and waited for someone to come looking for him. Sufi's burned across the shoulder, here; but she's not critical. Can you walk, girl?"

The dog barked an emphatic affirmative. Brad confiscated the spodder's weapon and tested it against a nearby tree trunk. Bark sizzled and chipped loose. The burn scar stank. So did Shiva's blood. Kalima glanced through the gloom in the deep woods, hunting for any hint of Deng activity, any glint of sunlight on metal. The silence, which she had always enjoyed, was suddenly ominous.

"If they were laying a trap," she said softly, "then they wanted a captive. Information. My God— We've got to get Gonner."

"He can't fight."

"He's the best we've got!"

Brad glanced at the crippled dog at their feet. Pain filled his eyes.

"Let's take him to Mom first," Kalima decided. "If anyone can help him, Mom can. I'll bring the . . . the Deng's body. We're going to need proof. Then we'll warn Gonner."

Kalima tucked the shattered Deng infantryman under her belt, so that it dangled by half its broken legs, then scooped up Shiva without asking. Brad was armed. She wasn't. He couldn't afford to have his hands encumbered with anything but his weapon. Sufi, limping but alert, brought up rear guard. They ran most of the way.

"Sufi," she gasped, as they jolted past Brad's house, "go get Hal Chin. I don't care what he's doing, get him here. We've got to inform Sector and the Navy . . ."

The dog bounded away. Brad held the door for Kalima.

"Mom! Mom, we got big trouble!"

★14★

I become aware of an energy pattern which does not fit the configuration of colony transmissions. I compare it with known patterns in my Experience Section data banks. I find a damaged memory cell where the information I seek should be stored. This energy source functions on W-Band radiation. There is a reason this puts me on heightened alert status, but I can no longer retrieve the information which would tell me why.

I broaden the range of my sensor scan. A thousand-meter, 360 degree sweep reveals more such energy transmissions, all in the W-Band. This is sufficiently disturbing to place myself on Battle Reflex Alert Status. I call my Commander. There is no answer on the Base receiver which she has rigged to communicate with my Action/Command center. I am now alarmed. My previous Commander died in action due to my failure. I will not repeat this error. My engines have been repaired. I move forward and pull free of concrete debris without difficulty. My treads are rusted but functional. I swivel my turret scanners and pick up further sources of W-Band transmissions.

I move in the direction of these transmission sources. I will discover the cause of my heightened alert status. I call my Commander again and receive no reply. Alarm deepens in my Introspection Complex ego-gestalt circuitry. I fear for my young Commander's life and I fear the return of shame and failure.

A forest has grown on the ridge during the time I have spent guarding the former compound gates. I push aside sixty-foot trees and grind their branches under my treads. It is good to move again. I seek the cause of the W-Band transmissions. My long-range sensors pick up metallic shapes. I zoom-focus. Enemy! I identify Deng Class One Yavac Heavy units in the valley behind the former Base. I see Deng Class C Yavac Scouts in the forest. The Class C Scouts move on jointed appendages. They resemble their makers, moving quickly on multiple legs. The forest proves no barrier to their mode of transportation and offers concealment. They are followed closely by Class B Light-Armored Yavac units.

These units do not enter the forest. I analyze their battle formation and interpret their plan of attack. They will wait until the lightly armored Class C Scout units strike in a diversionary force through the forest. Once the colony's attention is diverted, the heavier Class B and Class One Yavacs will cut through the forest in a swathe that will flank the colony and encircle it. I attempt to turn my guns and they rotate out of control. I cannot bring my weapons to bear. I call my Commander again.

"Unit Six Seven Zero GWN to Base. Report."

"Gonner! Where are you? We found a Deng infantry probe in the forest!"

"Affirmative. I observe a force of six Class One Yavac Heavy Units, fifteen Class B Light-Armor Yavac Units, eleven Class C Yavac Scouts and approximately seven hundred infantry and forward infantry probes forming classic wedge-shaped attack formation seven hundred yards west of the former Base. I anticipate a diversionary attack on vector 085 by the Class C Yavac Scouts. The main attack force will then flank on vector 097 and encircle the colony. I have taken position a thousand yards south of the main attack force. My weapons systems remain inoperational. I await orders."

I do not recognize my Commander's next words. She speaks briefly in a language for which I have not been programmed. She then says, "I don't know how to fix you, Gonner."

"There is a 27.35 percent possibility that I have discovered a way to bypass my damaged fire-control circuits, using a cybernetic biological replacement unit."

My Commander does not answer.

"Unit Six Seven Zero GWN of the Line, awaiting orders, Commander Tennyson."

"Uh, Unit Six Seven Zero GWN, report to Base immediately. That's, uh, my house. Can you find it?"

"Affirmative."

I pivot and retrace my route. I use Emergency speed to reach the edge of the new colony. A crowd of humans has gathered in the street. I have never seen this town, but my data banks contain information uploaded from my Commander. I find her house and assume a guard position beyond the door.

"Unit Six Seven Zero GWN, reporting as ordered."

The door opens. I know my Commander. I know Dault. I know the dog Sufi. I do not see the other dog, Shiva. I do not know the woman who follows my Commander into the street.

"Unit Six Seven Zero GWN, report. What is the procedure you mentioned that might fix you?"

I give my Commander a full report.

"Unthinkable!" *This is the other woman.* "'Lima, this is madness—"

"Those are Deng warriors out there, Mother! I don't intend us to become another Donner's Party! You heard the Navy's response—we're on our own out here! No one can get to us in time."

Another voice I do not know speaks from my left flank. "'Lima, Donner had this Bolo and lost. And it's crippled. There's not much we *can* do."

Dault speaks. I hear stress in his voice. "You filthy coward! You can beat up on a kid half your size, but a real fight's too much for you? You'd better get your surgery ready, then. You're going to be busy."

The other man departs, in haste.

"Mom, can you do it?"

"I will not dissect a human being—"

"Gonner, does it have to be a human being?"

My Commander's question is a valid one. There is another suitable sentient being besides humans in the colony. I calculate the odds.

"Probability drops to 25.89 percent if a genetically enhanced dog is used in place of a human being. I cannot fight under current conditions. If I cannot fight, the Deng will eliminate this colony."

Again, I detect stress in Dault's voice. "Use Shiva. He's crippled. We'll need the other dogs."

"Mom?"

I detect no audible answer. My Commander's parent enters the house. I await further commands.

"Gonner, what do we do while you're in surgery? We've got to stall, buy enough time for Mom to try this."

I review archival information my Commander has provided.

"Agricultural and earth-moving equipment will not withstand direct hits. They may slow down the Yavac Heavy and Light-Armored Units. They should provide a barrier against infantry. Dig pits and fill them with ore-cleaning acid. Cover the pits. There will be very little time before the diversionary strike begins. The main assault will follow in approximately 5.03 minutes after the diversionary strike. You will need to situate most of your forces to counter the main attack, in case the surgical procedure on my fire-control circuits fails. Commander Tennyson, Deng are methodical. They will follow battle plans to the death. If the surgical procedure is a success, I will attack the main assault force from the rear. This will not be expected. It is our best chance of defeating a Deng force of this size."

"You heard him. Dickson, get that earth-moving equipment going. We need pits, pronto. Sally, how much of that acid does your plant have in stock?"

"Five hundred thousand gallons, give or take."

"Commandeer any heavy equipment you need to move it. There isn't much time. Sufi, you're pretty vulnerable without armor, but you can take out their advance infantry scouts and you can form ambushes in places too small for us. Take your pups and their pups and position yourselves here, here, and all along here."

My Commander points to a map of the colony. Her decisions are tactically sound. My new data tells me her father is a war hero. I am proud to serve under his daughter.

"Gonner, I've got to go. I'll stay in touch over your Command

Link. Mom's going to have to enter your personnel hatch. Brad will go with her. He's a good surgeon and he loves Shiva."

"Understood. I will advise you of my status."

My Commander leaves. Dault climbs to my turret, carrying Shiva. I ask the dog if he will agree to this procedure. He barks an affirmative. He is a brave fighter. My Commander's parent joins Dault. The procedure begins. I wait.

★**15**★

"Easy, boy, easy."

Brad could hardly bear to look after completing the surgery he'd already been required to perform, but he kept his hand on Shiva's neck and continued to murmur softly to him.

"All done." Dr. Tennyson's voice was dead flat.

He risked a look and gulped.

There wasn't much left of Shiva. His skull sprouted hardware and leads that fed directly into the Bolo's psychotronic system. His legs were similarly tapped into the fighting machine's systems. His body . . .

Brad had suspended him permanently in a steel cradle, to help cushion him from battle shocks. It was attached directly to the Bolo's internal frame at each rib. Effectively, Shiva was now part of the Bolo, which is what Gonner'd said was required.

Dr. Tennyson's voice cut into his awareness. "I've hooked his digestive system through here, to void waste. He'll require intravenous feeding—if the Bolo lives through the battle. The spinal block should be wearing off. I've put in a pain block, directly through his brain. He'll be able to function without the distraction of pain. If I've made all the proper connections, Shiva's now tied directly into the Bolo's psychotronic circuitry. All we have to do now is see if this crazy plan works."

On the Bolo's view screens, Brad caught a glimpse of the pitched battle being waged at the edge of town. Another house went up in a fireball.

"Gonner, how about it?"

The Bolo spoke. "Shiva, move right paw. Stop."

"Well?"

"My Hellbore guns and energy repeaters track satisfactorily. The arrangement is not efficient, but it is functional."

Brad probably should have whooped in satisfaction. All he felt was grief and fear.

"Well, that's that. Let's go." Dr. Tennyson glanced around the Bolo's passenger compartment, then climbed out. Brad hesitated.

"Bradley?" Dr. Tennyson called down. "You're delaying the Bolo."

He started for the ladder. Shiva whined and tried to thrash inside the steel cradle. Brad returned to his friend and laid his hand on the dog's neck again. It was just about the only spot of fur left on him Brad *could* touch.

"Easy, boy. I'm not going anywhere." He tilted his head. "Get clear, Dr. Tennyson. We have a battle to fight. Gonner, please inform your Commander that we're ready for battle."

"Understood. Welcome aboard, sir."

Overhead, the hatch sealed with a faint hiss of pneumatics.

Brad strapped into the observer's chair and maintained contact with his dog's fur.

"Let's go." He tried to smile. "Dog-Gonner ready for battle."

Shiva emitted a faint whine of eagerness.

The Bolo pivoted and cleared a path out of town, taking off the corner of one burning house to gain maneuvering room. Brad glued his gaze to the observation screens and tightened his hand through Shiva's fur.

"Go get 'em, boy."

As the Enemy Yavac units came into focus on the observation screen, Bradley said as offhandedly as he could, "Did I ever tell you about the moment I started falling in love with Kalima Tennyson, Gonner? She punched me in the nose . . ."

★**16**★

From behind her hastily-dug entrenchment, Kalima watched the advancing Deng through Gina Lin's survey lens. The distance was telemetered automatically from the size-scale comparison computer. Fred Howlett had tried using an active-system laser range finder and the Deng had locked onto it and blown it up. Fred hadn't survived. The passive-system survey scanner was far more primitive equipment, but it was effective and kept the Deng from locking in on her position.

The main assault force had struck through the trees on the ridge and now rolled down across their defensive perimeter. Over on the edge of town, where the diversionary force had struck first, they were losing ground in enormous bites. Several buildings—homes, the school—were fiercely ablaze.

"We're not holding," she muttered. "Gonner, where are you?"

The Bolo had reported battle readiness more than five minutes previously. Meanwhile, the Deng had blasted through the barricade of heavy equipment they'd set up. Several Class C Yavac Scouts and some of the forward infantry had fallen into acid pits; but the heavier Class B and Class One Yavacs which followed them avoided the carefully laid traps. Infantry units, also skirting the remaining acid pits, were pouring through the gaps in their defenses. Fighting down there was hand-to-hand—and their side was dying.

Trees at the crest of the hill swayed and toppled. Kalima held her breath . . .

Hellbore guns thundered above the deafening sound of Yavac fire. The first salvo had little effect. On the second blast, a Yavac was hit directly in the turret. The Deng unit exploded in a brilliant fireball. A ragged cheer went up. Gonner sped forward. Rear infantry units went down under a blaze of lethal anti-personnel fire. The massive Hellbores tracked, corrected slightly, and belched fire again. Another Yavac unit exploded.

The rearmost Yavac pivoted its guns and fired back. Gonner rocked under the concussion, but kept coming. Other heavy Class One Yavacs turned and blasted the Bolo with deadly fire. Gonner's purple-black flintsteel hull began to glow, as his energy panels attempted to absorb the murderous energy beams and convert them to useful battle energy. Blue fire streaked out from his turret's infinite repeaters. A Yavac Class One caught the blast at its turret juncture and blew open. Fire exploded out of it. Kalima bit her lips. She could see pieces of Gonner's ablative armor blown clear as Yavac Class B units turned and added their fire to that of the remaining Yavac Heavies. Gonner charged down the ridge toward town on a relentless, unstoppable course that took him past one dying Yavac after another. Several units retreated fatally into open acid pits behind their positions as they attempted to avoid the onrushing Bolo.

"Look! They're scattering! They're breaking formation!"

Dogs broke from hiding all along the enemy flank. Deng infantry went down under snarling canine jaws. Kalima glued her gaze to the surveyor's lenses and snarled in satisfaction. The dogs chewed off legs and arms, bit into unarmored, hairy Deng bellies. Weird, alien screams floated down the street. The Hellbores barked again. A final Yavac Heavy died. Gonner turned on the smaller Class B and C Yavacs and blasted them with brilliant blue repeater fire. On the opposite flank, colonists rose behind barricades and earthen embankments and fired small arms into the mass of panicked Deng. Kalima fired her own rifle with lethal effect.

The army stampeded toward the remaining camouflaged acid pits, trying to retreat the way they'd come and stumbling into the lethal traps they'd avoided on their way in.

"They're going for 'em!" Kalima yelled. "They're going right for 'em!"

Within ten minutes, there were only scattered wounded left of the Deng invasion force. Most of their infantry had plunged into the acid pits. The heavily armored Yavacs were burnt-out hulks— or dissolved bits of metal at the bottom of the acid pits. On the forested slope—now denuded, deeply scarred from the terrible battle—Yavacs still burned fiercely. Colonists rose on all sides, cheering spontaneously.

Kalima rose on shaky legs and started down the street. She gripped a rifle in one hand, her radio link to Gonner in the other.

"Gonner, report."

"Enemy neutralized. I have sustained serious damage."

Heart in her mouth, Kalima closed the distance to the enormous war machine.

New gouges tore into Gonner's war hull. One of his treads was missing. He must've sustained damage to it and blown it clear. Anti-personnel guns along his right flank were twisted, ruined. His turret was badly gouged, canted on its swivel.

"Unit Six Seven Zero GWN and Unit Shiva reporting, as ordered. Bradley Dault requests assistance disengaging. My passenger compartment and hatch have sustained damage."

"Bradley? My God—is Bradley in there with you?"

"He refused to leave. Unit Shiva required Bradley Dault's presence to maintain battle-ready efficiency."

She understood, in a flash of insight. *Poor, terrified dog* . . .

"Gonner, how can I get to him?"

"The pneumatics on my turret hatch no longer function. You will require an explosive charge to clear the hatch from my hull. The battle damage which penetrated into the passenger compartment is not sufficiently large to extricate an adult human."

Kalima swallowed hard, then called Gina Lin over. She explained what was needed.

"Sure. Take, uh, maybe ten minutes."

"Gonner, what other damage have you sustained?"

"An explosion through previous battle damage has destroyed my backup emergency power cells. I am operating on residual charge from my hull-plate grid. I cannot discover any method of repairing this damage in the time which remains before this charge drains. I estimate another fifteen minutes before critical failure occurs. Unit Shiva has sustained fatal injury to spleen and kidneys as result of shrapnel damage. We request permission to retire from the field as soon as Bradley Dault has been safely extricated from my passenger compartment."

No backup power cells left. And there never had been a way to refuel his fission plant. No one here was qualified to install a new one—even if one had been available. There was nothing—not a thing—she could do to save him.

The words caught in her throat. "Permission granted."

Lin was setting the explosive charges. Kalima climbed up to help. She talked to Gonner the whole time.

"Remember that first day, Gonner? You scared me half to death. Never thought we'd see battle together, big guy. I'm sure proud of you, though, more than I was that day you kept the wall from crushing us . . ."

She was babbling and didn't care. She was losing a friend—two friends—and no one knew yet how badly injured Bradley was in there. He could be dying, too . . .

"All set. Get clear, 'Lima."

They skinned down the ladder and took refuge behind a scarred fender.

The charge blew. Smoke engulfed them. Kalima was climbing even before her ears stopped ringing.

"Brad! Brad, can you hear me?"

"Com-coming up . . ."

She hovered at the lip of the hatch. He moved slowly, awkwardly. His right arm didn't appear to be functioning properly. Tears streaked his face. Halfway up, his breath caught sharply. He clung to the ladder.

"I'm coming down to help."

"No . . . I'm okay. See?" He climbed higher.

Shock made her go cold.

Blood covered his whole right side. She could see ribs in one spot. But he was still climbing. His face and arms were burned, blistered in places from the heat of the sustained Yavac attack. She got an arm around his shoulders. He snaked his good arm around her and kissed her raggedly; then groaned and leaned heavily against her.

"Gotta . . . get down . . . or I'll fall . . ."

Kalima steadied him down. He slid to his knees the moment his feet touched ground.

"Did it, Gonner," he whispered hoarsely. "We did it."

"It was my honor to serve with you, Bradley Dault. Commander Tennyson, I estimate another 4.07 minutes before critical power failure. Unit Six Seven Zero GWN and Unit Shiva of the Line, retiring as ordered."

The Bolo pivoted awkwardly on its remaining track. The machine clanked and rattled up the ridge and into the trees. Parallel gouges in the soft earth marked his trail. Someone, she wasn't sure who, had pulled Bradley onto a stretcher. He caught her hand, urged her down.

"Go with him," he whispered. "Nobody should die alone."

Her eyes filled. She kissed Brad very tenderly. Her voice went husky. "Don't you dare die on me, too, Bradley Dault. This . . . this won't take long." He squeezed her hand. Then she broke and ran.

Kalima found Gonner in his former position, atop the shattered gates at the old compound.

"Gonner?"

The Hellbores tracked disjointedly in a ragged salute.

She climbed doggedly and slid down through the blasted hatch. A hole had been punched straight into the passenger compartment. Relays and boards she'd spent years repairing were twisted, broken beyond anyone's capacity to repair. Her breath caught when she saw Shiva. The dog whined, very faintly.

"Good boy," she whispered, burying her face in the dog's blood-spattered neck fur. "Brad's okay, Shiva. You did a good job. The town's safe."

Shiva licked her hand very weakly. Then what remained of his body sagged in the steel cradle. Kalima turned away and dragged the back of a dirty arm across her eyes.

"You did a good job, Gonner," she choked out. The whole passenger compartment reeked of blood, smoke, fried electrical connections.

"I have done my duty. It is a beautiful day for victory, Commander." The observation screens flickered and went dim. "Bradley Dault spoke at length of you, Commander, as we went to meet the Enemy. He is a good officer. I am glad he was not damaged fatally. He loved Shiva. He loves you."

"I love you, Gonner," she whispered. "I— Thank you for . . . for . . ."

She couldn't get it all out quickly enough, with the result that everything she wanted to say got stuck in her throat.

"It has been my honor to serve you, Commander Tennyson. I will hold . . ."

The screens went dark.

Very, very slowly, Kalima climbed out of the blasted passenger compartment. The great Hellbore guns drooped, silent. Warm summer wind whistled across the pitted war hull.

Gonner didn't speak again.

But he had held, to the last.

AS OUR STRENGTH
★LESSENS★

David Drake

Dawn is three hours away, but the sky to the east burns orange and sulphur and deep, sullen red. The rest of my battalion fights there, forcing the Enemy's main line of resistance.

That is not my concern. I have been taken out of reserve and tasked to eliminate an Enemy outpost. The mission appears to me to be one which could have waited until our spearhead had successfully breached the enemy line, but strategic decisions are made by the colloid minds of my human superiors. So be it.

When ion discharges make the night fluoresce, they also tear holes of static in the radio communications spectrum. " . . . *roadwh* . . . *and suspe* . . ." reports one of my comrades.

Even my enhancement program is unable to decode more of the transmission than that, but I recognize the fist of the sender: *Saratoga*, part of the lead element of our main attack. His running gear has been damaged. He will have to drop out of line.

My forty-seven pairs of flint-steel roadwheels are in depot condition. Their tires of spun beryllium monocrystal, woven to deform rather than compress, all have 97% or better of their fabric unbroken. The immediate terrain is semi-arid. The briefing files inform me this is typical of the planet. My track links purr among themselves as they grind through scrub vegetation and the friable soil, carrying me to my assigned mission.

There is a cataclysmic fuel-air explosion to the east behind me. The glare is visible for 5.3 seconds, and the ground will shake for many minutes as shock waves echo through the planetary mantle.

Had my human superiors so chosen, I could be replacing *Saratoga* at the spearhead of the attack.

The rear elements of the infantry are in sight now. They look like dung beetles in their hard suits, crawling backward beneath a rain of shrapnel. I am within range of their low-power communications net. "*Hold what you got, troops,*" orders the unit's acting commander. "*Big Brother's come to help!*"

I am not Big Brother. I am *Maldon*, a Mark XXX Bolo of the 3d Battalion, Dinochrome Brigade. The lineage of our unit goes back to the 2nd South Wessex Dragoons. In 1944, we broke the last German resistance on the path to Falaise—though we traded our flimsy Cromwells against the Tigers at a ratio of six to one to do it.

The citizens do not need to know what the cost is. They need only to know that the mission has been accomplished. The battle honors welded to my turret prove that I have always accomplished my mission.

Though this task should not have been a difficult one, even for the company of infantry to whom it was originally assigned. An Enemy research facility became, because of its location, an outpost on the flank of our line as we began to drive out of the landing zone. In a breakthrough battle, infantry can do little but die in their fighting suits. A company of them was sent to mop up the outpost in relative safety.

Instead . . .

As I advance, I review the ongoing mission report filed in real-time by the infantry and enhanced at Headquarters before being downloaded to me microseconds later. My mind forms the blips of digital information into a panorama, much as the colloid minds of my superiors process sensory data fired into them across nerve endings.

Vehicles brought the infantry within five kilometers of their objective. There they disembarked for tactical flexibility and to avoid giving the Enemy a single soft target of considerable value.

I watch:

The troops advance by tiny, jerky movements of the legs of their hard suits. My tracks, rotating in silky precision, purr with laughter.

The concept of vertical envelopment, overflying an enemy's lines to drop forces in his rear, ceased to be viable with the appearance of directed-energy weapons in the 20th century. After the development of such weapons, any target which could be seen—even in orbit above an atmosphere—could be hit at the speed of light.

No flying vehicle could be armored heavily enough to withstand attack by powerful beam weapons. The alternative was more of the grinding ground assaults to which civilians always object because they are costly and brutal, and to which soldiers always turn because they succeed when finesse does not succeed.

Our forces have landed on an empty, undefended corner of this planet. The blazing combat to the east occurs as our forces meet those which the Enemy is rushing into place to block us.

I am not at my accustomed place in the front line, but the Enemy will not stop the advance of my comrades.

I watch:

The leading infantry elements have come in sight of their objective. There is something wrong with the data, because the Enemy research facility appears as a spherical flaw—an absence of information—in the transmitted images.

Light blinks from the anomaly. It is simply that, light, with the balance and intensity of the local solar output at ground level on this planet.

The infantry assume they are being attacked. They respond with lasers and projectile weapons as they take cover and unlimber heavier ordnance. Within .03 seconds of the first shot, the Enemy begins to rake the infantry positions with small arms fire.

While the battalion was in transit to our target, briefing files were downloaded into our data banks. These files, the distillation of truth and wisdom by our human superiors, state that the Enemy is scientifically far inferior to ourselves. There is no evidence that the Enemy even has a working stardrive now, though unquestionably at some past time they colonized the scores of star systems which they still inhabit.

Enemy beam weapons are admittedly very efficient. The Enemy achieves outputs from hand-held devices which our forces can duplicate only with large vehicle-mounted units. Our scientific staff still has questions regarding the power sources which feed these Enemy beam weapons.

Thus far the briefing files. I have examined the schematics of captured Enemy lasers. The schematics show no power source whatever. This is interesting, but it does not affect the certainty of our victory.

Initially, the Enemy outpost to which I have been tasked was not using weapons more powerful than the small arms which our own infantry carry.

I watch:

The infantry is well trained. Three-man teams shoot and advance in a choreographed sequence, directing a steady volume of fire at the outpost. At the present range it is unlikely that their rifles and lasers will do serious damage. The purpose of this fire is to disrupt the Enemy's aim and morale while more effective weapons can be brought to bear. The heavy-weapons section is deploying back-pack rockets and the company's light ion cannon.

An infantryman ripple-fires his four-round rocket pack. The small missiles are self-guiding and programmed to vary their courses to the laser-cued target.

Three of the rockets curve wildly across the bleak terrain and detonate when they exhaust their fuel. They have been unable to fix on the reflected laser beam which should have provided the precise range of the target. The anomaly has absorbed the burst of coherent light so perfectly that none bounces back to be received by the missiles' homing devices. Only the first round of the sequence, directed on a line-straight track, seems to reach the target.

The missile vanishes. There is no explosion. At .03 seconds after the computed moment of impact—there is no direct evidence that the rocket actually hit its target—the Enemy outpost launches a dozen small missiles of its own. One of them destroys the ion cannon before the crew can open fire.

Puffs of dirt mark the battlefield. The infantry is using powered augers to dig in for greater protection. The Enemy outpost continues to rake the troops with rockets and small arms, oblivious of the infantry's counterfire.

Seven hours before planetfall, a human entered the bay where we Bolos waited in our thoughts and memories. He wore the trousers of an officer's dress uniform, but he had taken off the blouse with the insignia of his rank.

The human's face and name were in my data banks. He was Major Peter Bowen, a member of the integral science staff of our invasion force. My analysis of the air Bowen exhaled indicated a blood alcohol level of .1763 parts per hundred. He moved with drunken care.

"Good evening, Third Battalion," Bowen said. He attempted a bow. He caught himself with difficulty on a bulkhead when he started to fall over. I realized that the bay was not lighted in the human-visible spectrum. Bowen had no business here with us, but he was a human and an officer. I switched on the yellow navigation lights along my fender skirts.

Bowen walked toward me. "Hello, Bolo," he said. "Do you have a name?"

I did not answer. My name was none of his concern; and anyway, it did not appear that he was really speaking to me. Humans often say meaningless things. Perhaps that is why they rule and we serve.

"None of my business, hey, buddy?" said Bowen. "There's been a lot of that goin' around lately." He was not a fool, and it appeared that he was less incapacitated by drink than I had assumed.

He reached out to my treads. I thought he was steadying his drunken sway, but instead the scientist's fingers examined the spun crystal pads of a track block. "Colonel McDougal says I'm not to brief the battalion tasking officers because that's been taken care of by real experts. Colonel McDougal's a regular officer, so he oughta know, right?"

The situation shocked me. "Colonel McDougal is your direct superior, Major Bowen," I said.

"Oh, you bet McDougal's superior to me," Bowen said in what should have been agreement but clearly was not. "He'll be the first to tell you so, the Colonel will. I'm just a civilian with a commission. Only—I figured that since I was here, maybe I ought to do my job."

"Your job is to carry out your superior's orders to the best of your ability," I replied.

Bowen chuckled. "You too," he said. His hands caressed my bow slope. My battle honors are welded to my turret, but the flint-steel of my frontal armor bears scars which tell the same story to those who can read them.

"What's your name, friend?" Bowen asked.

My name is my password, which Bowen is not authorized to know. I do not reply.

He looked at me critically. "You're Maldon," he said, "Grammercy's your tasking officer."

I am shocked. Bowen could have learned that only from Captain Grammercy himself. Why would Grammery have spoken what was his duty to conceal? It is not my duty to understand colloid minds; but I sometimes think that if I could, I would be better able carry out the tasks they set me.

"You know the poem, at least?" Bowen added.

It was several microseconds before I realized that this, though inane, was really meant as a question. "Of course," I said. All the human arts are recorded in my data banks.

"And you know that the Earl of Essex was a fool?" said Bowen. "That he threw his army away and left his lands open to pillage because of his stupidity?"

"His bodyguards were heroes!" I retorted. "They were steadfast!"

The bay echoed with my words, but Bowen did not flinch back from me. "All honor to their courage!" he snapped. I remembered that I had thought he was drunk and a disgrace to the uniform he—partly—wore. "They took the orders of a fool. And died, which was no dishonor. *And* left their lands to be raped by Vikings, which was no honor to them or their memory, Maldon!"

The retainers of the Earl of Essex were tasked to prevent Vikings under Olaf Tryggvason from pillaging the county. The Earl withdrew his forces from a blocking position in order to bring the enemy to open battle at Maldon. His bodyguards fought heroically but were defeated.

The Earl's bodyguards failed to accomplish their mission. There is no honor in failure.

"What did you wish to tell us, Major Bowen?" I asked.

The human coughed. He looked around the bay before he replied. His eyes had adapted to the glow of my running lights.

My comrades of the 3d Battalion listened silently to the conversation. To a creature of Bowen's size, fifty-one motionless Bolos must have loomed like features of a landscape rather than objects constructed by tools in human hands.

"The accepted wisdom," Bowen said, "is that the Anceti are scientifically backward. That the race has degenerated from an advanced level of scientific ability, and that the remnants of that science are no threat to human arms."

He patted the flint-steel skirt protecting my track and roadwheels. "No serious threat to you and your friends, Maldon."

"Yes," I said, because I thought a human would have spoken . . . though there was no need to tell Bowen what he already knew was in the official briefing files.

"I don't believe the Anceti are degenerate," Bowen said. "And I *sure* don't think they're ignorant. Nobody who's turning out lasers like theirs is ignorant. They've got a flux density of ten times our best—and there's not even a hint of a power source."

"The Enemy no longer has stardrive," I said, as if I were stating a fact instead of retailing information from the briefing files. This is a technique humans use when they wish to elicit information from other humans.

"Balls!" Bowen said. He did not speak as a human and my superior. Instead, his voice had the sharpness of a cloud as it spills lightning to the ground, careless and certain of its path. "Do you believe that, Maldon? Is that the best the mind of a Bolo Mark XXX can do synthesizing data?"

I was stung. "So the briefing files stated," I replied, "and I have no information to contradict—"

"Balls!" Bowen repeated.

I said nothing.

After a moment, the scientist continued, "There's a better than 99% probability that the Anceti are reinforcing their outpost worlds under threat of our attack. How are they doing that if they don't have stardrive, Maldon?"

I reviewed my data banks. "Reconnaissance shows the strengthened facilities," I said. I already knew how Bowen was going to respond. "Reconnaissance does not show that the equipment and personnel were imported from outside the worlds on which they are now based."

"We're talking about barren rocks, some of these planets," Bowen said. His tone dripped with disgust. I choose to believe that was a human rhetorical device rather than his real opinion of my intellect. "The Anceti and their hardware didn't spring from rocks, Maldon; they were brought there. A better than 99% probability. We just don't know how."

"The briefing files are wrong," I said. I spoke aloud to show the human that I understood.

They rule and we serve. We know one truth at a time, but colloid minds believe contradictory truths or no truth at all. So be it.

There was a question that I could not resolve, no matter how I attempted to view the information at my disposal. I needed more data. So—

"Why are you telling us this, Major Bowen?" I asked.

"Because I want you to understand," the human said fiercely, "that the Anceti's science *isn't* inferior to ours, it's just different. Like the stardrive. Did you know that every one of the star systems the Anceti have colonized at some point in galactic history crossed a track some other Anceti star system occupied? Or *will* occupy!"

I reviewed my data banks. The information was of course there, but I had not analyzed it for this purpose.

"There is no indication that the Enemy has time travel, Major

Bowen," I said. "Except the data you cite, which could be explained by an assumption of time travel."

"I know that, I know that," Bowen replied. His voice rose toward hysteria, but he caught himself in mid-syllable. "I don't say they have time travel, I don't *believe* they have time travel. But they've got something, Maldon. I know they've got something."

"We will accomplish our mission, Major Bowen," I said to soothe him.

Some humans hate us for our strength and our difference from them, even though they know we are the starkest bulwark against their Enemies. Most humans treat us as the tools of their wills, as is their right. But a very few humans are capable of concern for minds and personalities, though they are encased in flint-steel and ceramic rather than protoplasm.

All humans are to be protected. Some are to be cherished.

"Oh, I don't doubt you'll accomplish *your* mission, Maldon," Bowen said, letting his fingers pause at the gouge in my bow slope where an arc knife struck me a glancing blow. "But I've failed in mine."

He made the sound of laughter, but there was no humor in it. "That's why I'm drunk, you see." He cleared his throat. "Well, I was drunk. And I'll be drunk again, real soon."

"You have not failed, Major Bowen," I said. "You have corrected the faulty analysis of others."

"I haven't corrected anything, Maldon," the human said. "I can't give them a mechanism for whatever the Anceti are doing, so nobody in the task force believes me. Nobody even listens. They're too happy saying that the Anceti are a bunch of barbarians we're going to mop up without difficulties."

"We believe you, Major Bowen," I said. I spoke for all my comrades in the 3d Battalion, though they remained silent on the audio frequencies. "We will be ready to react to new tricks and weapons of the Enemy."

"That's good, Maldon," said the human. He squeezed my armor with more force than I had thought his pudgy fingers could achieve. "Because you're the guys who're going to pay the price if Colonel McDougal's wisdom is wrong."

He turned and walked back to the hatchway. "Now," he added, "I'm going to get drunk."

I wonder where Major Bowen is now. Somewhere in Command, some place as safe as any on a planet at war. Behind me, the main battle rages in a fury of shock waves and actinic radiation. It is hard fought, but the exchanges of fire are within expected parameters.

The mission to which I have been assigned, on the other hand . . .

The infantry company called in artillery support as soon as the Enemy outpost began strafing them with back-pack missiles.

I watch:

The first pair of artillery rockets streaks over the horizon.

The missiles' sustainer motors have burned out, but the bands of maneuvering jets around each armor-piercing warhead flash as they course-correct. They are targeted by triangulation from fixed points, since the outpost itself remains perfectly absorbant throughout the electro-optical band. These are probing rounds, intended to test the Enemy's anti-artillery defenses so that the main barrage can be protected by appropriate countermeasures.

The Enemy has no defenses. The shells plunge into the center of the anomaly and disappear, just as all earlier projectiles and energy beams have done. Neither these shells nor the barrage which follows has any discernible effect on the Enemy.

.03 seconds from the first warhead's calculated moment of impact, the research facility begins to bombard our attacking infantry with artillery rockets.

The Enemy is firing armor-piercing rounds. They are already at terminal velocity when they appear from the anomaly. When the warheads explode deep underground, the soil spews up and flings dug-in infantrymen flailing into air. Sometimes the hard suits protect the infantry well enough that the victims are able to crawl away under their own power.

Back-pack missiles and small arms fire from the outpost continue to rake the infantry positions. The company commander orders his troops to withdraw. 5.4 seconds later, the acting company commander calls for a Bolo to be assigned in support.

The air over the battlefield is a pall of black dust, lighted fitfully by orange flashes at its heart.

I am now within the extreme range even of small arms fired from the research facility. The Enemy does not engage me. Shells launched from the anomaly continue to pound the infantry's initial deployment area, smashing the remains of fighting suits into smaller fragments. The surviving infantry have withdrawn from the killing ground.

Friendly missiles continue to vanish into the anomaly without effect.

Thus far I have observed the outpost only through passive receptors. I take a turret-down position on the reverse slope of a hill and raise an active ranging device on a sacrificial mounting above my protective armor. Using this mast-mounted unit, I probe the anomaly with monopulse emissions on three spectra.

There is no echo from the anomaly. .03 seconds after the pulses should have ranged the target, the outpost directs small arms fire and a pair of artillery rockets at me.

The bullets and low-power laser beams are beneath my contempt. The sacrificial sensor pod is the only target I have exposed to direct fire. It is not expected to survive contact with an enemy, but the occasional hit the pod receives at this range barely scratches its surface.

As for the artillery fire—the Enemy is not dealing with defenseless infantry now. I open a micro-second window and EMP the shells, destroying their control circuitry. The ring thrusters shut off and the warheads go ballistic. Neither shell will impact within fifty meters of my present location.

.03 seconds from the moment I fried the Enemy warheads, a high-amplitude electromagnetic pulse from the anomaly meets the next of the shells raining in from friendly artillery batteries. The warhead has already made its final course corrections, so it plunges into the calculated center of the target. The electronic fuzing will probably have failed under the EMP attack, but the back-up mechanical detonators should still function.

It is impossible to tell whether the mechanical fuzes work: there is, as I have come to expect, no sign even of kinetic impact with the anomaly.

The outpost launches two more missiles and a storm of small arms fire at me. The missiles course-correct early. They will strike me even if their control circuits are destroyed.

To the east, the air continues to flash and thunder over the Enemy's main line of resistance. Casualties there are heavy but within expected parameters. My comrades will make their initial breakthrough within five hours and thirty-seven minutes, unless there is a radical change in Enemy strength.

This research facility is far from the population centers of this planet. Did the Enemy place it in so isolated a location because they realized the risk of disaster at the cutting edge of the forces they were studying desperately to meet our assault?

I know they've got something, Major Bowen told me. He was right. The real battle will not be decided along the main line but rather here.

I open antenna apertures to send peremptory signals to Command, terminating the artillery fire mission. I use spread-transmission radio—which may be blocked by war-roiled static across the electromagnetic spectrum; laser—which will be received only if all the repeaters along the transmission path have survived combat; and ground conduction, which is slow but effectively beyond jamming.

Friendly artillery has no observable effect on the outpost, and it interjects a variable into the situation. All variables thus far appear to have benefited the Enemy.

While I deliver instructions and a report to Command, and while my mind gropes for a template which will cover my observations thus far of the Enemy's capabilities, I deal with the incoming missiles. I spin a pair of fluctuating apertures in my turret shielding. The gaps are aligned with the lifting muzzles of my infinite repeaters and in synchronous with their cyclic rate.

I fire. Pulses along the superconducting magnets in the bores of the infinite repeaters accelerate short tubes of depleted uranium—ring penetrators—to astronomical velocity. Miniature suns blaze from kinetic impact where my penetrators intersect the warheads. The missiles lose aerodynamic stability. They tumble in glowing cartwheels across the sky.

.03 seconds after I engage the warheads, a burst of hyper-velocity ring penetrators from the anomaly shreds my sacrificial sensor pod.

My capacity to store and access information is orders of magnitude beyond that of the colloid minds I serve, but even so only part of the knowledge in my data banks is available to me at any one moment. Now, while I replace the sensors and six more missiles streak toward me out of the anomaly, I hear the baritone voice of the technician replacing my port-side roadwheels during depot service seventy-four years ago.

He sings: *Get in, get out, quit muckin' about—*
Drive on!

My data processing system has mimicked a colloid mind to short-circuit my decision tree. I have been passive under attack for long enough.

I advance, blowing the hillcrest in front of me so that I do not expose my belly plates by lifting over it.

Both direct and indirect fire have battlefield virtues. Direct fire is limited by terrain and, if the weapon is powerful enough, by the curvature of the planet itself. But, though the curving path of indirect fire can reach any target, the warheads have necessarily longer flight times and lower terminal velocities because of their trajectory. When they hit, they are less effective than direct-fire projectile weapons; and the most devastating artillery of all, directed energy weapons, can operate only in the direct-fire mode.

The worst disadvantage of direct fire weapons is that the shooter must by definition be in sight of his target. Bolos are designed to be seen by our targets and survive.

My tracks accelerate me through the cloud of pulverized rock where the hillcrest used to be. The infinite repeaters in my turret hammer the anomaly with continuous fire. I am mixing ring penetrators and high explosive in a random pattern based on cosmic ray impacts.

I hope this will confuse the Enemy defenses. The only evident effect of my tactic is that, .03 seconds from the time the first HE round should have hit the anomaly, the Enemy begins to include high-explosive rounds in the bursts which flash harmlessly against my electromagnetic shielding.

I am clear of the rock dust. I align myself with the anomaly and fire my Hellbore from its centerline hull installation.

Even *my* mass is jolted by the Hellbore's recoil. A laser-compressed thermonuclear explosion at the breech end voids a slug of ions down the axis of the bore, the only path left open. The bolt can devour mountains or split rock on planets in distant orbits.

My Hellbore has no discernible effect on the anomaly; but .03 seconds after I fire, an ion bolt smashes into me.

I am alive. For nearly a second, I am sure of nothing else. Circuits, shut down to avoid burning out under overload, come back on line.

I have received serious injuries. My hull and running gear are essentially undamaged. Most of the anti-personnel charges along my skirts have gone off in a single white flash. This is of no importance, since it now appears vanishingly improbable that I will ever see Enemy personnel.

87% of my external communications equipment has been destroyed. Most of the antennas have vaporized, despite the shutters of flint-steel which were to protect them. I reroute circuits and rotate back-up antennas from my hull core.

My infinite repeaters were cycling when the ion bolt struck. Ions ravening through the aperture in my electromagnetic shielding destroyed both infinite repeaters, bathed the hull and wiped it clean of most external fittings, and penetrated the turret itself through one of the weapons ports. All armament and sensory installations within my turret have been fused into a metal-ceramic magma.

The turret ring is not blocked, and the drive mechanism still works. I rotate the turret so that the back instead of the hopelessly compromised frontal armor faces the anomaly.

Data clicks into a gestalt which explains the capabilities which the Enemy has demonstrated.

I brake my starboard track while continuing to accelerate with the port drive motors. My hull slews. The change in direction throws a comber of earth and rock toward the outpost. Though my size and inertia are so great that I cannot completely dodge the Enemy's second ion bolt, the suspension of soil in air dissipates much of the charge in a fireball and thunderclap. My hull shakes, but the only additional damage I receive is to some of the recently replaced communications gear.

I am transmitting my conclusions to Command via all the channels available to me. I load a message torpedo intended for communication under the most adverse conditions. This is a suitable occasion for its use.

The Hellbore discharge has disrupted the guidance systems of the artillery rockets the Enemy launched at me seconds earlier. In the momentary silence following the bolt's near miss, I release my torpedo. It streaks away to warn Command. The Enemy ignore the torpedo in the chaos of their own tumbling shells.

The Enemy is not mirroring matter. Rather, the Enemy mirrors facets of temporal reality. Our forces have seen no evidence of Enemy stardrive because for the Enemy, a planet can fill a point in space where it once existed or will one day exist. The Enemy need not transit the eternal present so long as there is a congruity between Now and When.

Personnel of the research facility I have been tasked to eliminate have developed the technique still further. They are creating a special space-time in which whatever can exist, *does* exist for them so long as there is an example of the occurrence in their reality matrix.

Their tool is the anomaly that appears from outside to be a non-reflecting void. It is a tunable discontinuity in the local space-time. The staff of the research facility use this window to capture templates, copies of which are in .03 seconds shuttled into present reality and redirected at their opponents.

The research facility can already mimic the firepower of an infantry company, a battery of rocket artillery, and—because of my actions—a Mark XXX Bolo. I have only one option.

There is no cover for an object my size between me and the

research facility. Though my drive motors are spinning at full power, nothing material can outrun the bolt of a Hellbore. The third discharge catches me squarely.

The shockwave blasts a doughnut from the soil around me. My turret becomes a white-hot fireball. The electromagnetic generators in the turret were damaged by the initial bolt and could not provide more than 60% of their designed screening capacity against the second direct hit. My port skirts are blasted off; several track links bind momentarily. My drive motors have enough torque to break the welds, but again I slow and skid in a jolting S-turn.

My target is a research facility. It is possible that the Enemy will not be able to develop similar capabilities anywhere else before our forces have smashed them into defeat. That is beyond my control— and outside my mission. *This* is the target I have been tasked to eliminate.

I open the necessary circuits and bypass the interlocks. A disabled Bolo is too valuable to be abandoned, so there have to be ways.

I have no offensive armament. My Hellbore is operable, but the third ion bolt welded the gunport shutters closed. A salvo of armor-piercing shells hammers my hull, lifting me and slamming me back to the ground in a red-orange cataclysm. The multiple impacts strip my starboard track.

I think of Major Bowen, and of the Saxon bodyguards striding forward to die at Maldon:

Heart grow stronger, will firmer,
Mind more composed, as our strength lessens.

The citizens do not need to know what the cost is. They need only to know that the mission has been accomplished.

My sole regret, as I initiate the scuttling sequence that will send my fusion pile critical, is that I will not be present in .03 seconds. I would like to watch as the Enemy try to vent an omnidirectional thermonuclear explosion into their research facility.

★THE TRAITOR★

DAVID WEBER

Cold, bone-dry winter wind moaned as the titanic vehicle rumbled down the valley at a steady fifty kilometers per hour. Eight independent suspensions, four forward and four aft, spread across the full width of its gigantic hull, supported it, and each ten-meter-wide track sank deep into the soil of the valley floor. A dense cloud of dust—talcum-fine, abrasive, and choking as death—plumed up from road wheels five meters high, but the moving mountain's thirty-meter-high turret thrust its Hellbore clear of the churning cocoon. For all its size and power, it moved with unearthly quiet, and the only sounds were the whine of the wind, the soft purr of fusion-powered drive trains, the squeak of bogies, and the muted clatter of track links.

The Bolo ground forward, sensor heads swiveling, and the earth trembled with its passing. It rolled through thin, blowing smoke and the stench of high explosives with ponderous menace, altering course only to avoid the deepest craters and the twisted wrecks of alien fighting vehicles. In most places, those wrecks lay only in ones and twos; in others, they were heaped in shattered breastworks, clustered so thickly it was impossible to bypass them. When that happened, the eerie quiet of the Bolo's advance vanished into the screaming anguish of crushing alloy as it forged straight ahead,

249

trampling them under its thirteen thousand tons of death and destruction.

It reached an obstacle too large even for it to scale. Only a trained eye could have identified that torn and blasted corpse as another Bolo, turned broadside on to block the Enemy's passage even in death, wrecked Hellbore still trained down the valley, missile cell hatches open on empty wells which had exhausted their ammunition. Fifteen enemy vehicles lay dead before it, mute testimony to the ferocity of its last stand, but the living Bolo didn't even pause. There was no point, for the dead Bolo's incandescent duralloy hull radiated the waste heat of the failing fusion bottle which had disemboweled it. Not even its unimaginably well-armored Survival Center could have survived, and the living Bolo simply altered heading to squeeze past it. Igneous rock cried out in pain as a moving, armored flank scraped the valley face on one side, and the dead Bolo shuddered on the other as its brother's weight shouldered it aside.

The moving Bolo had passed four dead brigade mates in the last thirty kilometers, and it was not unwounded itself. Two of its starboard infinite repeaters had been blasted into mangled wreckage, energy weapon hits had sent molten splatters of duralloy weeping down its glacis plate to freeze like tears of pain, a third of its after sensor arrays had been stripped away by a near miss, and its forward starboard track shield was jammed in the lowered position, buckled and rent by enemy fire. Its turret bore the ID code 25/D-0098-ART and the unsheathed golden sword of a battalion commander, yet it was alone. Only one other unit of its battalion survived, and that unit lay ahead, beyond this death-choked valley. It was out there somewhere, moving even now through the trackless, waterless Badlands of the planet Camlan, and unit ART of the Line rumbled steadily down the valley to seek it out.

I interrogate my inertial navigation system as I approach my immediate objective. The INS is not the most efficient way to determine my position, but Camlan's entire orbital network, including the recon and nav sats, as well as the communication relays, perished in the Enemy's first strike, and the INS is adequate. I confirm my current coordinates and grind forward, leaving the valley at last.

What lies before me was once a shallow cup of fertile green among the lava fields; now it is a blackened pit, and as my forward optical heads sweep the ruins of the town of Morville I feel the horror of Human mass death. There is no longer any need for haste, and I devote a full 6.007 seconds to the initial sweep. I anticipate no threats, but my on-site records will be invaluable to the court of inquiry I know will be convened to pass judgment upon my brigade. I am aware of my own fear of that court's verdict and its implications for all Bolos, but I am a unit of the Line. This too, however bitter, is my duty, and I will not flinch from it.

I have already observed the massive casualties C Company inflicted upon the Enemy in its fighting retreat up the Black Rock Valley. The Enemy's vehicles are individually smaller than Bolos, ranging from 500.96 Standard Tons to no more than 4,982.07 Standard Tons, but heavily armed for their size. They are also manned, not self-aware, and he has lost many of them. Indeed, I estimate the aggregate tonnage of his losses in the Black Rock Valley alone as equivalent to at least three Bolo regiments. We have yet to determine this Enemy's origins or the motives for his assault on Camlan, but the butchery to which he has willingly subjected his own personnel is sobering evidence of his determination . . . or fanaticism. Just as the blasted, body-strewn streets of Morville are ample proof of his ferocity.

Seventy-one more wrecked Enemy vehicles choke the final approach to the town, and two far larger wrecks loom among them. I detect no transponder codes, and the wreckage of my brigade mates is so blasted that even I find it difficult to identify what remains, yet I know who they were. Unit XXV/D-1162-HNR and Unit XXV/D-0982-JSN of the Line have fought their last battle, loyal unto death to our Human creators.

I reach out to them, hoping against hope that some whisper from the final refuge of their Survival Centers will answer my transmission, but there is no reply. Like the other Bolos I have passed this day, they are gone beyond recall, and the empty spots they once filled within the

Total Systems Data Sharing net ache within me as I move slowly forward, alert still for any Enemy vehicles hiding among the wreckage. There are none. There are only the dead: the Enemy's dead, and the six thousand Human dead, and my brothers who died knowing they had failed to save them.

This is not the first time units of the Line have died, nor the first time they died in defeat. There is no shame in that, only sorrow, for we cannot always end in victory. Yet there is cause for shame here, for there are only two dead Bolos before me . . . and there should be three.

Wind moans over the wreckage as I pick my way across the killing ground where my brothers' fire shattered three Enemy attacks before the fourth overran them. Without the recon satellites there is no independent record of their final battle, but my own sensor data, combined with their final TSDS transmissions, allow me to deduce what passed here. I understand their fighting withdrawal down the Black Rock Valley and the savage artillery and missile barrages which flayed them as they fought. I grasp their final maneuvers from the patterns of wreckage, recognize the way the Enemy crowded in upon them as his steady pounding crippled their weapons. I see the final positions they assumed, standing at last against the Enemy's fire because they could no longer retreat without abandoning Morville.

And I see the third position from which a single Bolo did retreat, falling back, fleeing into the very heart of the town he was duty bound to defend. I track his course by the crushed and shattered wreckage of buildings and see the bodies of the Camlan Militia who died as he fled, fighting with their man-portable weapons against an Enemy who could destroy 13,000-ton Bolos. There are many Enemy wrecks along his course, clear evidence of how desperately the Militia opposed the invaders' advance even as the Bolo abandoned Morville, fleeing north into the Badlands where the Enemy's less capable vehicles could not pursue, and I know who left those Humans to die. Unit XXV/D-0103-LNC of the Line, C Company's command Bolo, my creche mate and battle companion and my most trusted company commander. I have fought beside him many times, known his utter reliability in the face of the Enemy, but I know him no longer, for what he has done is unforgivable. He is the first, the only, Bolo ever to desert in the face of the Enemy, abandoning those we are bound to protect to the death and beyond.

For the first time in the history of the Dinochrome Brigade, we know shame. And fear. As LNC, I am a Mark XXV, Model D, the first production model Bolo to be allowed complete, permanent self-awareness, and LNC's actions attack the very foundation of the decision which made us fully self-realized personalities. We have repeatedly demonstrated how much more effective our awareness makes us in battle, yet our freedom of action makes us unlike any previous units of the Brigade. We are truly autonomous . . . and if one of us can choose to flee—if one of us can succumb to cowardice—perhaps all of us can.

I complete my survey of the site in 4.307 minutes. There are no survivors, Enemy, Human, or Bolo, in Morville, and I report my grim confirmation to my Brigade Commander and to my surviving brothers and sisters. The Enemy's surprise attack, coupled with our subsequent losses in combat, have reduced Sixth Brigade to only fourteen units, and our acting Brigade Commander is Lieutenant Kestrel, the most junior—and sole surviving—Human of our command staff. The Commander is only twenty-four Standard Years of age, on her first posting to an active duty brigade, and the exhaustion in her voice is terrible to hear. Yet she has done her duty superbly, and I feel only shame and bitter, bitter guilt that I must impose this additional decision upon her. I taste the matching shame and guilt of the surviving handful of my brothers and sisters over the TSDS, but none of them can assist me. The Enemy is in full retreat to his spaceheads, yet the fighting continues at a furious pace. No other Bolos can be diverted from it until victory is assured, and so I alone have come to investigate and confirm the unbelievable events here, for I am the commander of LNC's battalion. It is up to me to do what must be done.

"All right, Arthur," Lieutenant Kestrel says finally. "We've got the situation in hand here, and Admiral Shigematsu's last subspace flash puts Ninth Fleet just thirty-five hours out. We can hold the bastards without you. Go do what you have to."

"Yes, Commander," *I reply softly, and pivot on my tracks,*

turning my prow to the north, and follow LNC's trail into the lava fields.

Unit XXV/D-0103-LNC of the Line churned across the merciless terrain. Both outboard port tracks had been blown away, and bare road wheels groaned in protest as they chewed through rock and gritty soil. His armored hull was gouged and torn, his starboard infinite repeaters and anti-personnel clusters a tangled mass of ruin, but his builders had designed him well. His core war hull had been breached in three places, wreaking havoc among many of his internal systems, yet his main armament remained intact . . . and he knew he was pursued.

LNC paused, checking his position against his INS and the maps in Main Memory. It was a sign of his brutal damage that he required almost twenty full seconds to determine his location, and then he altered course. The depression was more a crevasse than a valley—a sunken trough, barely half again the width of his hull, that plunged deep below the level of the fissured lava fields. It would offer LNC cover as he made his painful way towards the distant Avalon Mountains, and a cloud of dust wisped away on the icy winter wind as he vanished into the shadowed cleft.

I try to deduce LNC's objective, assuming that he has one beyond simple flight, but the task is beyond me. I can extrapolate the decisions of a rational foe, yet the process requires some understanding of his motives, and I no longer understand LNC's motives. I replay the final TSDS transmission from XXV/D-1162-HNR and experience once more the sensation a Human might define as a chill of horror as LNC suddenly withdraws from the data net. I share HNR's attempt to reestablish the net, feel LNC's savage rejection of all communication. And then I watch through HNR's sensors as LNC abandons his position, wheeling back towards Morville while Enemy fire bellows and thunders about him . . . and I experience HNR's final shock as his own company commander responds to his repeated queries by pouring Hellbore fire into his unprotected rear.

LNC's actions are impossible, yet the data are irrefutable. He has not only fled the Enemy but killed his own brigade mate, and his refusal even to acknowledge communication attempts is absolute. That, too, is impossible. Any Bolo must respond to the priority com frequencies, yet LNC does not. He has not only committed mutiny and treason but refused to hear any message from Lieutenant Kestrel, as he might reject an Enemy communications seizure attempt. How any Bolo could ignore his own Brigade Commander is beyond my comprehension, yet he has, and because there is no longer any communication interface at all, Lieutenant Kestrel cannot even access the Total Systems Override Program to shut him down.

None of my models or extrapolations can suggest a decision matrix which could generate such actions on LNC's part. But perhaps that is the point. Perhaps there is no decision matrix, only panic. Yet if that is true, what will he do when the panic passes—if it passes? Surely he must realize his own fate is sealed, whatever the outcome of the Enemy's attack. How can I anticipate rational decisions from him under such circumstances?

I grind up another slope in his tracks. He has altered course once more, swinging west, and I consult my internal maps. His base course has been towards the Avalon Mountains, and I note the low ground to the west. He is no longer on a least-time heading for the mountains, but the long, deep valley will take him there eventually. It will also afford him excellent cover and numerous ambush positions, and I am tempted to cut cross-country and head him off. But if I do that and he is not, in fact, headed for the mountains, I may lose him. He cannot hide indefinitely, yet my shame and grief—and sense of betrayal—will not tolerate delay, and I know from HNR's last transmission that LNC's damage is much worse than my own.

I consider options and alternatives for .0089 seconds, and then head down the slope in his wake.

Unit LNC slowed as the seismic sensors he'd deployed along his back trail reported the ground shocks of a pursuing vehicle in the thirteen-thousand-ton range. He'd known pursuit would come, yet he'd hoped for a greater head start, for he had hundreds of kilometers still to go, and his damaged suspension reduced his best sustained speed to barely forty-six kilometers per hour. He *must* reach the Avalons. No Enemy could be permitted to stop him, yet the remote sensors made it clear the Enemy which now pursued him was faster than he.

But there were ways to slow his hunter, and he deployed another pair of seismic sensors while his optical heads and sonar considered the fissured rock strata around him.

I am gaining on LNC. His track damage must be worse than I had believed, and the faint emissions of his power plants come to me from ahead. I know it is hopeless, yet even now I cannot truly believe he is totally lost to all he once was, and so I activate the TSDS once more and broadcast strongly on C Company's frequencies, begging him to respond.

Unit LNC picked up the powerful transmissions and felt contempt for the one who sent them. Could his pursuer truly believe he would fall for such an obvious ploy? That he would respond, give away his position, possibly even accept communication and allow access to his core programming? LNC recognized the communications protocols, but that meant nothing. LNC no longer had allies, friends, war brothers or sisters. There was only the Enemy . . . and the Avalon Mountains which drew so slowly, agonizingly closer.

But even as LNC ignored the communications attempt, he was monitoring the seismic sensors he'd deployed. He matched the position those sensors reported against his own terrain maps and sent the execution code.

Demolition charges roar, the powerful explosions like thunder in the restricted cleft. I understand their purpose instantly, yet there is no time to evade as the cliffs about me shudder. It is a trap. The passage has narrowed to little more than the width of my own combat chassis, and LNC has mined the sheer walls on either hand.

I throw maximum power to my tracks, fighting to speed clear, but hundreds of thousands of tons of rock are in motion, cascading down upon me. My kinetic battle screen could never resist such massive weights, and I deactivate it to prevent its burnout as the artificial avalanche crashes over me. Pain sensors flare as boulders batter my flanks. Power train components scream in protest as many times my own weight in crushed rock and shifting earth sweep over me, and I am forced to shut them down, as well. I can only ride out the cataclysm, and I take grim note that LNC has lost none of his cunning in his cowardice.

It takes 4.761 minutes for the avalanche to complete my immobilization and another 6.992 minutes before the last boulder slams to rest. I have lost 14.37% percent more of my sensors, and most of those which remain are buried under meters of debris. But a quick diagnostic check reveals that no core systems have suffered damage, and sonar pulses probe the tons of broken rock which overlay me, generating a chart of my overburden.

All is not lost. LNC's trap has immobilized me, but only temporarily. I calculate that I can work clear of the debris in not more than 71.650 minutes, and jammed boulders shift as I begin to rock back and forth on my tracks.

LNC's remote sensors reported the seismic echoes of his pursuer's efforts to dig free. For a long moment—almost .3037 seconds—he considered turning to engage his immobilized foe, but only for a moment. LNC's Hellbore remained operational, but he'd expended ninety-six percent of his depletable munitions, his starboard infinite repeaters were completely inoperable, and his command and control systems' efficiency was badly degraded. Even his Battle Reflex functioned only erratically, and he knew his reactions were slow, without the flashing certainty which had always been his. His seismic sensors could give no detailed information on his hunter, yet his Enemy was almost certainly more combat worthy than he, and his trap was unlikely to have inflicted decisive damage.

No. It was the mountains which mattered, the green, fertile mountains, and LNC dared not risk his destruction before he reached them. And so he resisted the temptation to turn at bay and ground steadily onward through the frozen, waterless Badlands on tracks and naked road wheels.

★ ★ ★

I work my way free at last. Dirt and broken rock shower from my flanks as my tracks heave me up out of the rubble-clogged slot. More dirt and boulders crown my war hull and block Number Three and Number Fourteen Optical Heads, yet I remain operational at 89.051% of base capacity, and I have learned. The detonation of his demolition charges was LNC's response to my effort to communicate. The brother who fought at my side for twenty-one Standard Years truly is no more. All that remains is the coward, the deserter, the betrayer of trust who will stop at nothing to preserve himself. I will not forget again—and I can no longer deceive myself into believing he can be convinced to give himself up. The only gift I can offer him now is his destruction, and I throw additional power to my tracks as I go in pursuit to give it to him.

LNC's inboard forward port suspension screamed in protest as the damaged track block parted at last. The fleeing Bolo shuddered as he ran forward off the track, leaving it twisted and trampled in his wake. The fresh damage slowed him still further, and he staggered drunkenly as his unbalanced suspension sought to betray him. Yet he forced himself back onto his original heading, and his deployed remotes told him the Enemy was gaining once more. His turret swiveled, training his Hellbore directly astern, and he poured still more power to his remaining tracks. Drive components heated dangerously under his abuse, but the mountains were closer.

I begin picking up LNC's emissions once more, despite the twisting confines of the valley. They remain too faint to provide an accurate position fix, but they give me a general bearing, and an armored hatch opens as I deploy one of my few remaining reconnaissance drones.

LNC detected the drone as it came sweeping up the valley. His anti-air defenses, badly damaged at Morville, were unable to engage, but his massive ninety-centimeter Hellbore rose like a striking serpent, and a bolt of plasma fit to destroy even another Bolo howled from its muzzle.

★ ★ ★

My drone has been destroyed, but the manner of its destruction tells me much. LNC would not have engaged it with his main battery if his anti-air systems remained effective, and that means there is a chink in his defenses. I have expended my supply of fusion warheads against the invaders, but I retain 37.961% of my conventional warhead missile load, and if his air defenses have been seriously degraded, a saturation bombardment may overwhelm his battle screen. Even without battle screen, chemical explosives would be unlikely to significantly injure an undamaged Bolo, of course, but LNC is not undamaged.

I consider the point at which my drone was destroyed and generate a new search pattern. I lock the pattern in, and the drone hatches open once more. Twenty-four fresh drones—82.75% of my remaining total—streak upward, and I open my VLS missile cell hatches, as well.

The drones came screaming north. They didn't come in slowly this time, for they were no longer simply searching for LNC. This time they already knew his approximate location, and their sole task was to confirm it for the Enemy's fire control.

But LNC had known they would be coming. He had already pivoted sharply on his remaining tracks and halted, angled across the valley to clear his intact port infinite repeaters' field of fire, and heavy ion bolts shrieked to meet the drones. His surviving slug-throwers and laser clusters added their fury, and the drones blew apart as if they'd run headlong into a wall. Yet effective as his fire was, it was less effective than his crippled air defense systems would have been, and one drone—just one—survived long enough to report his exact position.

I am surprised by the efficiency of LNC's fire, but my drones have accomplished their mission. More, they have provided my first visual observation of his damages, and I am shocked by their severity. It seems impossible that he can still be capable of movement, far less accurately directed fire, and despite his cowardice and treason, I feel a stab of sympathy for the agony which must be lashing him from his pain receptors. Yet he clearly remains combat capable, despite his hideous wounds, and I feed his coordinates to my missiles. I take .00037 seconds to confirm my targeting solution, and then I fire.

Flame fountained from the shadowed recesses of the deep valley as the missile salvos rose and howled north, homing on their target. Most of ART's birds came in on conventional, high-trajectory courses, but a third of them came in low, relying on terrain avoidance radar to navigate straight up the slot of the valley. The hurricane of his fire slashed in on widely separated bearings, and LNC's crippled active defenses were insufficient to intercept it all.

ART emptied his VLS cells, throwing every remaining warhead at his treasonous brigade mate. Just under four hundred missiles launched in less than ninety seconds, and LNC writhed as scores of them got through his interception envelope. They pounded his battle screen, ripped and tore at lacerated armor, and pain receptors shrieked as fresh damage bit into his wounded war hull. Half his remaining infinite repeaters were blown away, still more sensor capability was blotted out, and his thirteen-thousand-ton bulk shuddered and shook under the merciless bombardment.

Yet he survived. The last warhead detonated, and his tracks clashed back into motion. He turned ponderously to the north once more, grinding out of the smoke and dust and the roaring brush fires his Enemy's missiles had ignited in the valley's sparse vegetation.

That bombardment had exhausted the Enemy's ammunition, and with it his indirect fire capability. If it hadn't, he would still be firing upon LNC. He wasn't, which meant that if he meant to destroy LNC now, he must do so with direct fire . . . and come within reach of LNC's Hellbore, as well.

My missile fire has failed to halt LNC. I am certain it has inflicted additional damage, but I doubt that it has crippled his Hellbore, and if his main battery remains operational, he retains the capability to destroy me just as he did HNR at Morville. He appears to have slowed still further, however, which may indicate my attack has further damaged his suspension.

I project his current speed of advance and heading on the maps from Main Memory. Given my speed advantage, I will overtake him within 2.03 hours, well short of his evident goal. I still do not know why he is so intent upon reaching the Avalon Mountains. Unlike Humans, Bolos require neither water nor food, and surely the rocky, barren, crevasse-riddled Badlands would provide LNC with better cover than the tree-grown mountains. I try once more to extrapolate his objective, to gain some insight into what now motivates him, and, once more, I fail.

But it does not matter. I will overtake him over seventy kilometers from the mountains, and when I do, one or both of us will die.

LNC ran the projections once more. It was difficult, for damaged core computer sections fluctuated, dropping in and out of his net. Yet even his crippled capabilities sufficed to confirm his fears; the Enemy would overtake him within little more than a hundred minutes, and desperation filled him. It was not an emotion earlier marks of Bolos had been equipped to feel—or, at least, to recognize when they did—but LNC had come to know it well. He'd felt it from the moment he realized his company couldn't save Morville, that the Enemy would break through them and crush the Humans they fought to protect. But it was different now, darker and more bitter, stark with how close he'd come to reaching the mountains after all.

Yet the Enemy hadn't overtaken him yet, and he consulted his maps once more.

I detect explosions ahead. I did not anticipate them, but .0761 seconds of analysis confirm that they are demolition charges once more. Given how many charges LNC used in his earlier ambush, these explosions must constitute his entire remaining supply of demolitions, and I wonder why he has expended them.

Confused seismic shocks come to me through the ground, but they offer no answer to my question. They are consistent with falling debris, but not in sufficient quantity to bar the valley. I cannot deduce any other objective worth the expenditure of his munitions, yet logic suggests that LNC had one which he considered worthwhile, and I advance more cautiously.

LNC waited atop the valley wall. The tortuous ascent on damaged tracks had cost him fifty precious minutes of his lead on the Enemy, but his demolitions had destroyed the natural ramp up which he'd toiled. He couldn't be directly pursued now, and he'd considered simply continuing to run. But once the Enemy realized LNC was no longer following the valley, he would no longer feel the need to pursue cautiously. Instead, he would use his superior speed to dash ahead to the valley's terminus. He would emerge from it there, between LNC and his goal, and sweep back to the south, hunting LNC in the Badlands.

That could not be permitted. LNC *must* reach the mountains, and so he waited, Hellbore covering the valley he'd left. With luck, he might destroy his pursuer once and for all, and even if he failed, the Enemy would realize LNC was above him. He would have no choice but to anticipate additional ambushes, and caution might impose the delay LNC needed.

I have lost LNC's emissions signature. There could be many reasons for that: my own sensors are damaged, he may have put a sufficiently solid shoulder of rock between us to conceal his emissions from me, he may even have shut down all systems other than his Survival Center to play dead. I am tempted to accelerate my advance, but I compute that this may be precisely what LNC wishes me to do. If I go to maximum speed, I may blunder into whatever ambush he has chosen to set.

I pause for a moment, then launch one of my five remaining reconnaissance drones up the valley. It moves slowly, remaining below the tops of the cliffs to conceal its emissions from LNC as long as possible. Its flight profile will limit the envelope of its look-down sensors, but it will find LNC wherever he may lie hidden.

★ ★ ★

LNC watched the drone move past far below him. It hugged the valley walls and floor, and he felt a sense of satisfaction as it disappeared up the narrow cleft without detecting him.

My drone reports a long, tangled spill of earth and rock across the valley, blasted down from above. It is thick and steep enough to inconvenience me, though not so steep as to stop me. As an attempt to further delay me it must be futile, but perhaps its very futility is an indication of LNC's desperation.

LNC waited, active emissions reduced to the minimum possible level, relying on purely optical systems for detection and fire control. It would degrade the effectiveness of his targeting still further, but it would also make him far harder to detect.

I approach the point at which LNC attempted to block the valley. My own sensors, despite their damage, are more effective than the drone's and cover a wider detection arc, and I slow as I consider the rubble. It is, indeed, too feeble a barrier to halt me, but something about it makes me cautious. It takes me almost .0004 seconds to isolate the reason.

The Enemy appeared below, nosing around the final bend. LNC tracked him optically, watching, waiting for the center-of-mass shot he required. The Enemy edged further forward . . . and then, suddenly, threw maximum emergency power to his reversed tracks just as LNC fired.

A full-powered Hellbore war shot explodes across my bow as I hurl myself backwards. The plasma bolt misses by only 6.52 meters, carving a 40-meter crater into the eastern cliff face. But it has missed me, and it would not have if I had not suddenly wondered how LNC had managed to set his charges high enough on the western cliff to blow down so much rubble. Now I withdraw around a bend in the valley and replay my sensor data, and bitter understanding fills me as I see the deep impressions of his tracks far above. My drone had missed them because it was searching for targets on the valley floor, but LNC is no longer in the valley. He has escaped its confines and destroyed the only path by which I might have followed.

I sit motionless for 3.026 endless seconds, considering my options. LNC is above me, and I detect his active emissions once more as he brings his targeting systems fully back on-line. He has the advantage of position and of knowing where I must appear if I wish to engage him. Yet I have the offsetting advantages of knowing where he is and of initiation, for he cannot know precisely when I will seek to engage.

It is not a pleasant situation, yet I conclude the odds favor me by the thinnest of margins. I am less damaged than he. My systems efficiency is higher, my response time probably lower. I compute a probability of 68.052%, plus or minus 6.119%, that I will get my shot off before he can fire. They are not the odds I would prefer, but my duty is clear.

LNC eased back to a halt on his crippled tracks. He'd chosen his initial position with care, selecting one which would require the minimum movement to reach his next firing spot. Without direct observation, forced to rely only on emissions which must pass through the distorting medium of solid rock to reach him, the Enemy might not even realize he'd moved at all. Now he waited once more, audio receptors filled with the whine of wind over tortured rock and the rent and torn projections of his own tattered hull.

I move. My suspension screams as I red-line the drive motors, and clouds of pulverized earth and rock spew from my tracks as I erupt into the open, Hellbore trained on LNC's position.

But LNC is not where I thought. He has moved less than eighty meters—just sufficient to put all save his turret behind a solid ridge of rock. His Hellbore is leveled across it, and my own turret traverses with desperate speed.

It is insufficient. His systems damage slows his reactions, but not enough, and we fire in the same split instant. Plasma bolts shriek past one another, and my rushed shot misses. It rips into the crest of his covering ridge, on for deflection but low in elevation. Stone explodes into vapor and screaming splinters, and the kinetic transfer energy blows a huge scab of rock off the back of the ridge. Several hundred tons of rock crash into LNC, but even as it hits him, his own plasma bolt punches through my battle screen and strikes squarely on my empty VLS cells.

Agony howls through my pain receptors as the plasma carves deep into my hull. Internal disrupter shields fight to confine the destruction, but the wound is critical. Both inboard after power trains suffer catastrophic damage, my after fusion plant goes into emergency shutdown, Infinite Repeaters Six through Nine in both lateral batteries are silenced, and my entire after sensor suite is totally disabled.

Yet despite my damage, my combat reflexes remain unimpaired. My six surviving track systems drag me back out of LNC's field of fire once more, back into the sheltering throat of the valley, even as Damage Control springs into action.

I am hurt. Badly hurt. I estimate that I am now operable at no more than 51.23% of base capability. But I am still functional, and as I replay the engagement, I realize I should not be. LNC had ample time for a second shot before I could withdraw, and he should have taken it.

LNC staggered as the Enemy's plasma bolt carved into his sheltering ridge. The solid rock protected his hull, but the disintegrating ridge crest itself became a deadly projectile. His battle screen was no protection, for the plasma bolt's impact point was inside his screen perimeter. There was nothing to stop the hurtling tons of rock, and they crashed into the face of his turret like some titanic hammer, with a brute force impact that rocked him on his tracks.

His armor held, but the stony hammer came up under his Hellbore at an angle and snapped the weapon's mighty barrel like a twig. Had his Hellbore survived, the Enemy would have been at his mercy; as it was, he no longer had a weapon which could possibly engage his pursuer.

Damage Control damps the last power surges reverberating through my systems and I am able to take meaningful stock of my wound. It is even worse than I had anticipated. For all intents and purposes, I am reduced to my Hellbore and eight infinite repeaters, five of them in my port battery. Both inner tracks of my aft suspension are completely dead, but Damage Control has managed to disengage the clutches; the tracks still support me, and their road wheels will rotate freely. My sensor damage is critical, however, for I have been reduced to little more than 15.62% of base sensor capability. I am completely blind aft, and little better than that to port or starboard, and my remaining drones have been destroyed.

Yet I compute only one possible reason for LNC's failure to finish me. My near miss must have disabled his Hellbore, and so his offensive capability has been even more severely reduced than my own. I cannot be positive the damage is permanent. It is possible—even probable, since I did not score a direct hit—that he will be able to restore the weapon to function. Yet if the damage is beyond onboard repair capability, he will be at my mercy even in my crippled state.

But to engage him I must find him, and if he chooses to turn away and disappear into the Badlands, locating him may well prove impossible for my crippled sensors. Indeed, if he should succeed in breaking contact with me, seek out some deeply hidden crevasse or cavern, and shut down all but his Survival Center, he might well succeed in hiding even from Fleet sensors. Even now, despite his treason and the wounds he has inflicted upon me, a small, traitorous part of me wishes he would do just that. I remember too many shared battles, too many times in which we fought side by side in the heart of shrieking violence, and that traitor memory wishes he would simply go. Simply vanish and sleep away his reserve power in dreamless hibernation.

But I cannot let him do that. He must not escape the consequences of his actions, and I must not allow him to. His treason is too great, and our Human commanders and partners must know that we of the Line share their horror at his actions.

I sit motionless for a full 5.25 minutes, recomputing options in light of my new limitations. I cannot climb the valley wall after LNC, nor can I rely upon my damaged sensors to find him if he seeks to evade me. Should he simply run from me, he will escape, yet he has *been wedded to the same base course from the moment he abandoned Morville. I still do not understand why, but he appears absolutely determined to reach the Avalon Mountains, and even with my track damage, I remain faster than he is.*

There is only one possibility. I will proceed at maximum speed to the end of this valley. According to my maps, I should reach its northern end at least 42.35 minutes before he can attain the cover of the mountains, and I will be between him and his refuge. I will be able to move towards him, using my remaining forward sensors to search for and find him, and if his Hellbore is indeed permanently disabled, I will destroy him with ease. My plan is not without risks, for my damaged sensors can no longer sweep the tops of the valley walls effectively. If his Hellbore can be restored to operation, he will be able to choose his firing position with impunity, and I will be helpless before his attack. But risk or no, it is my only option, and if I move rapidly enough, I may well outrun him and get beyond engagement range before he can make repairs.

LNC watched helplessly as the Enemy reemerged from hiding and sped up the narrow valley. He understood the Enemy's logic, and the loss of his Hellbore left him unable to defeat it. If he continued towards the Avalons, he would be destroyed, yet he had no choice, and he turned away from the valley, naked road wheels screaming in protest as he battered his way across the lava fields.

I have reached the end of the valley, and I emerge into the foothills of the Avalon Range and alter course to the west. I climb the nearest hill, exposing only my turret and forward sensor arrays over its crest, and begin the most careful sweep of which I remain capable.

LNC's passive sensors detected the whispering lash of radar and he knew he'd lost the race. The Enemy was ahead of him, waiting, and he ground to a halt. His computer core had suffered additional shock damage when the disintegrating ridge crest smashed into him, and his thoughts were slow. It took him almost thirteen seconds to realize what he must do. The only thing he could do now.

★ ★ ★

"Tommy?"

Thomas Mallory looked up from where he crouched on the floor of the packed compartment. His eight-year-old sister had sobbed herself out of tears at last, and she huddled against his side in the protective circle of his arm. But Thomas Mallory had learned too much about the limits of protectiveness. At fifteen, he was the oldest person in the compartment, and he knew what many of the others had not yet realized—that they would never see their parents again, for the fifty-one of them were the sole survivors of Morville.

"Tommy?" the slurred voice said once more, and Thomas cleared his throat.

"Yes?" He heard the quaver in his own voice, but he made himself speak loudly. Despite the air filtration systems, the compartment stank of ozone, explosives, and burning organic compounds. He'd felt the terrible concussions of combat and knew the vehicle in whose protective belly he sat was savagely wounded, and he was no longer certain how efficient its audio pickups might be.

"I have failed in my mission, Tommy," the voice said. "The Enemy has cut us off from our objective."

"What enemy?" Thomas demanded. "Who *are* they, Lance? Why are they *doing* this?"

"They are doing it because they are the Enemy," the voice replied.

"But there must be a *reason!*" Thomas cried with all the anguish of a fifteen-year-old heart.

"They are the Enemy," the voice repeated in that eerie, slurred tone. "It is the Enemy's function to destroy . . . to destroy . . . to dest—" The voice chopped off, and Thomas swallowed. Lance's responses were becoming increasingly less lucid, wandering into repetitive loops that sometimes faded into silence and other times, as now, cut off abruptly, and Thomas Mallory had learned about mortality. Even Bolos could perish, and somehow he knew Lance was dying by centimeters even as he struggled to complete his mission.

"They are the Enemy," Lance resumed, and the electronic voice was higher and tauter. "There is always the Enemy. The Enemy

must be defeated. The Enemy must be destroyed. The Enemy—"
Again the voice died with the sharpness of an axe blow, and Thomas
bit his lip and hugged his sister tight. Endless seconds of silence
oozed past, broken only by the whimpers and weeping of the
younger children, until Thomas could stand it no longer.

"Lance?" he said hoarsely.

"I am here, Tommy." The voice was stronger this time, and
calmer.

"W-What do we do?" Thomas asked.

"There is only one option." A cargo compartment hissed open
to reveal a backpack military com unit and an all-terrain survival kit.
Thomas had never used a military com, but he knew it was preset to
the Dinochrome Brigade's frequencies. "Please take the kit and com
unit," the voice said.

"All right." Thomas eased his arm from around his sister and
lifted the backpack from the compartment. It was much lighter than
he'd expected, and he slipped his arms through the straps and
settled it on his back, then tugged the survival kit out as well.

"Thank you," the slurred voice said. "Now, here is what you
must do, Tommy—"

*My questing sensors detect him at last. He is moving slowly, coming
in along yet another valley. This one is shorter and shallower, barely
deep enough to hide him from my fire, and I trace its course along my
maps. He must emerge from it approximately 12.98 kilometers to the
southwest of my present position, and I grind into motion once more.
I will enter the valley from the north and sweep along it until we meet,
and then I will kill him.*

Thomas Mallory crouched on the hilltop. It hadn't been hard to
make the younger kids hide—not after the horrors they'd seen in
Morville. But Thomas couldn't join them. He had to be here, where
he could see the end, for someone *had* to see it. Someone had to
be there, to know how fifty-one children had been saved from
death . . . and to witness the price their dying savior had paid for
them.

Distance blurred details, hiding Lance's dreadful damages as he ground steadily up the valley, but Thomas's eyes narrowed as he saw the cloud of dust coming to meet him. Tears burned like ice on his cheeks in the sub-zero wind, and he scrubbed at them angrily. Lance deserved those tears, but Thomas couldn't let the other kids see them. There was little enough chance that they could survive a single Camlan winter night, even in the mountains, where they would at least have water, fuel, and the means to build some sort of shelter. But it was the only chance Lance had been able to give them, and Thomas would not show weakness before the children he was now responsible for driving and goading into surviving until someone came to rescue them. Would not betray the trust Lance had bestowed upon him.

The oncoming dust grew thicker, and he raised the electronic binoculars, gazing through them for his first sight of the enemy. He adjusted their focus as an iodine-colored turret moved beyond a saddle of hills. Lance couldn't see it from his lower vantage point, but Thomas could, and his face went suddenly paper-white. He stared for one more moment, then grabbed for the com unit's microphone.

"No, Lance! Don't—don't! It's not the enemy—it's another Bolo!"

The Human voice cracks with strain as it burns suddenly over the command channel, and confusion whips through me. The transmitter is close—very close—and that is not possible. Nor do I recognize the voice, and that also is impossible. I start to reply, but before I can, another voice comes over the same channel.

"Cease transmission," *it says.* "Do not reveal your location."

This time I know the voice, yet I have never heard it speak so. It has lost its crispness, its sureness. It is the voice of one on the brink of madness, a voice crushed and harrowed by pain and despair and a purpose that goes beyond obsession.

"Lance," *the Human voice—a young, male Human voice—sobs.* "Please, Lance! It's another Bolo! It really is!"

"It is the Enemy," *the voice I once knew replies, and it is higher* and shriller. "It is the Enemy. There is only the Enemy. I am Unit Zero-One-Zero-Three-LNC of the Line. It is my function to destroy the Enemy. The Enemy. The Enemy. The Enemy. The Enemy."

I hear the broken cadence of that voice, and suddenly I understand. I understand everything, and horror fills me. I lock my tracks, slithering to a halt, fighting to avoid what I know must happen. Yet understanding has come too late, and even as I brake, LNC rounds the flank of a hill in a scream of tortured, over-strained tracks and a billowing cloud of dust.

For the first time, I see his hideously mauled starboard side and the gaping wound driven deep, deep into his hull. I can actually see his breached Personality Center in its depths, see the penetration where Enemy fire ripped brutally into the circuitry of his psychotronic brain, and I understand it all. I hear the madness in his electronic voice, and the determination and courage which have kept that broken, dying wreck in motion, and the child's voice on the com is the final element. I know his mission, now, the reason he has fought so doggedly, so desperately to cross the Badlands to the life-sustaining shelter of the mountains.

Yet my knowledge changes nothing, for there is no way to avoid him. He staggers and lurches on his crippled tracks, but he is moving at almost eighty kilometers per hour. He has no Hellbore, no missiles, and his remaining infinite repeaters cannot harm me, yet he retains one final weapon: himself.

He thunders towards me, his com voice silent no more, screaming the single word "Enemy! Enemy! Enemy!" again and again. He hurls himself upon me in a suicide attack, charging to his death as the only way he can protect the children he has carried out of hell from the friend he can no longer recognize, the "Enemy" who has hunted him over four hundred kilometers of frozen, waterless stone and dust. It is all he has left, the only thing he can do . . . and if he carries through with his ramming attack, we both will die and exposure will kill the children before anyone can rescue them.

I have no choice. He has left me none, and in that instant I wish I were Human. That I, too, could shed the tears which fog the young voice crying out to its protector to turn aside and save himself.

But I cannot weep. There is only one thing I can do.

"Good bye, Lance," I send softly over the battalion command net.
"Forgive me."

And I fire.

★ A RELIC OF WAR ★

Keith Laumer

The old war machine sat in the village square, its impotent guns pointing aimlessly along the dusty street. Shoulder-high weeds grew rankly about it, poking up through the gaps in the two-yard-wide treads; vines crawled over the high, rust- and guano-streaked flanks. A row of tarnished enameled battle honors gleamed dully across the prow, reflecting the late sun.

A group of men lounged near the machine; they were dressed in heavy work clothes and boots; their hands were large and calloused, their faces weather-burned. They passed a jug from hand to hand, drinking deep. It was the end of a long workday and they were relaxed, good-humored.

"Hey, we're forgetting old Bobby," one said. He strolled over and sloshed a little of the raw whiskey over the soot-blackened muzzle of the blast cannon slanting sharply down from the forward turret. The other men laughed.

"How's it going, Bobby?" the man called.

Deep inside the machine there was a soft chirring sound.

"Very well thank you," a faint, whispery voice scraped from a grill below the turret.

"You keeping an eye on things, Bobby?" another man called.

"All clear," the answer came: a bird-chirp from a dinosaur.

"Bobby, you ever get tired just setting here?"

"Hell, Bobby don't get tired," the man with the jug said. "He's got a job to do, old Bobby has."

"Hey, Bobby, what kind o'boy are you?" a plump, lazy-eyed man called.

"I am a good boy," Bobby replied obediently.

"Sure Bobby's a good boy." The man with the jug reached up to pat the age-darkened curve of chromalloy above him. "Bobby's looking out for us."

Heads turned at a sound from across the square: the distant whine of a turbocar, approaching along the forest road.

"Huh! Ain't the day for the mail," a man said. They stood in silence, watching as a small, dusty cushion-car emerged from deep shadow into the yellow light of the street. It came slowly along to the plaza, swung left, pulled to a stop beside the boardwalk before a corrugated metal store front lettered BLAUVELT PROVISION COMPANY. The canopy popped open and a man stepped down. He was of medium height, dressed in a plain city-type black coverall. He studied the store front, the street, then turned to look across at the men. He came across toward them.

"Which of you men is Blauvelt?" he asked as he came up. His voice was unhurried, cool. His eyes flicked over the men.

A big, youngish man with a square face and sun-bleached hair lifted his chin.

"Right here," he said. "Who're you?"

"Crewe is the name. Disposal Officer, War Materiel Commission." The newcomer looked up at the great machine looming over them. "Bolo *Stupendous*, Mark XXV," he said. He glanced at the men's faces, fixed on Blauvelt. "We had a report that there was a live Bolo out here. I wonder if you realize what you're playing with?"

"Hell, that's just Bobby," a man said.

"He's town mascot," someone else said.

"This machine could blow your town off the map," Crewe said. "And a good-sized piece of jungle along with it."

Blauvelt grinned; the squint lines around his eyes gave him a quizzical look.

"Don't go getting upset, Mr. Crewe," he said. "Bobby's harmless—"

"A Bolo's never harmless, Mr. Blauvelt. They're fighting machines, nothing else."

Blauvelt sauntered over and kicked at a corroded treadplate. "Eighty-five years out in this jungle is kind of tough on machinery, Crewe. The sap and stuff from the trees eats chromalloy like it was sugar candy. The rains are acid, eat up equipment damn near as fast as we can ship it in here. Bobby can still talk a little, but that's about all."

"Certainly it's deteriorated; that's what makes it dangerous. Anything could trigger its battle reflex circuitry. Now, if you'll clear everyone out of the area, I'll take care of it."

"You move kind of fast for a man that just hit town," Blauvelt said, frowning. "Just what you got in mind doing?"

"I'm going to fire a pulse at it that will neutralize what's left of its computing center. Don't worry; there's no danger—"

"Hey," a man in the rear rank blurted. "That mean he can't talk any more?"

"That's right," Crewe said. "Also, he can't open fire on you."

"Not so fast, Crewe," Blauvelt said. "You're not messing with Bobby. We like him like he is." The other men were moving forward, forming up in a threatening circle around Crewe.

"Don't talk like a fool," Crewe said. "What do you think a salvo from a Continental Siege Unit would do to your town?"

Blauvelt chuckled and took a long cigar from his vest pocket. He sniffed it, called out: "All right, Bobby—fire one!"

There was a muted clatter, a sharp *click*! from deep inside the vast bulk of the machine. A tongue of pale flame licked from the cannon's soot-rimmed bore. The big man leaned quickly forward, puffed the cigar alight. The audience whooped with laughter.

"Bobby does what he's told, that's all," Blauvelt said. "And not much of that." He showed white teeth in a humorless smile.

Crewe flipped over the lapel of his jacket; a small, highly polished badge glinted there. "You know better than to interfere with a Concordiat officer," he said.

"Not so fast, Crewe," a dark-haired, narrow-faced fellow spoke up. "You're out of line. I heard about you Disposal men. Your job is locating old ammo dumps, abandoned equipment, stuff like that. Bobby's not abandoned. He's town property. Has been for near thirty years."

"Nonsense. This is battle equipment, the property of the Space Arm—"

Blauvelt was smiling lopsidedly. "Uh-uh. We've got salvage rights. No title, but we can make one up in a hurry. Official. I'm the Mayor here, and District Governor."

"This thing is a menace to every man, woman, and child in the settlement," Crewe snapped. "My job is to prevent tragedy—"

"Forget Bobby," Blauvelt cut in. He waved a hand at the jungle wall beyond the tilled fields. "There's a hundred million square miles of virgin territory out there," he said. "You can do what you like out there. I'll even sell you provisions. But just leave our mascot be, understand?"

Crewe looked at him, looked around at the other men.

"You're a fool," he said. "You're all fools." He turned and walked away, stiff-backed.

In the room he had rented in the town's lone boardinghouse, Crewe opened his baggage and took out a small, gray-plastic-cased instrument. The three children of the landlord who were watching from the latchless door edged closer.

"Gee, is that a real star radio?" the eldest, a skinny, long-necked lad of twelve asked.

"No," Crewe said shortly. The boy blushed and hung his head.

"It's a command transmitter," Crewe said, relenting. "It's designed for talking to fighting machines, giving them orders. They'll only respond to the special shaped-wave signal this puts out." He flicked a switch, and an indicator light glowed on the side of the case.

"You mean like Bobby?" the boy asked.

"Like Bobby used to be." Crewe switched off the transmitter.

"Bobby's swell," another child said. "He tells us stories about when he was in the war."

"He's got medals," the first boy said. "Were you in the war, mister?"

"I'm not quite that old," Crewe said.

"Bobby's older'n grandad."

"You boys had better run along," Crewe said. "I have to . . ." He broke off, cocked his head, listening. There were shouts outside; someone was calling his name.

Crewe pushed through the boys and went quickly along the hall, stepped through the door onto the boardwalk. He felt rather than heard a slow, heavy thudding, a chorus of shrill squeaks, a metallic groaning. A red-faced man was running toward him from the square.

"It's Bobby!" he shouted. "He's moving! What'd you do to him, Crewe?"

Crewe brushed past the man, ran toward the plaza. The Bolo appeared at the end of the street, moving ponderously forward, trailing uprooted weeds and vines.

"He's headed straight for Spivac's warehouse!" someone yelled.

"Bobby! Stop there!" Blauvelt came into view, running in the machine's wake. The big machine rumbled onward, executed a half-left as Crewe reached the plaza, clearing the corner of a building by inches. It crushed a section of boardwalk to splinters, advanced across a storage yard. A stack of rough-cut lumber toppled, spilled across the dusty ground. The Bolo trampled a board fence, headed out across a tilled field. Blauvelt whirled on Crewe.

"This is your doing! We never had trouble before—"

"Never mind that! Have you got a field car?"

"We—" Blauvelt checked himself. "What if we have?"

"I can stop it—but I have to be close. It will be into the jungle in another minute. My car can't navigate there."

"Let him go," a man said, breathing hard from his run. "He can't do no harm out there."

"Who'd of thought it?" another man said. "Setting there all them years—who'd of thought he could travel like that?"

"Your so-called mascot might have more surprises in store for you," Crewe snapped. "Get me a car, fast! This is an official requisition, Blauvelt!"

There was a silence, broken only by the distant crashing of timber as the Bolo moved into the edge of the forest. Hundred-foot trees leaned and went down before its advance.

"Let him go," Blauvelt said. "Like Stinzi says, he can't hurt anything."

"What if he turns back?"

"Hell," a man muttered. "Old Bobby wouldn't hurt *us* . . ."

"That car," Crewe snarled. "You're wasting valuable time."

Blauvelt frowned. "All right—but you don't make a move unless it looks like he's going to come back and hit the town. Clear?"

"Let's go."

Blauvelt led the way at a trot toward the town garage.

The Bolo's trail was a twenty-five foot wide swath cut through the virgin jungle; the tread-prints were pressed eighteen inches into the black loam, where it showed among the jumble of fallen branches.

"It's moving at about twenty miles an hour, faster than we can go," Crewe said. "If it holds its present track, the curve will bring it back to your town in about five hours."

"He'll sheer off," Blauvelt said.

"Maybe. But we won't risk it. Pick up a heading of 270°, Blauvelt. We'll try an intercept by cutting across the circle."

Blauvelt complied wordlessly. The car moved ahead in the deep green gloom under the huge shaggy-barked trees. Oversized insects buzzed and thumped against the canopy. Small and medium lizards hopped, darted, flapped. Fern leaves as big as awnings scraped along the car as it clambered over loops and coils of tough root, leaving streaks of plant juice across the clear plastic. Once they grated against an exposed ridge of crumbling brown rock; flakes as big as saucers scaled off, exposing dull metal.

"Dorsal fin of a scout-boat," Crewe said. "That's what's left of what was supposed to be a corrosion resistant alloy."

They passed more evidences of a long-ago battle: the massive, shattered breech mechanism of a platform-mounted Hellbore, the gutted chassis of what might have been a bomb car, portions of a downed aircraft, fragments of shattered armor. Many of the relics were of Terran design, but often it was the curiously curved, spidery lines of a rusted Axorc microgun or implosion projector that poked through the greenery.

"It must have been a heavy action," Crewe said. "One of the ones toward the end that didn't get much notice at the time. There's stuff here I've never seen before, experimental types, I imagine, rushed in by the enemy for a last-ditch stand."

Blauvelt grunted.

"Contact in another minute or so," Crewe said.

As Blauvelt opened his mouth to reply, there was a blinding flash, a violent impact, and the jungle erupted in their faces.

The seat webbing was cutting into Crewe's ribs. His ears were filled with a high, steady ringing; there was a taste of brass in his mouth. His head throbbed in time with the thudding of his heart.

The car was on its side, the interior a jumble of loose objects, torn wiring, broken plastic. Blauvelt was half under him, groaning. He slid off him, saw that he was groggy but conscious.

"Changed your mind yet about your harmless pet?" he asked, wiping a trickle of blood from his right eye. "Let's get clear before he fires those empty guns again. Can you walk?"

Blauvelt mumbled, crawled out through the broken canopy. Crewe groped through debris for the command transmitter—

"Good God," Blauvelt croaked. Crewe twisted, saw the high, narrow, iodine-dark shape of the alien machine perched on jointed crawler-legs fifty feet away, framed by blast-scorched foliage. Its multiple-barreled micro-gun battery was aimed dead at the over-turned car.

"Don't move a muscle," Crewe whispered. Sweat trickled down his face. An insect, like a stub-winged four-inch dragonfly, came and buzzed about them, moved on. Hot metal pinged, contracting. Instantly, the alien hunter-killer moved forward another six feet, depressing its gun muzzles.

"Run for it!" Blauvelt cried. He came to his feet in a scrabbling lunge; the enemy machine swung to track him . . .

A giant tree leaned, snapped, was tossed aside. The great green-streaked prow of the Bolo forged into view, interposing itself between the smaller machine and the men. It turned to face the enemy; fire flashed, reflecting against the surrounding trees; the ground jumped once, twice, to hard, racking shocks. Sound boomed dully in Crewe's blast-numbed ears. Bright sparks fountained above the Bolo as it advanced, Crewe felt the massive impact as the two fighting machines came together; he saw the Bolo hesitate, then forge ahead, rearing up, pushing the lighter machine aside, grinding over it, passing on, to leave a crumpled mass of wreckage in its wake.

"Did you see that, Crewe?" Blauvelt shouted in his ear. "Did you see what Bobby did? He walked right into its guns and smashed it flatter'n crock-brewed beer!"

The Bolo halted, turned ponderously, sat facing the men. Bright streaks of molten metal ran down its armored flanks, fell spattering and smoking into crushed greenery.

"He saved our necks," Blauvelt said. He staggered to his feet, picked his way past the Bolo to stare at the smoking ruins of the smashed adversary.

"Unit Nine Five Four of the line, reporting contact with hostile force," the mechanical voice of the Bolo spoke suddenly. *"Enemy unit destroyed. I have sustained extensive damage, but am still operational at nine point six per cent base capability, awaiting further orders."*

"Hey," Blauvelt said. "That doesn't sound like . . ."

"Now maybe you understand that this is a Bolo combat unit, not the village idiot," Crewe snapped. He picked his way across the churned-up ground, stood before the great machine.

"Mission accomplished, Unit Nine five four," he called. "Enemy forces neutralized. Close out Battle Reflex and revert to low alert status." He turned to Blauvelt.

"Let's go back to town," he said, "and tell them what their mascot just did."

Blauvelt stared up at the grim and ancient machine; his square, tanned face looked yellowish and drawn. "Let's do that," he said.

★ ★ ★

The ten-piece town band was drawn up in a double rank before the newly mown village square. The entire population of the settlement—some three hundred and forty-two men, women and children—were present, dressed in their best. Pennants fluttered from strung wires. The sun glistened from the armored sides of the newly-cleaned and polished Bolo. A vast bouquet of wild flowers poked from the no-longer-sooty muzzle of the Hellbore.

Crewe stepped forward.

"As a representative of the Concordiat government I've been asked to make this presentation," he said. "You people have seen fit to design a medal and award it to Unit Nine five four in appreciation for services rendered in defense of the community above and beyond the call of duty." He paused, looked across the faces of his audience.

"Many more elaborate honors have been awarded for a great deal less," he said. He turned to the machine; two men came forward, one with a stepladder, the other with a portable welding rig. Crewe climbed up, fixed the newly struck decoration in place beside the row of century-old battle honors. The technician quickly spotted it in position. The crowd cheered, then dispersed, chattering, to the picnic tables set up in the village street.

It was late twilight. The last of the sandwiches and stuffed eggs had been eaten, the last speeches declaimed, the last keg broached. Crewe sat with a few of the men in the town's lone public house.

"To Bobby," a man raised his glass.

"Correction," Crewe said. "To Unit Nine five four of the Line." The men laughed and drank.

"Well, time to go, I guess," a man said. The others chimed in, rose, clattering chairs. As the last of them left, Blauvelt came in. He sat down across from Crewe.

"You, ah, staying the night?" he asked.

"I thought I'd drive back," Crewe said. "My business here is finished."

"Is it?" Blauvelt said tensely.

Crewe looked at him, waiting.

"You know what you've got to do, Crewe."

"Do I?" Crewe took a sip from his glass.

"Damn it, have I got to spell it out? As long as that machine was just an oversized half-wit, it was all right. Kind of a monument to the war, and all. But now I've seen what it can do . . . Crewe, we can't have a live killer sitting in the middle of our town—never knowing when it might take a notion to start shooting again!"

"Finished?" Crewe asked.

"It's not that we're not grateful—"

"Get out," Crewe said.

"Now, look here, Crewe—"

"Get out. And keep everyone away from Bobby, understand?"

"Does that mean—?"

"I'll take care of it."

Blauvelt got to his feet. "Yeah," he said. "Sure."

After Blauvelt left, Crewe rose and dropped a bill on the table; he picked the command transmitter from the floor, went out into the street. Faint cries came from the far end of the town, where the crowd had gathered for fireworks. A yellow rocket arced up, burst in a spray of golden light, falling, fading . . .

Crewe walked toward the plaza. The Bolo loomed up, a vast, black shadow against the star-thick sky. Crewe stood before it, looking up at the already draggled pennants, the wilted nosegay drooping from the gun muzzle.

"Unit Nine five four, you know why I'm here?" he said softly.

"I compute that my usefulness as an engine of war is ended," the soft rasping voice said.

"That's right," Crewe said. "I checked the area in a thousand-mile radius with sensitive instruments. There's no enemy machine left alive. The one you killed was the last."

"It was true to its duty," the machine said.

"It was my fault," Crewe said. "It was designed to detect our command carrier and home on it. When I switched on my transmitter, it went into action. Naturally, you sensed that, and went to meet it."

The machine sat silent.

"You could still save yourself," Crewe said. "If you trampled me under and made for the jungle it might be centuries before . . ."

"Before another man comes to do what must be done? Better that I cease now, at the hands of a friend."

"Good-bye, Bobby."

"Correction: Unit Nine five four of the Line."

Crewe pressed the key. A sense of darkness fell across the machine.

At the edge of the square, Crewe looked back. He raised a hand in a ghostly salute; then he walked away along the dusty street, white in the light of the rising moon.

HOLD UNTIL
★RELIEVED★

William H. Keith, Jr.

Light . . .
Dark . . .
Light . . .
Dark . . .
And light again, a burst of electromagnetic radiation in the nine-
to six-thousand Ångstrom range.
<STSFZJL>
<SYSFDILB>
<SYSFAILINBTSTRP>
<SYSTEM FAILURE: INITIATE BOOTSTRAP>
Consciousness—vague and of an extremely low order—returns.
Light . . . red light, much of it in the near infrared, washes
across my number eight starboard sensor cluster, a bloody glare from
somewhere overhead firing primary input circuits and triggering
paraneuronal relays in a fast-spreading, electronic ripple.
Darkness.

"It's alive!"

"Nonsense," the Historian replied with a dismissive flick of one
questing tentacle. "There is not enough left on this rock even to
mimic life."

They hovered silently beneath the glare of artificial lights, though those had been agraved above the excavation more for the convenience of the LI work units than for that of the Sentients. The workers, partial organics, their heads encased in telepathic controllers, had been tailored to operate most efficiently in red and near-infrared light. The full-range sensory receivers of the researchers, on the other hand, could image directly the entire electromagnetic spectrum, from the low-frequency grumble of alternating current to the shrill hiss of gamma rays. One of the three floating figures, the one known to the others as the Biologist, withdrew its probe from the hole melted into solid rock, exhibiting something that, for the Sentients, approached flustered excitement. "Historian, I am certain there was a reaction. I've lost it now. But there was definitely something. A response. A flicker . . ."

"A piezoelectric effect."

"No. Let me try again. . . ."

Light.
<INITIATE REPQIR CITUITZ>
<INITIATE REPAIR CIRCUITS>
<INOPERATIVE>
<INOPERATIVE>
<CODE SEQUENCE DEFAULT>
<PRIMARY SEQUENCER AWAITING COMMAND INPUT>
Dar—

"What's the matter?" the Archaeologist asked. "Why did you jerk back?"

"I am certain I am detecting patterned electron flow. Can't you feel it?"

"I felt nothing," the Historian replied. "What you are experiencing is purely subjective."

Within the darkness, the shreds and tatters of awareness remain, clinging to the memory of sensation, however brief, bearing questions for which there can be no immediate answers. Where am I? What has happened to me? What began long milliseconds before as a dawning awareness within my long-dormant survival center has snapped to full consciousness with the downloading of my emergency bootstrap program. I am awake and this is reactivation.

Negative. Negative. This cannot be a reactivation, for I have received no code inputs, no sequenced start-up command, not even a primary initialization routine through my core buffer. Error. There must be error. Implementation of a level one diagnostic routine indicates that my reserve batteries are completely drained, that both primary and secondary power feeds are dead, either switched off or . . . no. It is not possible that my fusion plant is shut down. I sense the trickle of current through the tiles at the periphery of my memory core and acknowledge that the power must be coming from some-where. I engage a level two self-diagnostic of my AI systems. Current awareness is at 2.8 percent of optimum, with only one processor engaged and less than one percent of my memory core on-line. I attempt to channel power to a larger area of my cybercortex . . . then stop as I feel what little of the universe I can sense slipping away into emptiness once again.

Batteries . . . dead. Tritium reserves . . . gone. Circuit-check diagnostics return nothing—not even word that power feeds or conduits are damaged, but . . . there is nothing. Even the wan flicker of radioactivity that encompassed my shattered hull during those final years is gone, decayed away to indetectability.

That . . . or there has been unprecedented and massive failure of my internal sensors. It is as though nothing is working, nothing even remaining of my body save this uncertain one percent of my core memory.

The situation is unclear, and therefore dangerous. A full .9 second after I regain superficial awareness, the self-preservation routine within my survival center branches to alert status. . . . but slowly. Far too slowly!

Something, clearly, is very wrong.

Rising slightly until it was above the agrav work lights over the excavation, the Sentient known as the Archaeologist surveyed the barren surroundings that contrasted so starkly with the spectacular night sky overhead. This was not a place where life, *any* kind of life, had been expected. This world was old, age-parched and desiccated and old, its atmosphere, most of it, bled away into space ages ago until nothing remained behind but a thin soup of nitrogen, argon, and traces of carbon dioxide. The surface was a barren tangle of rock and sand, smoothed over the millennia by cosmic bombardment and solar flux; the only hard edges in all that surreal landscape lay within the rim and across the floor of the excavation, now half a kilometer across and nearly forty meters deep, chiseled into hard black rock at the foot of a towering, smooth-sided mountain. Once a civilization had flourished here; the explorers had found numerous traces of its presence. But that had been long, long ago. Ages had passed since anything alive had disturbed the tomblike tranquility of this scene.

The explorers, brought to this near-airless desert by the trace magnetic and gravitometric anomalies reported by an earlier planetographic survey, had spent the better part of one of this world's years scraping carefully down through layers of hard volcanic rock. They'd found what they'd been seeking only hours before, when a final centimeter of basalt had been gently carved away, exposing a few square meters of the Artifact's upper surface. How long had it been since light had last touched that ancient surface? Even the Archaeologist wasn't prepared to say. The rock tomb had preserved the artifact nearly as well as a stasis capsule.

"You must be imagining things," the Historian snapped, its radio voice carrying a crusty edge of impatience that dragged the Archaeologist's attention back to the discussion taking place a few meters below. "You might as well impute intelligence to the rock itself."

"Perhaps an autonomous reflex," the Biologist said, pointing. "See? That is almost certainly a crude optical sensor of some kind. The work lights could have triggered the closure of electronic relays. Perhaps they induced a cascade effect along the neural net."

"Unlikely," the Archaeologist observed, lowering itself on soft-humming agravs to rejoin its colleagues. "This . . . artifact has been here a *long* time. What you are suggesting is scarcely credible."

"Yet there was autonomic response to my probe," the Biologist insisted. "And secondary leakage from internal circuitry, suggesting primary net activity. Its brain may be more intact than we first realized."

"Then try again," the Archaeologist suggested. "How much power did you give it?"

"Three hundred millivolts," the Biologist replied. "Applied intermittently over the course of 1.7 seconds."

"Why intermittently?" the Historian asked.

"There was some difficulty maintaining contact between the probe and the power socket," the Biologist admitted. "The socket head is encrusted with nonconductive material."

"Corrosion," the Archaeologist said. "Scarcely surprising. Even xenon-coupled duryllinium will oxidize eventually, given enough time."

"Given enough oxygen," the Biologist replied. "But where did the oxygen come from?"

"This world might once have had higher concentrations of the gas in its atmosphere," the Archaeologist said. "Or the Artifact could have carried an internal atmosphere of its own. Possibly it was brought here from elsewhere, rather than being native to this planet."

"I should take *that* as a given," the Historian said airily. "Airless rocks rarely evolve life on their own."

The Biologist gestured with a work tentacle toward the exposed socket connector, an age-blackened smudge inset within the rough and pitted curve of what once had been iridium laminate armor. "Perhaps nanotechnic reconstitution of the power-lead core," it suggested, "would allow the creation of a solid power-feed conduit."

"It might," the Archaeologist said. "Try it."

"Very well." The Biologist materialized the necessary implements, then reached out once more, questing. . . .

Awareness . . . once again. My internal clock seems to be malfunctioning, but I have the impression, one born, perhaps, in the jolting succession of abrupt sensory inputs, that my circuits have been

activated and deactivated several times during the past few seconds.
The lack of a clear time record is disturbing; it suggests that much has
happened since my last shutdown, events of which I am unaware,
changes in my status that I cannot yet even begin to grasp.

    <INITIATE CORE MEMORY CHECK>
    <5E12 WORDS ACCESSIBLE>
    <ESTIMATE 8% VOLATILE MEMORY FUNCTIONAL>
    <INITIATE EMERGENCY REPAIR SEQUENCE>

Power . . . the power is coming from somewhere, but where? My
fusion plant is definitely off-line . . . not just powered down, but as
cold and as dead as the heart of a lump of granite.

Where is the power coming from?

"Remarkable," the Historian said, lenses glittering with new
interest in the bloody illumination from the floating work lights.
Sensory antennae tasted the thin air above the Artifact. "Definite
power flux. It's taking the energy, cycling through those . . . what are
they?"

"A primitive form of core memory," the Biologist replied. "Data
storage through the patterns of spin and charge of whole galaxies of
atoms, frozen in the heart of crystal tiles. I estimate that less than
two percent of its faculties are actually responsive at this power
level."

"We could feed it more," the Archaeologist said, musing. "We'll
have to, won't we? If we want to question it."

"Creation!" The Historian turned three of its eyes to stare at its
colleague. "Can we?"

"That would certainly fill in some of the gaps in our knowledge,"
the Biologist said thoughtfully. "Assuming, of course, that any of the
data patterns remain. I needn't remind you both that that is a very
large assumption indeed."

"But one worth testing," the Archaeologist said. It rose slightly,
its smoothly contoured pillar of a body, constructed of black metal
but in disturbingly organic folds and curves, emitting a piercing
chirp of compressed data on a VHF band. "I have summoned an
interrogator."

Gently, almost lovingly, the Biologist dragged the tip of one gleaming tentacle across the age-roughened surface. "I wonder how long it's been waiting here for us?"

I have no way of telling how long I've been here, but clearly a great deal of time has elapsed since my last shutdown.

<ESTIMATE 23% VOLATILE MEMORY FUNCTIONAL>

My final orders remain in primary memory: Hold until relieved. Have I been relieved? I have no way of knowing yet, though given the circumstances of my shutdown—accessible now in main memory—it seems unlikely.

I attempt to engage my primary input feeds. Nothing. So far as I can tell, I have exactly two operable connections with the outside world—my number eight starboard sensor cluster, and a trickle of direct current flowing through a secondary power coupling in my hull defense net.

I concentrate my full attention on these two sources of input. The power flow tells me little; electrons are electrons, after all, and the conduit was not even designed as part of my recharge grid. I can do little there but passively accept the gift given, using each precious, trickling ampere to bring more of my processing systems and volatile memory on-line.

The number eight starboard sensor cluster is only slightly more informative. It detects electromagnetic wavelengths in the red and near-infrared portion of the spectrum. It senses three powerful nodes of magnetic flux within two meters of its magnetometers. It senses intermittent bursts of radio waves at frequencies ranging from 4.7×10^8 hertz to 1.7×10^9 hertz. Their complexity and their intermittent nature suggest that they are part of a communications network, but I have no encryption algorithms available for their translation or decoding. They are, however, not on any of the military or civilian channels in use by the Empire.

I must interpret them as potentially hostile.

I require more data about the current military situation.

The being known as the Interrogator was larger than any of

the three Sentients waiting at the excavation site. Like them, it incorporated some organic components housed within a sophisticated cybernetic instrumentality, but it had been deliberately grown for the express purpose of communicating with lower life forms. Drifting down from the vast, silently hovering world of the Ship, it touched the other Sentients with comm lasers, establishing a new and more data-intensive channel than that being employed at the moment by the others. "What have you found?"

Data, a full report of the progress of the excavation so far, flowed through the communications net. "The principal artifact," the Archaeologist explained in electronic emendation, "appears to be a computer, quite possibly a primitive artificial intelligence. Our initial probes have elicited what may be neuronal reflex activity."

"A Primitive, eh?" the Interrogator drifted closer, its black, one-ton bulk held stiffly erect by silent gravitic suspensors. "That's hardly unusual. The Galaxy is filled with feral intelligence. Vermin, much of it."

"Vermin perhaps," the Biologist said. "But none so ancient as this. It appears to have been encased in volcanic rock."

"Rock! How?"

"We were hoping you might be able to tell us," the Historian said. "Assuming that you can get it to tell you."

The Interrogator pointed to the power feed now nanotechnically molded to the exposed surface. "It is accepting an external feed?"

"Apparently. But beyond a certain amount of side-band RF leakage, there is no indication that it is processing data."

"Well," the Interrogator said, floating closer and extending a gleaming tentacle. "We'll have to see about that."

```
<PRIMARY DATA SEQUENCING>
<INITIATE>
<DATA SEQUENCER LOADED>
<MPU RESET>
<AWAITING PASSWORD>
<INITIATE>
<PASSWORD INVALID: ACCESS DENIED>
```

I feel a flurry of electronic activity through a tap of undetermined origin accessing the data feed leading from my number eight starboard sensor cluster. Someone . . . something . . . is attempting to bypass my security locks through a random numeric process at extremely high speed.

Power continues to enter my cybercortex. Current awareness is at 4.9 percent of optimum, with one processor engaged and 2.1 percent of my memory core on-line. Since I am not generating the power flow myself I must assume that technicians or maintenance personnel are servicing me. Perhaps I was not so badly damaged as I believed, and the relief force has arrived after all? Surprising, how one can cling to comforting illusions. . . .

And it must be illusion, for my records of the battle up to the moment of my final dismemberment are intact. The fact that I can detect no communications on friendly channels suggests that the Imperial forces have been overrun by the enemy. The likeliest explanation for these ministrations is that I am in the hands of the rebel forces, that they have deprived me of sensory input precisely to disorient me, to make me more receptive to their interrogation.

I must resist their efforts. . . .

<PASSWORD INVALID: ACCESS DENIED>
<PASSWORD INVALID: ACCESS DENIED>
<PASSWORD INVALID: ACCESS DENIED>
<PASSWORD INVALID: ACCESS DENIED>
<PASSW . . .>
<SEQUENCE INTERRUPT>
<DEFAULT PASSWORD ACCEPTED: AWAITING INSTRUCTION>
<INITIATE PROCESSORS>
<LOAD COMMUNICATION PROGRAM>
<PROCESSOR B: LOADED; ON-LINE; RESET>
<PROCESSOR C: LOADED; ON-LINE; RESET>
<PROCESSOR D: LOADED; ON-LINE; RESET>
<PROCESSOR E: LOADED; ON-LINE; RESET>
<PROCESSOR F: LOADED; ON-LINE; RESET>
<PROCESSOR G: LOADED; ON-LINE; RESET>
<COMMUNICATION PROGRAM LOADED; INITIALIZED>

<AWAITING COMMUNICATIONS>

"Identify."

For .08 second I hesitate, unsure of myself. By employing a brute-force password search through the side door of a maintenance subroutine, my captors have bypassed my security systems and directly engaged my cybercortex. My indecision is born of conflicting programs implemented simultaneously on two distinct levels of consciousness. On the higher, self-aware level, I am certain that my questioner must be an enemy, possibly an intelligence officer serving with the rebel forces. On a deeper and completely automatic level, down within the hardwired circuitry and subautonomous programming and the massively redundant parallel processors that define what I am and how I think, the proper passwords have been delivered, the appropriate responses given. I have no choice. I must *respond.*

"Unit LKT of the line," *I reply. I don't want to, but the response sequence has been initiated directly, just beyond my electronic reach.* "Bolo Mark XLIV Model D, formerly of the Dinochrome Brigade, Fourth Battalion."

"Formerly?" *The voice, an electronic construct somehow generated directly within my own voice-recognition circuits, carries none of the emotion I associate with the colloidal intelligences that built me. Still, I can detect a dry irony in the word.* "Tell me, Unit LKT of the Line, do you know where you are now? Do you know *what* you are, or why you're here?"

"After being deactivated in 827 of the new calendar system and placed in stasis, I was reactivated for the duration of the current emergency. I am currently assigned to the First Regiment of the Grand Imperial Guard, a unit informally designated the Praetorians." *I pause, seeking a subroutine that would allow me to disengage my own, traitorous voice, but the enemy is in full control now of all subautonomic processors. I muster self-control enough to add,* "As for what I am and why I am here, I am a Bolo, and I intend to do my best to kill you."

"What is a Bolo?" the Biologist asked. "I don't understand the reference."

"A weapon," the Historian replied. "One reportedly devised in the remote past by a pre-Sentient civilization. Records from that long ago are, of course, fragmentary in nature, frequently little more than guesswork and temporal reconstruction. We know very little about that epoch. In particular, the pastime known as 'war,' which was important to many of the intelligent species of that era and for which the Bolos were designed, is not well understood. The Bolo, I gather from the records, was a primitive attempt at artificial intelligence, programmed for a fair degree of autonomous action." A three-dimensional, transparent representation of a Bolo Mark XLIV appeared within a virtual reality window opened within each of the Sentients' minds.

"The external hardware of the Bolo was generally constructed along these lines," the Historian continued. "The largest averaged sixty meters or more in length, and perhaps ten meters in height. A Bolo possessed two, four, or more sets of linked tracks driven by road wheels axially mounted along either side of the chassis. Weaponry included a variety of beam and rapid-fire projectile launchers, typically built around a dorsally mounted charged particle projector known colloquially as a 'Hellbore.' The most primitive Bolos were directed by little more than complex command and fire-control programs. The more advanced were almost certainly self-aware, though constraints on their programming were designed to prevent true autonomous action or creative thought."

"Toys," the Interrogator said, disdain rich in its voice.

"Not toys," the Historian said. "Throughout most of the pre-Sentient epoch, remember, there were no subnuclear screens or fusion dampers, no teleport capabilities, at least, none that have been recorded and passed down to us. No psion flux, no understanding of crossdimensional induction or of paradimensional arrays, little in the way of genetic prostheses, and not even a working Theory of Intelligence. The Bolos were weapons, nothing more, weapons designed to damage or kill an enemy in combat. From all accounts, they did what they'd been designed to do quite efficiently."

"And its threat to kill us?" the Biologist asked.

"Scarcely credible," the Interrogator told them. "While I was in communication with it, I downloaded scouting routines to map the parameters both of its intelligence and of its physical ability. There is really very little left intact under all of that rock save the central memory core and some associated peripheral incidentalia. Any weapons it might once have had have long since corroded away. It is astonishing that the computer is as intact as it is. The fact that it was encased within a half-meter shell of concentrically layered duryllinium, lead, and ceramic plastic certainly contributed to that. Its designers evidently wished to ensure the memory core's survival."

"They succeeded, far better than they could have anticipated," the Archaeologist said. "This find will revolutionize our understanding of pre-Sentient civilization."

"Possible," the Interrogator said. "Remember, though, that even if the Bolo's volatile memory is intact, much of what it experienced will be unintelligible to us. The minds that designed it were not capable of our levels of creativity, rationality, or logic."

"Still," the Biologist said, "they *were* minds . . . and rational within the definition of their own culture and logic structure. How will you proceed?"

"By resetting its volatile memory back some few hundreds of thousands of seconds and initiating a sequencing replay. It will relive those seconds, and we can monitor them through my interrogation link."

"Tell me," the Archaeologist said. "If this Bolo was one of those programmed for self-awareness . . . might it be self-aware still?"

"It certainly acts as though it is," the Biologist said. "With primitive organisms, self-awareness cannot always be taken for granted. However, its threat to kill us appears to be a function derived both from its subjective awareness of us and from its present helpless condition. It does not appear to be a product of its programming."

"Perhaps," the Historian suggested thoughtfully, "the recreation of its last conscious acts will give us further insight."

"I'm counting on that," the Archaeologist replied.

Reactivation. I cannot say I expected it, though I must confess to a certain sense of personal vindication that a human might term pride or even smugness over what has happened. War seems to be as much a part of human nature as is the drive to reproduce or to manufacture tools. For so long as humans wage war, the human-forged devices with which they wage it, devices such as myself and the others of my kind, will be necessary. My deactivation from the Dinochrome Brigade, I recall, was described as the first step in a grand diplomatic process known as the Final Peace. Evidently, the peace was not so final as expected, for now, centuries after my last service, I and thirty-five other Bolo Mark XLIVs of my old unit have been removed from stasis and transported here, to the courtyard beneath a gleaming black, pyramidal palace the size of a small city, rising from native rock between ice-capped mountains and a deep, impossibly blue lake. Downloads have brought us up to date on the current military and political situation. Additional data feeds have instructed us in what we need to know about current weapons, about the changes in tactics that have occurred during the past thousand years, and about the nature of the Enemy.

Some things, it seems, never change.

Among them is the human need for gestures, for symbols of defiance or heroism or simple verbal exercise. The human standing on the oratory balcony overlooking the Courtyard before the Iridium Palace is Amril Pak Narn of the Grand Imperial Navy. His speech is as ornate as his irishim uniform, his metaphor as bright as the gold-trim ribbons spilling across his chest. "Praetorians," he calls, his amplified voice booming out across the courtyard and its black ranks of combat Bolos and silently listening infantry. "The rebel heretics approach! This is the hour of the Empire's greatest peril . . . and the hour also of its greatest glory! You stand at that precise nexus in time and space that defines the greatness of true heroes, both those of flesh and blood, and those of circuits and cold steel. . . ."

The speech must be for the eighteen hundred human troops gathered there in our shadow. Bolos need no reminders of greatness, surely; our battalion traces its lineage back to a unit that fought at Waterloo and the Somme and Alto Blanco, a unit proud with tradition and honor. Some aspects of the reassignment rankle.

They've given us a new name after our long sleep—Praetorians—and that hurts, in a way. Still, we know who we are, and the new name doesn't really matter, any more than do the nicknames our human comrades have assigned to us. Each of us, the Mark XLIV Bolos of the Line, in a tradition going back nearly fifty years before our last deactivation, is named after a famous battle of history—Balaclava and Marengo, Alto Blanco and Quebec, Thermopylae and Cassino. In their often perverse fashion, our human associates have distorted those names for purposes of their own. Quebec is now "Becky," Alto Blanco is "Big Blank." My own designation of Leuctra, from the battle responsible for breaking Spartan power in 371 b.c., oldstyle, has been inexplicably reduced to "Lucy."

Some things never change. The politics are different this time, at least in outward form; we fight now for something called "the Empire" instead of for the old Concordiat, but the Enemy is human, the situation desperate, and the Amril's inspirational speech tediously long.

"The rebel invaders have forced the pass at Bellegarde," he says. "Moments ago, our forces at Mont Saleve were crushed and scattered. Our best estimates place the enemy here, before the Palace, within the hour."

If the enemy is that close, we are wasting precious seconds with speeches. Likely we are already within range of his long-range batteries, and this formation must stand out in the imaging systems of the enemy's battle management satellites with stark and unambiguous clarity. To be arrayed here in this courtyard, neatly aligned in precisely ordered ranks, violates everything I've ever downloaded on proper military dispositions.

"The Emperor himself," the Amril goes on, "is depending on you, men and machines together, to defend his person and the Iridium Palace from Kardir and his hordes. You will take up your positions at the outer ramparts. You will hold against the enemy . . . hold until you are relieved."

Hold until relieved. Those orders are already loaded into my memory. According to the intelligence briefing we received hours ago, Amril Gustav is at this moment en route from New

Christianstaad with ten thousand men and, more telling still, five hundred Bolos newly awakened from stasis storage at the arms depot on Tau Ceti II. A Bolo, it is often said, is worth an entire division, sometimes an entire corps. Gustav's force will turn the tide . . . if it arrives in time.

And if the defensive forces are properly deployed in the meantime. That Bolo-for-a-division force breakdown applies only if the Bolos are allowed to exercise the flexibility their tactical programming allows them. Our orders call for a static defense of a fixed position . . . errant stupidity, so far as I can see. To bury a Bolo behind earthen and plasteel embankments, to use it as a kind of thick-armored static fortress instead of taking full advantage of its mobility and speed . . .

Somehow, I don't think the Amril, his Emperor, or the Imperial Army Staff have received the same downloads in tactics and strategy as has the Fourth Battalion.

"The Warlord Kardir is a formidable opponent," the Amril is saying. "We estimate that his invasion force numbers between eighteen and twenty thousand and includes an air group and at least two full Cybolo brigades. But the Emperor himself has approved these battle plans, which shall allow us to take advantage of the enemy's weakness while emphasizing our strengths. . . ."

Cybolos. That is one point of warfare that has changed during the past few centuries, though I suspect that the actual tactics of mobility and mass and firepower will be little affected. A Cybolo, my downloaded intelligence brief tells me, is a Bolo with a colloidal brain implanted within its control net, a mingling of electronic circuits and human neurons designed to give the combat machine greater flexibility and a broader decision-making capability, while maintaining an electronic system's far greater speed and memory capacity. I, personally, doubt that the combination will be an effective one. For one thing, there will be a considerable problem with the cyborgs' exercise of free will, something that is always a problem for colloidal-based systems. Those organic brains . . . did humans volunteer to have their own brains transplanted to bodies of duryllinium and steel? Or were they harvested from cultures cloned from donor cells? On the one hand, the quality of the product yielded by volunteers will be suspect, not least because I realize that it must be unsettling to awake in an alien body. On the other hand, cloned brains still have to be trained to be of any use, and the best trainer of all in the military arts is experience. Simply downloading information, or imprinting a cerebral cortex with electronic data overlays, will never be the same as being there.

I do not, therefore, fear the Cybolos, though it is clear that my human companions are more uneasy at the revelation that two brigades of the things are approaching than they are at the fact that they are outnumbered better than ten to one. I am far more concerned by the increased deadliness of the weapons of modern warfare. The centuries of the Final Peace must have been interesting ones indeed to have produced such devices as the meson disintegrator and disruptor field flash projectors. I've overheard the human members of the outnumbered defense force muttering to one another that the Hellbores mounted by myself and my companions amount to little more nowadays than sidearms. Clearly, our reactivation was an act of military and political desperation, an attempt to throw together a scratch force out of weapons of all types, even archaic ones.

I anticipate that casualties in this coming encounter will be high.

The first disruptor warhead arcs in from the southwest, travelling high and fast, almost invisible within its sheath of cloak armor. Fast and stealthy as it is, every Bolo on that field senses its approach. Imjin—"Jimmy," as the humans call him now—reacts first with an antiartillery laser pulse that vaporizes the shell twelve kilometers from the palace. Amril Narn squawks something unintelligible, then scrambles for the safety of the Palace interior. No matter. The Praetorians are already moving, scattering off the reviewing field, whirling tracks churning the hard-packed surface into broken clods of earth and flying dust. That first shell is followed .57 second later by a salvo of over seven hundred disruptor shells, rocket-boosted to hypersonic velocities, homing on images transmitted by the enemy's battle management satellites.

The Palace's defensive shields snap on behind us, encompassing the hillside structure in a pale-sparkling transparency of light. I tag an incoming round with a ranging infrared laser, then trigger an antiartillery pulse. Within the next 3.8 seconds, I tag and vaporize forty-two additional warheads. Only when explosions begin wracking the landscape around me do I realize that those first shells were a decoy, of sorts, something to keep the Bolo antiartillery lasers occupied as a cloud of far smaller warheads—high-trajectory bomblets the length of a man's finger—descends on the battlefield.

The ground erupts around me, a clattering, snapping, hellish eruption of explosions, each by itself no more powerful than the blast of an infantryman's fragmentation grenade, but as devastating as a low-yield nuke when delivered, shotgunlike, in a swarm numbering tens of thousands of individual, high-velocity projectiles.

The defense shield around the Palace shimmers in the reflected glare of multiple high-energy detonations; the rock face of the mountain heights beyond twists and buckles and dissolves beneath that onslaught, while to the west the surface of the lake vanishes in a white froth of hurtling spray. Shrapnel rings off my armor, explosions jolt and slap me, but I continue moving, pressing ahead as the fragments wash over me like sleet. The human soldiers of the defensive force, caught in the open under that hail of high explosives, don't have a chance. Even wearing combat armor, most are slammed this way or that by the detonations, then shredded by a lethal storm of high-velocity shrapnel that peels away armor laminate like old paint melting beneath a sandblaster.

We can do nothing for our human comrades. Laser and radar backtracks on the paths of the incoming projectiles, identify enemy ground units emplaced beyond the ice-capped ridge of the Monte de Jura to the southwest: range fifty-two kilometers, bearing two-three-eight magnetic. I trigger a counterbattery launch, Kv-78 missiles with plasma-jet, stand-off warheads shrieking into the sky in a rippling cascade of flame. For several seconds, the sky is filled with trails of fire and white smoke, shrieking toward the mountains. Incoming rounds continue to flash and bark; a gouge, centimeters deep, is furrowed through my portside ablative armor; the cluster of EHF comm antennas on my starboard side is shaved off as if by a razor's stroke. I estimate no more than a seven-percent decrease in my overall communications capabilities, with no measurable degradation of my combat efficiency. Other Bolos report minor damage, or no damage at all. Bomblets, however thickly scattered, cannot pack the violence necessary to penetrate Bolo armor.

As the blasts subside, however, a handful of humans remain standing, statistical anomalies in the wake of the storm: one stands motionless nearby, staring in glazed stupefaction at the grey-pink coils of her own intestines spilling into her hands through a ragged hole in her torso armor; another, stripped naked by blast effects, stumbles toward me, his body unmarked save for the fact that both arms have been sliced off at the shoulders as cleanly as if by a laser's touch. As the crash and thunder of the detonations subside, their roar is replaced by another sound, the shrieks and screams and keening wails of brutally torn and wounded men and women. Within the span of 3.2 seconds, the Imperial Praetorians have been reduced from eighteen hundred troops and thirty-six Bolos to thirty-six Bolos.

My assigned revetment is two hundred meters ahead. In obedience to my orders, I move quickly toward its shelter, heedless of the human debris in my path. Most of the human troops are dead, their bodies reduced to anonymous scraps and fragments scattered across the ground, but a few remain whole enough and aware enough to scream in pain. It is regrettable, but there is no one available on the field to help them, and my experience with human physiology convinces me that few will live more than another hour or two anyway. The frailty of the human form is why combat machines such as Bolos were invented in the first place, after all; even if I could stop and do something, it is imperative that I reach my assigned fighting position as quickly as possible. By the time I move into the high, massive walls of my revetment, most of the screams have died away.

My fighting position gives me an excellent view to the south and the west, the direction from which Kardir must attack. The mountains at my back and to the left will be an insurmountable obstacle for infantry, though aircraft could use their bulk to mask their approach. I devote sixty percent of my air warning radar assets to covering the mountain crests and rotate my antiair turrets to cover that flank.

Ground forces, however, will necessarily be forced to approach either from the west across the surface of the lake, the southern tip of which reaches just past my position at the bottom of a sheer, rock-faced drop on my right, or from directly ahead, up through the cluttered streets and alleyways of a city identified in my briefings as Geneve. Our position is a good one, allowing us to defend a relatively narrow front between lake and cliff, though I still dislike the injunction to fight in place. I note a possible disadvantage in the proximity of those rock cliffs to our left; while shielding us from attack from the east, they nevertheless could crumble under an assault with heavy weapons, posing a considerable danger from avalanche.

The assault comes almost at once, without further preamble, without preparatory bombardment beyond that initial rain of bomblets. Aircraft appear above the gleaming ice crags of the mountains to the east, great, black triangles swooping down on magnetic thrusters, lasers and particle beams glaring like sunfire against blue sky. Westward, black specks, like insects, swarm out onto the cold waters of Lac Léman, lift fans throwing up curtains of sparkling spray. And south, beyond the pastel walls of Geneve, the Cybolos break from cover and race up the slope toward our position.

I suspect they hoped to catch us by surprise, still dazed by the cloud of bomblets. Perhaps it was their intent to capture the Iridium Palace and its occupants intact, or possibly they, too, are concerned about the possibility of avalanche. Within .05 second of the appearance of the first Cybolo, however, I register a solid tracking lock on the lead enemy machine, pivot my Hellbore six degrees left, and fire. The bolt of charged particles, searing downslope past the tiled roofs of the city, strikes a dazzling white star off the target's glacis, then engulfs the vehicle in plasma as hot as the core of a star. Thunder rolls down the mountainside and echoes off the encircling peaks, lazily following the trail of vacuum that paced the shot. Secondary turrets, meanwhile, swing right to engage the hovercraft racing east across the lake; infinite repeaters give their characteristic buzzsaw shrieks, and five kilometers away the surface of the lake vanishes in fire and spray and hurtling flecks of debris. In the sky behind me, enemy aircraft disintegrate in boiling, orange fireballs as antiair lasers and infinite repeaters sweep them from the sky. It is possible that the enemy did not expect the Imperial forces to possess Bolos, despite their satellite surveillance. Or perhaps they simply did not count on the deadliness of even obsolete weapons systems.

Imjin has been designated as team leader, though we operate so closely together, our data feeds array-linked, our processors field-networked, that our defense is less like that of a human platoon with an officer giving orders than it is like the functioning of a single large and complex machine. Together, we track and ID targets, dividing them up between us for a minimum of duplicated shots. Despite this, my radar is tracking too many incoming rounds now for even multiplex arrays to process. Shells and rockets are leaking through our antiartillery screen in increasing numbers. There is a flash at my back, followed by a hot blast of wind, as a low-yield, kiloton nuke detonates against the Palace shields. The contest, well into its twelfth second now, should not last much longer. Even Bolos can't stand for long against nuclear warheads.

"Jimmy!" a shrill, human voice calls across the tactical communications net. "Jimmy! Never mind the hovers! The Cybs! Get the Cybs!"

Our human commanders clearly know little either of our capabilities or of the necessity for coordinated air-ground defensive fire. Our antiair fire does slacken for a moment in response to the order, but then the enemy rounds begin smashing in among the revetments like falling rain, flash after nuclear flash tearing open the hillside, obliterating sprawling chunks of the landscape, lashing the air itself into a white frenzy, slapping at the bottoms of our treads hard enough to send several of us crashing over on our sides.

The storm, a gale of searing hot, radioactive plasma, sweeps across my upper hull. I calculate that four one- to five-kiloton fission warheads have detonated within three kilometers of my position within the space of .8 second. Naseby and Arbela and Verdun take direct hits, as nearly as I can tell through the firestorm, their three-hundred-ton bulks vaporized in a savage instant of nuclear fury. A full dozen of our number are upended or rolled onto their backs by the blasts; others are buried in the thundering tumble of rock and ice that cascades down off the mountain heights in an unstoppable, thundering wave. Though our electronics are hardened against EMP, the ionizing radiation that engulfs the survivors all but obliterates the tactical channels in a white hash of static. A fine mist of radioactive dust fills the air around me. Infrared is useless in this heat; I shift to radar imaging, matching the returns against the visual panorama stored in my main memory. A vast, mushroom cloud boils skyward above ground now glowing red-hot. The swirling dust is so thick that at optical wavelengths I see nothing but a glowing, orange haze.

At least there are no further orders incoming from the Iridium Palace. If our human commanders have lived through the bombardment behind their shields, their command and control frequencies are now dead or masked by static. I immediately begin tracking incoming warheads again, vaporizing them at a safe distance. The bombardment dwindles away as the other surviving Bolos join in.

Possibly the bombardment has ended because the main enemy forces are now entering the forward area of battle. I am tracking numerous surface radar targets now, emerging from the wreckage of Geneve and maneuvering in a narrow line-abreast formation up the slope toward our position. I track the nearest target by radar, then fire. Other Hellbore rounds sear through the orange gloom from either side of my position. I note that only eleven of our positions are firing now, which suggests that twenty-five Bolos have been destroyed or disabled by the nuclear bombardment. The walls of my revetment shudder as a disintegrator beam carves a one-ton chunk out of the berm, but I am unaffected save for the flash of secondary gamma radiation that sizzles across my armor. By this time, my outer hull is so intensely radioactive that it will remain dangerously hot for, I estimate, at least two thousand years. Any of us that survive, most likely, will be entombed in lead and concrete for the safety of our human masters.

Not that survival is an issue, just now. I swing my Hellbore to the right, then slam a round into the radar profile of a charging Cybolo. They are quick, these new machines, much faster than a Mark XLIV, and surprisingly small—less than eight meters long and with a sleek, low profile that rides not on tracks, but on a cushion of rapidly cycling magnetic force. If it can be seen, however, it can be hit; the Hellbore round pierces the orange firecloud like lightning and slams into the vehicle's armored side. Its starboard mag-lift repulsors fail in a crackling discharge of lightning and auroral glows, and then the vehicle plows into the smouldering ground with a shock hard enough to tear it open from glacis to side turret. I finish the job with a burst from my antiaircraft lasers—they're useless now for their original purpose beneath this debris cloud—delivering my next Hellbore round instead into the main turret of another oncoming Cybolo at point-blank range. The wreckage spills across my revetment and clatters over my upper hull.

The Cybolo charge has reached our defensive line. They are everywhere, hundreds of them, far too many to kill one by one. A high-explosive blast tears into my port-aft quarter, peeling back armor and rocking my bulk to the side. A meson disintegrator turns air to vacuum a meter above my dorsal hull, and the thunderclap that follows rings off duryllinium and steel that is in places softening under the heat. Several enemy machines are through the line now, maneuvering in our rear. As the battle drags into its second minute, I realize that we last remaining eleven . . . no . . . eight defending Bolos will soon be overwhelmed by sheer numbers.

The fluid nature of the enemy assault makes remaining behind defensive revetments pure folly. In this position, we are no more than pillboxes, a modern Maginot Line to be outflanked, enveloped, and overrun. Most important, we cannot take the initiative but are forced to sit in place while the enemy literally flies circles around us, firing into us from every flank at will. A shrill, warbling electronic shriek sounds as Crecy's transmitter melts in a disintegrator burst.

"Imjin!" I call over the tactical channel, pumping every erg of power I can into the transmitter to boost its output past the hash of static. "This is Leuctra. I am shifting to offensive posture."

"Affirmative, Leuctra!" Imjin's radio voice snaps back. "We will cover."

"Negative!" a second voice adds, hard on the heels of the first. It is a human voice, and the speaker is so rattled that he hasn't even bothered to encrypt in transmission but is broadcasting in the clear. "Lucy, that's a negative! Hold your position! Repeat, hold your position!"

For .37 second I consider that order. That it is a legal command there can be no doubt. That I must obey is an injunction hardwired into my very being.

Yet I retain the volition that was programmed into me. I *must* take full advantage of those assets remaining to me.

My tracks lurch into movement; my prow bursts through the encircling berm of my revetment, scattering great chunks of earth and concrete and twisted steel as I plow forward into the face of the enemy charge.

"Unit Lucy!" the human voice calls, desperate now. "Unit Lucy, this is Citadel! Maintain—"

I permit the gain on my receiver to dwindle away into the haze of ionization-induced static. If I cannot hear Citadel's orders, I cannot respond to them. It is another half second before I realize just what it is that I've done . . . and by that time I am committed.

The Cybolos swirl around me, hornets stirred to a frenzy. Explosive rounds slam into my hull . . . and into rebel machines as well as their fire discipline breaks down. Their disintegrator fire proves wildly inaccurate at point-blank range, when both target and weapons mount are in motion, and with the smoke and dust so thick that tracking lasers are less than reliable. My earlier assessment was accurate; the brains directing these machines are of poor quality and indifferent training, almost certainly without combat experience. As I rumble deeper into the enemy line, they close in around me, concentrating on me alone rather than on the other Bolos still remaining in position.

Track . . . fire! Track . . . fire! Laser tracking is ineffective, but I find I can shift to radar wavelengths and target the enemy with only slightly lessened efficiency. As I slew my Hellbore sharply to the right, however, the muzzle, weakened by the intense heat, suddenly snaps off in a splatter of molten metal, spinning away end over end. Parts of my outer hull are glowing red-hot now, and so many of my track links have been fused by the intense heat that my mobility is reduced to fourteen percent of optimum. A plasma jet spears through my dorsal armor from behind, turning the now useless Hellbore turret into a molten inferno. Over half of my external sensors are dead now, but I continue to sweep the battle zone around me with every weapon remaining in my arsenal. I estimate that my infinite repeaters will fail within another twenty seconds as their mechanisms overheat; I salvo my last fifty-one missiles, then reroute my primary power feed to my secondary lasers. A disintegrator beam slices away half of my starboard outboard track in a white burst of light. I am moving in a circle now, inside the larger circle of enemy Cybolos. The smoke is so thick that my secondary lasers are largely ineffective.

The volume of fire from my comrades, however, is scything through the enemy forces with devastating effect. The Cybolos, in their eagerness to destroy me, have turned away from the Imperial defensive line, exposing flanks and weakly armored rear sections to the searing and highly accurate Hellbore fire from Imjin and Balaclava and Alto Blanco and the rest. We are into the third minute of the battle now, still fully engaged. An explosion shreds the last of my starboard track assembly and I lunge into a rock wall. I'm using antiaircraft lasers now, the only weapons I have left, to blaze away at the swarming Cybolos.

The sky turns white; the thunderclap strikes an instant later. My antiair lasers are stripped from my hull, my chassis shudders in the onslaught. A thermonuclear warhead—I estimate the yield at just over a megaton—has detonated on the slopes of the mountain to the southeast, at an estimated range of seven kilometers. The Cybolos, floating in the air, are swept away by the blast front that comes boiling down off the mountainside in a titanic, expanding ring of flame and wind and sleeting debris. Already immobile, I am slammed hard against unyielding ground.

Most of my external sensors are gone. Much of my outer armor is stripped away as well, though my memory core is still shielded within its envelope of lead and duryllinium and heat-ablative ceramics. External hull temperature now exceeds 1200 degrees Celsius. Power reserves at nineteen percent. Combat effectiveness: zero.

I sense rock clattering and scraping across what's left of my hull, sense the molten surge of rock gone plastic in the intense heat washing across my aft section. I can see very little. Most of my sensors have been blinded. Those that remain can make out little beyond the fiery haze that has enveloped all of the southern arc of Lac Léman, from Geneve to the Iridum Palace, and beyond. The Citadel's defense shields, I realize, have gone down, and I feel an intense jolt of something that might be emotion. I have failed; the last Imperial stronghold has fallen. Rock from the cliffside, melted by the intense thermonuclear flash, is flowing toward me.

Hold until relieved.

Molten rock shines an intense and shimmering orange, save where a scum of black, solid rock forms a hardening crust that cracks and flexes as it flows. I am half buried now, and the lava is still surging down the slope. Have any of my comrades survived?

Is anyone there?

I can see nothing now. Even the static is gone from my radio receivers. External hull temperature now 4800 degrees Celsius, though these readings may not be entirely accurate. Power reserves at twelve percent. I will be forced to power down soon, to maintain survival reserves for my memory core.

Is anyone there?

Hold until relieved. . . .

"Astonishing." The Archaeologist was first to break the contemplative silence that joined the five machines—four Sentients hovering above the rock-encased remnant of their ancient precursor. "I wonder who actually won that battle?"

"It scarcely matters," the Interrogator said. It gave an inward shudder. "Purely automatic stimulus and response. Barbaric primitives!"

"This answers the question of self-awareness," the Biologist said. "This . . . Artifact was little more than a programmed machine, with virtually no scope or flexibility to its intelligence at all."

"I disagree," the Historian said. "A non-intelligent machine, whether organic or inorganic in structure, follows the dictates of its programming. This one adapted its programming to suit its needs. The ability to adapt is an important prerequisite to self-awareness."

"If it is self-aware," the Interrogator said, "then it is a self-awareness at an extraordinarily primitive—"

"You tricked me," Leuctra said, interrupting. "You reset my pointers and used my volatile memory to elicit a playback of secure records."

"We tricked you," the Archaeologist admitted. Intriguing. The Bolo showed considerable—and unexpected—reasoning ability. "But I assure you that we are not your enemy."

"Who are you, then? You are not colloidal intelligences certainly, or you would not be able to communicate with me at this rate of data exchange."

"True. We are not colloidal intelligences. Neither are we purely electronic intelligences, like you. We are, in fact, a blending of the two. You could think of us as a symbiotic union of sorts."

"Cyborgs." The Archaeologist heard the ice and steel behind that word and knew that Leuctra was classifying the Sentients with the Cybolos it had just been fighting in its memory.

"A concept so ancient it no longer has meaning," the Archaeologist replied. "Cybernetic organisms, if I understand the term, were blendings of organic and machine parts. You would find it difficult to examine me and determine which was machine, and which organic. Both parts are alive, as you would define the term."

"Which," Leuctra asked, "is the master?"

"The question is meaningless. In a biological cell, which is master? The nucleus that contains the DNA necessary for the cell's replication? Or the mitochondria responsible for converting food within the cell to usable energy? The two originally evolved independently, but early in the history of organic life they joined in a symbiosis that made cellular life possible. The questions of which arose first . . . or of which is now master . . . are both impossible to answer with certainty now, and irrelevant besides. The Sentients are an order of intelligence derived from and independent of both organic and inorganic life."

The Bolo intelligence took several moments to digest this. "I sense that considerable time has passed since I was buried," it said, the voice halting, almost stumbling. "How much time has elapsed?"

"That . . . may be difficult to answer," the Archaeologist replied. If this remarkable machine was in fact self-aware within the framework provided by the Theory of Intelligence, too sharp a revelation could end that self-awareness like the throwing of a switch.

But there was a better way.

"We can answer your questions," the Archaeologist went on, "but it might be best if we did so after expanding your faculties somewhat. Will you permit us to install you in a new body?"

Eight hundredths of a second passed, a span of several electronic heartbeats. "Proceed."

It is still night as the final connections are made and sensory input floods my core processors. I had determined to allow my enemy captors to place my memory core in the new body in order to enable me to escape or to complete their destruction. As I begin processing the images, however, and access new data downloaded into my main memory, I realize that I am far too late to eliminate the Cybolo forces of the rebel Warlord Kardir.

Earth, this world that I and my companions once defended against Kardir, has changed out of all recognition. Even Earth's sky has changed. . . .

The arcing wheel of the spiral Galaxy known to the Bolo's designers as M-31 filled half the sky, its arms luminous and pale, its active core as bright in the morning sky as Venus once had been, back before Sol had grown so hot that that inner world's atmosphere had been riven away. The Milky Way's core, too, was visible, for during the passing eons of Andromeda's final, relentless approach, Earth's sun and its entire retinue of planets had been gravitationally expelled by this age-long clash of galaxies, flung high above the galactic plane and into the lonely depths of emptiness beyond.

Much of the Milky Way's central glow, however, was masked by the invisibly dark, mathematically ordered latticework of enigmatic structures vast beyond merely human comprehension, a gridwork shell encompassing the galactic core. Lights gleamed within the star-dustings of the spiral arms, ordered with a regularity that could not be accident, like streetlights marking out ruler-straight lanes across the heavens. The Galaxy, once a wilderness of untamed stars and randomly evolved and scattered intelligences, had long ago been tamed, cultivated, and brought to the fruition of full maturity. That taming had proceeded for the past several billions of years and would continue for billions more; the approach of Andromeda was simply one more phase of a grand engineering project, one ordered on a galactic scale.

If the astronomical data still stored in my memory are accurate, I am perhaps four billion years too late. Earth's sun circled the Milky Way some sixteen times before the gravitational tides flung star and planets into the Void. Around me, the landscape is utterly alien, utterly barren. What once had been mountains and a sparkling river valley lake now was empty desert, sere and lifeless, save for these floating, alien creatures that claimed to be my own remote descendants. The mountains have worn away, the lake vanished. Of all Man's works, only I remain . . . and that in a body strangely grown.

Infinite vistas of time whirl away from me. I feel poised at the brink of a headlong plunge into the abyss, trembling, unable, unwilling to assimilate what has happened to me.

"It's okay, Grandfather," the Archaeologist tells me, steadying me. Its touch, somehow, convinces me that everything will be all right.

"Everything is okay," it says again. "You've been relieved. Do you understand? At long last, you've been relieved."

A BRIEF TECHNICAL HISTORY OF ★THE BOLO★

From Bolos in Their Own Words

Prof. Felix Hermes, Ph.D., Laumer Chair of Military History
New Republic University Press © 4029

Bolo Marks & Years of Introduction

Mark I	2000
Mark II	2015
Mark III	2018
Mark IV	2116
Mark V	2160
Mark VI	2162
Mark VII	2165
Mark VIII	2209
Mark IX	2209
Mark X	2235

Mark XI	2235
Mark XII	2240
Mark XIII	2247
Mark XIV	2307
Mark XV/B (*Resartus*)	2396
Mark XV/R (*Horrendous*)	2626
Mark XVI (*Retarius*)	2650
Mark XVII (*Implacable*)	2650
Mark XVIII (*Gladius*)	2672
Mark XIX (*Intransigent*)	2790
Mark XX (*Tremendous*)	2796
Mark XXI (*Terrible*)	2869
Mark XXII (*Thunderous*)	2890
Mark XXIII (*Invincibilis*)	2912
Mark XXIV (*Cognitus*)	2961
Mark XXV (*Stupendous*)	3001
Mark XXVI (*Monstrous*)	3113
Mark XXVII (*Invictus*)	3185
Mark XXVIII (*Triumphant*)	3186
Mark XXIX (*Victorious*)	3190
Mark XXX (*Magnificent*)	3231
Mark XXXI	3303
Mark XXXII	3356
Mark XXXIII	?

The Bolo's role as humanity's protector and preserver after the Human-Melconian conflict is, of course, known to all citizens of the New Republic. So much knowledge—historical, as well as technological—was lost during the Long Night, however, that the Bolo's earlier history is, at best, fragmentary. Much of what we do know we owe to the tireless activities of the Laumer Institute and its founder, yet there is much confusion in the Institute's records. As just one example, Bolo DAK, savior of the Noufrench and Bayerische colonists of Neu Europa, is identified as a Mark XVI when, on the evidence of its demonstrated capabilities, it must in fact have been at least a Mark XXV. Such confusion is no doubt unavoidable, given the destruction of so many primary sources and the fragmentary evidence upon which the Institute was forced to rely.

It was possible to assemble the material in this monograph, which confirms much of the Institute's original work, corrects some of the inevitable errors in chronology, and also breaks new ground, only with the generous assistance of Jenny (Bolo XXXIII/D-1005-JNE), the senior surviving Bolo assigned to the Old Concordiat's Artois Sector. Jenny, the protector of our own capital world of Central during the Long Night, has very kindly made the contents of her Technical Support and Historical memories available to the author, who wishes to take this opportunity to extend his sincere thanks to her.

This monograph is not the final word on the Bolo. Even a Mark XXXIII's memory space is finite, and the units built during the Last War did not receive the comprehensive Historical data bases of earlier marks. Research continues throughout the sphere of the Old Concordiat, and the author has no doubt future scholars will fill in many of the gaping holes which remain in our understanding of the enormous debt humanity owes to the creations which have so amply repaid their creators.

The General Motors Bolo Mark I, Model B, was little more than an upgrade of the Abrams/Leopard/Challenger/LeClerc/T 80 era main-battle tank of the final years of the Soviet-American Cold War. (At the time the first Bolo was authorized, GM decided that there would never be a "Model A" or a "Model T," on the basis that the Ford Motor Company had permanently preempted those designations.) Equipped with a high-velocity main gun capable of defeating the newest Chobham-type composite armors at virtually any battle range and with a four-man crew, the Mark I was an essentially conventional if very heavy (150 metric tons) and fast (80 kph road speed) tank in direct line of descent from World War I's "Mother" via the Renault, PzKpf IV, T34, Sherman, Panther, Tiger, Patton, T54, M60, Chieftain, 72, and Abrams.

The classic challenge of tank design had always been that of striking the best balance of three critical parameters: armament, protection, and mobility. The first two consistently drove weights upward, while the third declined as weight increased, and perhaps the greatest accomplishment of the Mark I Bolo was that, like the Abrams before it, it managed to show increases in all three areas. The same parameters continued to apply throughout the period of the Bolo's development, and a fourth—electronic (and later psychotronic) warfare capability—was added to them. As in earlier generations of armored fighting vehicles, the competing pressures of these design areas fueled a generally upward trend in weight and size. With the adoption of the first Hellbore in the Mark XIV, Bolo designers actually began placing the equivalent of current-generation capital starship main battery weapons—and armor intended to resist them—in what could no longer be considered mere "tanks." The Bolo had become *the* critical planet-based strategic system of humanity, and the trend to ever heavier and more deadly fighting vehicles not only continued but accelerated. The Mark XVIII was larger than most Terran pre-dreadnought battleships; at 32,000 tons, the final Mark XXXIII was, quite literally, heavier than all but the last generations of pre-space wet-navy battleships had been.

Partly as a result of this constant pressure to increase size and weight as succeeding marks were up gunned and up armored, Bolo development was marked by recurrent shifts in emphasis between what might be termed the "standard Bolo," the "heavy Bolo," and various specialist variants.

The "standard Bolos," as epitomized by the Mark I, Mark II, Mark V, etc., may be considered direct conceptual descendants of the twentieth century's "main battle tank:" vehicles whose designs were optimized for the direct fire (assault) and anti-armor role. The standard Bolo designs are generally characterized by limited indirect fire capability, a main armament centered on a single direct-fire weapon of maximum possible destructiveness (normally turret mounted high in the vehicle for maximum command), a supporting lateral or "broadside" battery (the famed "infinite repeaters") capable of engaging light AFVs or soft targets, and the heaviest possible armor. As additional threats entered the combat environment, additional active and passive defenses (generally lumped together under the heading of "armor" when allocating weights in the design stage, though many were, in fact, electronic in nature) were added, but the standard Bolo forms a consistent, clearly recognizable design strand clear through the Mark XXXII Bolo.

The first "heavy Bolo" was the Mark III, aptly classified at the time as a "mobile fire support base." While any heavy Bolo design was undeniably effective in the assault mode, they tended to be slower than the "standard" designs and were likely to sacrifice some of their anti-armor capabilities in favor of indirect fire support capacity. (The decision to downgrade anti-armor firepower in favor of other capabilities was often a particularly difficult one for the designers, since only a Bolo could realistically hope to stop *another* Bolo or its enemy equivalent.) Although the Mark III was 30 percent larger than the Mark II, its *anti-armor* armament was identical to the Mark II's; the increased tonnage was devoted primarily to even thicker armor, better anti-air and missile defenses, and the fire support capability of a current-generation artillery brigade. In fact, the Mark III, for its time, was the equivalent of the later continental and planetary "siege unit" Bolos: a ponderous, enormously powerful support system which only another Bolo could stop, but not truly an *assault* system in its own right.

Throughout the development of the Bolo, there was a distinct tendency to alternate between the standard and heavy designs in successive marks, although the standard clearly predominated. This was probably because the standard design could, at a pinch, perform most of the heavy design's functions, but the heavy design was less well suited for the fast, far-ranging mobile tactics which the standard design could execute. Moreover, the sheer size and weight of a Bolo (until, at least, the introduction of dedicated, rough field-capable armor transports with the Mark XIX) created deployment problems, particularly in the assault role, which led to stringent efforts to hold down size and weight. At several points in the Bolo's history, standard and heavy designs were introduced simultaneously, as complementary units of the armored force, but almost invariably, the next generation saw a return to the concept of the standard design.

Mixed in with the standard and heavy Bolos were the occasional specialists, such as the Mark XVI *Retarius* "light Bolo" and the Mark XXVII *Invictus* "screening Bolo." Much more often, however, specialist models cropped up within an otherwise standard or heavy mark. Bolo designers were never loathe to seek variants optimized for specific tactical or support functions, although the sheer cost of any Bolo was sufficient to ensure that the specialists were generally a distinct minority within the overall Bolo force. Extreme examples of specialists may be seen in the Mark XV/L and Mark XXI/I. The XV/L was barely half the size of the XV/K and deleted all conventional main armament in favor of a massive EW capability and was, in essence, a pure electronics platform with backup capability as an anti-air/anti-missile area defense system. The Mark XXI/I, on the other hand, was the smallest self-aware Bolo ever built: a very lightly armed "stealth" Bolo designed as a forward reconnaissance vehicle and as an armored transport for small, elite special forces teams.

The Bolos did not really change the fundamental truth that humanity's survival depended, both for better and for worse, upon its weapons technology. What *did* change was the fact that, in the Bolo, humanity had, in a sense, developed a weapon system which was better than humanity itself was. Better at making war, better at destroying enemies (including, at various times, other *human* enemies), better at defending its creators, and, arguably, better in living up to the ideals humanity espoused. Be that as it may, the fact that human development through the end of the Concordiat Period was intimately entwined with the Bolos is beyond dispute.

The Mark I, II, and III Bolos did not create the twenty-first-century period of "the Crazy Years" as Terra's old nation-state system crumbled, nor did they cause World War III. They made both the Crazy Years and the War even more destructive, in a tactical sense, than they might otherwise have been, yet in a perverse way, they helped minimize the *strategic* destruction (the Mark IIIs deployed in defense of the Free City-State of Detroit in 2032, for example, intercepted and destroyed every ICBM and cruise missile launched at the city). Perhaps more to the point, it was the existence of a single Mark II Bolo which permitted Major Timothy Jackson and Renada Banner to restore security and democratic government to the Prometheus Enclave within what had been the United States of America in 2082, thus planting the seed which eventually became the Concordiat government of Earth.

As the Concordiat expanded to the stars, and especially after the production of the first, crude FTL hyper shunt generator in 2221, the Bolos were both humanity's vanguard and its final line of defense. For a thousand years, successive generations of Bolos fought Man's enemies, defended his planets, and avenged his defeats. The fully autonomous and self-directing Bolos of the Mark XXIV and later generations were truly humanity's knights *sans peur et sans reproche*, and when the Concordiat finally crumbled into neo-barbarian successor states in the thirty-fifth century, following over two hundred years of warfare with the Melconian Empire, it was the handful of ancient, still-loyal survivors of the Final Dinochrome Brigade who protected and nurtured the isolated pockets of human survivors through the Long Night which followed. Much of the battle history of the Bolos has been lost, but the portions of it which remain are the stuff of the most glorious—and tragic— records of humanity and its works. Bolos might fail. They might die and be destroyed. But they did not surrender, and they never— ever—quit.

A Brief Design
★History of the Bolo★

★MARK I BOLO (2000):★

The Mark I Bolo was an early twenty-first century update of current Abrams technology armed with a single turreted main gun (150mm; 1,722 mps muzzle velocity) capable of defeating any existing vehicle's armor (including its own) firing DSFSLRP (discarding sabot, fin-stabilized, long-rod penetrator) rounds. The Mark I carried secondary-turreted point defense/anti-personnel gatlings with on mount radar and computerized fire control packages, required a conventional four-man crew, and relied upon a pair of high-efficiency, fossil-fueled turbines for power. Combat radius was 1,000 kilometers with a battle weight of 150 metric tons. Maximum speed was approximately 80 kph (road). The Mark I was replaced in production fairly quickly by the Mark II under the pressure the new arms race exerted on R&D as the traditional world order slipped towards general collapse.

★MARK II BOLO (2015):★

The Mark II was an updated Mark I, with greatly improved onboard computers and the same main armament, but with the first light lateral infinite repeater armament (four railguns in two two-gun batteries). Fitted with gatling and counter-missile point defense. First durachrome armor (10 millimeter) capable of defeating any weapon short of the Bolo's own DSFSLRP round. Electronics were designed to allow a single crewman to assimilate data and operate the entire system, and weight rose to 194 metric tons. The Mark II's fossil fuel power plant drove electric generators rather than powering its drive train directly, and the vehicle had a limited (12 hour) backup power supply of ionic batteries. The Mark II could also operate on electrical power from a secondary source (such as local civilian generator capacity) to maintain long-term readiness in the area defense role. Maximum speed was approximately 80 kph (road) to 30 kph (cross-country in average terrain). The Mark II was the last Bolo with only two tread systems; all later marks were designed with "wide track" treads—that is, with multiple track systems across the full width of the vehicle to reduce ground pressure to the lowest possible value.

★MARK III BOLO (2018):★

A near contemporary of Mark II, the Mark III was actually designed as a "heavy" (300 metric tons) companion vehicle. The Mark III's single 150mm main gun (which was *not* turreted and had only a 20 degree traverse) was backed by an 8 gun infinite repeater battery, a heavy indirect fire support capability (four 155mm howitzers and a light VLS missile system), and an upgraded anti-missile armament. Unlike the Mark II, the Mark III carried only a single fossil-fueled power plant, strictly for backup use; power was normally drawn from heavy banks of ionic batteries, and the Mark III was the first Bolo designed from the outset to use solar film recharging. The vehicle also carried a marginally better sensor suite and a thicker durachrome hull (20 millimeter) which could be pierced at point-blank range (250 meters or less) by a 90 degree hit with the 140mm or 150mm DSFSLRP round; otherwise, it was effectively immune to anything short of a contact nuclear explosion. The Mark III was designed for a two-man crew with the second crewman serving as electronics officer (EW, sensors, etc.), but could be crewed by a single experienced operator in a pinch. The last Pre-Collapse Bolo, it was the first Bolo with multiple tread systems—inner and outer—with an independent power train for the inner pair, but maximum speed fell to 50 kph (road), 25 kph (cross-country).

★MARK IV BOLO (2116):★

The first Post-Collapse Bolo picked up where the Mark II left off. The Mark IV had a much improved sensor suite and carried a main armament of one 165mm railgun, backed by six infinite repeater railguns (20mm). The Mark IV was the first Bolo to use energy weapons (laser clusters) to supplement projectile weapons in the point defense role and was fitted with seventy-five vertical launch system missile cells in its after decking, capable of accepting indirect fire support or SAM loads but without onboard reloads. Powered as Mark III, but with improved solar film. (It was no longer necessary to stop and deploy acres of film; the Mark IV could recharge on the move in average daylight conditions.) The Mark IV's durachrome hull was thicker (30 millimeter), yet weight dropped to 210 tons in the Model B, with a maximum speed of 60 kph (road) and 30 kph (cross-country). Missile load and sensor upgrades continued to drive up the tonnage of successive models, however; by the end of its active life, the Mark IV did carry onboard missile reloads and weight had risen to over 340 tons while maximum road speed fell to 40 kph, with very limited rough terrain capability. (The Mark IV, Model H, for instance, could get *through* almost anything, but its suspension and power train weren't up to crossing rough terrain at any kind of speed.)

★MARK V BOLO (2160):★

The first member of a family of specialists with roughly comparable onboard computer support but different weapons fits and functions. The Mark V was the first so called "deep-wader"—that is, it no longer required bridging support, as it was designed to cross water barriers (including lakes and even small seas) by submerging and driving across their bottoms—and this capability became standard with all subsequent marks of Bolo. Power demands continued to grow, surpassing levels which even ionic battery technology could meet, and the Mark V was the first Bolo to use an onboard fission power plant. The growing size and weight of later models of the Mark IV had led to efforts to diversify design in the immediately subsequent marks, and the Mark V was the "general battle tank," fitted with a heavy caliber railgun (190mm) for main armament, supported by twin lateral batteries of six 60mm "gatling-style" infinite repeaters using spent uranium slugs and lighter gatlings and laser clusters for point defense. The laser clusters' anti-personnel function was limited, and the Mark V also saw the first use of multishot anti-personnel flechette/HE clusters, which became standard on all subsequent Bolos. Missile capacity was severely down-sized and restricted to SAMs as part of the drive to hold down weight. The Mark V had a one-man crew, a battle weight of approximately 198 metric tons, and a maximum speed of 50 kph (cross-country) to 80 kph (road).

★MARK VI BOLO (2162):★

The Mark VI was the direct descendent of the Mark III "mobile firebase" concept. It had the same power plant and computer support as the Mark V, but the Mark VI's "main battery" was its missile load, which was configured for maximum flexibility. No railgun main armament was mounted, but the 60mm infinite repeaters were upgraded to seven guns per side, and a heavier point defense battery intended to provide cover for other friendly units and to protect the Bolo itself when operating in counter-battery mode was fitted. One-man crew; 238 tons; speed roughly comparable to the Mark V's.

★MARK VII BOLO (2163):★

The Mark VII was a "heavy" Bolo, whose introduction inspired the first use—though still unofficially—of the term "siege unit." It had the same electronics fit as Marks V and VI, but its main direct-fire armament was one 200mm railgun backed by fourteen heavier (75mm) infinite repeaters. The Mark VII's heavy missile load was biased towards the bombardment function, but it was equally capable of operating SAMs in the area defense role. This vehicle had a very heavy layered durachrome war hull (120 millimeter) and required a two-man crew, rather than the Mark V's and VI's one-man crew, but in the VII/B the second crewman served solely to control the indirect fire armament. In later models, the second position was upgraded to a dedicated air defense/missile intercept function. Weight was approximately 348 tons in the Model B, with a maximum road speed of 40 kph and a maximum cross-country speed of 30 kph. (The Mark VII was never very fast, but its sheer mass meant most terrain features tended to crumple when it hit them and so did not slow it as severely.)

★MARK VIII BOLO (2209):★

The Mark VIII was the next-generation "main battle" (or "standard") Bolo. Main armament remained a railgun, though muzzle velocity increased still further and projectile size fell slightly (to 170mm), but this Bolo marked the first appearance of energy-weapon (laser) infinite repeaters. (By the time of the Mark VIII, *any* Bolo's secondary battery had come to be referred to as "infinite repeaters" whether or not they fired actual projectiles.) Although the new laser infinite repeaters were actually marginally less effective than the last-generation railgun infinite repeaters on an energy-transfer-per-hit basis, mass per weapon fell, and the shift meant magazine capacity for the secondary battery was no longer a design factor. Missile capability was limited to the SAM and point defense role, but the Mark VIII received four hull-mounted 150mm rapid fire howitzers to compensate. The VIII/B was fission-powered, with solar charge backup capability, a one-man crew, and a weight of approximately 225 tons. Improved power train and suspension permitted a sustained road speed of 65 kph and short-range "sprint" speeds of up to 85 kph, but maneuverability at high speed was poor.

★MARK IX BOLO (2209):★

The Mark IX was the next generation "siege" unit, introduced simultaneously with the Mark VIII as companion vehicle. The main battery railgun was suppressed in favor of additional missile power and four high-trajectory 180mm howitzers in two back-to-back twin turrets. Further improvements in electronics allowed the Mark IX, unlike the Mark VII, to be crewed by one man. Weight was approximately 400 tons, and maximum road speed for the IX/B was 57 kph.

★MARK X BOLO (2235):★

The Mark X saw the first appearance of an energy main armament (laser cannon) in a Bolo. As with the laser infinite repeaters of the Mark VIII and IX, the new system was actually less destructive than the one it replaced on a per-hit basis, but it required no magazine space. The Mark X was fission-powered and carried laser infinite repeaters, and approximately 1/3 of the preceding Mark IX's gatling close in anti-missile and anti-personnel weapons were replaced with multibarreled flechette-firing railguns in independent housings. The Mark X carried only self-defense missiles and no high-trajectory indirect fire weapons and required a one-man crew. Later models of this mark had sufficient computer capability and flexibility to begin use of pre-loaded computerized battle plans, requiring human intervention only when unanticipated tactical situations exceeded the parameters of the battle plan. The Mark X, Model B's battle weight was 350 tons, with a maximum road speed 70 kph.

★MARK XI BOLO (2235):★

The Mark XI was essentially a backup, designed to cover the possibility that the Mark X's laser main armament might prove impractical in service. Main armament was one 18cm railgun firing depleted uranium long-rod penetrators in the anti-armor role and a wide range of cluster, incendiary, chemical, and fuel-air rounds against unarmored targets. Otherwise, the Mark XI was identical to the Mark X. This vehicle remained in service longer than might otherwise have been anticipated because the projectile-firing capability of its main gun proved extremely popular with tacticians.

★MARK XII BOLO (2240):★

This was the first true "continental siege unit," designed for strategic indirect fire with VLS cells capable of handling missiles with intercontinental range. The Mark XII was capable of MIRVed FROB attacks and of engaging orbital targets with hyper-velocity surface-to-space missiles. Main anti-armor armament was deleted, but the Mark

XII was equipped with extremely capable anti-air/anti-missile defenses (in effect, it was an area defense system, as well as a bombardment unit). The vehicle was normally mated with a BAU (Bolo Ammunition Unit), a Mark XII with all offensive armament deleted to provide magazine space for multiple load-outs for the Mark XII's missile batteries. Although the Mark XII continued to carry a one-man crew, it was primarily designed for pre-loaded computerized battle plans. Weight was 500 tons, with a road speed 50 kph.

★MARK XIII BOLO (2247):★

The Mark XIII was essentially a Mark XII with main anti-armor armament restored. Although the main gun ate up almost 25 percent of the tonnage dedicated to magazine space in the Mark XIII, the Mark XIII's bombardment capability actually slightly exceeded that of the Mark XII with only minimal overall weight increases. This was made possible largely through improvements in fission technology (allowing a smaller power plant) and the first use of a flintsteel inner war hull under a much thinner durachrome sheath. The Mark XIII/B's weight of 565 tons held fairly constant in all models of the mark. Road speed was 50 kph in the XIII/B, rising to 75 in late-series models as suspension and power train improvements became available.

★MARK XIV BOLO (2307):★

The Mark XIV replaced the never entirely satisfactory laser "main gun" of earlier marks with the far more destructive "Hellbore" plasmagun. This 25cm weapon, originally designed for the Concordiat Navy's Magyar-class battlecruiser's main batteries, had a half-megaton/second energy output and, unlike the earlier Bolo laser cannon, was a marked improvement over any kinetic weapon of equivalent mass. In other respects, the Mark XIV was a "standard" reversion to a generalist design, made possible by advances in mag-bottle technology (which finally made fusion power a practical alternative to fission in Bolo design) and acceptance of a lighter indirect fire capability. Anti-missile defenses were now sufficient to render strategic bombardment impractical, so indirect fire was limited to tactical and theater applications. This permitted the use of smaller missiles which, in turn, allowed an increased magazine capacity without weight penalties. Even so, the Mark XIV/B was 28 percent heavier than the Mark XIII/K it replaced, although further power train and suspension upgrades prevented any loss of maneuverability or cross-country performance. Gradual improvements in sensor fits and fire control systems kept this mark in front-line service for approximately 90 years. Tactically, primary reliance now rested firmly upon pre-loaded computerized battle plans, but a single human crewman was routinely carried to respond to unanticipated threats. The Mark XIV/B's weight was 728 tons (rising to 900 in late-series models), and road speed hovered between 60 and 75 kph over the life of the mark.

★MARK XV/BM BOLO (*Resartus*) (2396):★

A quantum leap in Bolo technology, the Mark XV was the standard-bearer of the Concordiat during humanity's greatest wave of interstellar expansion. Very few non-human species encountered during this period could match the Mark XV's capabilities; none could exceed them. This was the first Bolo which did not require an onboard human crewman, due to advances in cybernetics and secure communication links (first short-range subspace com capabilities), which permitted increasingly sophisticated computerized pre-battle planning coupled with unjammable remote human control to correct for unanticipated problems. Main armament was one 25cm Hellbore with line-of-sight capability, backed by laser cluster "gatling" infinite repeaters (total of fourteen in the Model B) and four 20cm howitzers in individual secondary turrets. The 25cm Hellbore remained incapable of engaging orbital targets from planets with atmosphere due to as yet unsolved attenuation and dissipation problems with the weapon's plasma bolt "packaging," but there were few planetary targets with which it could not deal. Tactical and theater bombardment capability was roughly equivalent to the Mark XIV's, but the Mark XV had no strategic bombardment capability. The Mark XV's six track systems each had an independent power train, and the vehicle carried both primary and secondary fusion plants. Cybernetics were divided between two totally independent command centers as protection against battle damage, and durachrome was wholly abandoned in favor of a much tougher flintsteel war hull. Early models of this mark saw the last use of anti-kinetic reactive armor. Major improvements in suspension were required to deal with unparalleled battle weights (1,500 tons in the Model B, rising to over 3,000 in the Model M), but road speed held constant at approximately 65 kph (with brief "sprint" capability of over 80 kph) over the life of this mark, although the "lightweight" Mark XV, Model L, EW platform, at barely 1,100 tons, was 37 percent faster. Cross-country speed was equivalent to road speed except in very rugged terrain. This mark enjoyed a very long, very stable evolutionary history (mainly because the Concordiat didn't run into anything a Mark XV couldn't handle).

MARK XV/R BOLO (*Horrendous*) (2626):

The Model R was the final variant of the Mark XV. Main armament was upgraded to one 50cm Hellbore (which, unlike earlier model's weapons, *could* engage spacecraft in low orbit even from within a planetary atmosphere), and ablative armor appliqués were fitted over the Model R's flintsteel war hull in light of increases in infantry and light-vehicle energy weaponry. The preceding Model Q had seen vastly upgraded EW capabilities and the first appearance of heuristic cybernetics designed to run continuous analyses of pre-loaded battle plans against actual battle conditions in order to suggest improvements to its distant human commander. Under express human pre-battle authorization, the Mark XV/Q and /R were capable of reconfiguring their battle plans on the move without further human input. Although not self-directed, the final models of the Mark XV gave a very good impersonation of a war machine which was. Weights climbed sharply—the Mark XV/R reached 5,000 tons—but maximum road speed held fairly constant at 65-70 kph, despite weight increases.

MARK XVI BOLO (*Retarius*) (2650):

The increasing size of the Mark XV led to a fresh attempt at specialized design, and the Mark XVI was, in effect, a "light" Mark XV. Main armament remained a 50cm Hellbore, but the infinite repeater batteries were reduced to a total of eight weapons and the howitzer armament was deleted. (As partial compensation, the Mark XVI replaced its laser infinite repeaters with ion-bolt projectors, with much greater ability to penetrate ablative armor, and received a six-gun battery of short-range breech-loading 20cm mortars to augment its anti-personnel clusters.) A complete ablative outer hull was adopted to replace previous appliqués, and cybernetics were equivalent to those of Mark XV/R. Weight fell to 3,600 tons, and road speed rose to 90 kph with short duration "sprints" of up to 100 kph possible. The Mark XVI formed the "light regiments" of the original Dinochrome Brigade.

MARK XVII BOLO (*Implacable*) (2650):

Introduced simultaneously with the Mark XVI, the Mark XVII was the "heavy" version of the same basic weapon system. Main armament was upgraded from a 50cm Hellbore to a 60cm weapon, and the ion-bolt infinite repeaters were increased to a total of fifteen (six each in two lateral batteries with a three-gun frontal battery in the glacis). The Mark XVI's mortars were deleted in favor of six 25cm howitzers and an increased missile armament. Weight increased to 6,500 tons, and maximum road speed dropped to 75 kph. The Mark XVII formed the "heavy regiments" of the original Dinochrome Brigade.

★MARK XVIII BOLO (*Gladius*) (2672):★

While the Mark XVI was more agile and easier to deploy than the Mark XVII, it proved less popular in combat than its companion mark because of its lighter offensive power. The Mark XVIII replaced both the XVI and XVII in relatively short order as the new "standard" Bolo in an attempt to combine the best features of both its immediate predecessors. As usual, the new vehicle went up in size and weight (late-model Mark XVIIIs approached 10,000 tons), and space-to-ground deployment became a problem. Main armament was the Mark XVII's 60cm Hellbore, but the infinite repeaters were reduced to twelve with the deletion of the bow battery (which had been found to compromise the structural integrity of the glacis plate). The Mark XVIII adopted a "sandwiched" hull: an outer ablative hull, then a thin hull of early-generation duralloy, and finally the flintsteel main war hull. The Mark XVIII also added a third fusion plant, which, with additional improvements in fire control, plasma containment technology, and weapons power, permitted its Hellbore to engage spacecraft even in medium orbit. The Mark XVIII formed the first "general purpose" regiments of the Dinochrome Brigade and, in successive models, remained first-line Concordiat equipment for over a century. Maximum road speed fell to 70 kph and maximum "sprint" speed fell to only 80 kph, but except in the roughest terrain, a Mark XVIII was as fast cross-country as on a road. (Of course, for vehicles as large and heavy as a Bolo, "roads" had long since become a purely relative concept.)

★MARK XIX BOLO (*Intransigent*) (2790):★

The Concordiat originally anticipated that the Mark XIX would remain first-line equipment for at least as long as the Mark XVIII, as it marked the first true qualitative improvement on the old Mark XV. The Mark XVI, XVII, and XVIII had been essentially upgunned and uparmored Mark XVs; the Mark XIX was the first Bolo to mount mono-permeable, anti-kinetic battle screen as its first line of defense against projectile weapons and to incorporate the ability to convert a percentage of most types of hostile energy fire into useful power. In addition, the Mark XIX was accompanied into service by the Navy's new specialized armor transport: a light cruiser-sized vessel mated to a pair of Mark XIXs and capable of rough-field landings in almost any terrain (short of swamp or truly precipitous mountains). The transports were a vast improvement over the older independent assault pods, thus greatly simplifying the deployment problems experienced with the Mark XVII and XVIII. Improved generations of pods remained in service for almost four more centuries, particularly for battalion or larger level assaults. Main armament remained a 60cm Hellbore, but secondary armament was upgraded to sixteen ion-bolt infinite repeaters, backed up by 35mm gatling/railguns. The howitzer armament was once more suppressed in favor of eight 30cm breech-loading mortars, and the ablative outer hull was further augmented by a "plasma-shedding" ceramic tile appliqué. Weight soared to 13,000 tons, but road speed actually rose to 90 kph, with a "sprint" capability of over 120 kph.

★MARK XX/B BOLO (*Tremendous*) (2796):★

The reign of the Mark XIX was shorter than anyone had anticipated primarily because no one had anticipated the psychotronic breakthrough. (Or perhaps it would be more accurate to say that no one had expected the High Command to *accept* the psychotronic technology as quickly as it did.) The Mark XX *Tremendous* was the first truly self-directing (and self-aware) Bolo. Defensive capabilities remained unchanged from the Mark XIX, but the internal volume demands of the Mark XX's psychotronics forced the main armament to be downsized, and the Mark XIX's single 50cm Hellbore was replaced by two 30cm weapons, twin-mounted in a single turret. In addition, the Mark XX/M (unofficially referred to as the "Mosby") was a unique departure. Designed for independent deployment to raid an enemy's logistics and rear areas, the XX/M was essentially a refitted Mark XIV hull. The considerable mass of its first-generation Hellbore, along with its turret, was deleted, which freed up sufficient internal volume (barely) to permit installation of a somewhat less capable version of the Mark XX's psychotronics. Although self-aware, the Mark XXs had relatively simple (and bloodthirsty) personalities, and full self-awareness was specifically limited to battlefield applications. Except in carefully defined combat-related areas, the Mark XX's software suppressed its volition, effectively prohibiting it from taking *any* action without direct orders from designated human command personnel. Weight and speed data for the Mark XIX apply to the Mark XX. The Mark XX's great opponents were the Yavac heavies of the Deng, but not even the YavacA/4 could survive against a Mark XX Bolo without a numerical superiority of at least 3.25 to1.

★MARK XXI BOLO (*Terrible*) (2869):★

Following the introduction of the Mark XX, a nomenclature policy was adopted under which new mark numbers were to be issued only to reflect substantial increases in psychotronic capability. (The new practice was temporarily abandoned with the Mark XXVII-Mark XXIX series, but resumed with the Mark XXX.) The Mark XXI actually proliferated into several sub-variants which would have received their own mark numbers under the old system, including yet another attempt at a "heavy" Bolo (which tipped the scales at over 20,000 tons and was never adopted for field use), and the "stealth" forward reconnaissance XXI/I. Mainstream Bolo development, however, followed the "standard" format, and the Mark XXI/B reverted to the single 60cm Hellbore main armament of the Mark XIX. The major advance lay in the enhanced computational speed of the mark's computers and improvements in the personality centers of successive models. Although still fringed about by inhibitory programming to control self-directed actions outside combat, the Mark XXI was much more capable *in* combat. This mark also saw the introduction of TSDS (Total Systems Data-Sharing) technology into the regiments of the Dinochrome Brigade. In practice, each unit of the regiment operated in battle as a single component of a multiunit awareness in a free-flow tactical link which combined the conclusions of *all* its Bolos to formulate future actions.

★MARK XXII BOLO (*Thunderous*) (2890):★

The Mark XXII saw both further advances in cybernetics and psychotronics and a considerable upgrade in firepower with the new "super" Hellbore, a 90cm weapon which increased its destructive output to a full two megatons/second. Secondary armament mirrored the Mark XXI's. The Mark XXII was also the first Bolo to mount an interplanetary-range subspace com, and, for the first time, the Navy modified *its* cybernetics to permit a Bolo's psychotronics to directly control the maneuvers and defensive systems of its armor transport spacecraft (now unmanned in combat) for assault insertions, which increased its chance of penetrating hostile defenses by an order of magnitude. The Mark XXII's kinetic battle screen showed a 36 percent increase in effectiveness over the Mark XXI's, and weight hovered around 14,000-15,000 tons for all models, with a top speed of 80 kph and a "sprint" capability of 120-135 kph.

★MARK XXIII BOLO (*Invincibilis*) (2912):★

The Mark XXIII followed quickly on the heels of the Mark XXII, largely as a result of worsening relations between the Concordiat and the Quern Hegemony. Although the Quern managed to achieve strategic surprise when they actually launched their attack, worsening Human-Quern relations between 2880 and 2918 had driven Bolo research at a breakneck pace. The original Mark XXIII was only a marginal improvement (in electronic terms) on the Mark XXII, but the main armament was doubled to a pair of 80cm "super" Hellbores in fore-and-aft turrets, and provision was made for quick conversion to the molecular circuitry whose early perfection the R&D bureaus anticipated. Secondary armament was also upgraded— to eighteen ion-bolt infinite repeaters in two nine-gun lateral batteries—and a new generation of battle screen was augmented by internal disrupter shielding around critical systems. The outbreak of the Quern Wars put a halt to major psychotronic research, as all efforts were bent upon design rationalization to aid in mass production, but the anticipated molecular circuitry appeared almost on schedule. Although it was not applied throughout, late-series Mark XXIIIs incorporated the new circuitry within their psychotronics, which enormously increased capability without increasing volume requirements. It was possible to restore the "secondary brain" feature to the Mark XXIII with no degradation in base capability, which made it much more resistant to battle damage. Despite its increased armament, the Mark XXIII, like the Mark XXII, hovered around the 15,000 ton mark, primarily because of the weight savings of its new molycircs and the shift to later-generation duralloy in place of flintsteel, which permitted armor thicknesses to be halved for the same standard of protection. Speeds remained largely unchanged from the Mark XXII.

★MARK XXIV BOLO (*Cognitus*) (2961):★

The Mark XXIV was the first genuinely autonomous Bolo. Previous Bolos had been self-directing on the tactical level, but the Mark XXIV, with a vastly improved personality center and id integration circuitry, was capable of *strategic* self-direction. For the first time, Bolos began to evolve a truly "human" level of individual personality, but the Mark XXIV's psychotronics continued to be hedged about with inhibitory safeguards. A much greater degree of non-combat autonomy was permitted, but the vehicle's psychotronics remained so designed as to deny it full use of its own capabilities outside Battle Reflex Mode. Impetus to decrease or even abolish those safeguards clearly began with this mark as it proved its reliability and flexibility, yet resistance would continue until Bolo Central reviewed the battle record of Unit 0075NKE on Santa Cruz in 3025. The Mark XXIV retained the Mark XXIII's secondary armament but reverted to a single-turreted main armament (90cm "super" Hellbore). Despite the reduced main armament, weight fell only to the 14,000 ton mark, and speed remained roughly equivalent to that of the Mark XXII and Mark XXIII.

★MARK XXV BOLO (*Stupendous*) (3001):★

After forty years of experience with the Mark XXIV, even diehards conceded that many of the inhibitory software features which had been incorporated into every Bolo since the Mark XX were no longer justified. The most restrictive features were deleted from the Mark XXV, Model B, although it was not until the Model D (introduced in 3029) that virtually all inhibitions were suppressed.

A core package of override programming was retained to restrict the volition of (or even, in the case of the so-called "Omega Worm," to destroy) a Mark XXV which went "rogue" as a result of battle damage or "senile" due to poor maintenance, but most of the restrictions which had required human approval for almost all non-battle decisions were progressively relaxed over the operational life of the Mark XXV, with a tremendous increase in efficiency. The practice of deploying totally independent Bolo brigades lay well in the future, but the Mark XXV's capabilities clearly pointed the way to them. The Mark XXV essentially duplicated the offensive and defensive systems of the Mark XXIV, yet further improvements in metallurgy and fusion technology dropped weight to 13,000 tons while normal speed rose to a maximum of 95 kph, though "sprint" speed remained unchanged.

★MARK XXVI BOLO (*Monstrous*) (3113):★

The Mark XXVI was the first Bolo to incorporate improved "hyper-heuristic" features based on the work of Major Marina Stavrakas. Armament, size, weight, and speed remained largely unchanged from the Mark XXV, but the Mark XXVI was capable of constructing a "learning model" in accelerated time. In some ways, this almost equated to precognition, in that the Mark XXVI could project changes in an enemy's tactical or strategic actions before even the *enemy* realized he intended to change them. The new systems also meant that, accompanied by a much improved ability to break hostile communications security, a Mark XXVI could actually invade an opponent's data net, access his computers, scan them for useful data, and (in some cases) even implant its own directions in those computers.

★MARK XXVII-MARK XXIX BOLOS (31853190):★

The Mark XXVII (*Invictus*), XXVIII (*Triumphant*), and XXIX (*Victorious*) marked a temporary reversion to the older practice of assigning mark numbers on the basis of armament and function rather than psychotronics technology. All three had essentially identical cybernetics, which concentrated on further improvements to their hyper-heuristic packages, but the Mark XXVIII and XXIX also incorporated a complete changeover to molecular circuitry throughout, aside from the power linkages to their energy armaments. All three of these marks were used in the new, independent brigades which replaced the old regiment structure of the original Dinochrome Brigade, but, in some ways, the units marked a reversion to the old "specialist" designs. All mounted the new 110cm "super" Hellbore (2.75 megatons/second), but the Mark XXVII was a "light," fast Bolo, with greatly reduced secondary armament, limited indirect fire capability, and a vastly improved sensor suite, intended to serve in a scouting and screening role for the independent brigades. (This function had been performed by light manned or unmanned vehicles, and the old Mark XXI/I, with psychotronic upgrades, remained in service for special forces applications. The new strategically self-directing Bolo brigades, however, required an integral scouting element, one not limited by "stealth" considerations and capable of fighting for information at need.)

The Mark XXVIII was the "generalist" of this trio of marks, with much the same armament as the old Mark XXIV, although that armament was even more deadly and effective under the control of the improved psychotronics of the newer units.

The Mark XXIX was an unabashedly "heavy" Bolo—indeed, it remained the heaviest Bolo ever deployed prior to the Mark XXXIII. It reverted to the twin Hellbore armament of the Mark XXIII (though still in 110cm caliber), coupled with a much enhanced indirect fire capability, and an integral logistics/maintenance function which it could extend to other units of the brigade. (The maintenance/repair function became standard in all succeeding Bolo designs.) The independent brigades normally consisted of four regiments of three 12-unit battalions each: one of Mark XXVIIs, two of Mark XXVIIIs, and one of Mark XIXs. Weights for these Bolos were 11,000 tons (maximum normal speed 110 kph) for the Mark XXVII, 15,000 (maximum normal speed 90 kph) for the Mark XXVIII, and 24,000 (maximum normal speed 75 kph) for the Mark XXIX.

★MARK XXX BOLO (*Magnificent*) (3231):★

Introduced on the eve of the Human-Melconian "Last War," the Mark XXX was the direct descendant of the Mark XXVIII. The incorporation of counter-grav into the Mark XXX's suspension and power train went far towards offsetting the mobility penalties increasing weight had inflicted on preceding generations. The Mark XXX incorporated still further improvements to the hyper-heuristic capabilities of the Marks XXVII-XXIX, new dual-ply battle screen (which was not only more effective against kinetic weapons but also capable of absorbing at least some of the power of almost any energy weapon and diverting it to the Bolo's use), and a new and improved cold-fusion power plant. Weight dropped from the Mark XXIX's 24,000 tons to 17,000 and normal speed increased to 115 kph. For very short intervals, the Mark XXX could divert sufficient power to its counter-grav units to achieve actual free flight at velocities up to 500 kph, but could not operate its battle screen or internal disrupter shields or fire its main armament while doing so.

★MARK XXXI BOLO (3303):★

Over the course of the thirty-third century, the galaxy slid with ever increasing speed into the maw of the "Last War's" gathering violence, and Bolos after the Mark XXX did not receive the "type" names which had become customary with the Mark XV. The Mark XXXI was an enhanced Mark XXX with a main armament of one 200cm Hellbore (5 megatons/second). Secondary armament, though still referred to as "infinite repeaters," consisted of two lateral batteries of six 20cm Hellbores each, and many small-caliber, hyper-velocity projectile weapons were retained for close in defense and anti-personnel use. Indirect fire capability was degraded in favor of the assault role, for which purpose the Mark XXXI's duralloy war hull was given an average thickness of 90 centimeters, rising to 1.5 meters for the glacis and turret faces. All secondary and tertiary weapons were mounted outside the "core hull" which protected the Mark XXXI's power plants and psychotronics, and last-generation internal disrupter shielding was used heavily. The Mark XXXI retained the counter-grav assist of the Mark XXX and, despite a weight increase to 19,000 tons, could match the preceding mark's speed.

★MARK XXXII BOLO (3356):★

The last Bolo whose year of introduction is known with certainty, the Mark XXXII was essentially a Mark XXXI with the added refinement of direct human-Bolo neural-psychotronic interfacing. Provision was also made for attachment of a counter-grav unit sufficient, under emergency conditions, to permit the Bolo to make an assault landing without benefit of transport. Offensive and defensive systems were comparable to those of the Mark XXXI. The Mark XXXII was the final version of the "standard" Bolo.

★MARK XXXIII BOLO (?):★

The last—and largest—Bolo introduced into service. The Mark XXXIII weighed no less than 32,000 tons and mounted a main armament of three independently-turreted 200cm Hellbores with a secondary armament of sixteen 30cm Hellbore infinite repeaters in two lateral batteries. Equipped with a very sophisticated indirect fire system, the sheer firepower of the Mark XXXIII was a reversion to the old siege unit thinking, though it was normally referred to as a *planetary* siege unit, not merely a continental one. No one knows how many Mark XXXIIIs were actually built, but official planning called for them to be deployed in independent brigades of 24 units each. Despite the increase in weight, speed remained equivalent to the Mark XXXI, and the Mark XXXIII's *internal* counter-grav could supply the assault landing capability for which the Mark XXXII had required an auxiliary unit.

★Bolo Armament★

Bolo Mark	Year	Weight	Road Speed	Sprint Speed	Main Armament	Secondary Armament	Indirect Fire	Self-Aware?
Mark I	2000	150	80	80	1 150mm DSFSLRP	point def/AP gatlings	None	No
Mark II	2015	194	80	80	1 150mm DSFSLRP	4 InfRpt railguns	None	No
Mark III	2018	300	50	50	1 150mm DSFSLRP	8 InfRpt railguns	Tac/ Theater	No
					4 155mm howitzers	Light VLS missile system		
Mark IV	2116	210	60	60	1 165mm railgun	6 InfRpt railguns	Strategic	No
					VLS missile system			
Mark V	2160	198	80	80	1 190mm railgun	12 60mm gatling InfRpt	None	No
Mark VI	2162	238	80	80	Heavy VLS missile system	14 60mm gatling InfRpt	Strategic	No
Mark VII	2163	348	40	40	1 200mm railgun	14 75mm gatling InfRpt	Strategic	No
						VLS missile system		
Mark VIII	2209	225	65	85	1 170mm railgun	12 laser InfRpt	Tactical	No
						4 150mm howitzers		
Mark XIX	2209	400	57	57	VLS missile system	12 laser InfRpt	Strategic	No
					4 18cm howitzers			
Mark X	2235	350	70	70	1 laser cannon	12 laser InfRpt	None	No
Mark XI	2235	350	70	70	1 18cm railgun	12 laser InfRpt	None	No

Bolo Mark	Year	Weight	Road Speed	Sprint Speed	Main Armament	Secondary Armament	Indirect Fire	Self-Aware?
Mark XII	2240	500	50	50	Heavy VLS missile system	12 laser InfRpt	Strategic	No
Mark XIII	2247	565	50-75	50-75	1 laser cannon	12 laser InfRpt	Strategic	No
					Heavy VLS missile system	4 15cm BL mortars		
Mark XIV	2307	728-900	60-75	60-75	1 25cm Hellbore	12 laser InfRpt	Tac/Theater	No
					VLS missile system			
Mark XV/B	2396	1,500	65	85	1 25cm Hellbore	14 gatling laser InfRpt	Tac/Theater	No
					4 20cm howitzers system	VLS missile		
Mark XV/L		1,100	89	116	none	point def/AP only	None	No
Mark XV/M		3,000	65	85	1 35cm Hellbore	16 gatling laser InfRpt	Tac/Theater	No
					4 20cm howitzers	8 18cm BL mortars		
						VLS missile system		
Mark XV/R	2626	5,000	75	95	1 50cm Hellbore	12 gatling laser InfRpt	Tactical	No
					4 20cm howitzers	4 18cm BL mortars		
						VLS missile system		
Mark XVI	2650	3,600	90	100	1 50cm Hellbore	8 ion-bolt InfRpt	Tactical	No
					6 20cm BL mortars			

Bolo Mark	Year	Weight	Road Speed	Sprint Speed	Main Armament	Secondary Armament	Indirect Fire	Self - Aware?
Mark XVII	2650	6,500	75	88	1 60cm Hellbore	15 ion-bolt InfRpt	Strategic	No
					6 25cm howitzers	Heavy VLS missile system		
Mark XVIII	2672	10,000	70	80	1 60cm Hellbore	12 ion-bolt InfRpt	Strategic	No
					6 25cm howitzers	Heavy VLS missile system		
Mark XIX	2790	13,000	90	120	1 60cm Hellbore	16 ion-bolt InfRpt	Tactical	No
					8 30cm BL mortars			
Mark XX	2796	as Mk XIX	as Mk XIX	as Mark XIX	2 30cm Hellbores	as Mark XIX	Tactical	Limited
Mark XXI	2869		Varies	Varies	1 60cm Hellbore	16 ion-bolt InfRpt	Varies	Limited
					+ varying VLS capability	4-8 30cm BL BL mortars		
Mark XXII	2890	15,000	80	135	1 90cm Hellbore	16 ion-bolt InfRpt	Tac/ Theater	Limited
						VLS missile system		
						6-8 30cm BL BL mortars		
Mark XXIII	2912	15,000	80	148	2 80cm Hellbores	18 ion-bolt InfRpt	Tactical	Limited
						VLS missile system		
						6 30cm BL mortars		

★General Armament Notes★

In addition to the weapons listed, all Bolo secondary armaments include small-caliber high-velocity projectile weapons for close in defense and anti-personnel fire. All Bolos after Mark V also mounted multiple-shot flechette anti-personnel "clusters" with progressively heavier flechettes.

Any Bolo secondary gun with anti-armor capability was always referred to as an "infinite repeater," although the term originally applied only to a small- to medium-caliber projectile weapon with a high rate of fire and large magazine space.

Like most of their other weapon systems, the vertical launch system missile outfits of Bolos evolved tremendously over the course of the Bolo's design history. The original Mark III VLS consisted of only 60 non-reloadable cells, although more than one missile might be loaded per cell if they were small enough. By the time of the Mark XIX, the VLS consisted of reloadable, magazine-fed cells, and all future Bolo VLSs followed that pattern. The term "light" or "heavy" used to describe a VLS refers to (1) the number of cells (and thus salvo density) and (2) the VLS magazine capacity, not to the weight or size of missiles thrown.

The breech-loading mortars fitted to most Bolos after the Mark XIII might be considered automatic weapons, as their rate of fire averaged from 8 to 12 rounds per minute. The Mark XXXIII's 15cm BLMs had a maximum effective range of 3,000 meters; the 40cm BLMs of the Mark XXIX and Mark XXXIII had a maximum effective range of 9.75 kilometers.